WORLD WAR CTHULHU:
A COLLECTION OF LOVECRAFTIAN WAR STORIES

EDITED BY
BRIAN M. SAMMONS &
GLYNN OWEN BARRASS

DARK REGIONS PRESS, LLC
PORTLAND OREGON

World War Cthulhu: A Collection of Lovecraftian War Stories

Dark Regions Press, LLC
6635 N. Baltimore Ave., Ste. 241
Portland, OR 97203
United States of America
DarkRegions.com

Published by Chris Morey
Edited by Brian M. Sammons & Glynn Owen Barrass
Interior design by Cyrus Wraith Walker
Cover Design & Cthulhu Design by Irina Summer
Trade Paperback Edition
ISBN 978-1-62641-074-9

TABLE OF CONTENTS

World War Cthulhu: A Collection of Lovecraftian War Stories *is dedicated to the memory of C.J. Henderson.*

Rest in peace, friend.

INTRODUCTION

"Another race—a land race of beings shaped like octopi and probably corresponding to fabulous prehuman spawn of Cthulhu—soon began filtering down from cosmic infinity and precipitated a monstrous war which for a time drove the Old Ones wholly back to the sea—a colossal blow in view of the increasing land settlements."—H.P. Lovecraft, *At the Mountains of Madness*

World War Cthulhu. Lovecraft created war, and not only the wars between the dark horrors that toyed with our world mentioned in quote above. There was the incident described in his story "The Shadow over Innsmouth," in which the American government raids the town and battles its flock of mutated half-bred monsters. He also dealt with the horrors of Humanity's war with itself, as in "Herbert West: Reanimator," where the good doctor adds to the suffering of World War One by reanimating the corpses of dead soldiers, hideous Frankenstein experiments that contributed to his eventual downfall. Then there is "The Temple," which describes a lieutenant-commander in the Imperial German Navy during World War One, whose U-boat sinks a British freighter, and a certain icon owned by one of the dead sailors brings disturbing nightmares and real life horrors to all. Yes, Lovecraft was no stranger to war, be it eldritch races battling one another for dominion over the earth, or mankind locked in a desperate, futile fight for survival against titanic forces from beyond. War has been a part of the Cthulhu Mythos from the beginning, and here is a chronicle of that ageless, ceaseless conflict.

Of the individual tales, here is what you will find from our stalwart warmongers.

We begin the collection with a story by John Shirley, "Loyalty," the action taking place in a terrible future, in a place whose Pacific co-ordinates will be very familiar to Cthulhu Mythos fans. Stephen Mark Rainey follows with "The Game Changers," a tale of dark deals and deeds that bring soul-crushing horrors to the jungles of Vietnam. "White Feather," by T. E. Grau, set during the War of Independence, is a tale of a soldier and privateer's own personal apocalypse and battle for his soul. In "To Hold The White Husk," writer W. H. Pugmire takes a leaf from H.P. Lovecraft's story "The Temple," but turns the story on its head with the survivors of a u-boat attack encountering horror through a dead man's amulet. Robert M. Price follows, offering us an epic tale of Greek myths intertwined with the Mythos, "The Sea Nymph's Son" incorporating the legend of Achilles and Troy in a disturbing yet beautiful tale. Edward M. Erdelac then drags us back to the jungles of Vietnam, kicking and screaming, to encounter a thing called "The Boonieman." "The Turtle," by Neil Baker, returns us to the War of Independence, and a brave man's attack on the hated British from a small barrel-like submarine. Are the British really the only problem, though?

Next we have David Conyers, alongside his fellow recruit David Kernot, bringing us "The Bullet and the Flesh," a modern story of child soldiers in Zimbabwe. Then we're back in time, the Second World War, at the Swiss/German border, mountaineering across the Trollenberg range on the track of things that have taken a great interest in the affairs of man. William Meikle writes the admirable adventure "Broadsword." "Long Island Weird, The Lost Interviews," by Charles Christian, describes the history of a choice piece of real estate, the Gold Coast of Long Island, and details the horrors, both real and imagined, that have shaped its Mythos-tainted history. "The Yoth Protocols," by Josh Reynolds tells a story of a shadowy government agency's dark deals with beings that lurk underground, and the even darker being they use as an intermediary. In "A Feast of Death," by Lee Clark Zumpe, which is set during the First World War, a man is made prisoner in a horrible Turkish prison, only to be handed over to the Germans, encountering fellow prisoners that are not even human. Another take on the legend of Achilles follows, "The Ithiliad," by Christine Morgan, who, although using the same mythology as Robert M. Price, writes a very different tale with an unexpected ending. Troy has been exceptionally unlucky in this anthology.

Remember that little old location John Shirley wrote about at the beginning of the book? Konstantine Paradias returns us there in "The Sinking City," in a nightmare struggle of a violated mind fighting for sanity. A story set during the Second Mexican-American War follows, where a certain Lt. Col. Roosevelt and his men encounter a motley group of strangers in a hotel. Dark, ancient secrets abound in this: "Shape of A Snake," by Cody Goodfellow. Next, "Mysterious Ways," by C.J. Henderson, is a tale of a Roman centurion's terrible choice and a deal with an entity that will affect him, and Humanity, for all time. A disturbing, surreal treat follows in the shape of "Magna Mater," by Edward Morris. Here he incorporates the true events of a literary legend's experiences during World War One. Then we reach the story written by your humble editors. "Dark Cell," a contemporary tale where two unlikely heroes, an American CIA Agent and a criminal Army Intelligence officer, encounter the IRA and some ancient horrors they wish to invoke.

A collection like this couldn't be without an inclusion of the King in Yellow Mythos, and Pete Rawlik steps up to the challenge with "Cold War, Yellow Fever." The Cuban Missile Crisis is the setting, with some very familiar names out to save the world from itself. Darryl Schweitzer follows with "Stragglers from Carrhae," where two tired Roman soldiers set off on a journey across Asia minor with the most unlikely of companions. Another personal apocalypse, the tale of a veteran of World War Two comes next. In this, Tim Curran's "The Procyon Project," a crippled veteran exchanges the horrors of war for the horrors of mankind delving where it shouldn't.

We complete the collection with a story by Jeffrey Thomas, "Wunderwaffe" being a futuristic story where war, magic and religion blend together in an alien environment familiar to those that have read his Punktown books.

When we first contacted the authors for this collection, we asked them for 'stories of war, intermingled with the Lovecraftian/Cthulhu Mythos, set across all the ages including Roman Britain, the American Civil War, both World Wars, the Vietnam conflict, Afghanistan today, the far future, and anywhere else an author finds inspiration.' They brought us this, and more, in tales that blend both the horror of war and the madness of the Cthulhu Mythos in a collection we know you will find exciting, and terrifying; a collection you will never forget.

War never looked so good.

—Brian M. Sammons and Glynn Owen Barrass

LOVECRAFTIAN WAR STORIES FROM THE FALL OF TROY TO THE DISTANT FUTURE

LOYALTY

BY JOHN SHIRLEY

"Where are you taking me?" asked the man on the gurney. The old man had a hoarse New England accent.

"You go to call upon your master," Kline told him. "Relax, Professor Seekley. You're getting what you always wanted."

Seekley was silent for a time as Kline wheeled him along the steel corridor. The portable bed provided its own movement. Kline had only to put his hands on it. But high tech though it was the wheels of the gurney made a squawking sound with each turn. On the back of the gurney was a small metal basket with medicaments, water, and a CallTab.

"I smell the sea," said Seekley, lifting his head a little. The old professor's voice was feeble.

"Yes, we're near the balcony overlooking R'lyeh." Kline was mid thirties, strong, determined. His own voice had a sturdy determination about it. But inwardly he was cringing, as he thought about what was to come.

"The dreaming city..." Seekley muttered.

"Yes."

"What year is it, Dr. Kline?"

"It's the year 2087."

"Truly? I have slept a long time."

"You were in a kind of suspended animation. You were condemned to it, you remember?"

"I...almost remember."

"You were engaged in something inappropriate, at the time." Kline could hear the sea, now, pounding on the half sunken battlements of R'lyeh. "You nearly woke the giant. No one wanted that but you, not then. Now—it seems the only alternative..."

"I'm not sure this is what I wanted."

"You wanted to summon him. Here's your chance! We woke you up so you could do it."

"I wondered, at the end...if it was after all what I truly wanted. And then the men came and stopped me, just as he was stirring. Not that Cthulhu is truly a he... there is no gender, really, for one such as Cthulhu. But we devotees always used the male pronoun."

Kline noticed that Seekley pronounced the creature's name differently— Kline and his associates called the titan something like "Kuh-thool-hoo." Seekley pronounced Cthulhu something like "C'[tongue-click] -uh-hool-uh-y'oo"— inserting that barely audible tongue-click instead of a 't' sound. But it didn't matter how Seekley pronounced the titan's name so long as the old man knew his job.

They reached the end of the corridor, where the steel doors were already thrown open to reveal the purpling oceanic horizon and the darkening, cloud draped sky.

"Oh!" Seekley cried, startled, closing his eyes for a moment, as Kline pushed the gurney out onto the metal balcony overlooking the ruins.

Mightily reinforced—so its designers hoped—against any force coming up against it, the building from which the steel balcony jutted was just a great block of chromium-plated steel rising in stark anomaly from its foundation on an ancient reef that skirted one side of the sunken city. Built thirty years earlier to study R'lyeh and its slumbering inhabitant, the structure was nearly featureless on the outside, apart from a cluster of intricate antennae—the building had no windows, few visible vents. There was a tunnel-like entrance just below sea level, on the opposite side, for submarines; a helicopter landing pad occupied much of the roof, near a bristling apparatus. And there was this single observation balcony projecting out over the western edge of the city, about twenty meters above high tide.

"As you can see a part of the sunken city has elevated, since your time, all on its own, about twenty-five meters further above sea level," Kline remarked. "It's as if it were compensating for the rising waters of climate change. The creature's chamber has risen, somewhat, as well. He settled back into a slumber, after you disturbed him."

"How long ago now, has he slept in peace?"

"Oh, many decades. But it is a fitful slumber."

Seekley nodded, and added with soft reminiscence, "But you know—Cthulhu *has* risen, in the memory of modern man."

"I've heard that claim. I've read the account."

In fact, after many readings, the newspaper account was incised in Kline's memory: *The awful squid-head with writhing feelers came nearly up to the bowsprit of the sturdy yacht, but Johansen drove on relentlessly. There was a bursting as of an exploding bladder, a slushy nastiness as of a cloven sunfish, a stench as of a thousand opened graves...*

Seekley rubbed his eyes. "You say...you say summoning Great Cthulhu has become *necessary*, now?"

"Yes." Kline pushed the gurney close to the balcony's railing. "You know, I always thought the actual encounter with the creature, in that account, could have been made up by the journalist. The writer might have been inspired by reports of the idols, the old sculptures that turned up from time to time..."

"No, it was not fabricated." Professor Seekley raised himself on one elbow, grunting with the effort, to gaze down over R'lyeh. "Cthulhu returned to his slumber after that encounter. His regeneration was incomplete, you see. But in my own time, I was convinced the master was ready to arise for good and all. And so he *is*, now— he has far more strength, this time. I can feel it! The stars are aligned; his energies are attuned." He looked out over the sunken city and murmured, "And the air fairly quivers with it, at R'lyeh..."

The abandoned ruins of the primeval city, which could be mistaken for a mere tumble of boulders from the air, were located approximately at the "southern point of inaccessibility", known as Point Nemo. The nearest land, more than a thousand kilometers away, was the chain holding Pitcairn's Island, and, in another direction, farther, was Easter Island—its grim, hulking statues may well have been erected as a warning to go no further, in that direction, lest the mariner in time encounter R'lyeh.

Here stood its crumbling remains: Massive stones, some cut with an irregularity that seemed perversely intentional, loomed from the whispering waves. The bare outlines of a city--its crooked avenues, its harbor--could be ascertained, if one looked close. Few other artifacts had been found here. But an enormous underwater chamber, of surprising length and breadth, had been located. In it was an enormous, slumbering inhabitant, slumped on a gigantic throne carved from a single huge meteor...

"It's curious, how you and Cthulhu were both in a kind of doze, since the day you nearly woke him," Kline remarked, glancing at his watch. It was almost time. "You in Rio de Janeiro. He...*it*...in the wreckage of this old city..."

"Yes, it is curious," Seekley admitted, barely audible. He undid the buckles about his waist, and, grunting with effort, sat up to gaze out over the half sunken, broken shell of R'lyeh. "But in sleep, the master speaks to many who might someday be of use. *His* mind never sleeps, you see. Not really. And in my own sleep, these decades of coma...*sometimes great Cthulhu spoke to me!* He told me things I did not wish to know—so that when I woke I was no longer sure of what I wanted. I had seen, perhaps, a bit too much..."

The CallTab chimed. Kline took the tablet from the gurney's basket. "Answer."

John Shirley

Ihlala Gulahosi's face appeared on the CallTab's screen—clasping her long black hair was a red scarf picked out in gold thread; she was a dark woman with large brown-black eyes.

"Receiving," Kline said. The signal flickered, for a moment—few satellites were left intact—and he had to wait for it to stabilize.

"What's that, some sort of cell phone?" Seekley asked, looking over his shoulder. He blinked in the light from the declining sun glimmering over the top of the steel building.

"More or less," Kline said distantly.

"Who's calling?"

"A United World representative," Kline said. No time to explain the world government—a unity that had come about because of the invasion—nor Ihlala's work for its intelligence arm.

"They are closing in on your position," Ihlala said, in a New Delhi accent. "There are about ten screwplanes at the moment but they've sensed the anomalous activity and they seem be to bringing the Float Hive to bear."

"How much time do we have?"

"Their scouts will show up any moment. They'll probably wait for the near proximity of the Hive before they attack. This...this *summoning,* Kline...is it going to happen? Or is it not?"

"We're setting up for that. But if you're asking about success—I don't know."

"Place the communicator so I can observe, please."

Kline propped the CallTab on the nearer edge of the gurney, turning her camera toward the ruins. Then he looked at the graying professor. "Seekley, you must begin now."

"Why? I told you I wasn't sure I wanted to do it at all, anymore. I need time to think! Why must I summon him *now?"*

"Because..." A movement from the sky caught his attention. Kline pointed toward it. "See that, up there?"

Seekley looked. The screw-shaped vehicle, a thing of unearthly materials, glossy iridescence, seemed to be corkscrewing its way down from a cloud, leaving a trail of swirled mist. The craft was about as big as a fighter jet, but it tapered, at its aft, to a crystalline glowing stub like the coal of a cigar.

"That," Klein went on, "is a scout for the Takers. That's what they call themselves, at least in English. They invaded Earth about seven months ago. They used a translation device to demand our surrender. Everyone on the planet heard the demand, all at once—unconditional surrender. Those who surrendered are believed to have been subjected to experiments, then ground up for protein. No one is quite sure—no one's come back—" He broke off, pointing.

"—Ah, there's another advance scout!" They could see another corkscrewing vessel screwing its way through the air, in the distance. "The scouts usually come ahead of the Float Hive."

"Float Hive...?"

"Their mothership. The Hive does the large-scale destroying—the screwplanes scout and do the detail work of destruction. London is gone, simply destroyed. So are Beijing, San Francisco, New York, Paris, Mumbai, Bangkok, Hong Kong, Moscow, Tucson, Chicago, Rio, Melbourne, Houston, Washington D.C.—even Las Vegas! In fact Las Vegas was first to go—all the lights there seemed to draw their attention. And *we've* drawn their attention, Seekley."

Now seven screwplanes hovered, darted, corkscrewed along, over R'lyeh—and began to drift toward the balcony. Toward Kline and Seekley...

Professor Seekley gaped up at the alien vessels in awe. "Are they—the Old Ones?"

"We don't know if they're related to the so-called 'Elder Gods', Seekley. We've only managed to bring down three of those things and all three disintegrated with some kind of auto destruct before we could examine their interior. But we know they're operated from the Float Hive. And we think that Cthulhu...your master...may in fact be able to penetrate the Float Hive. We've tried everything else. There are indications that Cthulhu's body may be partly formed of a plasma which, theoretically, could penetrate their shielding. Especially in the monster's dispersal form."

Seekley looked at him in alarm. "Monster? You would *insult* Great Cthulhu... *here?* Do you not suppose he is listening?"

"Listening? You mean to me?" That hadn't occurred to Kline. "But he's...deep under the, ah...you know, he's inside a stone chamber and..."

Seekley snorted. "How do you think I am to *contact* him, you fool? Telepathy! The chanting is only to focus the mind! He listens as he chooses!"

"Just—*do* the damned thing, Seekley! Or humanity's done for. Finished!"

Seekley looked up at the approaching alien vessels. "I'm parched. I need some water. And if there's anything in that medicine kit to give me a little strength..."

Kline busied himself getting the water bottle and an injector ready as Seekley got to his feet, leaning on the gurney for balance. Then he lurched toward the balcony's metal railing.

"Be careful, Seekley! We don't have time for a cracked hip!" Kline said, as he brought Seekley the water.

Supporting himself with one hand on the rail, the old man drank thirstily. Then he tossed the plastic bottle aside as Kline applied the injector.

"I feel no injection," Seekley said, glancing at his arm. "No pain, no needle..."

"It's painless. Do you need me to hold you up?"

John Shirley

"No, the railing is enough... And I feel the drug now. I have some strength. Yes."

For several long moments they watched the screwplanes twist closer to the balcony; and closer yet, coming at them like flying drills.

Then a pulse of translucent red energy expanded from the coal-like tail of the nearest, ran forward along the screws, spinning as it went, and projected, a twist of living fire, down at the balcony, screaming with destructive glee as it came.

Seekley gasped—then one of the antennae on the roof behind them hummed and a shield of electromagnetic force appeared, up above, just in front of the twist of fire, dispersing it.

"You have a shield of some kind!" Seekley said.

"It won't work for long. It takes too much power...and we'll soon be overwhelmed. They'll blow us to bits! You must call your master!"

Seekley took a deep breath and began chanting. Mouth twisting unnaturally, he intoned, *"Ph'nglui mglw'nafh Cthulhu R'lyeh wgah'nagl fhtagn!"*...over and over.

Kline had heard a recording of a cult chanting that same wicked psalm. But now Seekley was incanting other words too guttural for Kline to understand. As he chanted the incantation his eyes rolled back to show only the whites, as if he were sinking into a profane ecstasy.

Abruptly the old man fell silent, head tilted, as if listening to the voiceless voice of great Cthulhu.

Another gleeful scream ripped the air above—a sizzling replied to it, as another bolt of energy chaos was deflected by the antennae. Several screwplanes fired at once and two of the antennae exploded...

In the distance, something loomed in the gathering dusk.

It had been given its human name based on its shape, like an old fashioned beehive, a cone made in layers of pearly material, crackling with electrical energies as it pressed through the atmosphere. It was mountainous, an unnaturally symmetrical mountain pocked with cryptic passages; it came skimming over the sea, spinning slowly, making the watery surface wrinkle and draw away beneath it. Its base was nearly as big as R'lyeh itself, bigger; big as midtown Manhattan. It was the Float Hive, the extraterrestrial mother ship.

Crimson energies rippled out from it, whiplashing up to the screwplanes, but not attacking them—nourishing them, reinforcing their energies, so that soon they would have the power to destroy this building, the balcony, and end humanity's last hope...

Then something glided into view, on Kline's right—the nuclear submarine which had brought him here. The sight saddened rather than heartened him—he knew what the outcome would be.

The submarine launched its cruise missiles. They chuffed into the air and soared up to strike at the screwplanes. They struck their targets--and had little effect.

The screwplanes regrouped, and angled to aim their corkscrewing tips down at the submarine.

All those men...

But they would serve their purpose. To delay the enemy, just long enough.

"Kline!" Seekley shouted, over the cacophony of the unleashed energies roaring around them. Crimson fire rained upon the submarine; cruise missiles hissed into the air. "Kline, I have called the master! I have reminded him that our world, which has sustained his organism for so long, deserves his loyalty. But Great Cthulhu says *no!* He declares it is *we* who must have loyalty—to him!"

"What the hell are you talking about, Seekley! Tell it to destroy that thing or it's going to be destroyed itself! The Hive will annihilate everything that could be any kind of obstacle!"

"The master doesn't care! How do you think Cthulhu came here? Now that he has regenerated, by that same means he can depart! *Unless!* You, speaking for humanity, must swear fealty to the master! You and all those you represent must swear your loyalty to Cthulhu! *All humanity must swear it!* Cthulhu will know! Once, in millennia past, humanity worshipped Great Cthulhu! *And must do so again!* The master demands our loyalty!"

Kline gaped at Seekley. What was he asking of them? "Perhaps, we...we might..."

"Are you thinking of destroying Cthulhu after he has done the deed, Kline? He is too strong now! And will become stronger with this act! If you try to betray great Cthulhu—you will trade one great enemy for a worse one!"

The submarine exploded, its hull snapping in half, gouting a roaring fireball of white and blue flame. Men's bodies spun into the air, burning...

There was so little time to decide. Kline writhed inwardly with uncertainty.

"*Kline!*" came the tinny voice from the CallTab. "I have been transmitting all of this to the United World! The delegates are unanimous! *We swear loyalty to Cthulhu!*"

"It cannot be undone!" Seekley shouted, eyes wild. "We have crossed into his world *and we are forever his!*"

Then Seekley turned to the sea and warbled his perverse hymn once more...

A roll of thunder boomed, then, followed by a massive crackling of unseen lightning; an echoing crash, like a hundred avalanches at once; a smell like hair burning, of electrical discharge, of a billion gutted fish...and the balcony shuddered under their feet. Kline staggered, caught the balcony railing beside Seekley just in time to see the slick, cracked blocks of R'lyeh shrug out of the way, pushed aside

John Shirley

from beneath...

The Float Hive drew nearer, glowing as it prepared to fire directly on the steel outpost.

Then a green titan emerged from the sea, rising up, tentacles waving furiously, throwing water and stone aside with equal ease.

Great Cthulhu reared up, higher and higher, many hundreds of meters high, tall as a skyscraper, exuding the smell of brine and burning electricity and bubbling acids, the odors washing over Kline in acrid waves.

Cthulhu's thin wings unfolded, and lightning, forking from the thickening clouds beyond, was seen through the emerald membranes. His gigantic body was both dragon-like and transparently gelatinous.

Seekley shrieked in mingled horror and ecstasy, falling to his knees, raising his shaking hands to his primordial lord.

Up, *up* rose Cthulhu, water streaming off his translucent green wings. His body quivered as he bellowed a challenge to the Float Hive; his beard of tentacles jittered with his rage. The spider-like cluster of eyes on his squid-like head glistened with malevolent intelligence; his scaly skin, transparent and yet murky, rippled as he waded out of the ruined city toward the approaching alien mothership: the mountainous cone of metal glowing ever brighter as it prepared to blast this new adversary...

"Aiiieee! Great Cthulhu!" shouted Seekley, spraying spittle in his excitement.

Kline watched, sickened and eager, as Cthulhu stalked toward the mothership—and suddenly flapped up into the air. The wings, looking too thin to support the giant body, seemed to stretch out, expanding to gather in more air, and they pulsed with a green energy that added its own lift...

And suddenly Cthulhu was flying.

The giant lifted up, streaming ocean water and seaweed, roaring with a sound that shook the world. His wings keened and hummed, almost invisible in their whipping activity. His tentacular "beard" writhed; gigantic talons stretched out...

The Float Hive fired. A beam of crimson energy big enough to melt a dozen aircraft carriers shot out of the mothership and in to Cthulhu's mighty breast...

And passed right through him.

It was as if the titanic body acted as a prism, separating out the energies of the red beam, keeping what Cthulhu wanted and conducting the rest out between his wings, to be dispersed in the sky. But yes—a wound, a green edged hole, had formed...and as Kline watched, it quickly sealed up. Cthulhu had taken what he wished from the beam, let the rest pass through, and had healed himself, all in an instant.

The screwplanes fired on Cthulhu—their energies, too, were refracted.

The ancient titan flew higher...and then, diving down from above, Cthulhu pounced.

The primeval colossus from the stars threw himself upon the Float Hive, attacking the mothership like some hideous parody of an eagle attacking its prey. Cthulhu clasped the alien spacecraft, arms and legs wrapped around the enormous cone. And the huge alien ship spun as if in impotent fury, gyrating Cthulhu about, perhaps trying to free itself with this desperate maneuver.

But instead of letting go, Cthulhu clasped tighter yet and—and then, abruptly... melted. Or so it seemed, at first. The gelatinous giant seemed to melt *onto* the Float Hive, becoming hundreds of seeking tendrils, each separate, but with one mind squirming their way into the mothership's cryptic openings, slithering into it...

Kline watched as Cthulhu sank into the giant alien craft.

And then, great Cthulhu vanished entirely.

Like an animal maddened by a wasp in its ear, the mothership spun recklessly about, wobbling, turning faster, faster—blurring...until at last it detonated from within.

A great shockwave rumbled out from the blast, coming visibly toward the balcony. Kline turned to run but the shockwave caught him and Seekley, threw them skidding across the balcony. Kline was stunned, dizzied as the shockwave flung him through the open doors, sliding into the steel corridor...

His body stopped moving, but his mind kept whirling...and he lost consciousness, sinking into a churning darkness.

The darkness was not comforting; indeed, it was not uninhabited...

"Kline..." came Seekley's croaking voice. "Kline!"

Head throbbing, Kline reluctantly opened his eyes. "What...has happened?"

"You must get up, Kline. There is more to do..."

Groaning, Kline forced himself to his feet. His every muscle ached; his head resonated like the speaker of an amplifier shaken by feedback. But he followed Seekley out onto the balcony.

The dusk was thickening; the clouds churned. The screwplanes were all down—some of them had crashed into the stones of R'lyeh, and their remnants melted away, disintegrating.

A noxious brown-black cloud was dispersing in the distance where the battle had been fought. Grisly wreckage floated on the sea, human bodies from the submarine blended horribly with wormlike extraterrestrial corpses from the shattered mothership.

And something else—was forming, out there. Something was taking shape in the cloud.

Kline remembered the account he had read of what had happened when a

John Shirley

steamship rammed giant Cthulhu: *...For an instant the ship was befouled by an acrid and blinding green cloud, and then there was only a venomous seething astern; where—God in heaven!—the scattered plasticity of that nameless sky-spawn was nebulously recombining in its hateful original form...*

And so it was now: recombining, Cthulhu sloshed ponderously toward them, wading across the surging sea, up to his scaly translucent hips in the waves, tentacles waving, the green feelers reaching out toward the two men...

"Oh, no, no," Kline said. "We mustn't..."

"But we have no choice," Seekley declared grimly. "We made a deal. *We agreed!* And so it must be. The master will have nothing less."

A few moments more, and then great Cthulhu was rearing over them like a cyclopean statue: reeking, dripping acid that hissed when it struck the stones of R'lyeh.

Seekley fell to his knees and clutched his head. "Yes, yes, I hear you, great one! I hear you, lord of all the Earth! You shall have one now!"

"Have...have one what?" Kline asked, his mouth paper dry.

"A sacrifice," Seekley said. "But it will not be you, you have another way to serve him." He reached out his arms toward the looming giant. "Lord Cthulhu! Take me as your first offering! Honor me—and take me first!"

Cthulhu bent—his hideous transparent head came within a dozen meters of Kline, who staggered back in revulsion. Then the giant feelers clasped Seekley, drew him into the gargantuan maw hidden behind the tentacles...

Seekley screamed.

Kline saw the man's form, his body, sinking head downward, visible in the semitransparent body of the giant as it swallowed him...

Whimpering, Kline turned away.

Then he heard a voice in his head. It was a wordless voice, and yet, somehow, it spoke clearly enough.

Kline took a deep, shaky breath. He must do what he must do.

He turned back to Cthulhu and threw himself to his knees. "Oh Great Cthulhu! You have destroyed our enemies! We will serve you! I myself will bring you offerings! We will offer up many to you, Lord Cthulhu! Many!" Kline salaamed to Cthulhu and cried out, "We give you our loyalty, great Cthulhu! Forever!"

And he found that he could pronounce the master's name, now, just exactly as Seekley had..

THE GAME CHANGERS

BY STEPHEN MARK RAINEY

We never saw or heard them coming. One moment, the squad was moving in a column along a narrow, muddy path through dense rainforest. The next, we were in the midst of deafening, blinding, bloody chaos. At some point, I discovered I was firing my M16 at anything that moved beyond the nearest trees, and I saw a flailing shadow topple and vanish in the surrounding green tangles. A terrific concussion rent the air, and, from behind, a blast of intense heat drove all the air from my lungs and sent my weapon flying. As I dropped first to my knees and then onto my chest, I felt something dancing and cascading over my shoulders—*flames*, I realized with horror. I threw myself onto my side and wriggled and rolled in the soupy mud, unable to turn fully onto my back because of my bulky pack, waiting for an onslaught of agony that somehow never came.

The daily rain I had been cursing for weeks had saved me from a fiery death.

As I rolled onto my stomach, my eyes swept the viscous earth for my M16. There—six feet to my right, its muzzle submerged in a small pool of steaming, standing water. I dug in with my elbows and scrambled toward it until I could throw out one hand, grab its sling, and draw the rifle back into my grasp.

By then, the firefight was all over.

There had been nine of us. Now there were four. Charlie was missing at least one, but for this round, he had won the body count.

"Fucking VC bastards." I recognized PFC Cothren's voice, but I didn't see him anywhere.

Behind me, a lanky silhouette tore itself from the mud beside the road. "Why the hell didn't they finish us?"

"Listen," came Sultan's voice again, and then I saw him, stumbling out from behind a partially uprooted cypress tree fifteen feet away. He gazed up at an expanse of deepening purple sky, and I heard a low, distant thunder.

Heavy jet-engine sound.

Corporal Maile, our M60 machine gunner, appeared next to Van Buuren, cradling an arm. I saw blood on his shoulder. "B-52s."

Van Buuren's eyes flicked toward me. "You all right, Timmons?"

I nodded. "Wind knocked out of me."

Van Buuren stumbled toward a couple of bodies lying next to the road. They were Delta, but I couldn't make out their faces. The sergeant snatched a few ammo magazines from the bodies.

"Coming this way," Maile said, his eyes still on the sky. "Low as hell."

A moment later, I saw them. Three giant black birds in the sky, one after the other, barely above the treetops, heading directly toward us. They were so big, so heavy, they seemed to hang in the air, virtually motionless. I could feel the rumbling beneath the soles of my boots.

Something was wrong. The second jet's wings were wobbling, and one dipped precariously, almost losing its lift before righting itself. Heading to Da Nang, I thought. It was the nearest airbase that could accommodate the heavy buffs. As the aircraft drew nearer, the engine noise pounded us like monstrous hammers, shattering all coherent thought. Gradually, the sound diminished, leaving my ears shrieking angry curses.

When I could hear again, Sultan was saying, "Radio's a goner." He held up a twisted bundle of metal and wire that I realized had been part of the PRC-25, aka the Prick, our portable radio unit. The damned thing was as tough as a tank; it must have taken a direct hit, probably from a Soviet-made SPG-9.

Which meant there was even less left of Hinkle, our Radio/Telephone Operator.

Four of us. Lost somewhere outside of Mai Loc, ten or more miles from the Demilitarized Zone. We were all that was left—as far as we knew—of 1st Platoon, Delta Company, 3/37th Infantry Regiment. October 29, 1969: our mission had been to patrol the jungle east of the Ho Chi Minh Trail. Our three squads left base camp at 0600, split up at 1040 when we took small-arms fire, and then lost contact with each other. Throughout the afternoon, we had been making our way eastward, back toward LZ "Sigmund," but the jungle, treacherous and devious, had outwitted us. Our maps worse than useless, we had only the vaguest idea where we were. So far, we hadn't encountered any booby traps, but we knew they must be out here, lurking like lethal vipers. Our advance, of necessity, had been slow and cautious, but it had given Charlie the opportunity to gather, hit us hard, and vanish in the shadows.

We were in rugged, mountainous territory, and Charlie held the high ground.

Yeah, I was scared. More than I'd ever been. In my three months here, I'd seen some action, but nothing like this sudden, devastating ambush.

Sergeant Van Buuren had grabbed from the dead whatever gear, ammo, and water we could use. Sultan, our M79 grenadier, had bandaged Maile's ravaged shoulder and was puzzling over our blood-and-mud spattered maps.

"This trail sure ain't marked, but there should be a road—southeast of here. Quang Tri ought to be seven, eight miles."

"Trail's taking us north," Van Buuren said, glancing westward. "We stay on this, we're sitting ducks. Jungle's a monster, but we've got to go east. We've got maybe an hour of daylight, so let's use it. Timmons, take the point."

Everything inside me screamed in protest, but I knew my duty. As we took up formation, I realized I still felt a subtle, almost subliminal rumbling beneath my feet, and it was becoming more distinct. Had the B-52s reversed course? The thundering grew louder, heavier, and a few seconds later, a single buff appeared directly above us, too low, banking too tightly. Its right wing dipped, pulling the fuselage over, and I could only watch in helpless horror as it began to spiral downward, scarcely a click to the east.

The impact threw us to the ground, and two seconds later, a terrific shock wave hammered us, toppling nearby trees and nearly rupturing my eardrums.

When the tumult inside my skull began to subside, I raised my head to see a cloud of black smoke roiling through the green canopy toward us. Then, from the distance came a silent, brilliant flash. Not fire or flames, but a blinding burst of color—purple, blue, gold, red, silver—all at once, like nothing I had ever experienced.

We lay there for untold moments, dazed and bewildered.

Corporal Maile was the first to speak. "What the hell were they carrying?"

Sergeant Van Buuren finally regained his feet, pointed toward the crash site, and then at me. "There'll be teams crawling over that scene soon enough. Let's be there to meet 'em."

"What if Charlie gets there first?" Sultan asked.

Van Buuren hefted his M16. "What do you think we do? We shoot him."

⊙ϟ≑ⅼⅼ

By the time we advanced a click through the jungle, the sun was gone, but the strange light ahead blazed like a beacon, sending misty, curling tendrils of indefinable color creeping through the trees. I kept wondering if something might be wrong with my vision, but we were all seeing the same thing: waves of shifting spectrums; coalescing masses of silver-green-violet light; strobing bursts of black energy that turned the whites of our eyes to bulging, luminous discs. I felt we were walking into a cloud of fallout from some new, unknown doomsday bomb, though if we had been radiated, it was far too late to escape its effects.

Surprisingly little fire and smoke remained now; the aircraft's fuel tanks must have been near empty when it went down. We couldn't yet see any wreckage, and I wondered whether the jet had mostly vaporized on impact. But a hundred meters farther on, I saw a distinctive, angular silhouette standing out against the spreading glow: the B-52's vertical stabilizer.

The crash site was a smoldering clearing at least a hundred meters in diameter, over which the bizarre glow crawled and shimmered like living, phosphorescent liquid. Pieces of twisted wreckage littered the terrain like huge, charred tinfoil scraps. Of trees in the circle, only a few blackened stumps remained. We could see no sign of life, human or otherwise. Van Buuren directed me to move a dozen meters to my right, while Sultan went left, brandishing his M79 grenade launcher. Maile, in obvious pain from his shoulder wound, knelt next to the sergeant, who raised his M16 and started toward the edge of the open area.

"Sergeant," Maile said, his voice low and hoarse. "Hold up. Look." He pointed to his left, past Sultan. I saw it then: a luminous, misty mass, creeping like a ghostly centipede toward the trees. As the thing reached the standing trees, its color gradually faded from view, as if the thick foliage had somehow drained its vitality. For several moments, nothing further happened.

Then we heard a low, barely audible creaking, like an ancient wooden door swinging back and forth.

Though I felt nothing, I believed a breeze must have picked up as the uppermost branches of the trees I was facing began to sway back and forth—rhythmically, hypnotically. Then, as if in supplication, the branches, in unison, lifted themselves skyward, their leaves shivering and vibrating, their tips bending and twisting until they too pointed at the sky. A subtle tickling began in my ears, intensifying until it adopted a kind of cadence, giving me the impression the tree was somehow *singing*.

"More over there," Van Buuren said, pointing to my right, and I saw more tongues of luminous, living mist worming into the jungle.

Within three minutes, most of the trees around us had raised their branches and begun to sing to the black night above.

Another hint of sound caught my attention, and, shortly, the deep growling of a diesel engine invaded the night like the voice of an angry tiger. However, we detected no lights or movement, and after a few moments, the engine sound shuddered into silence. From somewhere in the darkness behind me, I could hear the eerie wailing of a nightjar. Not one of us moved, spoke, or breathed.

Then, from the far side of the crash site, a dozen or more figures swept out of the jungle like giant, predatory insects, their sudden appearance as shocking to our senses as an enemy ambush. All wore uniforms we could not yet identify, each body limned by the ghostly color that oozed from the charred earth. They seemed unaffected by either the heat from the smoldering wreckage or the glow itself. None carried lights of any sort. As we watched, several of them appeared to sniff the air like curious dogs, and I realized something about the proportions of their bodies seemed *off*. To the man, their arms and legs appeared uncannily long and spindly, their heads oversized.

Van Buuren moved back toward me, holding one finger to his mouth. We crouched in tight balls behind the broad roots of a towering kapok tree and watched several tendrils of shimmering color waving at us as if sentient, some twenty meters away.

"ARVN uniforms," Van Buuren said, indicating the newcomers were South Vietnamese Army. "But something doesn't look right about them."

I nodded my agreement. "Where the hell did they come from so fast?"

"Gotta be a road out there." He gave a low snort. "Shows how good our maps are."

From nearby, I heard a weak but high-pitched "*treep-treep*" sound: a passable, familiar imitation of a barn owl. Van Buuren and I looked toward Maile, who was pointing toward the far side of the clearing. From his pack, the sergeant produced a pair of binoculars and peered across the blasted

Stephen Mark Rainey

expanse at a new arrival to the scene. A single figure, dressed in fatigues but, judging by his poised demeanor, a person of authority.

"American," Van Buuren said. "Officer. Can't make out his insignia. I don't recognize him."

The tallest of the South Vietnamese approached the Caucasian officer. One overlong arm rose and gestured with a strange arcing, twirling motion, and I could hear a gruff, querulous voice rattling across the distance, too indistinct to make out any words.

Another barn owl cry, sharp and insistent, came from my left — Sultan, trying to get our attention. A number of shimmering filaments were crawling with unmistakable deliberation toward his hiding place. The thick foliage shook and churned as he turned and beat a hasty retreat into the jungle. The weird tendrils curled and quested at the base of a huge tree before slithering beyond my line of sight.

To my right, more fingerlike projections of misty color were forming and snaking toward the underbrush, and I realized with horror that this living, *sentient* plasma was moving to flank us. Sick with revulsion, both Van Buuren and I backed into the surrounding clusters of ferns. I could see Maile leaning against his tree, his face a death mask in the alien glow. Blood was oozing from his shoulder again, and his knees were sagging, ready to collapse. His wound was worse than I realized.

Van Buuren started toward him, but Maile shook his head and motioned him back. I noticed now that several distant heads had turned our way, and one of the nearest figures, some sixty meters away, was pointing in Maile's direction. They had spotted him, if not the rest of us.

Maile signaled us to stay put, and then he stumbled forward, just to the edge of the charred ground — less than a dozen meters from the nearest fingers of swirling, menacing color.

"Hey," he called out, his voice weak. "Hey! I'm an American. I need help!"

I heard a sudden, deep rumble, like thunder, but I was certain it had come from *beneath* the earth. The nearest tendrils quivered and writhed. One of the distant figures disappeared into the trees, only to reappear moments later, carrying an object of some sort, which he handed to the American officer.

A megaphone.

"Stay where you are," came a rasping, tinny voice. "Do not step into the crash area. We will come to you."

"Shit," Van Buuren whispered. "Don't move. Don't make a sound. I don't want those bastards to know we're here."

"What about Maile?"

"He won't give us away."

A few seconds later, Sultan emerged from the darkness, his eyes brighter than flares. "God almighty," he said, looking back the way he had come. "The trees! The trees are fucking moving."

"We saw."

"No," he said, and I realized tears were streaming down his cheeks. "They're coming out of the ground. Like … they're *walking*!"

We both stared at him, disbelieving. I heard another rumble and then a series of creaks and groans, as if something huge were pushing its way through the jungle.

Our eyes reverted to Maile, who stood exposed, visibly shivering.

The amplified voice came again. "Someone will be there to help you in a few moments. Stay where you are."

Out of the corner of my eye, I glimpsed a rapid movement—a shadow streaking through shadows—and a second later, Maile vanished, ripped from his place by something faster than a striking cobra. A sharp scream followed, mercifully cut short, and we heard a thudding, ripping sound as something dragged his body into the jungle. Moments later, everything went silent. Everything but the low, rhythmic creaking of trees, seemingly getting closer.

"That's it, we're moving out of here," Van Buuren whispered. His face reflected the ghostly pallor of the mist creeping toward us through the plane wreckage. He jerked a thumb to his right, back to the southeast. "This way."

Sultan and I fell in behind him, crouching low but moving at a clip, ignoring the prospect of booby traps or other hazards. However, I had barely gone a dozen paces when something snagged my left ankle and sent me sprawling. I went down hard, clenching my eyes shut, anticipating the quick, final sound of a grenade blast, or the agony of punji sticks piercing my chest. For several seconds, I lay in the cool mud, barely believing I was alive. Glancing at my feet, I realized I had stumbled over a thick, leafy vine.

I dragged myself upright, only to discover that Sultan and Van Buuren had passed out of sight. New terror hit me like a hammer blow, for despite my arduous physical and mental training, I had never truly conceived of being lost in the jungle alone. I *had* to quell the panic before it got the better of me. I knew Sultan and the sergeant couldn't be more than ten paces ahead, and I could still see the leaves of the nearest vines swaying from their passing. I scrambled forward, keeping low, trying to regain my wits, intent on catching up.

Then I froze, as several meters in front of me, a pair of black shapes emerged from the foliage. Not Sultan and Van Buuren, but two of *them*—the uniformed strangers—as stealthy as spiders creeping up on their prey. They were not coming toward me but following the others. *They had not seen me fall.* My instincts screamed that these strangers had to be hostile. But rather than shoot them, I dropped to the ground and gave a loud, insistent barn owl trill. I didn't know whether it would fool the pursuers, but it might afford Van Buuren and Sultan at least a moment's warning.

I could only pray I hadn't given myself away.

A second later, a single gunshot exploded in the night. A .45 pistol—Van Buuren's, I guessed. Then I heard a scuffle, a grunt, and the *crack-crunch* of branches breaking.

Then only complete, baffling silence.

I wanted to scream. I'd had a split-second to open fire on the interlopers, and I had let them pass. I listened for several more seconds, heard nothing, and trilled a barn-owl query.

No response.

To my left, a rustling rose amid the foliage, and then something gurgled, or growled. An animal? It couldn't have been human, or so I thought, until I realized the guttural noises were forming syllables. Not English, and I didn't think it was Vietnamese. But it was clearly speech, of a kind.

A second later, in English: "Bastard." Sultan's voice.

A deep *thump* and nothing more.

At least Sultan was—or had been—alive.

There was only one thing left for me to do.

⊙ᵠᗄⵀ

I should have run blindly into the jungle and taken my chances. That is what I told myself. Yet, somehow, the prospect of fleeing alone through the malevolent darkness terrified me more than dying in a bitter firefight.

It was a bad choice, an awful choice, but marginally less horrifying than the alternative.

I skirted the eastern edge of the smoldering hollow, where the ghostly radiance had not yet spread. I clung to the belief that Van Buuren and Sultan were both alive, that we would all yet make it back to Mai Loc Base. Ten to one they were being interrogated even at this moment. So far, the strangers remained ignorant of my existence, and I was certain my life depended on keeping it that way.

The "road" was a narrow dirt track through the jungle, barely wide enough for a truck to pass. Fifty meters ahead, numerous points of light moved like lazy fireflies against the black backdrop. I could hear low voices, as well as occasional thumping and hammering. Behind and to my left, the alien glow continued to creep and curl like morning fog, still potent, still *alive*. I did not for one minute believe these strangers were a legitimate crash team, nor that they would be the sole responders. A cynical voice told me they had come to keep everyone else out—even our own military—presumably by force.

I wondered: had they anticipated, or even directed, the unknown horror that had killed Maile?

I moved at an agonizing crawl toward a thicket near the boundary of what I took to be a base camp in the works. Soon, I detected a pair of voices speaking English. One belonged to the American officer. The other was the same gurgling, growling, buzzing voice I had heard before.

No human vocal cords could ever produce such deep, resonating noises.

"You thought you could control it. We cannot control it. It is beyond control. Your ignorance will be your undoing and ours."

"You accepted our terms."

"Extortion."

"Insurance. You would have used it on us, eventually. We know this."

I couldn't make out much that followed — until, after a long, disconcerting silence, the officer's voice said, "Given time, it may collapse on its own. Until it does, we cannot know."

I kept hoping one or the other would speak of Van Buuren and Sultan, but the figures moved away from me so I could no longer hear them. From somewhere distant came a low, rhythmic pulsing, like a heavy drumbeat, and when I eventually raised my head to peer through the wall of ferns toward the hub of activity, I realized a thin layer of luminous, violet mist hung a dozen feet or so above my head, like a translucent film spreading over a layer of denser air.

Once again, I heard the American officer's voice. "What is this?"

"No one knows. As we warned you."

"Bring out the prisoners. Let's see what comes of it."

This was it.

I felt myself tensing. To my right, I made out the rear portion of an M35 truck, and I figured the strangers must be holding my squadmates in there. Sure enough, a few seconds later, both Van Buuren and Sultan appeared,

Stephen Mark Rainey

their arms bound, escorted by two uniformed figures, all made into ghosts by the pervasive glow. Van Buuren looked all right, but Sultan's face was covered in blood, his body slumped in pain and fatigue. Both were gazing at something to my left, in the direction of the crash site. I could barely refrain from raising my head to look for myself.

Then the American officer materialized before them, and for the first time I saw him clearly. He was thirty, maybe thirty-five years old, solidly built, with black hair below the brim of his helmet, narrow eyes, rather oversized ears. His helmet and the collar of his fatigues bore the silver eagle insignia of a colonel. His dark eyes roved over his captives but did not meet their gazes.

The bastard was a coward.

From behind me, the heavy pounding sound grew heavier, more insistent. It dawned on me it might be a kind of signal, a herald of some new unknown. And these strangers, who were in some fashion responsible for it, by their own claim had no idea what they had wrought.

I had loaded a fresh 20-round magazine in my M16 and carried two spares.

I tucked away my fear, my anger, my uncertainty — everything that made me vulnerable—and focused on my targets, some ten meters before me, trusting my peripheral senses to detect any oncoming threat. Apart from Van Buuren and Sultan, there were four figures in view, and I anticipated another four to eight within twenty meters or so. Those would be the ones who could take me out as I made my move. Even so, my gravest concern was that Sultan might be unable to make it out on his own.

Best I could do was give him a fighting chance.

Deep breath.

Go.

I sprang to my feet, finger taut on the trigger, and popped off two quick rounds. The two nearest figures went down, writhing, as the fragmenting rounds ripped through soft tissue. Two more shots took down the next closest. With my first shots, Van Buuren and Sultan had hit the deck. The colonel spun around—he hadn't seen me and, from his bewildered expression, still couldn't identify the origin of the attack.

That damned ethereal glow, I realized. *It had dazzled them so they couldn't yet focus on me.*

I used my advantage and sprayed half my remaining rounds at the moving shadows beyond my squadmates. A hellish scream shattered the night—an unearthly sound, something between the howl of a wounded wolf and the frantic trilling of some monstrous insect.

The Colonel had drawn his .45, and I knew he could see me now. At point-blank range, I popped off a single shot, putting it just above his left knee. Crying out in shocked agony, he spun and tumbled to the earth, out of my sight. I rushed forward, my eyes locking on Van Buuren's prone figure. His eyes were blazing, searching the darkness for the source of the sudden confusion. When he realized it was me, a shadowy smile passed over his face. I sprayed the magazine's final rounds into the brush at the edge of the road, yanked the spent box, and popped in the next. Then I rushed to Van Buuren, unsheathed my KA-BAR knife, and sliced the cords binding his arms.

In two seconds, he was on his feet. "Give me the knife," he growled. "I've got Sultan."

I slapped the knife in his hand, raised my M16, and cut down a pair of figures that emerged from a thicket to my right.

Then I turned and gazed down toward the crash site—and froze as if a giant, icy hand had taken hold and pinioned me. I sensed movement off to my right, but no shots came, no shadows leaped out of the darkness to take me down. All eyes had turned to the nascent spectacle at the edge of the jungle, some three hundred meters away.

I was gazing into a massive ring of swirling, silver-purple mist, two-hundred feet or more in diameter, hanging in the air like a gaping mouth, its center blacker than black. Not just dark but *vacant*, like a portal to the remotest depths of outer space. I felt a moment of vertigo, a sense of falling into the abyss, so I turned my eyes toward my feet. I had to, or this *thing* would swallow me. I felt my heart hammering all the way into my throat.

My eyes locked on another pair staring up at me from below. It took some seconds to realize they belonged to the American colonel, the enigmatic figure I had been forced to take down. His wound was severe but hardly mortal—yet his eyes burned with that awful awareness that comes only in the instants before death, as I had learned too well in this place.

"We had no choice," he said, and his voice sounded like cracking glass. "So past time to finish the game. We had the means—the meteor. Like it came from God."

I didn't understand, but I had heard enough to put at least a few puzzle pieces together. I pointed into the darkness, away from the gaping portal. "Who are they—the strangers?"

"The enemy. The *true* enemy. But we used them. We had to use them."

"South Vietnamese?"

"Found them here. But not *from* here."

Stephen Mark Rainey

After several moments, I realized someone was tugging my sleeve. Glancing around, I saw Van Buuren, his eyes near-panicked but still lucid. Sultan, dazed and barely able to stand, clung to his other arm. "Come on, Timmons. Time's running out."

"We should drag this bastard with us."

"Don't you know what's coming?"

Despite my every instinct warning me against it, I knew I had to look back at that cavernous breach. I drew away from the colonel, overtaken by a sudden, almost irresistible desire to put a bullet in his head. This was a place beyond madness—around me and within me.

I turned and looked.

Inside the shimmering, slowly revolving ring of unearthly color, the blackness remained complete, darker than the deepest cavern beneath the earth. Yet, within it, I discerned something even blacker. Moving. Shifting. Emerging.

I had been wrong to fear falling *into* the abyss.

The pounding that had begun some time before was rising to an earthshaking, nauseating rumble.

I perceived movement around the base of the ring, and I realized it was the trees. From the largest to the smallest, the kapoks, the cypresses, the palms, all were bending and writhing, like worshippers praising their god, their trunks and limbs driven by seemingly deliberate motor impulses.

A clattering-crunching sound nearby alerted me to someone or something approaching from my right. I gave Van Buuren's shoulder a shove, urging him to get Sultan out of here. "Go on, Sergeant. Get clear."

He knew better than to argue or attempt to haul me with him. In two seconds, he was gone. I had little ammo to waste, so I raised my M16, trigger finger tense, but held my fire.

When the figure burst into view, only a few feet away, the glow from behind me illuminated his—*its*—face.

It wasn't human.

I was on the verge of shooting it, but something stopped me. The uniformed, manlike *thing* carried no weapons that I could see. Its features resembled an insect's—an ant's, or a bee's—with large, bulging black eyes, no nose or nostrils, and a pair of small, thorny-looking mandibles shielding a thin slit of a mouth. Unlike an insect's eyes, however, these gleaming black spheres expressed feeling, intelligence—perhaps even emotion. When its gaze met mine, I felt a sudden rush of sickening, debilitating terror, and then a bizarre, dizzying exhilaration as this insane, incongruous image seared itself into my brain.

Though certain my next breath might be my last, I felt no more fear. Just a burning, overwhelming curiosity.

"Stay and die," the thing growl-buzzed at me, and I noticed a small, metallic object fastened to the underside of one of the mandibles. *That*, I realized, was how I could understand its speech. "Not by my hand."

The appendage it lifted more resembled a huge, pale spider than a human hand.

The creature gestured to itself. "Attempted fragment recovery, intercepted by yours. Gave portion, yours to return remainder. But did not." I could sense contempt even in the translation of the inhuman voice. "That—" the hand pointed to the glowing, cavernous ring behind me— "your work."

I could *almost* follow its words. The colonel had made some "arrangement" with these beings but double-crossed them, ultimately resulting in *this* event. Then a sudden, terrific concussion caused the ground to lurch, and I lost my balance, almost toppled. When I regained my footing, the stranger had vanished.

Another heavy impact rattled my teeth, and a cool, dank draft passed over me, accompanied by a reek like charred flesh. Seized by a new, crushing dread, I could barely summon the nerve to look upward. But I did, and I saw it: a massive, black shape passing slowly overhead, blocking out portions of the star-filled sky. The thing reflected no light, its contours moving and shifting endlessly, preventing me even guessing at its actual size and shape.

I heard creaking and groaning around me, and a quick glance revealed trees, vines, grasses—*all* the foliage—swaying and writhing, animated by this otherworldly force the B-52 crash had unleashed.

Several more thudding impacts made the ground quiver and crack. *Footsteps*, I realized, and, around me, numerous huge, tree-sized stalks, which must have been its legs, appeared, vanished, and then reappeared some distance away.

There was nowhere to run, no direction that wasn't blocked by the sentient trees and vines or the advancing black titan.

I dropped and hugged the ground, forcing my mind to remember its cold, regimented military training. This was an air strike, an assault by a powerful enemy, an attack beyond my ability to counter.

Stay alive until the opportunity to alter my circumstances presented itself.

Somewhere beyond the drum-like thumping, a droning whine or wail began to rise, growing rapidly louder, washing over me, encompassing me.

Stephen Mark Rainey

Almost the timbre of a human voice, it seemed, yet amplified beyond any natural or technological possibility. Its ringing tones pierced my eardrums, penetrated my skull, as painful as a thrusting stiletto, and after some time I realized I could no longer hear or sense the repetitive booms. Even stuffing gobs of mud into my ears did nothing to mute this onslaught of sound.

Then it was over.

Only silence remained; not even a hint of echoes or ringing aftertones.

Had I gone deaf?

I found myself immersed in new, unbroken darkness, and I feared I had gone blind as well. But no. Shortly, I was able to discern the vague shape of the thicket a few feet away, and, peering upward, I made out a dim cluster of stars against a midnight backdrop. The heat and humidity of the jungle, however, had been replaced by a startling, shocking cold. I found my fingers aching as if they were submerged in ice water.

Had the level of hell I had previously occupied given way to an unknown new one?

I rose on shaky legs and tried to assess my situation. No lights showed anywhere around me. All traces of that unearthly glow, the color from beyond space, had vanished. No more earth-shaking footsteps. As best I could tell, none of the trees were moving.

Apart from the awful cold, the jungle seemed itself again.

I felt an inexplicable certainty that not one stranger remained nearby.

Praying it was in the direction of the road that had led those *others* here, I began to move, hoping against hope at least one of their trucks might remain.

My choice earned out. The first thing I saw was an M35 rolled onto its side, smashed, the suggestion of a human body hanging from its cab. But a short distance farther on, I came upon another truck, this one intact—and empty.

Though I knew I might end up in the hands of the Viet Cong or even the North Vietnamese Army, it scarcely seemed to matter. As I had too-well discovered, there were many levels of hell, and all I knew now was that I intended to quit this one.

ᎿᎽᎨ

I never learned what happened to Sergeant Christopher Van Buuren or PFC Jeremy Sultan. No one ever saw either of them again, and both were desig-nated MIA, presumed dead. I was the only surviving member of my squad;

ironically, all but two members of the other squads from which we had gotten separated survived that day's patrol.

When I returned to the United States six months later, it was with a Purple Heart and a Silver Star Medal for exceptional valor in combat against the enemy. I can safely say that, after my uneventful return to Mai Loc Base on that night, I no longer possessed the slightest regard for my own life. Almost half a century later, my last vivid memories of Vietnam come from what I call the Night of the Game Changers. During those subsequent months, I am certain I existed in a state of deep if undiagnosed shock.

In the early 1970s, I went to work for the U.S. Department of Defense, initially in various low-level capacities, though after a period of years I attained the position of senior librarian in the department of records, with security clearance sufficient to access certain classified documents.

Despite years of diligent effort, I never found any documentation of the events I witnessed that night in 1969. The only relevant notations indicated that a single B-52, on its return to Da Nang from a bombing mission over North Vietnam, experienced catastrophic engine failure and crashed; and that a certain Colonel Everett M. Boothe, a liaison officer working with the South Vietnamese Army, had vanished under unknown circumstances. Personal experience has convinced me that the only explanation for such a deficit of information would be that these events never occurred or were being deliberately suppressed.

Officially, no record existed of any attempt to weaponize an element of unknown properties, which had likely originated with a meteorite. Or of the U.S. military interacting with any personnel, indigenous or otherwise, aware of such an element.

Outside allusions to similar interactions came only from what most reasonable human beings might attribute to works of fantasy or outright fabrication, despite correlating observations by numerous, unaffiliated witnesses, spanning many decades.

Five years ago, on several occasions, I viewed no fewer than four individuals observing me, most frequently in the areas around my workplace and near my home. I can unequivocally state that, despite the distances from which I saw them, based on their unique anatomical proportions, they were of the same type as the ARVN-uniformed beings I encountered in Vietnam.

I am convinced that my investigations, discreet as they were, somehow drew these beings' attention to me. However, since my recent retirement, which put an end to most of my inquiries, I have observed no further sign of the strangers.

Stephen Mark Rainey

Those "other" sources I discovered relating to the enigmatic color, the inter-dimensional portal, and the entity that emerged from it, however archaic, have convinced me of the existence of another realm of time and space—another *reality*—ordinarily hidden from the living. By way of some unknown element from interstellar space, brought to Earth by a meteor and used by our military in an ill-conceived attempt to create a weapon, a bridge between this reality and our familiar sphere of existence came about—in this case only temporarily because, to paraphrase those beings I have termed the "gatekeepers," the element *cannot* be controlled. I should not hazard a guess as to the horrifying consequences had we been more "successful."

Those same source materials suggest the black entity that emerged from the portal is something that resides in a realm known only to the dead. Given these accounts, as well as the evidence of my own senses, I absolutely cannot, *must not* discount such a premise. My nerves in recent days have begun to fray, and I believe my time left to live is running short, for this simple reason:

Increasingly, I have begun to hear the trees around my home creaking and groaning in the darkness, and my every sense assures me not a single breath of breeze is moving them.

WHITE FEATHER

BY T.E. GRAU

he glass of cider arrived without ceremony, set several feet from the tall figure standing at the counter. The barkeep crossed his arms and waited.

The man reached over and picked up his drink, placing a coin in the center of the circle of liquid left on the oaken tavern top. The barkeep made no move to retrieve it.

Chilton held the glass to his nose, working through the alcohol and molasses and smelling the subtle perfume of Newtown Pippins before they were picked, smashed, and ordered to rot. Back when they first emerged as springtime buds from the lifeless branch, so full of promise. This was the aroma of his home, of a particular wind and soil that knew him and held no judgment. He wished he were a boy again, before his father lost his leg and his mother her will, before the responsibilities of adult life solidified a legacy that was as permanent as history written by the bloody victorious. Before his last raid on Nova Scotia.

Chilton wasn't a drinking man, but he wanted very much to taste this cider today. A warm bloom of past life while all in the present was cold and dark and mutely watching him instead of groping for his neck.

"Finish that and be on your way."

Chilton opened his eyes, not realizing they were closed, and looked at the barkeep, who glared at him, eying the Indian war club at his waist. Gad Richardson was his name. Little Gaddy, all grown up and bulging his success over imported purple trousers, filling up a bit larger every day inside the walls of the Broken Pony. The walls Chilton had helped him build. They'd known each other since they were lads, running the untamed forests and creek beds around New London, looking for arrowheads and fighting imaginary skirmishes against the savages. They always played the British then, swaddling themselves in red fabric and brandishing muskets of birch. Today, and ever after, they were strangers. Battle makes heroes, and it makes goats. It all depends on who survives.

"I'll be moving on presently," Chilton said, gazing into the golden fluid, drawn to the dance of sediments arranging themselves in curious patterns at the bottom of the glass.

Richardson wiped down the bar, moving past Chilton. "A good Christian never turns away a thirsty man," he said quietly. "But I don't think all my customers are so charitable in their adherence to Holy Scripture."

Chilton followed the jut of his chin to the patrons clustered in small groups and huddled over their mugs at tables throughout the room. No one spoke, and every eye watched him with varying levels of hatred and disgust. He nodded, finished his applejack in one pained gulp, and headed for the door, shouldering his pack and donning his black felt hat as he exhaled fire, blinking his eyes quickly to reorient the fading room. Gad spiked his cider with grain alcohol, which kept his tables full and the neighborhood pillory well populated.

"Ger damn 'em bloodybacks what left ye alive."

He recognized the voice, but couldn't find the face in his mind. Everyone was the mob now, every word the jeering chorus. Chilton's hand pawed at the door latch. It clicked and gave but the hinges stuck tight, frozen over from the icy brine outside, forcing him to put his shoulder into the wood. He banged a few time before the door finally creaked open, framing a very ungraceful exit for the famed New England privateer, Captain Mark James Chilton.

꒦ᛁᕼᏩᏒᚩᚠᛁᚯ

Chilton stepped outside and clenched every muscle in his body, as much against the bracing cold as the bullet he assumed would pierce him like sackcloth through the back—a leaden spine-check to make sure he still had one, or ever had. Chilton was curious himself, and almost hoped for the hot stab of whistling death to put his suspicions to rest.

At any rate, his nerves were shot, and his gait now unsteady. He couldn't well remember the days just before the incident, although they were only a few months prior. The midnight missions up the coast, the sinking of the British frigate after a vicious battle that cost him most of his men and a good portion of his foremast. The Caesar's welcome the survivors received upon limping back to dock, battered but triumphant. Captain Chilton, slayer of the Tories, subject of song and pamphlet churned out to raise morale amongst the rebels, which it did. They now felt like adventure stories written about someone else, read in his mother's voice when only just a lad, and therefore fuzzy around the edges. But the looks inside the Broken Pony assured him that they were just as real as his last raid on that uncharted Nova Scotia cove. The legacy of the past made the present fall from grace all the more jarring, and the once-proud locals all the more vicious. When times are bad and sustenance dwindling, the starving eat their heroes first.

Chilton never wanted any of it, but providence finds those that it needs, regardless of cost. Indeed, Mark James, eldest child of native son Elias Chilton and exiled Ulster aristocrat Ms. Charlotte Flannery Fitzpatrick, was hailed as the bravest lad ever sired in New London, who grew into the bravest man to ever join the Connecticut militia. On a dare, or even without one, he'd climb the tallest tree to fetch a swarming honeycomb, take on a rogue bear with nothing but a patch knife, or drop his shirt and prizefight for a half-plug of tobacco. He wasn't much of a shot with a musket, but loved a tussle more than anyone around. A natural-born pugilist with a chin made of granite. Old-timers would just sit back and shake their head with a smile, wondering if he was dropped on his noggin when he was born, or just too naturally muddleheaded to consider consequences. Or too Irish. But Chilton was that sneaky kind of smart that made him a good soldier, and an even better ally, and your worst enemy if you crossed him, which fewer and fewer people did as he added years and the city dug deeper into the forest.

His father Elias was once a gentlemanly farmer of rye, potatoes, and apples, proudly tilling his uneven plot situated as far outside of New London as the council would allow. He wanted the challenge of taming the land, and providing room for what he hoped would be a large family. But it turned out that he was too far from town, as a raiding party of Mohegans caught him while cutting trees on the backside of his expanding property, taking off his leg with the same pit saw that had felled the acres of maple and birch. He cauterized his wound in the glowing ashes of a stump fire, dragged himself back to the family home, locked himself in his room with a dusty case of whiskey, and emerged two weeks later a different man. Freed from his cage of empty bottles, smears of dried blood, and piles of human filth, he fashioned a crude wooden leg from the last red maple tree he cut, and went right on farming without another word about the incident, or any word for his family in general. That next harvest, he sold what he needed to rear his family and dumped what was left into the smoking brass still set up in the barn after slaughtering all the animals and leaving their corpses to rot in the yard, dooming the family for fresh meat.

He said the sound of them bothered him, so he brained each in turn with a bush hammer. Every day after he'd spend the daylight hours trudging across the fallow fields, combing the forest for Indians, avoiding human contact, and making rare few trips into town. At night, he'd take turns on his wife and his two children, depending on the moon and the quality of the spirits bubbling into maturity out in the darkness, telling them that it was his divine right as *pater familias* to sleep where he saw fit. Charlotte took exception to this, and was beaten with a length of firewood until she could no longer speak, or do much of anything aside from drool, her eyes now crossways and the light inside her gone. But she still had enough wherewithal to drown her only daughter in the horse trough, lest Elias get to her one more time. After making a dinner of stewed hare and turnips——her husband's favorite——she hung herself from the support beam over the kitchen table that night, discovered by Mark James upon returning from town after selling off the family heirlooms for salt and flour. After taking in the scene, the son stirred the pot over the fire, sending the aroma of bubbling meat up the chimney, sat at the table, and waited.

Mark James, who soon became just Chilton in the absence of Elias amongst the populace, killed his father slowly and carefully with the same piece of firewood that stole the life of his mother and eventually his sister, and loaded his battered remains into the still in the barn. He spiced the batch with a pot of stew and added wood to the fire. He took the wooden peg back into the house and carved it down into an Iroquois war club. That morning at dawn, he put torch to the house, mounted the family horse, and galloped into town. He left his father's whiskey fermenting in the barn for the creatures of the forest, both human and not. Everything gets thirsty, especially those that call the wilderness home.

New London gossip whispered about the occurrence at the Chilton farm, but no official inquiry followed. The British Magistrate was unconcerned with the disappearance of rurals, and the underground leadership committee was uniformly sympathetic to the younger Chilton to a man, while always scornful of Chilton the elder. An outbreak of yellow fever was eventually blamed, and the property shunned, but no one knew from where this story originated. Interest in this local mystery was soon eclipsed by the rumblings of war, as revolution was taking hold amongst the colonies. Forces were agitating in Boston, and more redcoats were sent in from across the ocean, together with new laws to strangle the unruly subjects back into airless servitude. Although Chilton cared little about discovery of those events that took place on the final night at his childhood home, or the capital repercussions, the timing of these major events moved minds away from such domestic matters. Nothing erases memories faster than war, as those within band together against those without. That both of these groups were mixed together up and down the colonies just made the growing situation all the more explosive.

During this upheaval in the day-to-day doldrums, Chilton found a new home on the New London docks. He'd hop any ship that was leaving harbor, often taking lower wages and sleeping on deck amid the elements, just to get away from the sweaty grip of the land behind him and learn his new life as a swab. The salted air was cleansing, at least on the outside, adding color to his cheeks and a sharpness around his round Black Irish eyes. Standing on the prow in the early morning hours while the rest of the crew slept, he sucked in as much brine as he could, hoping it would take care of what was curled up inside.

Now a dyed-in-the-wool wharf rat, whose already sizable reputation for courage and grit only grew with each excursion upon the waves, Chilton soon netted a wife—a wispy clothier's daughter named Agnes Warren—and set up house on Bank Street. From this close vantage point to the harbor, and the marked increase in often-late-night voyages, Chilton quickly secured ownership of a merchant vessel he re-christened the *Sea Hag*, which he embellished in wide, bold black lettering on the stern, making sure everyone on the docks knew the name. A local artisan painted a terrifying visage of an aged crone, horns dripping kelp, mouth running red with blood. Rumors spread that the moniker was inspired by his notoriously frosty mother-in-law Eleanor Warren, who had provided the loan to purchase the ship, most likely to keep Chilton away from her daughter. Two years on, with Chilton spending more time at sea than at home, and Agnes without child, the investment seemed to have paid off for Eleanor. Either way, both parties seemed happy, or at the very least mollified.

After several seasons of stocking New London with rum, sugar, and what many thought were unseemly spices from the Caribbean and shadowy spots further to the southwest, the Intolerable Acts of the British finally pressed too deeply on the colonists, and the Revolution broke out in earnest, changing everything. Maritime activity turned from mercantile to martial, as all of New England, and New London, rallied to the saber-rattle of war against the British crown, at the behest of a steely Virginian named General George Washington.

Chilton was drafted into the newly minted American Navy an hour after he declared his soldiering intentions. He was officially granted the rank of captain by the Second Continental Congress, receiving his first commission to command the *Sea Hag* as a privateer against the ravaging patrols of the British fleet off the coast of New England.

Living in New London, Chilton was in prime position to raid the southeast Canadian coast and rebuff hostile moves against the heart and soul of the Revolution. It was 1776, and a year into the war, American losses were mounting, both on land and at sea, helped in no small measure by the constant flow of reinforcements from England by way of Canada. After a dozen successful incursions that inflicted notable losses on the Crown, the Royal Navy pulled back, avoiding the *Sea Hag*'s usual radius. Sensing a change in the tides, and eager to push the battle lines further into enemy territory, Congress issued Captain Chilton an express order to break up the supply routes and staging areas of Nova Scotia. Chilton rounded up his best veteran crew members and a gaggle of greenhorns inspired by promises of honor, spoils, and much righteous violence, refitted his vessel with new cannonry fresh from the smiths of Philadelphia, and set off up the coast to a hero's farewell. The last sight Chilton beheld on shore was the stooped and shaking figure of Agnes. She was weeping into her hands. It was the first and last time he saw her cry.

≵ⴳⵝⵓⵔⵏⵕ

Chilton walked down Pequot Avenue, passing School Street and on to Thames Street Portage. The cider in his belly shot fire down his legs and into his feet, melting footprints into the lightly blown snow, leaving a steaming trail behind him.

He avoided a look to his right toward Bank Street and the empty shell he once called his home, and all of the ghosts moaning in those empty rooms that had never been filled, no matter how many trinkets and furniture he had stuffed inside. Further out of town, the Chilton farm lay still and quiet, unmarked graves in the overgrown potato field leaching off the buried bodies of mother and daughter. He was glad they had been spared from what had happened, only wishing that his father still remained to witness what was coming. Chilton touched the club at his waist and felt a twinge of unexpected regret. Pa had died too soon, he decided, with too little horror to aid his passing.

Crossing Thames Street brought Green Harbor into view, and the outline of the *Sea Hag*. He watched the gentle sway of his vessel, noting every slope and angle that was engraved into his mind like the body of an immodest lover. His ship was the only craft moored to the wharf at Green Harbor. No others wanted to be within a hundred feet of her.

He tightened up his kerchief and continued down the street, passing the tiny Mariners' Church that teetered on a rocky outcropping near the graving docks, between the foundry and the fish house. A set of weathered stairs led up to the doorway, which stood wide open. This let in the cold, but also kept the congregation awake, while sending the message that God closes the door on no man, no matter the transgression, either at sea or lands immediately adjacent. A resonant voice boomed from the populated darkness inside. Even though he couldn't make out the words, he knew the sermon was coming directly to him.

"Today's message was first centered in the generous spirit of the Christian soul," intoned the barrel-chested Reverend from behind the pulpit fashioned from prow and rigging. "But recent developments have moved me to speak about courage, and of cowardice." Murmurs rippled through the crowd. "For a craven soul stands amongst us now. A shirker, a soft liver holding up a spine made of Goodie Holman's poorly baked bread." Mrs. Holman blushed in the front row, surrounded by a few laughs tinged with a constrained anger.

"It is written in Second Timothy," The Reverend continued, "that God hath not given us the spirit of fear; but of power, and of love, and of a sound mind. We were born into fear upon receiving the knowledge of good and evil, but through God's divine grace, and his protection, we now ... fear ... *nothing*."

"Nothin' 'cept a coward!" someone called out from the back row.

"Indeed, indeed, Goodman Pratt. For the Proverbs state that the wicked flee when no man pursueth: but the righteous are bold as a lion."

The congregation rumbled their consent. Heavy boots thumped the floor.

"And forget not the writings of the Revelation. Chapter 21, Verse 8: 'But the fearful, and unbelieving, and the abominable, and murderers, and whoremongers, and sorcerers, and idolaters, and all liars, shall have their part in the lake which burneth with fire and brimstone: which is the second death.' I say to thee, good people, that Hell awaits the fearful of all things that are not the Lord our God!"

A laugh cut through the shouts of agreement, turning every head in every pew toward the open door at the back of the church, where Chilton stood, holding a small statue of Jesus on the cross.

"Unhand our Christ," the Reverend commanded.

Chilton glanced around the room. "The last church I was in," he said quietly, "looked nearly identical to this one." He looked down at the occupied crucifix in his hand, absently rubbing the figure's feet with his thumb. "Except for this."

He shrugged and tossed the cross to the floor, where it landed face down. Half of the room shot to their feet, gasps and curses knitting together in a seething ball of fury.

"Blast ye!" the Reverend hissed, pointing down from his place on high. "Blast ye and burn ye."

"Piss on yer coward soul, Chilton," snarled Mr. Pratt, rushing toward the lone man in the doorway.

Chilton pulled a flintlock from his breeches and shoved the barrel into the advancing man's mouth, stopping him cold. Chilton rattled the metal around Pratt's teeth, knocking out a rotting molar that dripped to the floor.

"He wouldn't dare kill a man in church!" a woman sobbed, gripping her husband tight.

"No, I wouldn't kill a man in church," Chilton said, his voice flat. "But I would kill this one right here, right now, because he be no man, and this be no church."

"You blaspheme!" thundered the Reverend, nearly shaking apart the pulpit under his whitening knuckles.

"Oh, I do more than that," Chilton said. "I speak the truth hidden beneath the blasphemy, because I surely seen it, plain as day and the stars at night. Hell be no fiery place. Hell be dark, and wet, and glitters with white gold."

Men rushed at Chilton, who cocked the hammer on his pistol. Urine ran down Pratt's trouser legs, collecting in a steaming pool around his boots, creeping toward the statue.

"Hold!" the Reverend shouted, stalking up the aisle, shoving aside tensed bodies, unsheathed knives. He stood before Chilton, holding out his worn Bible like a talisman. "Begone, yellow demon. Your reckoning awaits you, outside these doors."

Chilton glanced behind him. "I reckon it does." He tipped his hat and looked down at the floor, flipping over the cross with his boot, facing Jesus to the ceiling. "He won't be coming down to save you." Chilton took in each pale face in the room, engaging every wide or squinted set of eyes. "Because the other ones are coming up for you first."

No one said a word, the silence broken by the thud of a woman who fainted in the back row. Chilton walked out the door, a black silhouette against the blinding daylight.

Outside the church, Chilton descended the steps slowly, pulling the war club from his breeches and twirling it with his free hand. Below him on the street a crowd waited, led by a core group of hard-bitten men and a few slatternly women who had followed him from the Broken Pony. They were arranged at the bottom of the stairs in a ragtag formation, pipe smoke dancing up into the icy sky. All of them regarded him squarely, ginned-up courage hardening their bloodshot eyes and tightening their grip on musket iron, daring him to raise the pistol. Even outside, over the breeze, he could smell their fear underneath the stink of alcohol and sweat. He knew that smell, and hated it. His senses were heightened after his last night at sea, and what he saw there. A survivor's wisdom, he told himself, never believing it for a second.

Chilton stepped off the stairs and parted the crowd, heading toward the waiting *Sea Hag*.

"A pox on you, Captain Craven," came a gravelly female voice from the crowd.

He turned to the woman, aged beyond her grief by strong drink and late nights in various alehouses around town, and no doubt a few swinging hammocks as well. Chilton's eyes narrowed, drawing up the hollows underneath like two tiny curtains. His lips curled sideways. "A pox on all of us, Widow Embree."

Invectives spewed out of the tavern patrons, while more shocked gasps issued from the church doorway that was emptying out the congregation, encircling Chilton on all sides. Hands fluttered hex signs, while men held their women close and covered the eyes of their children. A few of the more modest citizens of New London hurried on their way, sensing trouble. Most stayed, hoping for the same.

"You speak the language of witchcraft," Samuel Ennis said from the crowd, swinging his musket down from his shoulder.

"O that witches were real, and their sorcery at our disposal," Chilton said, casually scratching his growing beard. The crowd moved back several steps in each crescent, as if pushed by an invisible hand instead of the outrage of fear. "But alas, we are alone in this universe of monsters."

Mrs. Embree conjured up a ball of phlegm from deep within her wasted being and spat on the ground as she staggered forward, dragging her gnarled left foot behind her. She groped inside her untied bodice, digging between flattened breasts, and produced a damp white hen feather, holding it out in front of her body as if poisonous. Stopping in front of Chilton, she reached up and buried the pointed quill into the loosening wool of his topcoat lapel. He looked down at it, the soft tendrils along the shaft dancing slowly by the cold breeze off the ocean.

"Only medal yer'll ever wear."

Chilton nodded once, turned on his heel, and left the crowd standing huddled together, the steam of their quick breathing twisting and disappearing into the whistle of the building gale.

It was thus that the citizens of New London sent off Captain Chilton, who boarded the *Sea Hag* alone, cut the mooring ropes short from the cleat, and headed off to sea.

꒰ᐢ⑅ᐢ꒱

The *Sea Hag* carved the waves with an almost perceptible eagerness as it headed north, just as it had done the last time, when the deck was crowded with singing mariners busying themselves with battle preparations. Today the ship held only one man, which was all it seemed to have room for now.

T. E. Grau

At the helm, Chilton listened to the creak of the rigging, the flap of the topsails, trying to find solace in the familiar sounds. He looked up at the crow's-nest, where young Paul Wiggan once held vigil, day or night, only coming down to eat and often taking his meals high above the planks. He had wanted to be a captain someday, just like *the* brave Mark James Chilton, who assured him that without question he'd be Commodore in a free American republic before his twentieth year. All he had to do was keep his eyes sharp and his instincts whetted. Wiggan promised that he would, and meant it, yet when the time came, he never saw them come up from the sea, because he wasn't at his post. No one was, and so no one did see them, as they moved from sea to air without a sound, parting the water as if it were a silken curtain and climbing up the side of the ship like bloated crickets. But the day before, the lad had been in the nest, keeping constant watch for the dread Nova Scotian Colonel Alexander Godfrey, who never materialized on the horizon as Chilton thought he would. He even had the night watch burn torches, in hopes of drawing out Godfrey from the blackness, but to no avail. The Colonel wasn't in the area, or if he was, he chose not to engage. A disappointing turn of events for the crew, and no less to Chilton, who was itching for a fight, and a chance to hobble the Brits.

With a strong tailwind and favorable current, they made good time. On their port side passed Massachusetts, New Hampshire and Popham Colony country in upper Maine. The whole of the trip north, they encountered no resistance, allowing them unfettered and almost leisurely ravaging of the suspect fishing communities once they hit the islands of Nova Scotia, starting with Yarmouth and working their way up the northeastern coastline, jagged with inlets and the jut of peninsulas piled with massive boulders. While unarmed villagers watched helplessly from a distance, Chilton and his men sank suspicious ships at harbor, dumped a portion of the fish haul, and restocked their barely depleted supplies from larders as they worked their way to Halifax, where they knew a proper battle awaited, possibly with help from additional American privateers that constantly prowled the nearby waters. The triplet grouping of Halifax, Spryfield, and Burnside were always fattened by their British masters and begging to be plucked. Chilton was only too eager to do the plucking, and had cleared out space in the lower hold of the *Sea Hag* for pillaged goods. He felt like a proper pirate, a regular John Halsey on a divine mission, and wished there was a little more bend and heft to the saber at his side.

On the morning of the day they were to reach Halifax, Wiggan spied the thin, delicate steeple of a church peeking over the rise of a high cliff face walling off a hidden cove. As sure as an arrow stuck in the ground, the spire gave away the location of the beating heart of a community, tucked away from the sea, that wasn't logged on any of their charts. This was indeed queer, as they were using smuggled British maps certified by the King's royal cartographer. Chilton immediately took it for a secret British military base, hastily built to give the appearance of a bucolic fishing and herding community.

Chilton's heart soared as he instructed his men to arm heavily, loading up extra powder and ball, as what they were about to find on shore would dwarf any domestic goods they burned or pillaged in Halifax, and wouldn't come willingly. "We've found a nest of vipers, lads," he said with a laugh. "So bring your biggest sticks."

The raiding party arrived on shore in the late afternoon, just hours before sundown. After encountering some difficulty scaling the cliffs that led from the rocky beach, they moved quickly into the rundown village. The streets were empty, the houses timeworn and ramshackle, looking barely livable. Everything smelled heavily of rotted fish, although no catch lined the empty stalls in the cramped market square. As they crept from building to building, they found not a living soul, discovering instead several large smelters installed in various innocuous-looking warehouses. The town seemed deserted, although recent habitation was evident from the filthy conditions. All was quiet as a tomb. No birds sang in the trees, no dogs barked behind fences or sniffed the gutters. The trees had been cleared from every rutted sidewalk. Yards were only tamped-down mud. It was a depressing place, lorded over by the high steeple of the church that sat on the hill just above town, a small belfry window giving a clear view of the sea. The citizens must have seen the approach of the *Sea Hag*, and had fled.

The small scouting teams returned to the square and gave their reports, regrouping around their captain.

"There's nothing here, sir," reported Lt. Jeffrey Scott, Chilton's first mate, who was the last to return. "No weapons, no supplies, no—"

"—No people," Chilton finished, his gaze resting on the church. He walked toward it, climbing the smoothed dirt pathway that lead to the plateau above town. Scott nodded and followed, checking the breech on his Brown Bess and affixing his bayonet. The men did the same, pulling out ramrods and falling in line behind the man in front of him.

The church was infinitely older than the rest of the town, and seemed to be built right into the granite—or out of it—with the wooden frame and shingles acting as more of a masking agent than necessary architecture. No windows lined the walls, giving the impression of a strong box instead of a house of worship. The twin doors were shut and no sound came from inside, but the structure had a weight to it, a populated heaviness that seemed to hum.

T. E. Grau

"There aren't no cross up there," Wiggan said, squinting at the shape topping the steeple point. "It's a star."

"Byzantines," spat an old scarred sea dog named Boone. "In league with the Tommies."

A slight tapping came from behind the doors. Muzzles rose. Boone moved to the door, and Chilton nodded. Boone turned the iron latch and pulled back the heavy wood.

A cold stink issued from the church like a punch, squeezing groans from the sailors. Chilton raised his kerchief over his nose and mouth and entered, waiting for his eyes to adjust to the near absence of light. As vision slowly returned, he found what must have been the entire village—close to a hundred people—peering back at him. Men wore hats low over their faces, women were veiled like brides, their features hidden under gray and green lace, but hinting at large, strangely colored eyes and wide lips. A man removed his hat and smoothed back wispy black hair over the smooth skin of his unnaturally streamlined head. A smile seemed to play on his toadish lips, but it might have been the curvature of the mouth high up the cheek. His hazel pupils were flecked with gold and appeared to push out from his skull with each quick, labored breath he took.

Chilton took a step back, shocked at the unnatural appearance of the faces, the waxen expressions, that stared back at them.

"What's wrong with these people?" whispered Scott.

"Inborns," someone said.

"Celestials," Boone said.

"Innsmouth folk," said a sailor named Burdoo, who had grown up in the woods north of Boston. His face was pale and his trigger hand shaking.

Chilton had heard of the secretive village of Innsmouth, tucked away in a narrow fold of the Massachusetts coast, although neither he, nor anyone he knew—save maybe Burdoo, by all accounts—had been there. It was a closed community of religious and cultural abnormalities, founded long before the rest of the colony. The crew must have stumbled upon another outpost of the Innsmouth clan, or perhaps the other way around. Either way, Chilton thought, there certainly weren't any British sympathizers here.

"Look at the ceiling!" Wiggan said, his voice far too loud.

Above them, the vaulted ceiling was covered in images and pictograms set amid a heavenly scene of what first appeared to be aquatic life playing amongst stars and fanciful planets unlike anything Chilton had seen in the schoolhouse astronomy texts. The entire rendering glistened, made entirely of pale gold, studded with gemstones the size of a man's fist.

"We're rich!" Boone shouted. A few of the men cheered.

"Return to ship," Chilton said, cutting through the excitement, trying to keep the creep of fear out of his voice. He had never been afraid before, but the gnawing chill in the pit of his stomach surely must be it. It felt as if the ceiling were watching them. "We have no business here."

"But Cap—"

"Return to the goddamn ship!" Chilton ordered.

The men hesitantly turned to the door, one taking Boone by the arm, but the door was no longer behind them. Several of them turned back around, and discovered the way out was now across the room. The congregation just stood and silently watched.

"What is this?" Chilton whispered aloud, his voice rising in pitch.

No one in the room uttered a word. His men began to mutter, and Chilton felt as if he had to say something, and was about to blurt either a salutation or an order to fire—he didn't know which—when a small robed figure emerged from the collection of villagers and shuffled toward the sailors. He or she was no larger than a child, but moved with the pained effort of extreme old age. When it reached the men, a hand emerged from the folds of heavy fabric and stretched out to the club at Chilton's waist, revealing a spindly arm covered in flaky, desiccated skin.

"Leper!" Boone breathed.

Chilton knocked the hand away with the butt of his musket, and at that instant the congregation came alive with a sudden outburst of barks and croaks, surging forward like a swarm of locusts. A boom echoed off the high rafters, and then another, and a dozen more. Smoke choked the air and bodies slammed to the floor.

"Back to the ship!" Chilton shouted into the haze, burnt saltpeter stinging his nose. He charged through the confused mass of leaping and fallen bodies toward the last location of the door. Something snatched his musket from his hands while the man at his side was pulled to the ground. Chilton pulled his pistol and fired at the writhing figures in front of him, swinging his club at anything that didn't fall.

He reached the door and kicked it open, pulling out each of his battling men to the last, before slamming the door shut and leaning into it with his full weight, soon joined by several of the larger crew members.

Hands slapped at the door from inside; the slaps quickly became heavy lunges. The door bowed and the thick rusted hinges creaked, but held. Scott and three other men pushed a weathered buckboard in front of the entrance, and the men stood back, breathing heavily while reloading their muskets.

"What do we do, Captain?" Wiggan said, face pale.

Chilton listened to the inhuman sounds coming from inside the church, terror shriveling his insides, stealing his voice, melting the iron of his past.

"Captain?" Scott said.

"Burn it," Chilton finally managed. "Burn it all."

፠ᕯᕲᕱᕯᑐ

The *Sea Hag* raised anchor and crept back out to sea. Chilton stood on the quarterdeck and watched the last rays of daylight frame a dozen funnels of black smoke that joined together into a growing cloud above the burning town. He didn't move until the sun was gone, and the sea and the sky became one.

The crew was silent on the voyage home. No hoots and hollers and drunken brags about feats of barter and sexual conquest once they reached New London. Boone even stopped talking about the pool of melted gold collecting in the burning ruins behind them, never mentioning a return plan to collect it. The ship was full of plunder, but this was forgotten. The mugs hung empty and the grog stayed in the barrel. Everyone to a man seemed drawn inside themselves, contemplating what they had just seen. Hands made the sign of the cross, or clenched together in rusty prayer. Even after all duties were complete, no one slept. Wiggan didn't climb the crow's nest that night, huddling instead down in the hold. He didn't want to see anymore. Chilton walked the deck, trying to conjure up the right words to share with his men, to reassure them, but he had nothing to say. Instead, he retreated to his cabin while Scott took the helm.

፠ᕯᕲᕱᕯᑐ

It was hours into the silent journey home, and just before dawn, when the *Sea Hag* suddenly stopped in the water, pitching man and cargo headlong across the ship.

Ships on open sea, miles from shore and nowhere near pack ice, never just stop, but the *Sea Hag* did, freezing on the main as if grabbed by a giant hand below the waves. Sails billowed and the masts groaned angrily, but the craft held fast while everything simply *stopped*. No waves lashed at the waterline. Scott regained his feet, ran to the railing and looked down, finding the sea smooth as glass, like a frog pond. The texture of the water mesmerized him. He could see down deep into the ocean, spying a light that filtered up from the murky depths. A pale golden glimmer of something very deep, but quite vast.

Chilton had been thrown into his dressing closet, and was frantically fighting through the maps that covered him when he heard the first shout. By the time he reached the door to his quarters, the shouts had turned to screams.

He dashed out on deck just as the ship was overrun with lightening speed. Shadows leaping out of shadows, hopping and scuttling, extinguishing torches that reflected off bulging white eyes, slick mottled skin. Musket fire flashed in the darkness, etching scenes of dismemberment in stark relief. This was something that should not be. An impossible sight, ripped from fever dreams buried deep within the brain and deeper in the human race, clotting men's marrow with dark truths that retreated from evolution outside the caves, waiting in forest glades and beachside caves for those who remembered the old ways guided by the Elder Knowledge.

Chilton staggered from the inside out, feeling his grip on sanity loosening by the moment, helped in large measure by the fact that the things grabbing his men and pulling them into the water made no sound at all. They slaughtered in silence and with a cruel efficiency. All he could hear was the one-sided screams of horror ripped from the throats of his crew, and the splashes as they hit the water, carried down by the things that had boiled up from the deep. His men called out to him for help, pleading, but Chilton stood frozen in place, his courage rendered down to a glue that fastened his boots to the deck timber. He just stood and watched as the ship was cleared, one shrieking man at a time, until all were gone.

After several tortured moments, a lone creature leapt down from the yardarm, landing heavily. It rose partially erect and looked in Chilton's direction, then brought itself to its full height, thin muscles rippling strangely under its glistening skin. As if showing the man it could do so. It could stand like him, taller than him. It could beat him—and had. The face born at the bottom of the sea seemed vaguely human, in some respects. More than the faces of the other ones that had taken his men. Walking in a loping manner, it approached Chilton, carrying something small and glittery in its webbed hand. He set it down in front of the captain, turned, and leapt over the rails, disappearing under the water without so much as a splash.

Chilton gazed down at the object resting at his feet.

The *Sea Hag* was empty. All that remained was her captain, who stood on deck, waiting to go down with a ship that remained afloat.

ᎫᎾᎧᎶᏫᎦᎻᎠ

To live is sometime to die, to leave behind the world you once knew and to journey, transformed, into the Hell of displacement, separated from everything you knew and loved. This was the hero's journey, and the course on which Chilton was unknowingly traveling, as the *Sea Hag* sliced through the ocean waves toward that locus of nightmares.

T. E. Grau

Just as he had returned home, he arrived again at his destination, alone on an empty ship. He consulted the chart spread out on the deck, checking his sextant one last time, then dropped anchor.

Chilton went to the railing and discarded his pistol in the water, then his compass, and finally his club, testing its heft one last time before casting it into the sea.

With great effort, he unmoored a cannon and dragged it to the center of the upper deck. He sponged out the bore and dried it with great care, then packed the chamber with an extra portion of black powder and wadding, before loading the heaviest ball on ship. He cut the wick of the slow match short and wound the strands tight.

Leaning against the cold iron of the neck, Chilton reached into his pack, pulling out a small crown. By its size, it could have been a tin children's toy, or a priceless diadem for a boy king, made of intricately intersecting wires of pure white gold. He removed the white feather from his lapel and stuck it into the top of the crown, before placing it on his head. Then he slowly disrobed, piling his unwashed clothing into a heap that he sprinkled with gunpowder and set ablaze from the lantern he placed nearby.

His offerings made to the sea, and the signal fire set, Chilton waited.

It didn't take long. Just enough time for the sun to set over the land behind him, washing the thin clouds in pink and yellow, and once again merging sea and sky.

Then they were there, emerging from every concealed spot on the ship and standing in a loose formation. Like a military raiding party.

Chilton got to his feet, his naked flesh quivering in the biting cold, and looked over the group of creatures. How pale and hairy he seemed in comparison to their smooth, colorful skin, flared with splotches of red and stripes of yellow. Natural war paint. When he finally spotted the one that had given him his crown, he nodded.

In one movement, he picked up the lantern and straddled the lip of the cannon, forcing down the muzzle toward the deck under the weight of his body. With one last look at the tall creature, he turned and smashed the lantern over the wick, and seconds later the cannon fired, sending its charge down deep into the guts of the *Sea Hag,* which were packed with a privateer's fortune in gunpowder.

The ship exploded like the floating bomb it had become.

A shower of wreckage descended through the dark water, drifting gently down toward the waiting golden hive, which was already marshaling for a war for which the land dwellers weren't prepared. This would be a revolution of a different kind.

Amid the debris, the small crown tumbled, the white feather gone.

TO HOLD YE WHITE HUSK

BY W.H. PUGMIRE

The enemy submarine had torpedoed our warship, and my frantic memory of the event was smoke and fire and men screaming as Roberts and I managed to free one of the lifeboats, which crashed into the churning waters below us. We dove into those waters and manned the small boat, preparing to row from the sinking ship, when we noticed a body floundering in the water, a body we identified as Gustav Sturhman. Moving our vessel to him as he momentarily sank beneath the water, we hauled him in, and then, struggled to row away from the scene of disaster. I watched Sturhman open his eyes and nod at me, and I didn't like the glassy look of his eyes—that half-dead glaze. We had managed to move a good distance from the warship that was almost submerged when we heard further explosions and screams.

"They're torpedoing the lifeboats!" Roberts yelled, with terror dancing in his eyes. It came to me then, the low queer sound of singing. Looking at Sturhman, I saw that one of his hands had clasped the jade amulet that he always wore; his eyes were closed and his lips moved slightly as he moaned a song in the Dutch language. I often thought of how ironic it was, that this very young man, whose family had moved to America and become citizens thereof, was now fighting in a war in which his Dutch nation was not involved. His eyes suddenly opened and his speech grew in volume; words spilled from his mouth that were in a language—if it could be called that, for it seemed more like vocal retching than anything else—that felt like pinpricks on my brain. I was aware of the thick coils of black cloud that began to spin around our boat, coils that rose from the water and sank from above us until our vessel was completely cloaked. I was aware of the violent noise coming from beyond our black cloud, explosions and screaming; but I was far more attentive to how this cloud was affecting my senses, for it smelled like nothing I had ever encountered, and when I sucked wisps of it into my nostrils and mouth I was confused by the twin sensations of sweetness and a kind of rottenness.

Sturhman began to cough violently, and Roberts bent over him to smooth a piece of white cloth over the young man's face. The Dutchman had removed the amulet from around his throat and he now offered it to Roberts. "It's a very old family heirloom," Sturhman rasped, "centuries old, Johnny. Please try and return it to my family." He then became very still, and his eyes lost the light of life. I don't know how long we floated there, in silence, before the black cloud finally dissolved. We were alone on the waters; no other lifeboats or their shattered remnants in sight. We prayed over the corpse of our young mate, and then we carefully lifted him out of the boat and into the water. We did not watch his sinking body, but stretched our aching limbs and moaned, and shut our eyes, and dreamed unsettling dreams.

I was awakened by an odd cry, which I thought had come from my companion; but when I pushed upward with my elbows I saw that Roberts was asleep, with Sturhman's odd amulet clasped within closed hands. Our lifeboat moved through a thick mist that made it impossible for me to detect the time of day. Bending to the small cabinet that had been built into each lifeboat, I removed the canteens of water and tins of jerky that were always kept there, and I nudged my companion awake and offered him sustenance. We ate in silence, and as he ate Roberts examined the amulet.

"It's damn old," he said, nodding to himself. "It reminds me of a pendant I once saw, an old silver sphinx charm from South India that a swami was trying to peddle. But the facial expression on that was benign—this is pure malevolence. Made out of jade, I think. The wings suggest that it's supposed to be some kind of sphinx, or maybe some outlandish winged hound effigy." He finished his jerky and seemed to notice the mist for the first time. "Weird. I was just dreaming about a mist like this and something hovering above the boat that I couldn't quite make out, something that bayed and flapped huge wings. Don't usually remember my dreams. How come you're so silent?"

"I'm listening. Do you hear it? The sound of waves on a surface?"

My words seemed to act as conjuration, and the dim form of an island broke through the mist. Without thinking, I grabbed hold of the length of rope that was tied to a metal ring on the bow of the lifeboat and dove into the water, swam to where a little plot of sand was surrounded by an outcropping of rock. Struggling onto the land, I heaved the boat toward me. Roberts finally jumped from the vessel and joined me in pulling it to the surface of white sand. Exhausted, we sat and heaved heavy breaths, and I examined the landscape. There were no signs of human occupation, enemy or otherwise. Although the foggy air made it difficult to see the land fully, what was revealed seemed strange and surreal.

"What a riot of colors!" Roberts exclaimed. "It's like a Klimt painting come to life."

"Who?"

"He's a controversial artist I met some years ago in Vienna," my companion explained as we continued on our way. "Look at those trees just ahead, at how their upper branches conjoin and form a kind of tunnel—and those trees have such an eerie, almost sinister form. And there beyond them, you can just make it out through the fog—some kind of ruins."

Roberts had come from money and had lived a rather Bohemian existence before being called to serve his country; but to hear him talk of relics found in India, of foreign painters met in Vienna, was a bit unreal to a guy who had been raised in poverty. But I understood what he was trying to get across. The trunks of the trees on each side of us resembled stout crones out of some medieval fairy tale, and the way their sinister-looking branches reached over us and met would be unnerving to one who had a sensitive imagination. The multicolored leaves on those trees were like nothing I had ever beheld, and the way they littered the ground made me feel as if I was treading on the spilled contents of some outlandish kaleidoscope.

"It's like we're walking through a dreamscape," young Roberts went on. "If I touch you, are you really there?" He reached out to lay his hand on my shoulder, and I was so unnerved by his weird behavior that I playfully locked his head in my arm and roughed him up a bit.

"We're real enough, buddy," I assured him; yet when I laughed and looked into his eyes, I was nonplussed by their expression, which seemed to belong to a haunted soul.

Escaping from the canopy of sinister trees, we stood before the ruins, which looked to me like the mausoleum of some slumbering giant. It appeared to be constructed with huge blocks of sandstone, and one sensed that it had been erected centuries ago. We entered one of the three arched thresholds, and I was glad that the muted daylight fell through those portions where the roof had fallen. We stepped over debris and down a pale stone stairway, into a kind of antechamber, past thick columns and a mammoth black statue that depicted a faceless winged demon. This was not a place of buried and discarded treasure, but more like a pit of decay and wreckage; and we did not want to touch any of the relics that littered the ground as we walked to the thing that squatted on its dais of circular green stone—that enormous figure that seemed vaguely familiar. I heard my companion's breathing and turned my head to squint at him; and when I saw that his hands clutched the strange amulet fastened to twine that encircled his throat, I suddenly recalled where I had seen the likeness of the mammoth statue before us. The difference between the two carved creatures was that the forelegs of the statue on the dais were raised so as to hold their burden of white flesh, that shapeless bundle of something that might once have been human.

"All hope abandon ye who enter here," Roberts whispered, quoting something that I suspected was from the Bible, a book I've never read. Although I wasn't religious, I had a sense of sin, of that which went against what was good and right. "This temple isn't real, and we're not really here. No, don't look at me like that. This is some kind of crazy hallucination that has plagued us, from fatigue or lack of sustenance. Look around you—this place is mad delusion." The location wherein we stood was indeed all wrong. There were too many walls, and several of them were at odd angles and made you dizzy if you stared at them for too long a time.

W. H. Pugmire

Hieroglyphs had been etched onto some of the walls and columns, but the alphabet was puzzling and somehow revolting. It seemed an outlandish coincidence that the huge statue before us should so resemble the amulet that had been worn by our dead comrade. My brain grew tight with pain as I tried to figure it all out, and I rubbed my eyes with one hand in an attempt to soothe the discomfort away. I was vaguely aware that Roberts was moving to the three levels of the dais that might have been meant as steps. I watched in silence, my head pounding with pain, as he went to the misshapen bulk of flesh held by the statue; and I moaned a little as Roberts raised his arms and used them to lift the dead thing from the carven thing and place it, almost reverently, on the surface of the dais. Fragments of penetrating light, a manifestation of faintness, pierced my eyes; but I ignored my discomfort and staggered to the dais, climbed its steps and knelt beside my friend. I regarded the white thing, and I knew that Roberts was right—we had entered some kind of macabre dream.

The husk of pale flesh was flattened and utterly void of color. Even the places where the flesh had been ripped—bitten into, I think—were bleached. But the head of the thing was bloated, round and puffy—and it wore the face of Gustav Sturhman. "This cannot be," I moaned.

"It isn't. I told you, we're hallucinating. Maybe the jerky was bad and we've been poisoned."

"This isn't a dream, Johnny," I answered. "It's diseased reality. This stone that we kneel on is real, look how my fingers bleed after I've scraped their flesh across its surface. Funny; I feel no pain."

I rammed my fist down on the floor of the dais, again and again as I screamed insensibly, until Roberts stopped me and clutched my bleeding hand. He then grew as white as the husk of flesh before us, as some shadow passed over the portions of roof that had not fallen in ruin. We heard the baying of some nightmare thing as the smell of my blood coiled to our nostrils.

Roberts began to chuckle—or maybe it would be best described as chortling. He had removed the amulet from around his throat and was working its cord over the bloated head of the dead thing. A current of noisome breath propelled from the corpse, an exhalation that contained a kind of language. I shuddered at the sound of it, and at the sight of Roberts bending low so that he could press his ear against Sturhman's distended lips, those lips that subtly parted. I shivered violently as Roberts began to mimic the language that was whispered to him, the insane chanting that was an epitome of evil. The air *quivered* at the unholy utterance, and I sensed again that winged thing, hungry and hidden, that beat its wings above the edifice. I watched, with eyes that began to burn as if they had been doused in acid; and I trembled, as the dead thing below us raised one arm so as to hold its awful amulet to Johnny's mouth, to those lips that moved as they continued to chant in whispered voice the nameless words of outrageous idiom. I could not flee or scream as the dead thing's mouth moved to Roberts' throat and began to feast. I could only laugh like a mad fool, and dig my fingers into my face, and cry like crazy as I plucked out my smoldering eyes.

THE SEA NYMPH'S SON

BY ROBERT M. PRICE

1

Etchings and Odysseys

ear, my friends, and I shall relate to you the strife of titans and heroes. Of King Agamemnon, great general of the Argive hosts, the second Theseus, slayer of the Man-Bull in pitched combat. And of mighty Achilles, invincible son of the sea-nymph Thetis and scourge of all men. It was boasted that he possessed nigh-invulnerability to weapons, his divine mother having dipped him into the flow of the Styx, forgetting only the heel by which she gripped the infant tightly so he might not slip from her grasp and perish in the icy waters. But none had seen such powers displayed for the very good reason that their supposed possessor was so skilled in battle that his opponents collapsed to the ground inert before any might lay a hand or sword upon his person. Invulnerable or not, Achilles was surely gifted with more than mortal prowess. Days before, all had witnessed a dispute between the two heroes as great Achilles professed himself too high and too mighty to take orders from a mere mortal.

Agamemnon had at first refused to give in to Achilles' petulance, then repented in vain once Achilles refused to lead the army onto the field of battle against their Trojan foes as formerly. The general dreaded the hobbling of his men by the gloom that must settle upon them if the Son of Thetis did not lead them. Thus great was his astonishment the following dawn when Achilles emerged, fully armored, from his tent and wordlessly mounted his mighty stallion, awaiting Agamemnon's command with uncharacteristic humility. Agamemnon wondered whether the face beneath the visor of the other man's helm registered emotions of resentment or of stolid resolve. But the king's relief made all doubts and fears flee like wind-blown leaves.

He ordered the men to advance to the plains outside the city.

The Achaeans cut through the defensive lines of King Priam, following Achilles' lead as a great ship divides the waves before it under the figurehead atop its prow. And so the battle went until that happened which no man dreamed possible.

Achilles fell.

As word spread, the Achaeans hesitated and the Trojans rallied. Achilles' blood scented the air, and the tide turned. It was all his compatriots could do to retrieve his corpse and retreat to their ships, the rear guard keeping the vengeful Trojans from their flanks as they fled in shameful disarray.

And today the rites of mourning were in full swing in Agamemnon's camp. He walked slowly to the tent of the fallen hero now, in order to collect some mementos which should become prizes in the games to be held later in the day to commemorate the slain champion. There were subtle sounds of motion inside, and Agamemnon drew his sword, thinking to surprise some jackal looting the tokens of Achilles. He drew back the tent flap.

And beheld Achilles.

His massive back faced Agamemnon, and he did not at once turn to greet him. But he did speak, and the voice was truly his. "Things did not go well yesterday, O great Agamemnon, did they?"

The stunned general stammered in reply. "But you were … all thought you slain … How…? Your corpse awaits the pyre even now"

"It is the body of Patroclus. Know you not his face?"

"In truth, I do not. *Did* not. But neither have I seen your own face, mighty Achilles." For indeed the Son of Thetis was never seen without his helmet, except by a select few, such as Patroclus, a common Myrmidon, but Achilles' favorite; some whispered, even his lover.

"Foolish Patroclus liked not to displease you, nor to disappoint his fellows. And so he begged the use of my armor to play his doomed masquerade, and I allowed it. Do not permit some young pup to win it in your games, Agamemnon. I'll be wanting it back. I mean to use it tomorrow."

With that, Achilles turned to face Agamemnon, for the first time with no concealing helmet.

Agamemnon gasped and hastened from the tent, his royal bearing gone.

2

An Unexplainable Couplet

Inside Priam's palace, most lamps had been snuffed out, though torches aplenty lined the battlements of the city walls, lest the treacherous Argives should seek to murder Troy's innocents in the night. By the light of a single candle, already mostly consumed, Prince Hector donned his armor—again. He had fought long and hard most of the day. Some of his bandaged wounds still bled, and his aches and bruises besieged him. He had done good, red work in the fields of combat, killed more than enough of the invaders for one day, but, instead of taking needed rest before the mêlée should resume at cockcrow, here he was strapping on breast plate and helm once more.

There was no way to armor himself quietly enough not to wake his wife Andromache, and now she stirred. For a moment she watched him silently, so that Hector did not at once know she was awake. But then she spoke.

"My darling, where are you bound? What business takes you away from our bed?"

"Beloved," he said, as he sat beside her on the bed's edge, "word has reached me that Achilles still lives. It was not he who fought and died before our city gates, but another. One dear to Achilles, and he will surely seek bloody revenge on the morrow. He will know that it was I who killed his man, and his sword will seek my blood. I go now to the Oracle to inquire of the battle and its outcome."

"But I know the outcome, great Hector. You will strike his head from his shoulders. You shall kill him as you killed his double."

"Aye, I shall meet him, sharing the joy of battle. But I fear I know the outcome better than you, so well that I require no oracle for that. I am no match for his supernatural prowess."

"But surely that is superstition; he is a man, albeit a mighty one. And so are you, my husband."

"Do you not see? It matters not if he be demigod or mortal man. He fights with strange and godlike skill in either case. In the end I cannot stand against him."

She was weeping now. Between her sobs she asked, "Then why leave me if this is to be our last night? What use in seeking out Apollo's soothsayer?"

"Our gods are deaf as well as mute. The priests face me with empty stares. I must know what fate awaits you, and my father, and the city. Best to know ahead, so we may plan for the worst."

"Have we not planned for that already?"

"My father and his counselors think they have, but I fear they have not reckoned with just how terrible the worst may be. Now I go to supplicate the Cabiri." (Which, being interpreted, means "the Old Ones.") "They are older than the Titans and, it is rumored, know what even the gods do not. What I do now is the last good thing I may do for Troy—and for you, beloved Andromache."

Withal, Hector strode from the room, as Andromache stood and watched him from the door frame.

An hour later, he emerged from a secret tunnel as yet undiscovered by Achaean scouts. He had arranged for a guide who now stepped forth from a shadow into the moonlight. Following him wordlessly, Hector soon found himself stumbling through the darkness. He was little helped by the unsteady light from the smoking torch borne by the robed and hunched dwarf. The diminutive form led him down rocky paths he had never before seen, though, as Prince of Troy, he believed himself familiar with every foot of his kingdom's territory. He prayed it was not a trap. He knew his death was imminent, but he hoped to live at least long enough to face Achilles and to die a glorious death. His guide made no intelligible sound.

At length the mismatched figures slowed to a stop before what appeared to be a mere fissure between boulders. It turned out to be a cave mouth through which mighty Hector could barely squeeze his frame. When he got through, the dwarf was already well ahead of him on the scarcely navigable trail downward. There were no torches bracketed to the wall, but as Hector climbed and jumped his way along, he came to realize that there were in fact smooth channels, worn by countless feet, but they ran along the *sides* of the cave walls. He tried not to think of what denizens might frequent this corridor. He was glad his silent guide had advanced so far ahead of him, given his greater familiarity with the passage. Hector did not care to see how the fellow found the going so easy.

When the tunnel gave out, it opened onto a huge grotto, the ceiling of which was too remote for the eye to see. The space was filled with a great black lake. Far out into the still water stood a small island. Hector's guide was nowhere to be seen, but two new figures populated the rocky outcropping. One stood, his torch revealing nothing beneath his overhanging hood. The other sat or squatted, it was hard to tell which because of the way he, or she, was robed. This one's face was covered, too. The standing figure spoke a single word, which penetrated the gloom so clearly, it seemed to Hector that it had been spoken directly into his ear by someone standing in concealment beside him, so that he turned to make sure he was alone on the bank.

"*Ask.*"

The prince bowed both knee and head and spoke. "O Oracle of Kronos, I would learn the secret of the morrow: who will prevail in battle? What will become of the vanquished?"

Now it was the seated figure who spoke, if it really was speech. What it uttered did not sound at all like any tongue known to the well-traveled Hector. It was guttural and bubbling, more like gargling than speaking. Whatever the intended meaning, this saying could do him no good. But then the standing figure spoke, and Hector understood. It was even as Apollo's oracle at Delphi: the seeress would speak in unknown tongues, and the attendant priest would interpret in mortal dialects.

"The one who supplicates R'lyeh
Shall perish but shall win the day."

When Priam's son raised his head to look, both figures had disappeared, though neither before nor now had he seen any boat pulled up to the tiny island. He could not suppress a shudder, but his soul was eased of its burden. His city and his loved ones should survive his death—because he had thought to visit the oracle He had been wiser than even he suspected.

3

Spawn of Thetis

Hector had wept with his wife as he embraced her for what both knew to be the last time. But as he strode into the midst of his brave Trojan soldiers, his mood lightened. He realized he had become elated. It was as if knowing his fate beforehand drained all worry and uncertainty from him. He felt free to fight his hardest, to fight for fighting's sake. Indeed, did not every true warrior feel the same deep down, since at the last all must fall to the sword of some foe? Any one of them might be Hades' agent come to claim him. No prowess could save a man from that. And if this Achilles were to prove the scythe of Hades today, what of it? Yes, he would thrust and swing with pure abandon for as long as the Fates assigned him to play the game.

His men seemed to expect something full of import. Some clapped him on the back with admiration and affection, disregarding his royal gravity for this moment that made them alike, brothers of the blade. Hector could read in the eyes of many that they knew the outcome as well as he did and were starting to mourn already. For their part, the advancing Argive host was rejuvenated, singing lusty battle chants, knowing now that their demigod champion was alive after all, doubly convinced of his invulnerability. It was hard to defeat men like these, who seemed already to rejoice in a victory that no oncoming events might steal from them.

The dance of death given and taken began, as it always did, with a largely ineffective exchange of arrows, though ever fewer as supplies waned. Upraised shields frustrated their descent, making a sound like hard rain on a roof above. Cast lances did more damage, but by now these were scarcer, too, and most were saved for the thick of combat, where more accurate aim was possible. Still, using spears as lances made them more unwieldy in such close quarters, where swords were easier to heft and swing. The twin armies met with an impact like rival cloud banks crashing together. The compact masses of both armies held locked for a moment before small rivulets of men began to trace twisting channels through the living wall of the enemy, until permeation became vitiation, and the solid continents of men shattered into a multitude of island knots of hacking and thrusting swordsmen. Men imagined they were hallucinating as blurs of orange and red clouded their vision, but the blurs were very real splashes of blood and woven lattices of darting bronze swords.

The pattern changed yet again when the carnage retracted into a rough circle, its center occupied by a pair of men so similar in stature and build that they might have been Castor and Pollux; only the Dioscuri were not believed to try to slay one another as these did. Achilles had appeared, striding a path carpeted thick with blood, facing a gore-spattered Hector who had arrived in much the same style. Swords drawn, the two stood still in the eye of the hurricane that raged around them, none of their men daring to take their curious eyes off their own struggles.

Hector charged, sword and battle axe performing glinting acrobatics in the air. Achilles somehow met both with his single sword, then jabbed at Hector's chest, pulling his blow at the last second, laughing. He was toying with Priam's son, who smiled at the jest, as he was equally rejoicing in the sport.

Hector let the fight take him, use him as its sword against great Achilles. Before he consciously recognized it, Hector had aimed a razor blow that hacked off Achilles' right hand. He saw it drop to the ground and felt stunned with new hope: this Achilles was by no means invulnerable! In that moment he noticed a faint greenish tint on the severed hand as it bounced in the bloodied dust. Could it have begun to decompose so quickly? Surely not. But this astonishment was at once replaced by a fresh one, as he saw *another* right hand, with the same tint, reach down to retrieve the sword from the loosening grip of the lost fist. His foeman had grown a new limb in a moment! Thus did Hector discover the secret of Achilles' invincibility. He could be wounded, and seriously, but, like some reptile, he could replace what he had lost.

The Prince of Troy cursed himself for becoming distracted, though he could scarcely help it. He set his attention again on Achilles. As he calculated the best course in view of what he now knew, he was again nonplussed, this time at the sight of Achilles reaching for his encompassing headgear and removing it.

The face revealed was not that of any tribe of man, he was sure of that. Thetis' son had no hair on his head, no lordly beard, no lips, even. His eyes bulged and showed no emotion, did not even blink. His wide mouth opened, showing no teeth. And from it rushed a nebula of purplish mist. Hector involuntarily breathed in the noxious cloud and found himself instantly paralyzed. He wondered for a second whether the stuff would also have the effect of numbing the pain of the death blow he was about to receive. And thus he went down, cruelly sundered.

The news of Hector's defeat spread like wildfire back along the lines and over the walls of Troy. Andromache did not seem to take the report with the shock and hysteria all expected. She only shook her head in resignation, as if she had already seen this section of the Fates' tapestry. She alone knew that she had. Likewise, she alone knew of Hector's visit to the forbidden prophetess. The oracle had given her no hope for her husband, but now she prayed the rest would come true, that Hector's sacrifice should somehow win Troy's salvation.

4

The Gift of the Gods

The contest between the Achaean alliance and Troy had stretched on for so long, a decade so far, that few remembered the cause of it. And those who did resented the fact that so many had spent their lives for nothing, for mere revenge in a domestic melodrama. For the whole crusade had been mounted to recover one Helen, the adulterous wife of King Menelaus. She had abandoned the unhandsome man for a young lover, himself of dubious virility, named Paris, a dandy visiting from Troy, who had bewitched Queen Helen with a cock-and-bull story about a dream in which he had been chosen to compare three beauties: Aphrodite, Athena—and Helen. He had given Helen the crown, and, once informed of this oneiric victory, she had given him her heart—at least her body—and the pair of fornicators had escaped to Troy. The Greek kings had agreed that they should all lose face if one of their number were allowed to be cuckolded without punishment. Their wives shook their heads in disbelief at the men's childish plan but knew they dared not protest. And so the Achaean fleet sailed.

But the Trojans had even greater cause to bemoan the foolishness of their warring. All resented the presence in their city of the Greek adulteress, whom they regarded as little more than a common harlot, and wondered how it counted as a matter of honor for Troy to defend her and her girlish paramour against the Achaeans, who were clearly in the right. No wonder the war was going so badly; what self-respecting deity should reckon Troy worth defending in these circumstances? Their only comfort was that their opponents' gods must be equally disgusted with them, hence the endless deadlock where no battle was ever decisive. It was like a dream, where the same thing happened over and over again.

If it was looking like a stalemated child's game, perhaps it was appropriate that a child's toy should beak the logjam. For one morning the Trojan watchers on the ramparts scurried to report to the grieving Priam that one of the gods' playthings had fallen from Olympus onto the plain just outside the city gates. It was a huge wooden horse of crude but unmistakable design. The king called in his most trusted priest who read the fresh entrails of a dove and announced that the giant, wheeled effigy was indeed a gift from the gods, a token of their blessing and favor, and victory was surely within sight. They need only open the gates and wheel the thing in, and the protection of Zeus and Hera would be theirs. Priam, ever one to heed the guidance of the gods, considered this plan and quickly agreed. He had no reason to suspect that his priest had only days before received a talent of gold from an Achaean envoy.

There was great rejoicing in the streets of Troy when the gates were opened and the horse pushed through. The king and his nobles sat upon a hastily erected dais wide enough to support several thrones. They watched excitedly as Priam's chaplain intoned the ancient psalms of thanksgiving and slit the throats of sacrificial beasts. Ritual dancers gestured and swept their limbs with contorted grace. Flutes and lyres added to the festivities—until a trapdoor in the equine belly swung loose and, like foals exiting a mare's womb, a squad of Achaean soldiers poured out and hit the ground running. The priest knew what was coming, but he was nonetheless quite surprised when the first thrown lance skewered him through the back like a gigged frog, in mid-prayer.

The crowds scattered like panicked sheep upon the appearance of a wolf. The Achaean wolves played their part and set to the slaughter. Priam and his retinue were clapped in chains, though the universal belief in numinous charm surrounding any and all royalty, whether or not one's own, protected them from further rude treatment, at least for the present.

The invaders quickly opened the wall again, and their comrades poured in like a flood through the sluice gates. The Trojan warriors had been caught completely off guard and mounted no greater resistance than an occasional armed struggle in an alley. The city was occupied in only a few hours. There was an initial wave of executions, but these had ceased, and the nobles prayed there would be no more. It was not long before Trojans and Achaeans alike settled into an uneasy peace, awaiting further decrees of fate.

In this relative calm, the one exception was Achilles. His breach with Agamemnon was easily forgotten, his sadness at Patroclus' passing mitigated by the glorious death his friend had died. And now he set about tying up the only remaining loose end. He began to look for the craven Paris, who was hiding somewhere in the corners of the city, perhaps even within the palace. No one opposed him; indeed, most Trojans blamed Paris for the ills that had befallen them. They were pleased enough to see whatever justice Achilles and Agamemnon might deem fit for him. Some Trojan troops gladly volunteered to join in the search, or as they viewed it, the hunt.

The search was systematic; Paris eluded his pursuers for a week or so only because he had a few retainers and servants loyal enough to report to him the movements of the searchers. At length, however, the reports were that Achilles and his party were closing in, and that mere minutes remained to Paris. Helen had been taken from him, and he knew he would die alone. He waited like a condemned prisoner in his cell, but an idle peek out his curtained window galvanized him to reckless action. There below him in the street stood Achilles, still helmeted, talking in a friendly manner with Helen. His armor was impenetrable even if he were not physically invulnerable. But his heel! Did not the story have it that his right heel could be wounded?

Paris turned back to his chamber and quickly scanned the interior. Yes, there it was: his hunting bow and a single arrow in the quiver. He thought of the poison draught he had prepared lest he fall alive into the hands of the vengeful Achaeans. He crossed the room and withdrew the sturdy shaft, then poured most of the chemical on the arrowhead. Then he notched the arrow on his bow and used his best hunter's aim.

Like an ambushed deer, mighty Achilles crumpled to the pavement, the potent drug coursing through his screaming veins. Helen screamed her lungs out, drawing the attention of nearby soldiers, half of whom dragged her struggling form away, the others attending to the stiffening body of the demigod. They pulled his ever-present helmet off to aid his breathing, but quickly stumbled back away from the visage now revealed. A few heard Achilles' last words, though all anyone could afterward recall was the mention of his mother's name. Was he calling to her? Praying to her?

Word was secretly passed to the deposed princess Andromache that her husband's slayer had met with justice, but she did not appear gratified, as they expected. For she remembered the words of the Cabiri seeress, whom men called Cassogtha:

"The one who supplicates R'lyeh
Shall perish but shall win the day."

Perhaps, she pondered with terrible dread, her Hector was not the one intended in those equivocal words. And perhaps Troy's fate would be more fearful than she had imagined....

Robert M. Price

5

Black Gods of R'lyeh

If Andromache and Priam lamented the slain Hector, Achilles was by no means without mourners of his own. The rites begun when the Achaeans thought the slain Patroclus to be Achilles were now resumed. His armor was made the prize in the contest of champions. Ajax the Greater won it, and in centuries to follow it would come into the possession of Goliath of Gath and of Roland of the Franks, and others still. But wailing for Achilles was not confined to the world of poor mortals, for, deep beneath the ocean caverns, no unblinking eye but her own beholding her, Thetis, the mother of the godling Achilles, floated motionless in place before a great pylon encrusted with barnacles. She had often come here over the centuries to pay homage to Great Kronos who dreamt and tossed and turned within, stirring up the waters to a churning boil on the surface of the Great Sea. But now she had come for a different purpose in the wake of her son's cowardly murder. In the forgotten tongue of Galiyeh, which is also R'lyeh, she bubbled forth the primordial summons which, being interpreted, is *"Release the Kraken!"*

The Achaeans had gotten what they came for. Menelaus' honor was restored, though men still whispered jests at his expense, and Agamemnon decided it was time to go home again. He left a contingent of troops in the city and laid down terms for tribute to be paid by the Trojans by way of war reparations. But none would ever be paid, for Troy was soon in no position to pay them. As the last of the remaining Achaean ships (many had been burned or else dismantled for the wood to build the Horse) sailed safely away, Agamemnon thought his fleet had entered the shadow of a mighty cloudbank. This he could not fathom, as the skies had been brilliant blue and mercilessly sunny only moments earlier. Then he raised his eyes aloft, as did many of his men. None of them spoke thereafter of what they thought they saw swiftly sailing through the heavens above them, toward defeated Troy. It was vaguely human in outline, suggesting an elephant on its hind legs, but with wings spread like sails to the wind currents. But the worst was the mammoth squid atop its shoulders, with hooded orbs like liquid black jewels.

Across the waters, a single man out in the fields, a man named Aeneas, saw the vast cloud-like shape approaching Troy and took off running.

THE BOONIEMAN

BY EDWARD M. ERDELAC

irebase William stood on a bare hill shorn clean of the emerald jungle that covered the remote Chý Prông District. Five years ago in '66, Sikorsky CH-54s had played the barber with ten-thousand-pound daisy-cutters. Buzzing Chinooks had dropped in the men, trenchers, and bulldozers that had finished the job, adorning the hill with a ring of sandbags, berms, and barbed wire. The whole shebang had been capped off with six 105mm Howitzers arranged in the standard star pattern, one in the center to fire illumination rounds during night attacks, five at the points. Designed as a temporary fire support base for special missions near and occasionally over the Cambodian border, William had for some reason remained when its garrison had changed from marines to Army Special Forces. Now it was home to an element of the Army of the Republic of Vietnam, or would be, once the A-Team of American MACV-SOG advisors officially turned the place over to Captain Dat Quách next month.

Lt. Jatczak wondered how long the ARVN would hold out before the North Vietnamese Army overran William. Nixon was pulling the plug on Vietnam, and the NVA was wondering how committed the US was to withdrawal. They'd been dropping sporadic, harassing mortar fire on William for the past two weeks; nothing serious, just trying to goad their jumpy southern cousins into expending the precious ammunition Major Dyer was writing off as 'field lost'.

The major had been at William longer than anybody. He claimed to have suggested the name of the place to the original CO after his uncle, who'd been a geologist and explorer. Nobody knew if it was Bravo Sierra or not. Dyer had served with the 1st Marines in Korea and done five combat tours in 'Nam: two as an Airborne Ranger, and three in the 10th Special Forces Group attached to various units, including a stint in the A Shau valley. He looked it, too, with his odd shock of white beard crisscrossed by wandering scars like old wagon trails, and eyes that looked as if they'd never found anything funny, ever. He was a real boonie rat and didn't bullshit.

Intelligence anticipated a big push by the NVA on the ARVN II Corps here in the central highlands. General Abrams was telling everybody and anybody he could about it, but it was being dismissed as the wailing of a brat who was having his war toys taken away.

As far as Jatczak was concerned, they were welcome to this miserable country. North, South, he didn't really care who won anymore. He had grown to hate the fucking bush, the stink of it, the summer heat, the punji sticks dipped in shit, and the way you couldn't even trust a little kid without getting your ass blown to hell. The 'Nam didn't scare him anymore. He was bored with it. His only fear was of not being able to leave it behind. He didn't wanna wind up one of those jumpy Section 8 saps shrieking into his pillow in the middle of the night. He wished he was back home in Calumet City, eating a drippy Schoop's burger and sucking down a milkshake. He was sick of C-rats for breakfast and cigarettes for dinner.

Jatczak was smoking in the TOC bunker watching Major Dyer, Chief Beems, and Captain Quách iron out details for the turnover when Albarada came in with a harried-looking man leaning on his shoulder.

Jatczak recognized him straight off as Beo, a Montagnard native from the little village on hill 231 in the boonies west of William.

He gave up his bench for Beo. Jatczak was the liaison officer, and had worked with 'yards for much of his tour. He knew the people, knew their lingo. They were good men, these highlanders. There'd always been some around the base, hired on as laborers. A few like Beo went out on missions with SOG, since they knew the terrain best. If you did them a kindness they'd step in front of a tank for you. They'd tripped a minefield once over the Cambodian border and Jatczak had gone back for Beo, guiding him out. Later, when he'd been on a fire mission over in Ratankiri Province and had caught a round through the calf, three 'yards he didn't even know had jumped on his body to shield him from getting hit again. He liked the 'yards, almost as much as he hated the gooks.

Case in point, Captain Quách. The sweaty little REMF in the aviator sunglasses was everything that was wrong with Vietnam. More of a politician than a soldier, always on the lookout for a bribe or an easy out. Who had Quách pissed off back in Pleiku to get this detail, and what the hell had MACV-SOG done to deserve him?

Beo looked like hell in a hand basket. His green t-shirt was sweaty and torn, and his loincloth was filthy. His rangy, muscled legs were slashed by elephant grass. He looked exhausted.

"He came up the hill out of the jungle," said Albarada. "'Asked for you, Major."

"He shouldn't be in here," Quách said testily, lighting a Black Lotus cigarette. "This is no place for him."

Jatczak unscrewed his canteen and passed it to Beo. *De oppresso liber, my ass,* he thought. The hippie that he might have been, the one that smoked grass and read Dee Brown behind the communications bunker, got testy, and the Green Beret he was itched to punch Quách in the trachea. The Vietnamese did the 'yards the same way the US had done their Indians, pushed them to land they didn't want until they realized they really wanted it after all, then caused them all kinds of grief trying to get them to move. Hell, the hill tribes didn't even call themselves Montagnards. That was a French word. The local tribe was Gia Rai. They didn't know what a 'monatagnard' was any more than a Lakota could tell you what 'Sioux' meant.

"It's still a place for him while we're here, Captain," rumbled Dyer, in that John Wayne way he had of putting an amen on things.

"What's the matter, Beo?" Jatczak asked him in his own language, when he'd finished drinking.

"NVA. I don't know how many. 'Couple companies."

Beo was no simple rice farmer given to exaggeration. Like Dyer, he was an old soldier, and had fought with the French back when they'd tried to run the country. But there was real fear in his eyes, and 'yards didn't fear for themselves.

"They were headed for my village," he gasped.

Jatczak relayed the information, mostly for Beems' benefit, as he knew Dyer spoke Gia Rai.

"Could be intel's big offensive," said Beems.

Dyer rubbed his scarred chin, frowning.

"Get on the horn to Pleiku, Chief."

Beems left, making a beeline for the communications bunker.

Quách looked as if he were about to shit a brick.

"We should pull out."

"No time. That ville isn't that far away," said Dyer. "We hold here."

"Sir, case in point," Jatczak piped up, standing, "permission to take a bird and check the ville."

"We can't spare a helicopter. We need every available man," Quách blurted.

Edward M. Erdelac

Jatczak looked over Quách's head at Dyer and raised his eyebrows.

Dyer nodded. "All right, Lieutenant. Go tell Wurlitz to warm up his ship. Have Sgt. Hale pick two volunteers from the ARVN."

"Major, I protest," said Quách. "The village is of no strategic importance and has probably already been ..."

"You're wrong there, Captain. That ville's more important than you know. Lieutenant?"

"Sir?"

He took Jatczak by the shoulder like an old college buddy and led him to the doorway, speaking low in his ear.

"Keep me apprised of the situation. I want to know the condition of the village as soon as you get there. Report anything out of the ordinary."

Jatczak nodded, though he didn't know what Dyer expected him to find aside from bodies.

Beo got up.

"I go too."

"You'll need a guide, el-tee," Dyer assented.

"Thank you, sir," Beo gasped.

As Jatczak turned to go, Dyer pushed something into his hand.

"Take this for luck."

Jatczak looked down at the trinket. He had seen it on Dyer's desk before and had always taken it for a paperweight. It was about the size of his palm and shaped like a starfish, made out of some dark, polished mineral.

Jatczak half-grinned, but the major's expression was, as usual, totally serious.

"Yes, sir."

Funny to think that Dyer, after all the shit he'd been in, put any stock in boonie voodoo. Jatczak supposed everybody had their Bravo Sierra, after all.

Twenty minutes later Jatczak, who had cross-trained as a Huey pilot, was dressed in chicken plate and riding Peter P next to Lt. Wurlitz, the team's flyboy. Wurlitz had once nearly killed Jatczak trying to prove he could loop a Huey. After stalling out at 3,000 feet and recovering at the last second, he'd tersely attributed his failure to the 'extra weight.'

They were flat-hatting the tree tops, bearing straight for a faint, discouraging plume of inky smoke curling over the jungle. Hale was on one of the door guns, singing Barry Sadler with a complete lack of irony. He was Alabama-born, fourth-generation Army. He bled O.D. green. Beo was in the back, looking as if he'd jump out and flap his arms if the Huey went much slower. Two green-as-grass ARVNs, Thu and Phom, rode along. Phom leaned forward and puked over the barrel of his M60 the first time the Huey tilted at a cross wind and righted itself.

"Jesus Christ!" Hale snarled, slapping his helmet on over his green beret.

But it wasn't the cherry's cookie popping that had inspired him to blaspheme.

The rotor wash blew a gap in the forest canopy below and the sinking sun shown down on a mass of brown clad bodies flowing like a muddy river in the opposite direction.

"NVA regulars!" Hale shouted.

More than a couple companies. Maybe a battalion.

Jatczak keyed the radio to call in the position back to William. A half a second later the M-60s were chattering, spitting 7.62 mm rounds earthward, raking the long line of marching troops as Wurlitz pulled back on the stick.

Something came streaking up from between the trees, trailing smoke.

Jatczak yelled 'incoming' just as it struck the tail rotor like a sledgehammer, tilting the ship so badly Phom nearly tumbled out, straining against the monkey harness as Beo hauled him back in.

Wurlitz cursed and fought the stick, opening up the throttle to escape the barrage of small arms fire that lit up from the columns, rattling like gravel on the underside of the ship and punching holes in the cabin floor. The central pedestal took a round and exploded in the cockpit.

Jatczak looked back and saw white smoke streaming behind them.

"How bad?" Wurlitz hollered.

"I can't tell," Jatczak said, glancing down at the ruined instruments between them. "Radio and the transponder are shot, anyway. How's she handling?"

"Like a fuckin' dump truck on a wet road! I gotta bring her in. I can't stay up here."

"We're past the midpoint to the village," Jatczak said.

"I know it."

It meant bringing the chopper down on the hill and maybe having to hump it back to base if they couldn't get it in the air again. And if there were more NVA coming …

The Huey bucked and dipped like a roller coaster, the RPM alarm wailing like a breakout at Alcatraz, indicators across the top of the panel flashing.

The village loomed. It was situated much like William on a bare bit of hill upthrust from the jungle proper. The NVA had done a number on it. The tranh grass roofs were burning, the communal longhouse billowing black smoke. The hootches, the animals in the pens, even the ground looked scorched.

Edward M. Erdelac

Wurlitz set the chopper down roughly on the east side of the village, just past the barbed wire wall. The first thing Jatczak saw was the little guardian totem carved out of pine, a squat, grimacing figure with an approximation of a beret atop its head and a white painted beard, just like Major Dyer's. He cringed inwardly. It wasn't just the ARVN that were getting left holding the bag once they pulled out. The 'yards had fought under the Americans against the VC and NVA for years. What would happen to them when Uncle Sam pulled up stakes? Was that why he'd volunteered for this detail so readily, to salve his own conscience? How would his burger taste back in the world, knowing Beo and his people were still here, dealing with the consequences of having collaborated with Americans?

Drive on.

As the engine wound down, Jatczak took off his helmet and unbuckled, jumping out of the cockpit to inspect the damage.

Beo bounded out of the back and collided with him. His eyes were wild, his cheeks streaked with tears. He had a wife and daughter. He pushed away from Jatczak and ran pell-mell up the slope.

Behind him, Hale and the ARVNs clambered out. Hale had his XM177 and tossed one to Jatczak. The ARVNs were armed with Special Ks and looked terrified.

Beo was almost to the top.

"Lock 'n' load!" Hale said to the ARVNs and covered the jungle. "Watch that treeline!"

"Where the fuck's your buddy going, Mike?" Wurlitz yelled as he marched to the rotor.

"Guy's got family up there. I'm going too."

"What about the goddamned rotor?" Wurlitz called.

"*Xin loi*, man!" Jatczak called, huffing up the hillside after Beo.

The sun was orange. The jungle was alive with the calls of birds and terrified insects. Mosquitoes buzzed in his ears and he saw the little bastards swarming in clouds around the edge of the smoke.

"Beo!" he called.

The 'yard paused at the entrance to the village.

Jatczak caught up with him. He took out his .45, chambered a round, and gave it to Beo.

"Easy, dude," he said.

Easy. What the hell did Beo have to be easy about? It looked like the NVA had marched through with flamethrowers, like the VC had done at Dak Son in '67. Every hootch was burned. Black bodies lay contorted everywhere in the dirt, the cooked flesh dripping off their charred bones. The smell was of barbequed meat. He remembered the first time he'd come to this village. Beo had killed a pig and cooked up some *chocon* for them.

His belly rumbled.

Christ. He needed a smoke. He reached in his pocket and found the stone Dyer had given him. He ran his thumb over it. There was a design on there, invisible because of the dark color. A circle with a warped star in the center, and an intricate little burning eye or branching column or something in the middle. Weird shit. He put it back in his pocket and got out his Lucky Strikes.

The storehouse was still blazing. It looked like they hadn't even taken the goddamned rice. Even the *yang pri*, the sacred stand of five precious *sua* trees in the center of the village, was burned.

He thought about Dyer's orders to radio him about the condition of the village ASAP. The ship radio was fucked, but there was an RT secured in the back.

He lit his cigarette.

They trudged through the ruins, kicking up ash. They passed the tombs, the little totem-surrounded huts packed with offerings and the belongings of the deceased. These abodes of the spirits were untouched, and he could imagine the dinks rubbing that stinking tiger balm on the backs of their necks and refusing to desecrate them, while not hesitating to immolate anything with a pulse. They had burned children alive with no concerns about angering any ghosts or demons.

Report anything out of the ordinary, Dyer had said. *Nothing out of the ordinary here, Major. Just the 'Nam. Bravo Sierra.*

Jatczak followed Beo to the ruins of his hut. The walls and ceiling had fallen in and were nothing more than a heap of firewood now.

"You too late," came a guttural voice.

Three men stepped out from among the tombs like ashen ghosts. They were 'yards, and Jatczak knew the one who had spoken, a squat man in a red head wrap and loincloth, with a black VC shirt and a necklace of weird silver spirals. His name was Rin, and he was the village *be gio*, or sorcerer. A tough bastard, more than a little *dinky dau*. He'd once seen Rin cut a VC's heart out and slip it still beating into a bag for God only knew what purpose. The Gia Rai grew their hair long, because cutting the hair damaged a man's soul. Rin kept his head shaved. Beo had told Jatczak once Rin's grandmother had been a Tcho-Tcho, but he didn't know what that meant, and Dyer had said only that the Tcho-Tchos were Cambodians and 'bad news.'

The two men on either side, he knew only by their nicknames, Lyle and Tector. They'd once screened the movie *The Wild Bunch* at the base and these two had eaten it up, hollering and hooting in the back row to beat the band, declaring they wanted to meet their deaths the same way as Warren Oates and Ben Johnson. Lyle smoked a long-stemmed pipe, probably packed with *koon sa* from the skunky smell and the red haze in his eyes. Tector had a spread of suppurating sores creeping up the side of his face, maybe leprosy. All three were armed. Tector had an AK-47, Lyle a homemade crossbow, and Rin a sharp, curved Cambodian *dha*.

Beo sank to his knees and clawed the black dust. He sobbed.

"How'd you escape?" Jatczak asked the others, slinging his rifle.

They came closer.

"They catch me, march me through bush, but I get loose, *tre bien*," said Rin. "These two, out fishing when gooks come."

"We've got a chopper," Jatczak said. "It's damaged, but maybe we can get you back to William."

Rin chuckled, showing his black and yellow Indian-corn teeth.

"No … we stay, lieutenant."

Yeah, William was probably the last place anybody would want to be in another half hour.

"What'll you do?"

"*Mut bong pao*," said Rin.

A sacrifice. They'd adopt a water buffalo into the tribe and then kill it. Everybody present would eat some of it. The Gia Rai were big on sacrifice to the *caan*, the evil spirit of the mountain on which they lived. The *caans* slept in the rivers and the rocks and had to be appeased regularly, particularly in times of misfortune. Beo had told him once that every family killed its first-born child for the *caan*, to ransom the spirit of the next. He'd taken it as *koon sa* talk, as they'd been sharing a pipe of the local homegrown at the time.

"I don't see any animals," said Jatczak.

"How many men you bring?" Rin asked. He was standing too close.

"Just Hale and …"

There was something off about the look in Rin's flat eyes. He looked through Jatczak.

"I'll go tell 'em you're here," said Jatczak.

"Glun will go," said Rin.

Lyle, the pipe smoker, nodded and walked off with his crossbow on his shoulder.

Rin went to Beo and put his hands on the man's heaving shoulders.

"I hear the ghosts of our people screaming," he said in Gia Rai.

"We can do nothing," sobbed Beo.

"*We* can do nothing," Rin agreed. "But the servant of Shugoran may."

Beo straightened slowly and looked up at Rin, blinking away his tears. "Shugoran?"

"The *caan*. The *yang pri* are burned," Rin said, pointing to the smoldering stand of *sua* trees with his sword. "Even now it stirs, smelling death."

Suddenly, from the east end of the village, down by the chopper, there came the clatter of Hale's XM177 on rock-and-roll, and the popping of the ARVNs' .45s.

"Contact!" Jatczak heard Hale yell.

He unslung his rifle and started to run, but Rin's narrow ankle jutted out and tripped him. He fell sprawling on his belly. The next minute his weapon had been kicked away. Tector loomed over him, covering him with his AK.

"What the fuck?" he yelled. "Beo!"

Beo still knelt in the dust.

"Come with me," Rin said to Beo, turning away from Jatczak.

The firefight continued on the side of the mountain. He had thought it was the NVA doubling back on the chopper, or maybe the reinforcements they'd feared, but he heard no returning fire at all. Then it was just Hale's XM177, and him yelling 'Get some!'

Then nothing.

Beo stood up and followed Rin to the sacred grove. Rin hacked at the bases of the damaged trees with his sword. Beo stuck Jatczak's pistol in his waistband and uprooted the spindly, blackened *sua* one at a time.

Out of the smoke to the east came Phom, limping, an arrow through his left leg. Lyle walked behind, Phom's submachine gun aimed at his back, the crossbow over his shoulder again. He was still smoking.

"Beo! What the fuck's going on?" Jatczak yelled, as Phom was flung down beside him.

Beo said nothing. When they had worked the last tree out, Rin called the others. Phom and Jatczak were hoisted to their feet and dragged over.

The five sacred trees lay scattered. The ground they had occupied was a black hole now. Jatczak knew it couldn't be that big, but the darkening shadows gave it the illusion of depth. A rotten smell rose from the hole, like decomposing vegetation and fish.

Edward M. Erdelac

They were forced to their knees.

Phom yammered shrilly in Vietnamese, asking what was going to happen over and over. Jatczak only shook his head and repeated that he didn't know.

Rin raised the sword and chopped through the back of Phom's neck with a single whack that sent his gobbling head bouncing into the hole.

Lyle lost his grip on the ARVN's jerking body and it lurched to its feet, the stump spewing a diarrhetic surge of blood that plopped warmly down on Jatczak.

It stumbled a few steps, tripped in the hole, and crashed to the ground, jerking and emptying itself into the black dirt and its khakis.

Rin chased it down and hacked it with the sword, the sound like wet kindling being chopped. He cut furiously, the sword swishing in the air, blood and meat flying up over his shoulder.

"Oh *Jesus!*" Jatczak whispered.

Rin stood up and turned. There was a hunk of something dripping in his hand, and he pushed it up to his face and bit into it.

Mut bong pao.

Jatczak felt for his knife in the dark.

He watched Rin hand the chunk of meat to Tector, who partook before passing it to Lyle.

Lyle put the scrap of the dead ARVN to his lips. Jatczak looked across at Beo. The man's face was a mask of disgust and wide-eyed terror. In that moment their eyes met. Jatczak remembered giving Beo's pretty little daughter a Hershey's bar, soft from being in his pocket, and asking her name. *Fumier.* Suspecting an embarrassing mistranslation, he had asked Beo if he knew what the word meant in French.

"Manure," Beo had confirmed. "Because she's such a beauty, she must be kept humble."

Jatczak had laughed at that, and he grinned now, insanely, as a blood-smeared Rin advanced on him with the sword raised. This fucking country. In one month he would've been on the freedom bird. He was gonna buy it in the bush after all, and it wasn't even a gook that was doing him.

He pulled his knife and rammed it to the knuckle in Tector's gut, for what it was worth. There was a gunshot. Rin toppled over, grimacing. Jatczak's .45 was in Beo's hand. The second bullet went through the hunk of flesh in Lyle's teeth and blew out the back of his skull.

Rin rolled over, groaning beside the hole.

Jatczak got to his feet.

"Christ, man."

"Sorry, lieutenant," Beo said. He handed the pistol over.

Jatczak took it and covered Beo, not sure what he was going to do next.

"We should leave, sir," Beo said.

"*We?*" Jatczak exclaimed, backing away.

"*Now*, sir," Beo said, staring down at Rin.

Jatczak spared a glance.

Beo hadn't been looking at Rin. He was looking at the hole, at Phom's head emerging from the shadows.

Jatczak couldn't understand what was happening. Phom's body was lying cut up a meter from the hole. How was his head moving?

It rose out of the dark, a slack jawed, drawn expression, drooping, dead eyes. The lids fluttered, and the eyeballs rolled weirdly in their sockets, as if they were being operated by a brain unused to the interface. The head turned back and forth slowly, the eyes screwing in unnatural directions.

"The fuck is *that*?" Jatczak shrieked, every hair on his body from his scalp to the tops of his feet uncurling.

"The *caan*," said Beo, backing away.

Jatczak trained his pistol on the head and emptied the clip at the thing, cutting it dead center in the sagging face.

It shook with each impact, and the skull trembled and cracked beneath, dribbling a surprisingly little amount of blood and a considerable volume of some sticky, greenish black ichor that spurted over Phom's cheeks and out his nose and the corners of his downturned, disapproving mouth.

The ground jolted so hard beneath Jatczak's feet it nearly knocked him on his ass. Beo grabbed his elbow.

"Let's *didi*, lieutenant!"

But Jatczak lingered, fascinated as the head rose clear of the hole on the end of some undulating substance he couldn't quite make out in the twilight. It was a viscous, glistening sludge. It flowed over Rin, who managed a weak moan as it pulled him close, like a child gathering a favored toy in its slumber. The ground cracked and crumbled and more of the stuff bubbled up. Even as Rin rolled into the thing, it reached out to the mutilated body of Phom and the corpses of Tector and Lyle.

Beo would wait no longer and jerked him nearly off his feet.

Jatczak ran alongside him, down the length of the village, the crisp bones of the dead snapping beneath his boots, through the gate and down the hillside to the chopper.

Hale and Thu lay dead near the skids, crossbow bolts in their chests.

Edward M. Erdelac

Wurlitz was on his knees, still in front of the tail rotor with his toolkit spread out alongside him.

Had he hid during the shooting and crept out to finish his repairs? No. As Jatczak got closer he saw Wurlitz was pinned to the tail by a bolt through the back of his neck.

Beo broke the arrow and pushed Wurlitz's body away.

"Will it fly?" he asked, squinting mystified at the rotor in the dark.

"Hell if I know!" Jatczak said, running for the cockpit.

The earth shook again. Lightning lashed the sky in a jagged arc over the village. Black clouds funneled upward from the middle of the village, and a hard, cold wind kicked up that made the trees bend almost double. Thunder rolled.

Jatczak slid into the pilot's seat. He toggled the engine control and engaged the main rotor. It whined to life as he flicked the overhead switches and lit the cockpit.

Beo jumped in the back and shouldered into the monkey harness, manning the right-side M60.

The rotor whipped the air now. Jatczak grabbed the stick and eased the ship into the air, praying Wurlitz had fixed the tail rotor before he'd bought the farm.

He glanced to his right and wished he hadn't.

The thing lumbered out of the burned village, a great dark mound wavering on two thick, indistinct legs. Just as it had gathered the corpses of the 'yards and Phom to it, it had also pulled all the burned villagers together, and now wore them, the twisted limbs of charred men, women, and children interlaced like some horrific suit of corpse mail. It had no arms, no features, but in its center there was a deep, swirling fissure, a terrifying throat-like tunnel of glistening dark slime. The hurricane winds that seemed to emit from the throat tore the planks of the wrecked hootches loose. Bamboo and wood were sucked into the black swirl and then swiftly absorbed and distributed to its swelling outer layer. The trees splintered and joined it too.

He felt the winds pulling at the Huey.

The bodies of Hale, Wurlitz, and Thu rolled and slid uphill toward it.

Beo cut loose with the M60, raking the thing with bullets, but though the bodies erupted and bled, and the thing shed bits of plank wood and bamboo, it didn't slow.

Jatczak tested the rotor pedals. The Huey turned sluggishly. He banked away and hauled ass east for William, climbing and weaving out of the thing's path.

"Jesus Christ, Beo! How do we stop it?"

"Don't know!" Beo yelled against the rush of the wind and the chopping of the rotor. "The sacred trees kept it sleeping! The sacrifices! Now there's nowhere to go!"

Jatczak looked down on it as they climbed.

It was descending from the hill now, tearing up rocks, dirt, the whole jungle, getting bigger every step it took and leaving a bare swath of stumps and flattened foliage behind it. He heard the trees ripping free, even above the engine.

It looked like the hill had come alive. It inhaled bats, birds, a tiger, even the lightning, which rippled down into its empty face as if it were nursing from the ponderous thunderheads overhead. It was a monarch conscripting all its vassals. A wild, hungry vortex building a patchwork suit of armor from vegetation and animals. It howled like a lonely monsoon as it came.

Jatczak struggled to keep ahead of it. Beo held the trigger of the shuddering M60 so long it began to heat up and cook off, the bullets popping in the belt so that he had to rip it free, nearly losing his hand in the process.

"Beo!" Jatczak yelled, fighting to keep a scream from erupting through his lips. "Get on the radio!"

Beo knew how to work the portable RT. In a few minutes they heard the panicked chatter of Captain Quách going back and forth with his superiors. They could clearly hear explosions and gunfire amid the squelching.

Beo brought the RT up to the cockpit and Jatczak yelled into the receiver.

"Pot Shot to Chilly Willy, Pot Shot to Chilly Willy ..."

After a few minutes, they heard Dyer's voice.

"Pot Shot, this is Chilly Willy actual. We got our hands full here. What's your situation? Over."

"Sir ... I got ... there's something ... big. Sir, I don't know how to explain this.... I don't ..."

Jesus, he couldn't even keep it together on the radio. How to describe the thing? It was as if somehow all the blood of all the children they'd doused in napalm, all the malformed defoliant babies, all the lost limbs the VC had hacked from their own people, all the blown-off fragments of all the men and women and the hate and bile of this whole freak show had seeped down into the ground; and the earth, she had puked up something, something concocted from all that heinous shit. Something that was coming to consume everything and everyone.

Dyer's voice came back, surprisingly calm.

Edward M. Erdelac

"Easy, Pot Shot, easy. Have you still got that good-luck charm I gave you? Over."

The what? Jatczak had forgotten the star-shaped stone charm. He didn't have it. It must have fallen out of his pocket at some point. What the hell did he want to know that for?

"Uh ... negative, Chilly Willy. Over."

There was a long break.

"Pot Shot, has the boogieman left the hill? Over."

It sounded like he said 'boonieman.' That's what this was. The Boonieman. The boonies come alive. The 'Nam on foot. The whole goddamn war given a clumsy, monster's body with punji stick teeth, toe-tag eyes, and napalm breath to shamble around in.

"Pot Shot, I say again, has the boogieman left the hill? Over."

Dyer knew about the thing in the hill. Jesus, why hadn't he told them? He fought down his panic.

"Chilly Willy, affirmative. It's comin' your way, sir. Over."

Another maddeningly long break.

"Pot Shot, understood. Be advised. Do not attempt a landing. Over."

Landing? Jesus, it was the last thing he wanted to do. Still, there was Beems and Albarada and the others. They were his brothers.

"Chilly Willy, that thing's not stopping. If you pop us some smoke I can come in for evac. My ship's practically empty. Over."

Then all of a sudden there was a hell of a lot of feedback and Quach's voice came through, spluttering.

"Yes! Yes! Come and get us!"

Then Dyer was back.

"Pot Shot this is Chilly Willy actual. Do not. Say again. Do not attempt a landing. Our lines are failing. You can't tell the cowboys from the Indians down here. Just get yourself a nosebleed seat and watch the fireworks. Over and out."

He understood. Dyer would call in an air strike. That would take care of the thing. Had to.

Five minutes later, with the Boonieman dogged on their six, they spied William.

It was a Chinese fire drill down there, lit up by intermittent explosions, and the flickering pulse of a drifting parachute illumination round from the center artillery. The ARVNs scurried all through the compound like ants in a rainstorm, transporting ammo, relaying orders, bearing wounded away. The bunkers poured green tracer fire outward as wave after wave of NVA regulars rolled inward from the tree line and collapsed in the trenches or got hung up on the barbed wire or were cut off at the ankles by claymores or flung into the air by mortars.

The Howitzers fired in succession, the ARVN crews scrambling frantically over them. Jatczak saw the 105 shells crash into the jungle, trying to crush the attack at the source. It was no use. The NVA were coming in from every direction, and as they watched, a squad of belly-crawling coal-black sappers blew a new hole in the wire and sandbag perimeter on the south side with improvised Bangalore torpedoes on bamboo poles. The enemy poured into the gap.

In that instant, the Boonieman broke through the tree line. It was immense, as tall as the hill on which FSB William sat. Behind it, leading all the way back to Beo's village, was a wide path of bare earth like that left behind when the C-123's dumped Agent Orange. He could barely stand to look at the slimy hole in the middle of it, as if he would be compelled to aim the nose of the chopper for that opening and fly right in.

When it reached the lines of NVA, they were swept screaming into the dark sky, tumbling end over end like swarms of bugs caught up in a vacuum. Their equipment was sucked up too, guns and mortars crashing along with the rush of men, mashing together in a grotesque amalgam of steel and flesh, vegetable and bone, wood and rock.

Beo gibbered in the back, something about his family.

They orbited the chaos helplessly. The chopper gave a lurch as one of the pedals locked up. Jatczak panicked, thinking the rotor had gone out again, but he felt down beneath the panel and found something wedged there.

It was that paperweight the major had given him. It had fallen down there. Why had Dyer asked about it?

Below, the attackers tried to flee or fight, but it was fruitless.

However, the NVA who were already inside the wire, fighting the ARVN's and the SF at close quarters, stayed where they were. No one inside the perimeter of William seemed affected by the Boonieman's whirl and suck.

The gun crews lobbed round after round at the thing, but the shells only sank into its mass and exploded with a far-off, muffled sound somewhere within.

Though it shuffled voraciously at the edge of Firebase William, the Boonieman didn't enter the perimeter.

Each time it tried to advance, it stopped short, as though it had run into something. And something else, a trick of the light maybe, but the shape of the layout of the base, the star pattern of the 105s, the circle of barbed wire in which they sat, the placement of the center gun with its illumination rounds, like a burning eye. It all suddenly coalesced in Jatczak's mind. The arrangement of the base was the same as the sign on Dyer's good-luck charm.

He heard Dyer's voice on the radio again.

"Elder Sign priority! I say again! Elder Sign priority! Boogieman at the wire! Broken arrow! Broken arrow!"

Jatczak pulled back, putting the firebase between himself and the Boonieman.

"What does it mean?" Beo asked, clinging to the back of his seat.

"I don't know what Elder Sign is, but Broken Arrow's a call for any aircraft in the area to dump their payloads on the base."

"Everyone will die," Beo said.

"That's the idea, man." It was some cowboy shit. *Adios, Dyer.*

He flung the stone charm on the co-pilot's seat.

Beo snatched it up.

"What is this?"

"I don't know. Something the major gave me."

"It reminds me … of a carving on the *yang pri* trees," Beo said, stroking the engraving in the center.

"Here they come!" Jatczak hollered, hearing the buzzing of engines.

They roared in from the southeast. Prop-driven A-1E Skyraiders up from Pleiku, four of them, with South Vietnamese Air Force markings. If the flyboys took exception to the Boonieman, they didn't show it. They loosed a storm of 20mm rounds, peppering the ground and the Boonieman. All four dropped all their hardpoint ordnance, including napalm. FSB William was murdered by explosions and draped in a shroud of liquid fire. The *caan* was splashed with a 2000-degree tidal wave of burning hell.

But even as the flaming gel spread up its body, two of the Skyraiders passed too close to the thing and were plucked spinning right out of the air. They fishtailed into the black maw and collided, exploding. The Boonieman inhaled the fire and the fragments of the two fighters rattled into place on its growing outer bulk.

The air strikes had obliterated William. The Boonieman trudged to the top of the hill, no longer hampered by whatever had kept it at bay. It stood howling, coated entirely in blazing napalm, a towering beacon visible in the darkness for klicks around.

Jatczak shuddered. It was unstoppable. Irresistible. Where could they go that it wouldn't follow? It was slow, but it was as inevitable as death. It was a gaping mouth, patiently, indifferently, but assuredly waiting to be glutted.

He urged the chopper to bank and descend. The wet mouth of the Boonieman spiraled repulsively. The mantle of corpses, the machinery, the jungle: all that was just the trappings of the hunger that waited in there, as it always had. What were the odds that he would be here this night to see this? How long had it slept beneath the hill, waiting for the war to come and wake it, anticipating him? Why should he avoid it? It seemed crazy to live full of dread. Who the hell was he, to deny the Boonieman?

He felt the stick move of its own volition in his fist and let go. The chopper was drawn toward the Boonieman.

Good.

He heard a clink behind him and he looked back to see Beo unstrapping himself from the monkey harness.

He had the major's charm held to his chest. The wind was whipping his shirt and long hair, and the light cast him in flickering orange.

He caught Beo's glistening eyes a moment before the 'yard stepped out the open door.

Immediately Beo was caught up in the sucking wind and whipped past the cockpit, freefalling toward the Boonieman.

A surge of jealousy flared in Jatczak's heart. No, he had to be first. *Come back here you fucking dink.* He wrestled with his seatbelt.

But it was too late. Beo became a spread-eagled silhouette, like a doll. His clothes and hair caught fire. He disappeared somewhere in the wet black throat.

The Boonieman shuddered. The throat quivered and collapsed. Tons of stone, flaming wood, bodies, and machinery tumbled down in a great avalanche, and just as suddenly, the chopper, released from the strange wind, went into an erratic spin.

Instinctively Jatczak gripped the wild stick and wrestled with it. He planted his boots on the instrument panel, screaming with the effort of contending against the more familiar insistence of gravity. Finally the ship nosed up and leveled again.

He looked down at the fiery wreckage strewn across the smoking remains of William. The sight was a snapshot of hell. Thousands of broken corpses lay strewn amid piles of twisted metal, broken timber, and shattered stone.

The bones of the Boonieman.

Edward M. Erdelac

Had Beo killed it with Dyer's charm, or doped it back into slumber with his own life, as the 'yards had done for God knows how long?

More likely the latter, because Jatczak realized he was circling the hill, scouting hard for a place to land. He kept seeing the black spiral swirling behind his eyes, hearing the monsoon howl like an insidious call over and over in his head, drawing him down.

He pulled up and *didi*'d after the Skyraiders, his heart hammering in his ears, mumbling to himself just to drown out the noise in his head.

The wind had gone, but the pull was still there.

He wondered if it would ever let him go.

THE TURTLE

BY NEIL BAKER

ergeant Oliver Schulte clenched his buttocks and lifted his knees no more than two inches, but this tiny gesture yielded great results and he sighed with relief as his cramped limbs tingled with renewed blood-flow. He peered through the front porthole into the gloom of a most disagreeable evening; bellicose clouds grumbling overhead, their saturated bellies threatening to dip into the very bay itself. The lack of moonlight and the omnipresent mists reduced visibility to less than ten feet, and Sgt. Lee did not like that one bit. No sir. Not when bobbing in a modified barrel in dark waters said to be teeming with godless fishfolk. *No sir, not one bit.*

He wistfully considered how Bushnell's face would contort upon hearing his beloved submersible referred to as a 'barrel'. Indeed, after his invention's maiden voyage, Bushnell himself had called the device *The Turtle,* but Oliver knew what it really resembled; a coffin. A pear-shaped, vertical coffin, just waiting to be flooded or blown out of the water. Oliver had accrued the most hours in Bushnell's device. He had unsuccessfully attempted to screw a powder keg to the underside of *HMS Eagle,* both men blaming each other for the failure of the mission, but this effort had so captivated General Washington that their commander-in-chief had insisted on repeat attempts. The deployment of floating mines and surreptitious hole-making in the hulls of British barges had been satisfying enough, but none of these would be as crowd-worthy as the sinking of a frigate, and it just so happened that *HMS Cerberus* was moored in Niantic Bay for the evening. Double pay and the promise of relocation for his family from the shanties of Old Lyme, threatened by the fevered masses who worshipped a rumored sea beast, to the inland town of Hartford had been enough to get him back into the crate, a freshly sealed powder keg strapped to the exterior of the submersible, mere inches above his head.

He cranked the handle next to his right leg with slow, deliberate effort, feeling the resistance of the water against the paddle-blade mounted on the front of the submersible. The pear-shaped craft lurched forward with a barely audible splash and soon Oliver settled into a steady rhythm which propelled him forward at a little under walking pace, leaving no wake in his path. His left hand gripped the rudder bar and he steered slightly to starboard, into the relentless push of an annoying current that desperately wanted to spill him out into the Sound. The soporific rolling of the *Turtle* always managed to calm Oliver before a mission, but just as his mind began to drift along with the submersible a small black object fell from the roof, brushing his nose on its descent. He recoiled with a start and looked down only to see a beetle, no bigger than his thumbnail, rocking on its carapace, its legs bicycling in the air.

"How did you get in here?" Oliver said to the helpless bug, his voice deafening in the cramped vessel. He raised his heel, hovering it over the helpless form, watching the insect's desperate attempts to right itself. After a few seconds his foot came down upon the beetle with a faint crunch and he turned his gaze back to the circular window. An insignificant life snubbed out, just one more casualty of war. In the morning he would have words with Bushnell about the cleanliness of this craft.

After a few minutes a yellow smear of shore lights began to emerge from the blackness, and then Oliver saw three columns of flickering lantern flames that seemed to rise from the water and disappear into the clouds; the central masts of the *Cerberus*. Oliver's mouth instantly dried and he took a swig from a water pouch hanging from the rudder bar. This was the night to show what he could do in Bushnell's *Turtle*: a chance for redemption, fishfolk be damned.

His more recent sabotage attempts had been impeded by the insidious spread of the sinister cult that festered along the Massachusetts coastline, corrupting good people and transforming them into bilious shadows of their former selves; webbed hands stretching to grasp at unfortified townships that were easily converted. With Washington devoted to repelling the British threat, it had been no surprise to see Ben Franklin step up to tackle this new problem. The biological, theological and political aspects of this new issue were like opium to the old man, and he had thrown himself into negotiations with the sea cult's human representative, a shifty young man named Birch. Despite Franklin's efforts, the cult continued to infect the eastern coastal regions, and glassy-eyed agents of the new order now infiltrated the waters as far south as New Haven. This prompted Franklin, on orders from Washington, to advance troops by land and sea to Long Island Sound in a final attempt to stop the ghastly advance of the aquatic monstrosities and their demonic rituals. Naturally, the British had capitalized on this new threat to the eastern coast and remained thoroughly disinterested in a combined effort to stamp out the cult, for it had rapidly transpired that the fertile land was much more important than the corruption of good Christians.

Sgt. Lee, however, was a good twenty miles from the nearest friendly ship and was increasing that margin with every turn of the propeller crank. He slowed until he was drifting about eighty feet away from the stern of the vessel and then turned the handle backward until the *Turtle* stopped dead in the water, bobbing silently, its lethal cargo scraping gently upon the rounded shoulder of the craft. The *Cerberus* was moored a little more than a hundred feet from the shore, her bow pointed inland as if she wanted to escape the inky waters. He stared intently at the top rear decks of the ship, straining for signs of life, but none materialized. This was odd. Welcome, but odd. Every fiber in him yearned to crank forward quickly and secure his payload to the exposed rump of the British warship, but he felt compelled to sit tight, and so removed his hand from the paddle crank, pausing to take another drink while he watched his target closely.

There. Movement! A lone figure ran to the back of the ship, a lantern held high and swinging wildly. Oliver could now see that he was a naval officer and he watched intently as the man looked out over the aft railing while running the considerable width of the deck back and forth, his movements frenzied and erratic. For a second Oliver thought he had been spotted, but then the officer turned without any indication that he had seen the submersible and sprinted back toward the mizzenmast. It was obvious the British were distracted by something; perhaps Washington had surprised them with an attack from the shore. If so, the General had kept that plan close to his chest. Oliver briefly entertained the notion that the wide-faced fishfolk were the cause of the Navy's consternation, but the warship would have been too well armed for those religious deviants to be of any concern, and so he began his preparations for what was rapidly turning into an easy mission.

Rotating about on the wooden bench, Oliver checked his clearance through each of the six tiny portholes that haloed his head and, noting that he was indeed a solitary body in the water, he screwed in the water-tight bung above his crown, smearing lukewarm tar from an insulated tin by his feet around the seal. He now had just thirty minutes to deliver the keg and return to safety; any longer and he would suffocate inside the wood and steel-banded egg.

Oliver reached down and grabbed hold of the descent control, yanking upward on the steel lever until the sound of water rushing into the tank roared loud in his ears. Immediately the tiny submersible began to sink and Oliver counted off five seconds, a period of time that should equate to two fathoms, then pushed down on the lever, shutting off the bilge tank, and waited to see if he had indeed achieved the equilibrium he desired. Satisfied he could detect no further vertical motion he slowly began to crank the propeller handle, sharking silently toward his quarry. Even at this shallow depth it was pitch black and Oliver relied on his compass to keep him true as the *Turtle* gently rocked from side to side, swimming for all the world like its namesake toward the hull of the *Cerberus* until Oliver could see it quite clearly; a sharp-edged mass in the middle of the murk. He piloted the submersible closer still until, even in the gloom, he could make out the crosshatched beams of live oak that formed the plump underbelly of the ship. Oliver gently nestled the *Turtle* in the angle formed by the immense rudder against the frigate's stern and pulled briefly on the bilge lever which caused the sub to dip suddenly. This action forced a row of iron hooks on the submersible's exterior to bite into the soft hull of the slumbering giant, anchoring it securely.

Oliver held his breath, but no shouts came from above; no thumps from the berth deck on the other side of the hull walls. He shimmied around inside his submerged tomb and located the tiny L-shaped handle by his left ear. This controlled the screw that would secure the keg to the hull of the frigate and next to it dangled a thin, hemp rope, soaked in bitumen and end-capped with a brass ball. Pulling on this rope would strike the covered flint bolted to the underside of the explosive barrel and then Oliver would have precisely two minutes to disengage the craft and paddle to a safe distance as the coiled fuse of wax-coated paper slowly burned. He pressed his cheek against the left-most porthole, trying to see whether the keg screw was facing in the right direction, but silt flurries and gloom hampered his vision and he knew he would have to risk using artificial light. Oliver reached down to the floor of the submersible and flipped open a small lockbox, pulling out a shrouded lump that he unwrapped to reveal a block of cork. The block was coated with a fungal layer (on the recommendation of Franklin), and this fungus instantly filled the chamber of the submersible with a soft, green foxfire. He pushed the cork block onto a short spike that hung down from the entry hatch and then pulled down a polished mirror attached to a brass arm, twisting it to direct some of the glow through the forward windows.

The biological light source was dim but manageable, and all that was required was a slight turn of the lateral prop to line up the eight inch screw attached to the powder keg with a spot on the hull level with the base of the warship's rudder. If the explosion didn't sink her, at least she would not be leaving any time soon. Oliver began the slow turn of the screw handle, feeling the submersible tilt back slightly as the screw tip bit into the soft outer hull. This was another of Bushnell's better ideas, a steel screw with gaps in its razor-sharp thread which would help it chew through the planks, resulting in a fastener that was near impossible to remove.

As he continued the slow grind, Oliver thought back to the previous night's meeting with Bushnell, Ben Franklin and General Washington's representative, a squirrely officer from Vermont, called Hooper. The evening had yielded no surprises from Hooper, who delivered Washington's order to sink the *Cerberus* with clipped efficiency and waved away Bushnell's assurances of success with a request for *'results, rather than promises'*. However, Benjamin Franklin's latest revelations regarding the fishfolk had chilled the briefing room with such efficacy that not even the old man's finest brandy could take the edge off. Franklin had reported how his negotiations with the young representative had already stalled, Birch seemingly blinkered to any rational discussion, and instead had focused on the physiology of the cultists. Two live specimens representing both genders, the result from a recent skirmish on Nantucket Island, had provided him almost eighteen hours of scrutiny before they had turned on each other in their holding cell, chanting loudly as they had ripped at each other's neck flaps, asphyxiating in the clean air of the hospital. Franklin had gone into extreme detail regarding their anatomical defects, but Oliver had been too distracted with thoughts of the mission to fully comprehend what was said. The old scientist maintained that growths on the subjects' lungs permitted an amphibious lifestyle, befitting the structural mutation that gave the cultists their vaguely caecilian features; bulbous, black eyes drifting apart, drooping translucent jowls framing obscenely wide mouths that smacked and drooled constantly, peppering the air with salty froth as they chanted in their mesmeric states. Hooper had scoffed at Franklin's findings, having not personally encountered the cultists himself, but Bushnell had silenced him with recounted reports of a horrifying creature spotted off the east coast. Reports of a vast, humanoid shadow rippling just beneath the waves; upended fishing vessels claiming to have run aground with nary a rock nor reef in sight. The group had retired late and, though he couldn't speak for the others, Oliver Lee knew full well that nobody slept soundly that night.

Neil Baker

The resistance on the screw handle disappeared, which meant the powder keg was in place, and Oliver returned his attention to the job at hand. All that was left to do was detach the *Turtle*, prime the fuse and beat a hasty retreat. By the glow from the foxfire his pocket watch indicated that he had around ten minutes of air left, more than enough time. Oliver twisted on the bench and reached down for the cloth-wrapped handle of the hand pump, ready to eject enough water from the bilge tank to release the anchoring hooks, but before he could securely grasp it he was thrown to the side of the submersible as a tremendous shudder shook the little craft, hitting his head on the rim of a porthole which split the skin above his right eye. A second tremor, this time longer, almost turned the submersible onto its side and Oliver had to push himself away from the curved wall to prevent further injury. As the *Turtle* righted itself, he scrambled to the observation hatch and looked through the sextet of windows, trying to ascertain what was happening. Astonishingly, the submersible was still securely hooked onto the stern of the frigate, which meant whatever was tilting his tiny craft was doing likewise to the *Cerberus*. He craned his head and looked to the surface of the water at the far edge of the hull, straining to make out shapes in the darkness beyond. Oliver thought he heard muffled screams, and then multiple objects broke the surface with dense splashes, streaming down through tunnels of tiny bubbles before suspending briefly in a frozen dance of death; the torn and crushed bodies of sailors. A tongue of flame spewed from the port side of the frigate, briefly illuminating the bodies which were already rising to the surface and trailing dark ribbons behind them. A sudden volley of cannon fire erupted from the starboard side, shaking the hull once more, imbuing the waters with orange and yellow hues. In the moments of sudden light, Oliver could make out a colossal mass moving from the bow toward the stern, each cannon flash picking out a new detail; a tree-like limb here, a serpentine tail there, monstrous appendages that seemed to reflect the flames with the intensity of cut glass.

On instinct, Oliver yanked sharply on the pump handle, forcing water from the bilge as fast as he could. The fungal cork block had shaken free and fallen to the base of the submersible, its green bioluminescence picking out tiny puddles; signs that the sub had suffered a slight rupture. The *Turtle* bounced up slightly and the external hooks tore free from the hull of the frigate allowing the tiny sub to rise swiftly to the surface. Oliver suddenly lunged and grabbed the brass ball attached to the end of the fuse rope, wincing as his closed fist jammed between the ball and the interior of the sub. With his free hand he wiped blood and sweat from his eyes before he fumbled for his pocketknife, drawing it up and sawing frantically at the slippery fuse rope.

Now that the submersible had breached the surface, the sounds of destruction and battle were all too clear. He heard screams, rifle shots and cannon fire. He also heard a low drone, that of a multitude of low voices chanting over and over, their tones thick and garbled, the words nonsensical.

The brass ball tore away from the last few fibers of the rope and he tossed it to the floor as the frayed hemp strands slithered out through a brass gasket and the tiny sub began to drift away from the *Cerberus*, riding on choppy waves as the waters churned around the ship. Oliver could feel a dull ache slowly seeping up from the base of his neck, a combination of being tossed around and the thinning of the air. He pulled on the six latches that held the entry hatch secure and used both hands to heave it open. The hatch flipped over with a resounding clang and Oliver inhaled sharply, unprepared for the unseasonal chill of the night air. He stood on the wooden bench and raised himself up, then gripped the edge of the circular hatch with terror as he absorbed a scene cut from the fabric of his mind's darkest recesses.

The *Cerberus* was ablaze, her rigging and sails now webs of flame. As the *Turtle* drifted left of the warship, Oliver could plainly see the fore-mast, snapped in two like a twig and hanging forlornly over the side while the main and mizzenmast smoldered. The top deck was alive with scurrying sailors; some trying to reload the cannons, others throwing pails of water onto the flames, still others throwing themselves into the bay. On the far side of the frigate, an immense shape came crashing down, sending splintered deck and bone spinning into the sky. The flames revealed a colossal, flabby forearm, adorned with weeds. The hand at the end of the arm was as large as a schoolhouse and the individual fingers, as fat as the mast they were reaching for, ended in bulbous, pruned tips. The hand grasped the mainmast, and the warship rolled as the rest of the creature heaved itself further out of the water. Men were dashed against the starboard railings and several heavy cannons smashed through the already-weakened wood, one firing uselessly into the water, as the port side rose into the sky. The sound of the shattering mast cracked like thunder as the *Cerberus* flopped back into the water, sending frothy spouts high into the air and spraying flotsam in all directions. The *Turtle* rocked violently as debris-laced waves crashed over it, and Oliver almost lost his grip, but his knees were hooked under the neck of the submersible, and he steadied himself as he watched the sea beast approach the rear of the ship.

The abomination was vast, its toad-like head blending into its bloated torso with the merest hint of a neck tucked away behind a sagging throat pouch that swelled and deflated as the creature swallowed great gulps of hot air. Above the gaping maw, which was lined with thick, yellow tusks, two pale

Neil Baker

moons sat unblinking in their sockets. The beast's thick arms were covered with layers of rippling skin that jiggled as it moved and yet the muscularity beneath the gray-hued exterior was well defined, swelling as the broken mast was lifted high into the air and brought crashing down into the middle of the deck. The way it moved suggested it was walking on the seabed, which put its height at around one hundred and twenty feet and Oliver could see a short, gelatinous tail unfurling and slapping the surface behind it as it reached the stern. The giant began to tear away at the hull of the broken ship as a child might rip into a birthday present, determined to get to the prize hidden within. It still had not seen him, and Oliver glanced toward shore, exploring his best passage for escape. It would not be by land.

The entirety of the Niantic shore was lined with figures, some holding lanterns, other waving crude torches, all of them chanting as one. In the glow from the lights their features and attire were perfectly visible and Oliver saw that the throng was entirely comprised of fishfolk, the term fittingly applied to both male and female, such was the ambiguity of their gender. The former humans were in varying states of metamorphosis; some were fully-formed, miniature versions of the monstrosity destroying the *Cerberus*, others were in mid-change, their hair still in place, shreds of clothing hiding their lingering modesty. The crowd whooped and croaked with glee at each shattering blow upon the ship, and some had scrambled into the surf to scoop up exhausted sailors, ripping the unfortunate men to shreds. Oliver was thankful that the foxfire had fallen to the bottom of the *Turtle*, for the green glow did not reach the hatch nor the portholes, and so he remained somewhat invisible. He toyed with the idea of descending, but recalled the puddles on the floor and the hole where the fuse line had snugly sat. *The fuse line!*

Oliver looked back upon the creature reducing the warship to pulp and saw that the powder keg was still intact, Bushnell's screw was working admirably and the bomb was untouched, tucked into its resting spot between the stern and the rudder. His initial revulsion had passed, now Oliver knew only anger. This was no way for men to die, British or not. He located the point where the fuse rope was attached to the keg and followed it into the water, tracing its winding path through islands of spume and human wreckage until he could see the end that he had cut free. It wriggled in the water a short swim away from his position, but that meant leaving the submersible, exposing himself to the elements, both natural and otherwise. He could just silently paddle back the way he came, back toward Fort Saybrook where hopefully Hooper and his soldiers would be waiting for him. The *Cerberus* was destroyed anyway, he would receive credit for his actions, his family would still be relocated, and yet …

The water was shockingly cold but Oliver did not attribute the chattering of his teeth to the temperature in the bay, but rather the close proximity of the toad monster as it peeled back the roof of the berth deck, plucking screaming men from their hiding places like berries from a bush. He reached the tattered end of the rope and pulled hard on it, but the rope merely lost a few of its loops. He grimaced as he bit down on the hemp, the bitterness of the greasy bitumen on his tongue making him retch, and turned back to the submersible. He wished now he had paddled over to the rope, but he could swim twice as fast, and the creature behind him was almost at the rudder. His shoulders burned with pain as he pulled himself back into the *Turtle*, almost sinking the craft as he did so. Then he turned and began to gather in the rope, watching the curves straighten in the water until it finally raised clear of the surface, water droplets sparkling in the apocalyptic glow of the warship's demise. Oliver pulled sharply on the line and saw the end fall out of the powder keg. Had it worked? An eternity passed.

The monster was now at the rudder, ripping it upward, and Oliver feared that the explosives would be flung away with it. As the creature stepped to one side he saw with relief that the barrel was still attached to the hull, next to a gaping gash where the rudder had once been and pressed against the monster's belly. Then a tiny wisp of white smoke, proof that the fuse was alive and burning, snaked from the hole in the side of the keg, and Oliver dropped down into his shell, pulling the top hatch down and securing it with two of the latches. Through a porthole blurred with foam and soot he watched as the behemoth lifted both arms ready to deliver the final blow, and then the keg exploded. With its belly pressed against the charge, the toad monster took the entire force of the explosion directly into its torso and for a fraction of a second the effect was almost comical as the beast swelled like a balloon before its entire midsection blew out in a glorious blossom of fire and black meat. Its top-section fell forward onto the deck of the *Cerberus*, lifting the bow of the ship high into the night, almost brushing the low clouds, before sinking into the bay, monster, ship and all.

The chanting on the shoreline had stopped. Guttural murmurings and angry cries now filled the air, but Oliver Lee had no intention of waiting around to listen. As the aftershock of the explosion rocked his vessel, he settled back onto the bench and took hold of the paddle handles, turning the craft away from the bubbling carnage behind him and facing due south. The *Turtle* creaked a little and listed to port, but she would still get him home. Oliver smiled, relishing the prospect of the report he would give Franklin in

Neil Baker

the morning. With no evidence of American involvement in the destruction of their frigate perhaps now the British would re-evaluate their stance, allying with their human brothers to drive back the menace of this sea-devil worshipping cult once and for all.

The sky finally opened, dimpling the dark waters with fat, clean raindrops, and Oliver made himself as comfortable as he could. This was going to be a long night.

THE BULLET AND THE FLESH

BY DAVID CONYERS AND DAVID KERNOT

amouflaged in military issue fatigues overlaid with body armor, Harrison Peel sprinted with stealth along the savanna rise. Ahead, a Zimbabwean farmstead burned like a pagan bonfire in the reds and oranges of a pre-morning light. Dark columns of smoke twisted and contorted skyward. Flames licked like mad tongues from square holes where there had once been windows.

Up close, Peel crouched, gazed along the scope of the cocked M4A1 assault rifle on full automatic fire. He could smell blood, the aftermath of a killing, almost unbearable in its obviousness. The scent of scorched petroleum was stronger.

Advancing, Peel discovered the first body. The well-dressed man in civilian clothes had been cut down by a volley of bullets, but the empty gun holster highlighted that the victim was experienced in violence. The wounds in his chest were close together, suggesting the work of professional soldiers.

Peel marched on, suspecting an ambush at any moment. Instead, he counted further bodies: two, three, four … all put down by precision gunplay. He identified a shiny shard of glass clutched in the hand of the fourth dead man, recognized it as a diamond of significant size. Not sure what to do with it, Peel pocketed it. Diamonds were the currency of a war-torn Africa, and this one had to be worth a hundred thousand US dollars or more.

Frantic movement, thrashing from under a pile of corrugated iron sheets startled him, unnatural sounds as if something wet and long-shaped had flipped upon the earth under it. He imagined a survivor rolling in their own blood, but the noise was all wrong.

Cautiously, terrified, Peel stepped toward the discarded metal.

In a bizarre circle around the shaking iron were more corpses. Unlike the other bodies there were no bullet wounds; rather, death had been by dismemberment, flesh ripped from their bodies and scattered near and far. An arm here, a leg there, Peel identified a Zimbabwean National Army corporal chewed from the waist down, the lower part of him missing. It was as if he had been eaten.

None of the body parts moved as they should. The only sound came from under the corrugated iron sheet. Whatever it was, it had rattled its cover and tried to remain hidden. It was too small to be a man. Perhaps a young child?

Peel raised his rifle when he heard another man run toward him from behind. He turned quickly, weapon leveled, and relaxed when he spied his field partner, Emerson Ash, who had approached the carnage from the opposite direction to Peel.

"All clear," Ash stated for the record. "I count three down, two ZNA soldiers and Abdul Farzi."

"Shit!" Peel nodded. The man they had come to extract was now a corpse. "Farzi, you say?"

Ash nodded. "'Fraid so."

This was bad news, but in this moment Peel focused on securing their position. He trained his weapon back in the general direction of the iron that continued to rattle.

"Something still alive?" Ash pointed his M4A1 assault rifle on the iron and took a cautious step forward. He too was decked in dappled green camouflage fatigues and body armor. Both men were former Australian Army soldiers—they knew how to run military ops by the books and could plan the basics of any tactical military operation in their sleep—but their roles in the current geopolitical environment were as covert operatives, field agents employed by global intelligence organizations. Different sides of the same coin, thought Peel.

The flopping wet shape wouldn't let up thrashing. It sounded increasingly to Peel like the death throes of a snake with its head cut off, and tapped randomly against the curved iron shell covering it. It was too big to be a snake, too small to be a man. He didn't want to go near it, but he had to.

"Cover me," Peel said to Ash and edged forward cautiously, weapon raised and his eyes fixed on the view through the weapon's advanced-combat optical gunsight. The sweat on his shaved head was almost unbearable as it rolled along his face and hung precariously off his nose and chin in an irritating way.

"Roger that," said Ash.

At the sheet, Peel kicked it over.

The shape was like a headless snake, but it was no snake. The thrashing thing became violent and aggressive, now that it had been exposed. It resembled a branch or a vine, a moss-covered tentacle tapered at one end, shredded by bullets at the other, and lined with a dozen snapping, salivating mouths in place of branches. It thrashed like a whip at Peel, narrowly missing him, unable to gain purchase because whatever it had been attached to was long gone, but still very much alive and threatening.

Peel and Ash didn't hesitate; they released volley after volley of 5.56mm rounds into the mass until it was cut to pieces. Now it thrashed as smaller, less effective parts.

Yet the mouths still snapped and salivated.

Ash took a thermite grenade from his webbing and looked to Peel. "Fire in the hole?"

Peel nodded and they both moved backward from the threat. Ash lobbed the grenade and the two men sprinted. The galvanized iron and the creature detonated in a flash of heat, flames and debris, incinerating whatever it was they had discovered until it was no more.

"Did you smell petroleum?" Ash asked after the flames had died down.

Peel nodded and reloaded his weapon.

"I reckon the ZNA took out that farmstead with man-portable flamethrowers," said Ash. "I reckon that's what the petroleum smell is from."

"Maybe they used flamethrowers to put down the rest of this creature."

"Maybe."

They strode from the destroyed remnants of the farmstead, and Peel admired the striking contrast as the sun rose above the distant rolling hills, dappling the African savanna, the granite kopjes, and the wooded landscape in vibrant earthy colors. The landscape was pristine and unspoiled in comparison to what they had just witnessed.

Peel stopped at the top of the hill. "We were too late," he said, voice a low, barely audible growl. "I wanted Abdul Farzi in custody ... before he gave up whatever weapon he was selling to the ZNA."

"We will have to find another way, Major," said Ash.

"I'm no longer a Major," said Peel.

"And I'm no longer *Sergeant* Ash, and yet here we are, sir."

Peel nodded, recognizing Ash's desire to revert to military protocol. This was a military field op, and how things were done. "The weapon; did you see it?"

The former sergeant shrugged. "Nothing I recognized."

Peel paced, his frustration grew with each second they did nothing. "Intel said Farzi was selling a weapon of the ESB kind, an Extraterrestrial Sentient Being. In other words, an alien horror like we just saw."

"Yes," Ash's eyes lit catching Peel's meaning. "You think we just found part of it?"

"Seems likely. So the buyer, Colonel Nambutu, has it? The rest of it?"

"I'm guessing so."

"And the blood is fresh."

"Also correct, sir."

Peel took in another quick scan of their surroundings. The landscape of undulating savanna woodlands, low rolling hills and granite outcrops would be perfect for an ambush, and yet … Peel had an idea.

"Ready the Jeep, I'll be back in a minute."

"Roger that." Ash took off in a double march down the hill to where they had hidden their vehicle. Peel didn't wait and sprinted up a granite rise. He clambered onto the suspended layered boulders that were like pinnacles, and scared away the baboons who used the rocks for the same purpose he wanted, as a lookout.

High on a rock, Peel scanned the savanna. It didn't take long to spot the dust trail of three Zimbabwean National Army troop trucks. He took their position and general direction, and scrambled back down to where Ash gunned their vehicle.

Peel clambered into the passenger seat and set his assault rifle down. "I've got him." He gave Ash the coordinates of Colonel Nambutu and the trucks, and they took off at breakneck speed along a dirt road.

Peel wiped the sweat from his head and remembered why they were here. It had started with an unexpected telephone conversation in London, then a National Security Agency briefing in Cyprus where Peel had met up with Ash, followed by a military flight direct to Francistown Airport in Botswana. After that the two had crossed into Zimbabwe illegally, because surprise was required, time was against them, and their presence had to be deniable.

"Ash, tell me. The Cambodians develop a covert biological weapons program involving extracted alien matter from hell knows where. The Saudis buy it. They sell it to the Zimbabweans via Abdul Farzi. But why the ZNA? They have no money."

Ash shrugged. Peel knew he concentrated on the road because they were driving fast and the deep potholes threatened to flip the vehicle.

Peel massaged his forehead. He didn't need a headache today. "I'm sick to death of fucking governments playing with alien horrors they can never control."

"Perhaps it's not what the Zimbabweans have now, but what they might have to offer in the future. This is a potential diamond-producing region, right?"

Peel nodded. He touched the stone in his pocket; he liked how Ash could put incomplete puzzle pieces together and see a discernible picture anyway. "This region is rife with resistance fighters, backed by Botswana diamond-mining companies."

"And Colonel Nambutu wants to eliminate them," said Ash. "So the Zimbabwean State mining companies can come in and set up instead—"

"—and so Nambutu decides he'll finish off the resistance the easy way … with Farzi's weapon." Peel completed his field partner's sentence.

Ash grinned. "There are two RPG-7s in the back. You might want to prep one, sir."

Peel grinned with Ash, and they sped on. Peel had a lot of time for the sergeant, finding the man quick to assess any situation, and he always had Peel's back. More importantly, they shared a similar sense of humor.

Not far in the distance, dust trails from the three trucks ahead swirled skyward. Despite the gunned-down ZNA soldiers at the farmstead who'd been a part of this group, Peel and Ash could still expect at least a couple of dozen more ZNA soldiers to contend with. Not great odds, but the end result if they didn't at least try to stop Nambutu were too hideous to consider. Nambutu might think an ESB weapon could solve his problems, but reality was that he would soon create a bigger mess than anyone, anywhere, could conceivably control. Peel had an inkling of what kind of weapon the Cambodians had placed on the market: xenobiological, because Peel had stolen samples of something similar from that country long ago. He'd thought he'd put that threat down, but maybe not.

The former-major-turned-NSA-consultant reached in the back for a rocket launcher, loaded a HEAT, or high-explosive anti-tank warhead, and then stood precariously in the roof top hatch, balancing the seven-kilogram weapon on his shoulder while they bounced along the rickety road to catch the convoy.

Until now, Nambutu and his men had failed to spot them, but Peel soon realized he was overconfident. Automatic gunfire peppered the front of the vehicle; the windscreen fractured, headlight glass shattered, and lead penetrated the radiator, but Ash maintained speed and course.

With the last truck in the convoy in his sights, Peel fired the weapon. The rocket launched, and light gray-blue smoke erupted around him. He felt no recoil, as was often expected by novices who used the weapon, and watched the HEAT warhead accelerate away at three hundred meters per second.

Whoomp!

The missile struck the last truck low. It shattered with a sound that hurt Peel's ears, and the truck spun in the air, sending ZNA troops into the sky with it as flapping body pieces.

Then the truck thudded onto the earth, rolled, and kept rolling toward Peel and Ash at an alarming speed.

Ash overcompensated, hit an obstacle, a pothole maybe, or perhaps he panicked in response to the fiery, gutted hull of a heavy military truck bowling toward them.

In that instant the Jeep rolled, and Peel was thrown from the vehicle. He instinctively curled into a ball before thick scrub broke his fall, and hundreds of the African bush thorns cut his skin.

Peel sat, momentarily stunned, and pain nodules erupted all over his body from the thorny cuts and bruising. He forced himself onto his feet and checked for broken bones. Thankfully nothing was.

He half-ran, half-limped to the wreckage of the Jeep, finding his M4A1 in the dirt nearby. He smiled: something had to go right today.

The Jeep had rolled, doing a complete flip but ending up righted when it had come to a rest. Emerson Ash was still buckled into his seat, bloody and bruised, when Peel reached him. His wounds didn't seem too serious, but one could never tell just by looking.

"What happened?" Ash asked groggily.

"Stupid-private mistake, I fired too close. Are you okay?"

Ash checked himself over. "I'm good, Major."

"Then let's get to work."

Ash climbed from the wreckage of the Jeep, readied his M4A1 and grabbed a case of thermite grenades. He divided them between him and Peel. "I think we are going to have to be generous in giving today."

"I think you're right." Peel smiled.

"I'm also thinking about that tentacle, Peel."

"Roger that. We can't assume it was the only one."

They took to the road, covering each other in turns as they advanced upon the wreckage of the decimated ZNA truck. The other two trucks had stopped a hundred meters or so down the road and soldiers were disembarking, ready for gun battle. What at first appeared to be men, were smaller, lighter people. They readied Uzi submachine guns and AK-47 assault rifles.

"Child soldiers." Peel hissed through his teeth like it hurt to join those two words together. "Nambutu's more of an asshole than I thought."

"I'll let you kill him then, sir, if we get that choice," Ash responded sarcastically, which made Peel chuckle. "I don't care what Nambutu's bought, I'm not killing children."

"Well then, we're agreed," said Peel through gritted teeth. They had likely already murdered children when they destroyed the first truck. That was enough innocent blood on his hands for one day. Peel didn't want any more.

One child fired his assault rifle wildly, more to scare than to do any real damage. In response Peel and Ash ducked behind the wrecked truck. It was instinctive to return fire, but they couldn't, not if they were to keep their words.

"Fucking fucked-up Zimbabwe," Ash exclaimed.

"You can blame President Mugabe for this country falling behind the rest of Africa," Peel countered as he glanced toward their advancing foes. The young boys had already covered half the distance between Nambutu's forces and the wrecked truck. Their only option was to disappear into the scrub and run for it. But that left Nambutu with his ESB weapon. That would be a whole lot worse.

More gunfire, shots that sounded concentrated on a specific target that wasn't them. Peel snuck a look when the bursts silenced momentarily. Between the children and the truck wreckage was an oil drum he had not noticed earlier. It had rolled from the truck wreckage, metal coils encased it with a strapped-on battery. It looked as if it was intended to generate a magnetic field.

The tallest boy in the group was close to the drum now, and fired his Uzi. He didn't miss, and the drum split open. Peel half-expected it to explode as the oil inside ignited, but that wasn't what the drum contained.

A tentacle, moss-covered and overrun with snapping mouths, tore out of the split drum casing, then another, and another, until dozens of the slimy, vegetative limbs thrashed widely. The pseudopods were too large to have fitted inside the drum, and Peel wondered if it was some kind of dimensional-folding contraption that had contained the creature. He had witnessed similar abominations in Pakistan not that long ago.

The monster finally broke free and the drum exploded around it, sending metal shards flying in all directions as blast shrapnel. Peel crouched low and hit the dirt, as did Ash.

Thud!

A sheet of the drum embedded into the truck right next to them, saving Peel from instance decapitation. It reminded Peel of the corrugated iron at the farmstead.

The gunfire had ceased and Peel looked up again. Child soldiers were running everywhere, probably terrified of the creature from their darkest nightmares they had released. It was fully free now, standing more than fifteen meters high upon three legs that resembled fern stems but ended in hooves. At the top of its body were branches of tentacles, some thirty or forty meters in length above its central mass, which was covered in snapping mouths. It had no eyes that Peel could see, and probably didn't need them.

Several of the children were already dead, crushed or swiped by the angry creature. Peel watched as another boy was stomped underfoot by the monster, and there was nothing he could do to save him. The surviving children had dropped their weapons in fear and fled into the thick savanna woodlands.

"Oh, fuck!" exclaimed Ash when he took in the enormity of the alien horror before them. He fired his weapon at it, emptying the clip. It did nothing.

What they had seen before at the homestead was tiny in comparison. It had not been allowed to grow as this one had.

"What the fuck *is* that?" Ash exclaimed again, looking pale and shaken.

"I don't know, but the classified Code 89 files that cross my desk suggest it might be referred to as a Dark Young of Shub-Niggurath."

"And what the fuck is *that*?"

"Something fucking scary, not of this Earth, and probably the weapon Nambutu just bought himself."

"He's got more?"

Peel shrugged. "He needed three trucks."

Ash nodded, but he seemed wary of Peel. Although he and Peel were friends and colleagues, they worked for different masters. Ash was an Intel cyber-analyst with the Australian Defense Force, while Peel was an Intelligence consultant with the U.S. National Security Agency. Both worked to put down Extraterrestrial Sentient Beings wherever they appeared across the globe, but with different databases to draw their knowledge from. There was no knowing what each other knew, outside of their shared bilateral arrangements.

"I encountered something similar in Cambodia a long time ago," Peel said and wondered what they should do now.

A tentacle thrashed toward them, collided with the truck and sent it rolling away. Peel and Ash stood exposed.

"Run!" Peel yelled and bolted, following the path of the child soldiers. He didn't have time to look back to see if Ash followed.

Under the cover of the scrub, Peel kept sprinting, but he could hear the creature behind them, crushing trees and foliage as it ploughed through the semi-tropical forest.

He saw a boy in front of him, no more than ten and dressed in camouflage and terrified. Peel lifted the boy under one arm without a second thought and kept sprinting.

"Let me go, Mabono!"

The boy struggled but Peel ignored him. He then bit Peel, forcing the Australian soldier to drop his human cargo. Peel tripped on a root, and fell with the boy.

"*Musudhu! Pamhata! Dambe!*" He leapt onto Peel, punched and kicked him.

"Stop it!" Peel yelled, and protected himself with counter blocks, still reluctant to hit or restrain the boy into submission, even though it would have been simple enough to do.

The boy stopped, pale, and looked up over Peel's shoulder.

Peel turned. He realized he had dropped his weapon somewhere. But he wasn't really looking for the M4A1, instead staring up, struck dumb by the huge, hideous monster that followed them with blood and sap-like goo dribbling from its many mouths. Its tentacles still thrashed wildly, while fifty or more nostrils huffed and snorted, smelling the air. He could smell it too,: an odor like a fern forest gone moldy.

Peel knew he was a dead man.

Then it moved off, crashing through the undergrowth on its huge, fern-like legs, and Peel couldn't understand why.

The boy tried to run, and Peel had just enough sense to grab him and hold him in a lock until the boy gave up the will to resist. When his captive's breathing slowed, Peel talked to him in calm tones. "I'm not here to hurt you. I'm here to save you from that monster and Colonel Nambutu. He took you from your family, right?"

The boy gave up fighting Peel's grip, so Peel released him. The boy stood alone and Peel half-expected him to run, but he didn't.

Peel scanned the bush for any signs of the sergeant, but there were none, and he resisted calling out while the monster was so close. He'd tried Ash through their radio mic to no avail, but he hoped Emerson Ash was alive; his friend was a smart individual and could take care of himself.

"Nambutu sent you to release that monster, knowing you'd die when you did."

"How do you know that, Mabono?"

Peel tensed. He instincts screamed at him to flee this place before the monster returned, but he also wanted to save this boy and as many of the boy's friends as he could. "I know what men like Nambutu are like."

"You wear a uniform like the Colonel. You are no different."

"I am different. There is a UNHCR refugee camp in Botswana, just across the border where you can be processed and, hopefully, reunited with your parents. I can take you and your friends there."

The boy hesitated, wanting to believe Peel, but afraid.

Peel noticed his M4A1 lying in the dirt. He desperately wanted to pick it up, to give him some level of comfort that he could protect himself, but he knew if he did he'd scare the boy.

"My name is Harrison. I'm from Australia. You heard of Australia?"

The boy shook his head. Chances were he'd never seen the Internet, or a computer, or any form of technology that could put him in contact with the rest of the world, or understand what he did not have in his dictatorship-destroyed country.

"My name is General Velempni!" the boy exclaimed proudly.

"Velempni?" Peel asked. "That's a fine name." He didn't want to imagine what tortures the boy had been subjected to. A favored trick of despot warlords like Nambutu was to have children practice firing assault weapons while blindfolded, not realizing that they were killing bound and blindfolded men, women and children in the target range. The shock of what they did numbed them, terrified them, and so they became indoctrinated through the allocation of powerful names that made them feel like powerful soldiers. That was likely where the title 'General' came from.

Peel would not use that title.

He heard screaming, more gunfire, and in the distance, the monster flung a body far and high across the sky.

Peel lifted his assault rifle, readied it, and he took Velempni's hand. "We have to find your friends. Get us all out of here."

Velempni didn't resist as they took off in a brisk pace. Peel found a trail where a dozen light-footed individuals had trampled through the undergrowth ahead of them. No doubt more young boys forced into soldiering.

They passed acacia, ziziphus, and mopane trees. When they crossed over bare granite rock, tiny lizards with rainbow-colored reflective skins darted for cover. The trail was simple enough to follow, with bare footprints and boot prints in the dirt to lead the way, and occasional drips of blood. All the time they could hear the monster never far away, tearing through the undergrowth searching for more victims to trample and consume. They heard stampedes, kudu antelope or zebra most likely, fleeing the creature.

Ahead, Peel could see the trail led to a rise of domed granite and balancing rock formations. Someone in the group ahead was smart enough to realize they might find cover there. Peel wondered again what had happened to Ash and tried the radio with no luck. The sergeant still wasn't responding.

At a corner in the thick scrub, a volley of bullets ripped the air above Peel. He ducked instinctively, readied his weapon, and crept forward to find a dozen boys ranging from ten to maybe sixteen huddled together. The eldest was the only one with a weapon, an AK-47 and he had just depleted the clip. When he saw Peel with Velempni, his eyes grew wide with surprise.

"Sizabantu!" Velempni yelled loudly calling his friend's name. "The Mabono helped me."

"I can help you all," Peel spoke loudly taking the opportunity to win their 'hearts and minds,' as the Americans liked to phrase it. "I can get you away from here, all of you." He pointed at the eldest boy. "You, Sizabantu your name?" Despite almost being shot, Peel kept his voice calm and authoritative. "Are you in charge?"

The eldest boy nodded. Although he was trying to be brave, he let his guard down for a moment and expressed relief that an individual other than himself was taking charge. Peel didn't doubt for a moment that in the back of all their minds, all these children expected him to transform into a tyrant at any moment, like every other corrupt soldier in this destitute land. He had to treat them with respect and caution. He was also thankful he was the only one with a weapon that worked.

"Any of you hurt?"

Sizabantu pointed to one of the smallest boys, who had a deep wound on his leg, the source of the blood they had been following. "Ngqobile got cut by the exploding drum."

Peel moved forward and checked the laceration. It was deep and bleeding fast. He took his first-aid kit, wiped down the cut with iodine, and used strip bandages to hold the wound in place. Peel took a tube of skin glue he always carried for emergencies, and sealed the wound.

"Can you walk, Ngqobile?"

The boy shook his head.

"I'm going to carry you, okay?"

He nodded, so Peel lifted him. The boy was lighter than he expected; malnourished, most likely. That would make his work easier and his hatred for Nambutu stronger.

"We head for that granite dome. We should find cover there."

They took off at a brisk pace, and Peel was relieved to see that everyone kept up. He counted their number at eleven. If he could save these eleven children, then he would have done some good this day.

Peel heard the Mil Mi-24 helicopter gunship before he saw it, flying low from the northeast, from Bulawayo. He could just make out the Air Force of Zimbabwe insignia. It cut through the air fast in their general direction.

Up on the rise now, scrambling through the granite rocks, Peel could see down into the valley from where they had fled. The creature was also easily visible, rising above the tree line with its head of thrashing tentacles, about a kilometer from them now. It moved with alarming speed, faster than their Jeep could drive, and the undergrowth did nothing to slow it. It still hunted.

The gunship flew low in the direction of the monster. It fired a high explosive anti-tank missile—not at the creature as Peel had hoped—but near it, sending the scrub into a torrent of energetic flames. The creature moved away from the heat, toward Peel's location.

Colonel Nambutu was herding it toward them.

Peel readjusted his grip on the uncomplaining Ngqobile and picked up the pace. The rise they headed to was sharp and wide. If they could get over the rocks, perhaps the creature would be too cumbersome to follow them, and they could escape.

Meanwhile the gunship fired another missile, closer this time, to inform the creature they meant business. It had the desired effect, forcing the Dark Young to move toward Peel and his group.

What the gunship didn't expect was the range of its tentacles, and one whipped out faster than Peel could register. It smashed the Mi-24 with enough force to crumble the cabin.

The gunship fell like a rock out of the sky. The overhead blades, still spinning, sliced at the offending tentacle, severing it and the monster screamed with many mouths in unison. Peel had never heard a sound so chilling.

Neither the crew nor the gunship could survive the incineration on impact with the savanna forest. The creature, however, did.

Peel's gut went cold; a wall of fire and a monster on one side, a high rise rocky peak on the other. Then the creature trotted toward them. It had nowhere else to go, and the scent of their flesh had caught its attention.

"Run!" Peel bellowed with all the volume he could muster.

The group split, scrambled up the rounded granite rocks. The closer they reached the peak, the steeper the track climbed. Peel lost his M4A1 without remembering when, and Ngqobile seemed heavier with each step. He checked his holster, finding the 9mm Glock handgun ready should he need it. He checked for thermite grenades, found three.

Then Peel had an idea.

"Run!" he yelled again to the last of the boys he could see, who were ahead of him now. "Get over the rise, head southeast and I'll come after you."

He sat Ngqobile on a rock and caught his breath. His chest hurt with the exhaustion of constant, rapid breathing to oxygenate his complaining muscles, and he wondered again where the hell Ash was right now.

Peel turned to the small boy. They were alone now. "You should follow your friends."

The young boy shook his head. "I can't."

"Your leg still hurt?"

He nodded.

Peel nodded too. "Okay, we'll go together."

The sounds of sizable trees being crushed underfoot grew loud as the monster advanced upon them. It could probably smell them: human flesh. Peel appreciated the fear that grazing antelopes faced upon the African savanna; the horror of knowing that in the end their death would be one of being eaten alive. He didn't want to go out like that.

Peel took the three grenades, primed them and threw them one by one in a fan pattern. Each detonation created a wall of flames, deterrent enough—he hoped—to send the creature in a different direction.

"You ready to go again?"

Ngqobile nodded. He even managed the slightest of smiles. "Thank you," he said quietly, "for saving us."

Overcome with emotion, Peel didn't know what to say. So he lifted the boy with both hands now, and strode up the steep path. If they could just get over the hill, he kept telling himself, they would survive this.

All too soon the flames behind them burned out, and the creature advanced again to hunt them.

Peel wanted to demand that the boy run, but he couldn't ask that of him.

So he pushed harder, until all the muscles in his legs and back screamed for him to rest, and he ignored them.

He couldn't find an easy path that led upward, and soon Peel found he was cornered, in a granite ravine where the walls were too steep and too smooth to climb.

"Fuck!"

He was going to die. They were both going to die.

He put Ngqobile down.

"Are you okay?" the boy asked.

"We'll be fine," Peel lied. "The monster didn't see us head this way."

Then they saw the tentacles, rising above the forest, no more than fifty meters from them. There was a boulder in its way, several dozen meters wide. The creature rolled it out of the way with a single pseudopod as if it was nothing more than a silk curtain blocking its path.

Peel's whole body felt like jelly. Normally he had some kind of plan, even a crazy plan, but right now he had nothing, and only seconds to find one if he were to see this day through to its end.

He had nothing.

Ngqobile wrapped himself tight around Peel, gripped for life that wasn't there. "I don't want to die like this, taken by the devil."

The Dark Young advanced. Its hundred nostrils snorting as it sensed them, moved in slowly for a precision kill. The rest of the creature was stationary while the head of tentacles thrashed with the same madness as when it was first released.

Ngqobile helped Peel take his handgun from the holster, until Peel held the muzzle directly over the young boy's heart.

Peel hesitated. He had always promised himself, if he had a choice he would rather take his own life than let an abomination like this one claim him. But never had he expected to have to make this decision for another, and a child at that.

"DO IT!" the boy screamed, tearing Peel from his melancholy to the horrors about to transpire. The monster was close now; only a dozen meters separated them. Peel felt the creature's hot breath on him, like the stench of a lion after a feast.

The boy grabbed Peel's trigger finger, and the weapon went off. Ngqobile fell lifeless at Peel's feet as a mist of red sprayed him.

Shocked, the Australian spy turned toward the monster, placed the hot muzzle against his forehead, and willed himself to pull the trigger.

But he couldn't do it.

He closed his eyes and tried again. There had to be a way out, and suicide was a path open to him.

And he still couldn't pull the trigger.

A blast of heat from an explosion shocked Peel. He opened his eyes and saw the Dark Young on fire, burning from its central mass outward. The tentacles above still thrashed, but with anger and pain now, and a dozen mouths poured out that horrific scream. In that instant, Peel was sure his ear bones shattered.

He watched Emerson Ash stand from the undergrowth. He dropped the shell of a second RPG-7 and lobbed several grenades into the central burning mass of the creature. He was killing it, slowly, after no one else had been able or willing to do so.

In a state that felt like slow-motion, Peel lifted his Glock 9mm and fired, every last bullet landing in the creature. He didn't know if he did any good, but he didn't want any bullets left over. *The bullet and the flesh.* He still might do it, kill himself, after the atrocities he had caused. With his weapon depleted, the choice would not be his to make.

The creature fell, burning like a pyre, and twitched now rather than thrashed. Ash walked up beside Peel and handed him the M4A1 he had dropped earlier. "You'll need this, mate."

Peel nodded, went through the motions of checking, then loading, a round into the chamber. He couldn't talk. He couldn't respond. He was going into shock, and even though this realization was clear to him, he couldn't stop himself from embracing that dark place.

"Major!" Ash exclaimed. The cyber-analyst looked at the dead boy, then back at Peel again. "You did what you had to do, Major; now let's get out of here."

Peel couldn't move. His legs wouldn't respond.

And then he was sick, dry-retching only because he hadn't eaten in over twelve hours. Being sick was all he could do to remind himself he was human, so he took his time.

꙳ᚲ·�

Peel and Ash returned to the trucks and discovered a savanna littered with the fleshy remains of human and animal corpses, Zimbabwe National Army soldiers and zebra being the highest amongst the body count. The Dark Young of Shub-Niggurath had been thorough, hunting down all that moved on two or four legs. The ZNA soldiers left protecting the two surviving trucks had not stood a chance; the monster had decimated them quickly and cleanly.

Peel had never seen so much blood.

More uncanny, perhaps, were the two trucks themselves. They had not been touched; not even a scratch.

They advanced with their assault rifles ready, unsure what to expect. Then Ash raised a hand and indicated that Peel should slow. He pointed under the closer of the two trucks, to where a man hid.

"Come out or I'll shoot," Ash commanded.

"The m-monster?" the man exclaimed.

"Gone," Ash answered sharply. "Now move."

When the soldier refused to comply Peel fired a bullet into the chassis of the truck, just above the enemy soldier. The man moved quickly then, clambering to his feet with his hands raised high. He was as scuffed, bruised and bloody as Peel and Ash, and just as terrified.

Peel noticed the insignia on the man's shoulders. "Colonel Nambutu?" he asked.

The despot nodded.

Peel didn't hesitate and put three bullets into the man's chest, dropping Nambutu into a rapidly expanding pool of his own blood.

Ash faced Peel and raised an eyebrow. "That was unexpected."

"Do you have a problem with it?" Peel asked in all seriousness.

"I promised you could have him," said Ash.

Peel stepped forward over the twitching corpse. Just to make sure, he put three bullets into the man's head and shattered the skull and the brains inside until it became a pulped mess of meat.

He had hoped to feel better, killing Colonel Nambutu, but he felt nothing. He couldn't remove the image of Ngqobile's last pained expression as he pulled Peel's finger on the trigger. He couldn't stop analyzing that he was more willing to let one of those monsters take his life than take his own. Killing the Colonel had done nothing to silence the darkness within him. Revenge was a hollow promise.

"Major, we should check the trucks," said Ash quietly. "Find out why they were untouched."

The former Australian Army officer nodded and the two men peered cautiously into the back of the first, and then second of the trucks. There were six oil drums in each, each coupled with magnetic-field-generating batteries.

"We should destroy these," said Ash.

Peel nodded through the dark fog that clouded his mind.

"I guessed that creature sensed more of its own, either afraid to hurt them or wary of more predators taking over its patch.

Unsure how to respond, Peel searched the trucks' inventories and the corpses, gathering grenades and explosives, enough to set up a large detonation in each truck. In the vehicle they had toppled earlier, they discovered an additional four barrels. Together he and Ash packed the explosives into three clumps around each truck's fuel tank.

Hours passed before they completed their work and stood far back, ready to run should they need to. The goal was to destroy, not release the creatures, but they would only know which it was when they executed their plan.

"Ready?" Ash asked.

Peel nodded.

Ash lifted his weapon, stared down the sights, and shot the first petrol tank. The explosion was loud, hot, and intense, and it sent the second nearby truck into an all-consuming fireball. Ash fired one more shot, incinerating the first truck they had toppled earlier that morning.

Peel and Ash stared down their scopes, ready for more of the horrors to materialize from the flames, but none did: they had caught them early.

They marched from the scene of carnage. Their work was done.

⅜⦂Ⅱ⦂ↄ⦂ↆ

After consuming some rations, rehydrating, pulling forgotten thorns from their flesh, and cleaning their wounds, Peel and Ash marched again. They picked up the trail of the former child soldiers, followed them across the granite dome rise, and headed southwest toward Botswana.

Upon the peak, with the sun setting ahead of them, the two Australians stared down at the carnage they had been party too. Peel couldn't believe they had survived, and wondered if he had deserved to.

He shook his head at the thought, hating it. He couldn't let negative chatter get the better of him, because that was the path of madness. But he needed an action to undertake to appease his soul because revenge was not the answer. Otherwise he wasn't certain he would survive this day with any mental fortitude left in him.

"Africa's beautiful." Ash stated it as if it were a matter of official record. "If you don't count those corpses over there, and those flames, and that blast site … oh, and the corpse of the creature … and …"

Peel could see Ash trying hard not to laugh, and the man was right, because all they could see before them was the carnage and aftermath of battle. Nothing majestic about it at all.

"Mate, shut the fuck up," Peel muttered.

"Is that an order, sir?" Ash almost chuckled.

Peel sensed the man was relieved Peel was finally talking again.

Peel wanted to laugh too. He really did. He wanted the world to go back to the way it was before today, when he didn't have the blood of children on his hands.

"Damn straight it's an order."

He felt a sharp object rub against his leg, and he remembered the diamond he'd recovered earlier. He'd forgotten that he had a hundred thousand dollars in his pocket.

"Sergeant?"

"Yes, Major?"

"You think we can catch those boys before the border?"

Ash grinned. "Sure."

Peel smiled, an action he thought he'd never be capable of again, but he had been wrong. Redemption came not from spilled blood, but offering possibility to deserving others.

"Let's go, then. I have something very important I need to give those boys to help them on their way."

BROADSWORD

BY WILLIAM MEIKLE

"Broadsword calling Danny Boy, come in please, over."

I let go of the button on the mike and waited. There was still nothing on the line but hiss and crackle.

"Broadsword calling Danny Boy, come in please, over."

"Leave it, Sandy," Captain Dave Collins said. "It's the mountains getting in the way. We'll try again at higher ground."

I looked up the Trollenberg. The top was obscured by thick cloud, and I had a bad feeling that was refusing to go away. Whatever waited up there, it wasn't going to go well for us.

The captain seemed to have no such qualms. He hefted his rucksack and started off along the tree line to our left. I packed up the radio, strapped it on my back, retrieved my rifle from where I'd leaned it against a tree, and trudged after him.

It had already been a long haul; we had come across the Swiss-German border after midnight and walked all night—ten miles through high passes in thick snow just to get to the foot of the mountain. My feet felt like frozen lead, my shoulders ached from the weight of the radio, and the blinding white all around had brought on a headache like an ice pick stabbing behind my left eye. But I couldn't falter—not now that we were so close.

Our future depends on it.

That's what they told us when they hauled us off our exercise on Dartmoor and laid on a train, just for the two of us, to get us first to London, then Biggin Hill airfield. I knew it was something big when the Brigadier himself was on hand to brief us.

"A bit of a flap on, lads," he said. "Winnie's had an ultimatum—stop fighting, or we all die—bit of a rum do if you ask me, but the brass are taking it seriously. What you're about to see is so hush-hush you can never tell anyone, and if you do, it'll be denied at the highest levels."

A projector whirred into life, the lights went down, and a flickering image came into life on the wall. Winnie was front and center, standing behind his desk. A pale, nebulous thing seemed to hang in the air in front of him. It was almost formless, pulsing in and out of vision every few seconds as if the camera could not quite catch it. It seemed composed of strange angles, misshapen and grotesque. I saw wings and claws, too many arms and not enough heads; there was only a fleshy pyramid of quivering tissue where a face might have been. It was an impossibility, as faint as a ghost but, if the picture was to be believed, it was most definitely there. It spoke, heavily accented, and lisping so thickly so as to almost obscure the words completely. But I caught the meaning well enough.

Stop this war or die.

Winnie's instantly recognizable voice rose in an indignant reply.

"And who the hell are you to make such a demand?"

"Some of you call us the Mi-Go," came the answer, calm and slow, as if it were addressing a child. "We are your destiny, should you choose it. Stop this war. Or you will die."

A new image appeared, superimposed over the top of the PM's desk, like a miniature, moving panorama. I did not recognize the city it portrayed, but it teemed with life—at least at first. The screen filled with a blinding flash of light, and when normality returned the desk was overlaid with a view of a smoking ruin, not a single building left standing, not a single living thing moving in the rubble.

"Stop this war. Or you will die."

The lights went up and the Brigadier addressed us again.

"Now you know the Jerries; they're a devious lot. This might all be a cunning bit of propaganda when it comes down to it. But the destruction you saw was real enough. Turin is gone, in a flash like you just saw. Winnie can't ignore a weapon like that. The boffins have tracked the source back to the Trollenberg range. There's a plane waiting. No time to lose. Get over there and report back, on the double. Our future depends on it."

ᛞᛟᛟᛟ

And now, thirty-six hours later, we were at the base of the Trollenberg, still no wiser as to what we might encounter, but resolute in our determination to find out.

We started the climb with a diagonal traverse of the northern face. We climbed swiftly over steep, icy terrain with some spots of fresh snow, making good time until the foot of the summit pyramid—and some easier climbing—was only a cliff climb away above us. But we still had some work to do. We had known from our view from below that this would be one of the most taxing parts of the ascent.

It proved to be worse than we could have imagined. The rock face was nearly a hundred feet tall and loomed over us in one massive slab. The captain seemed daunted by the sheer enormity of the task ahead of us, and for my part, it seemed at least as tough as any face I had ever attempted. But Winnie was waiting in London, and the outcome of the war might depend on our actions in the next few hours.

I set to it with a will. I had thought that Pillar Rock in the Western Fells would prove the toughest challenge of my climbing career, but the Trollenberg proved tougher still. All that long afternoon I fought it, with the captain creeping up cautiously behind me, following my every move. Back and forth I went, and from side to side. Several times I had to retrace my route for long periods.

But I would not be defeated. Just as day turned to dusk, I hauled myself up over the last lip, which had been proving a bugger for an hour, and lay gasping at the foot of the pyramidical slope that led to the summit.

I helped the captain up beside me. We just had enough light remaining to see that our route to the top led via a forty-five degree snow slope, which would take us directly to the summit ridge. It was only after we caught our breath that I realized we were not the first to reach this spot. Two sets of tracks led upward five yards to the left of us. I hadn't seen any sign of other climbers on the way up the cliff, but another man could have taken a different line to the top and evidence of his passing would easily be missed.

The captain went over to examine the tracks.

"Jerry-issue boots," he said. "Either the Brigadier was right, and they're at the bottom of this, or they're just as panicked as we are and have come to take a shufti. Whatever the case, we're not alone up here."

I took the hint and had my rifle ready as we made our way up the last slope.

ᴣ૧ᑎᏽᴵ

It was relatively easy going, and almost peaceful in a strange way. Night fell around us, and a cloudless sky filled with stars. There was no sound apart from the crunch of our footsteps in the snow.

We followed the tracks to where they crested the ridge that led directly to the summit; then, I had to stop quickly as the captain bent to examine the snow at his feet.

William Meikle

I saw the problem immediately. Both pairs of tracks just stopped, seemingly mid-step. It was as if the two climbers had been plucked, ever so neatly, off the face of the hill, leaving no further trace of their presence.

"A sudden gust of wind?" I asked, but I knew already that anyone good enough to come up the cliff would not be stupid enough to let the wind take them down again.

The captain agreed with me.

"No. It wasn't the wind. But I'm buggered if I can figure this one out, Sandy. Let's just press on. The answer's here somewhere—I can feel it in my water."

We heard the hum before we had gone another step. It started low, a deep bass vibration that I felt in my stomach even before I heard it. The tone rose quickly to a buzzing whine. The snow at our feet slid away below us as the rock beneath it tilted, threatening to drop us back down the slope. We had enough presence of mind to throw ourselves to the ground as the ridge opened up in front of us, revealing not rock, but a metal dome, silver and glistening beneath the stars.

Ice cracked loudly in the night air. Snow flurried all around us and I was all too aware of the long drop that waited at our backs should we slide any further down the slope. Luckily for us the movement of rock and snow slowed and came to a halt.

There was a new feature on the mountain's summit. Instead of a rocky outcrop, there was now the high silver dome, partially opened to the sky along a central ridge. The captain motioned me forward and I followed, as quietly as I was able, up to where the opening in the dome was closest. We were able to look over the lip with ease, and down into what seemed to be an empty laboratory of some kind. A twenty-foot long tube of silver, brass, and glass coils dominated the space. I had no idea how it might work, but I immediately knew I was looking at the weapon that had destroyed Turin.

The captain pulled me back away, and whispered urgently.

"We're going in. If that's the new weapon, we need to find out as much as we can. Leave the radio here. We're traveling light."

I divested myself of the radio, and shucked off the parka and snow trousers. I saw the captain pull his balaclava down over his face and I followed suit. We were now two black outlines against the white of the snow.

"Rifles?" I asked.

He shook his head. I had a revolver, four grenades, and a long knife—more than enough to do a lot of damage if need be. I laid the rifle down beside the radio and the parkas, making sure everything was weighted against any wind, and followed the captain over the lip to drop gently down into the dome.

We met no resistance. The laboratory, if indeed that was its function, was quiet and empty. I had a closer look at the *weapon* but its means of operation continued to elude me. The metals I had taken to be silver and brass seemed on closer inspection to be harder than either, colored alloys with which I was completely unfamiliar. And what I had taken to be glass was instead a peculiar form of opaque crystal containing minute speckles of rainbow flakes. The whole apparatus vibrated and thrummed to my touch, and I pulled my hand away sharpish as it began to glow.

I motioned to my grenades, then to the weapon. The captain shook his head.

"Later," he mouthed, and motioned me toward a cave mouth to our left, the only entrance to the room. We moved quietly into the darkness and started to follow the passage.

We went down, into the mountain.

ᗡᑫᑎᕼᐧ

It was not long before we heard the sound of activity rising up from below. At first it echoed around us, like a great many sibilant whispers. As we descended it grew louder, and we heard it for what it was.

An interrogation, of sorts, was going on; one voice asked questions in a language we could not even begin to fathom, being all sibilant tones and glottal stops. But the other was all too familiar; a male German answered—and the voice was that of a man in mortal terror. He repeated the same thing to every question— Gerd Brunke, Colonel, 734561.

Name, rank and serial number.

The captain and I crept slowly down the tunnel. The German colonel's replies turned to wild screams that were far more discomforting than the previous whispers. The screams didn't last long before being replaced by a pitiful sobbing that was somehow even worse.

We moved faster—the speaker might be German, but his pain was human, and something neither of us would allow. We arrived soon afterward at an opening and looked out over a wider chamber that was artificially lit by a blue globe hanging high above. It cast dancing shadows across a scene from a nightmare.

The German soldiers lay on a long trestle that ran along the far wall from where we stood. The chamber itself was full of equipment built of the same brass and silver shaded alloys we had seen up in the dome, along with a great deal more of the rainbow-flecked crystal. But it was something else that caught our full attention. We had seen its like before, standing in a shimmering image before Winston's desk in the film we had been shown. But here it was in the flesh.

It was the size of a man, but looked more like a hideous shrimp than any

William Meikle

human being. The body was segmented like that of a crustacean, but this was no marine creature—for a start, it had membranous wings, currently tucked tightly at its rear, but judging by their size, more than adequate to lift its weight into powered flight. There were no arms or hands to speak of. I counted four pairs of limbs. The pair the thing used as legs—I use the word loosely here—were more stout and thicker than the rest, each being tipped with three horny claws extended to balance its weight at the front, while a segmented tail completed the tripod behind it. The other appendages looked more flexible and nimble, and as I watched, the thing leaned forward and delicately picked up a tool from the trestle. I got a good look at its face—or, rather, lack of one. Instead of features there was only a mound of ridged flesh, pale and greasy, like a mushroom toward the end of its cycle. A multitude of thin snake-like appendages wafted around the head and I took these to be the equivalent of sensory organs, although quite how they might function, I had no idea.

I did, however, know exactly what it was doing—it was torturing its prisoners. The German colonel screamed again, and the captain and I moved at the same time, running forward and freeing our knives from their sheaths. The thing *sensed* us coming somehow and turned toward us, but that only served to give me an opportunity to go for its throat. My knife went through the flesh as if it were indeed some kind of fungus, and the beast fell in a heap at my feet, twitching once, then falling still.

The captain gave it a kick to make sure it would stay down, then clapped me on the shoulder.

"If they are that easy to kill, this should not be a problem," he said softly.

"Do not make the same mistake I did," a German-accented voice said from behind us. We turned toward the sound. It came, not from the man's body, but from a screen on the wall. It showed his face, staring straight at us. The captain nudged me and pointed at the prone bodies. It was only then that I saw the apparatus on each side of them—more of the silver, brass and crystal and—most horrifying of all—*the brains of the two men hanging suspended inside tall glass jars.*

The image of the German officer was still speaking, and I struggled to pay attention.

"You must do something," he said. "They know we will not bend before them without coercion. They mean to show us again that they are serious. They want us to stop the war."

"But what are they?" the captain said, looking down at the dead thing at our feet.

"There's no time," the German replied. "They are from—somewhere else—a dark planet in deep space. They say they have many things to teach us, many wonders to enrich our lives, if we would just lay down our arms and submit. But they have no compassion, no *humanity*—they are like insects, writhing in their warrens in dark places. The *Fuehrer* will never sanction a treaty with such as these—they are beneath us, despite their knowledge. They are impure."

"I can't see old Winnie giving them the time of day either," the captain said softly, giving the thing another kick. "But what do you mean about them being serious? Are they planning something big?"

The Colonel's image was fading away, and his voice was now little more than a whisper.

"They mean to destroy London and Berlin. You must stop them."

⊱⊰⊹⊰⊹⊱⊰

The Colonel's image faded from the screen. I walked over to the men's bodies. Both had the top of their skulls removed and the brains extracted. There was no life in them. If the men were still awake, still aware, locked inside their brains in those glass jars, it was not a fate I would wish on anyone, enemy or not. The captain guessed at my thoughts.

"Let's give them some peace," he said. "Then I think it will be time for a little mayhem of our own."

He took the German colonel's jar and I took the other, aware even as I lifted it that I didn't even have a name to give to the poor chap. In unison we smashed the jars on the ground. The brains lay there, dead meat. I followed the captain's example and lifted the fleshy ball at my feet to place it back in the skull cavity. It was all we could think to do for them.

"This is not war," the captain said, more to himself than to me. "This is barbarism. I won't stand for it."

He looked over at me as he drew his revolver. His face was grim.

"Get topside and call in the strike," he said. "I'll see what I can do about putting a spanner in the works."

I knew better than to argue—indeed, I agreed with the plan. I made my way back up to the dome, creeping quietly, listening at every step for any sound of pursuit, or for any indication that the captain had got himself into trouble.

I arrived in the dome room with no mishap. The weapon—for that was surely its purpose—sat quiet and still. The only sound was the whistle of wind from outside. I pulled myself back out over the lip of the opening and immediately felt the chill bite at my bones. I had to retrieve my parka from under a new covering of snow, and my already-stiffening fingers fumbled to get it zipped up.

There was a bad moment when I thought the radio was jammed, frozen solid, but the thin layer of ice on the dials cracked readily enough under my fingers. And this time Control came through loud and clear in answer to my call.

I only needed to say one word.

"Hammerstrike. I repeat, Hammerstrike. Over."

"Broadsword, this is Danny Boy. We read you. Twenty minutes. Over and out."

Our spanner in the works was going to have to be inserted quickly; in little over a quarter of an hour enough bombs would rain down on this mountain to lower the summit a good few yards. I crawled back up to the lip of the dome, intending to head back inside and join the captain.

He was already there, just below me, held tight between two of the lobster-things. A third one of them was standing next to the long tubular weapon. I fetched my rifle, intending to start some of the mayhem the captain had promised, when he looked up, straight at me, and shook his head.

"Not yet," he mouthed.

I gave him the OK sign with finger and thumb, made sure I had secure footing, and watched what transpired beneath me.

They had taken the captain's revolver; it was lying on the ground off to one side, but they had not taken his grenades. They were still there at his belt—either the things did not know their purpose, or they thought that they had the captain under too close control for him to make a move. They didn't know the man as I did.

For the moment, the captain seemed calm—almost relaxed, as he watched the third creature make some movements above the metal and crystal tube with its clawed appendages that seemed to pass for hands. It spoke, alternately hissing and guttural, completely unintelligible. But the meaning was clear enough as, once again, three- dimensional images formed in the air between the captain and the weapon.

Winnie stood in front of Parliament, and I well remembered the words he spoke, for they had stiffened the resolve of a nation.

"We shall go on to the end. We shall fight in France; we shall fight on the seas and oceans, we shall fight with growing confidence and growing strength in the air. We shall defend our Island, whatever the cost may be; we shall fight on the beaches, we shall fight on the landing grounds, we shall fight in the fields and in the streets, we shall fight in the hills; we shall never surrender."

The picture changed, showing battlefields, mass graves, plumes of smoke from the burning of the dead, prison camps with skeletal figures, villages, towns, cities, all flattened.

"We shall go on to the end." Winnie said again.

The picture changed—another leader, another parliament. Adolf was shouting again.

"Those who want to live, let them fight, and those who do not want to fight in this world of eternal struggle do not deserve to live."

More moving pictures followed in quick succession—armies, vast and implacable, hell-bent on annihilation of each other; a world in flames until there was naught left but a burnt out cinder floating in space.

For a last time the scene changed and split in two. I recognized both cities—London on the left, Berlin on the right. I remembered the German's words.

They mean to show us again that they are serious.

I saw the captain stiffen, readying himself. And I saw something else, an indecision I did not expect to see, as the creature by the weapon waved a limb and the tube started to glow and throb. I saw the captain look from London to Berlin and back again, and I believe I understood his thought. If the creatures blasted Berlin first, the war could be finished in one stroke—all we had to do was wait and see before acting. And therein lay the danger, for if we waited, it might be London that was taken first, and all we had fought for these past years would be undone.

As for myself, I was only too aware that *Hammerstrike* was getting ever closer. The captain and I came to our respective decisions at the same time. I hefted the rifle, aimed at the creature bent over the weapon. At the same instant that the captain swiveled and tugged, pulling one of the beasts off balance. I fired; my target stumbled but did not fall, so I put another round in it, trying for the head this time.

As I was preparing for a third shot, the moving picture shifted again to show a night sky and three Lancasters approaching. *Hammerstrike* was indeed coming—and the beasts knew about it. The long weapon glowed ever brighter and a loud hum rose to an almost deafening pitch. My target was still standing over it.

The captain was busy, fighting off the other two creatures—he had one of them on the floor and was tussling with the other, but I had no time to help him. I fired two more quick shots. The beast fell away—but not quickly enough. A blinding flash filled the room. I blinked, and looked down just in time to see one of the Lancasters explode and crumple to fall away in flames. The long tube pulsed again, the glow brightening, the hum rising.

"Time to go," I shouted. The captain obviously had the same thought. He pulled a pin on a grenade and lobbed it under the weapon, in the same movement making a lunging jump to the opening where I stood. I lobbed one of my grenades down to almost the same spot and managed to pull him up and out of the dome to roll away just as the twin concussion blasted the top off the structure.

We slid, out of control, down the steep snow slope as another explosion blasted rock and snow and metal to fly all around us. The night was filled with

William Meikle

sound and fury that got even louder as the roar of the bombers came to us.

We came to a sliding stop on the very rim of the sheer cliff we had come up.

"Heads down," the captain shouted, and we cowered, unable to do little else, as the bombers went overhead, and seconds later, the top of the mountain was blown clean away.

༄༅༅།

It took me a while to realize we were still alive, and longer still before I could hear much beyond the rumbling echo of the explosions in my head. The captain tapped me on the shoulder and turned me around to look at what had happened.

The top level of the summit above the snow slope had been completely obliterated to leave only a pile of rock and rubble that was still smoking. There was no sign that any structure had ever been there.

We sat there for long minutes, catching our breath, peering in the dark, waiting to see if there would be any movement. But it seemed we were the only things left alive on the mountain.

"Looks like the job's done, old chap," the captain said after a while. "Let's go home."

"Would you have let them do it?" I asked. "If it had been only Berlin, not London, would you have let them do it?"

He didn't even think before answering. "No. Actually, I was considering letting them do both—it might have been the only way to finish this bloody thing once and for all. But whatever nefarious reasons those creatures had for stopping the war, I doubt they were doing it for the good of humanity. Remember those two jars we smashed? I wouldn't wish that death on another living soul—and if they had got their way here, a similar fate might have befallen all of us in time."

I will not tell of the descent—I will only mention that it was almost as terrifying as the events that took place under the dome. But we survived. I reached the bottom first and looked up. The captain was still climbing down, still focused on the rock face, so he did not see it. Indeed at first I wasn't sure I had either—it was merely a darker shadow against the night sky.

Then the wings opened out, obscuring the stars behind them. It launched itself off the cliff and into the sky.

The last I saw of it was as it crossed the face of the moon, heading yet higher, the wings unfurled and soaring, far from any war or thought of war.

I envied it in that moment—and I envy it still.

LONG ISLAND WEIRD – THE LOST INTERVIEWS

BY CHARLES CHRISTIAN

I n the course of the Congressional hearings into the so-called "Long Island Incident" and the subsequent loss of over [data redacted on the orders of the Department of Homeland Defense] lives, the following files were located on cloud storage archives. The first eight files are transcripts of interviews conducted by an unknown individual. The ninth file is part of a police Missing Persons report. The tenth and final file is a preliminary autopsy report.

1

The Skipper's Story

If you want to know anything about the Gold Coast of Long Island, I'm your man. I've been running boat trips and supper cruises for tourists around Long Island Sound since I was a kid.

Okay, that's a bit of an exaggeration. I used to help my Pappy run boat trips back when he left the Coast Guard after World War Two. After I came back from my tour of duty in 'Nam, he retired and I took over the business. Now I'm retired, and my son Jimbo took over the business after he came back from Iraq. I guess if Jimbo ever wants to retire, Uncle Sam's first going to have to find a new war for his son to fight in!

They don't call it the Gold Coast because any gold was ever found there. No; it's because of all the big houses the millionaires built along its shore during the late 19th and early 20th centuries. The Vanderbilts, the Astors, the Whitneys, the Morgans, the Pratts, the Hearsts and the Guggenheims all spent fortunes building opulent mansions and mock chateaux along the north shore of the Island during the era Mark Twain called *The Gilded Age*. The glory days of many of these properties is now long gone, and they've either fallen into disrepair or been converted into condos. And those are the lucky ones that have avoided being demolished! But there's still plenty enough to see to make the Gold Coast a great location for a nice supper cruise.

Anyway, you were asking about Beacon Towers....

That was one of the last mansions to be built and the first to be demolished. Built in 1918 for Alva Belmont, the ex-wife of a Vanderbilt and a multi-millionairess socialite in her own right, it was a gorgeous property, right on the shore, with its ramparts rising out of the sand. It was supposedly based on an Irish castle but looked more like a French chateau to me. William Randolph Hearst bought it in 1927, apparently because he wanted a castle on the East Coast to match his San Simeon property in California! Well, at least that's what people say, but in 1942 he sold Beacon Towers to its final owners, who had it demolished just three years later, in 1945.

Yes, there is an interesting symmetry there, built at the close of World War One and demolished at the close of World War Two.

Beacon's heyday was undoubtedly the Belmont era. In fact it is all down to one of her house guests—the writer F. Scott Fitzgerald—that anyone remembers the place today. Fitzgerald based Jay Gatsby's West Egg mansion in *The Great Gatsby* on Belmont Towers. The words Fitzgerald uses to describe West Egg and how it was an "imitation of some Hotel de Ville in Normandy, with a tower on one side" leave no room for doubt.

But that was in 1923. Twenty years later it was a different story. Hearst had to sell the property to a bunch of Wall Street bankers to settle some mortgages, and while they tried to find a buyer or, anyway, decide what they were going to do with the place, the 140-room property was put in the hands of caretakers. This is where the story starts to get weird, though you have to remember that, back in the first half of the 1940s, I was still a kid in grade school, and a lot of what I heard about Beacon Towers came from either classroom gossip or stories my Pappy told when he was home from Coast Guard duty.

According to the scuttlebutt, the caretakers were either an extended family of Eastern European refugees or they were Italian refugees now working for one of the New York crime families. Whatever the truth, during those last three years there were some odd comings and goings around Beacon Towers.

What were they, you ask? Those who believed the caretakers were Eastern Europeans were convinced they were fifth columnists working for the Nazis, and Beacon Towers was being used to land spies and bombs from

German U-boats cruising the Sound. However, if you subscribed to the Mafia theory, then they were using the Towers as a clearing house for mobsters smuggling in black-market contraband from Canada.

There was also a suggestion that the place was haunted, although that was down to the weird lights that could sometimes be seen shining out from there. I saw them myself a few times—and this was during a war, when there were supposed to be strict blackout restrictions along coastal areas. After all these years it's still hard for me to describe those lights. They were simultaneously a vibrant sickly green, flickering with violet, and a color I don't ever before recall seeing in the spectrum. A regular little Northern Lights they were.

As for the so-called caretakers ... Well, they kept themselves to themselves. We never saw them in town shopping for vittles or at the drugstore, and they certainly never showed their faces at the movie house or social events. Then again, if you looked like they did, you'd have kept out of sight.

I saw them just the once. I was out on the Sound in my Pappy's boat—he was back home on leave—fishing for sriped bass, when he suddenly passed me his binoculars and said "Look over there, on the rocks in front of Beacon Towers."

I took the glasses and looked. There were four of them sitting there. Thinking about it now, I suppose they reminded me of lizards warming themselves in the sun. They were squat, stocky people, and their skin had a yellowish tinge. They were bald, and through the glasses I could see they all had tiny little ears and large, bulbous staring eyes. Their faces were more like those of a fish or a frog than a human.

"Gee, Pa," I said, "do you reckon they're Nips?" as we'd all seen newsreels about the Japanese and knew they were a race of ugly, deformed, semi-human yellow people. I hope you'll excuse my political incorrectness, but that's how the Japs were depicted in wartime propaganda.

He said, "No, son, they're not Japs. They've all got the 'Innsmouth look'; they must be some of those inbreds from Massachusetts. I thought the Feds rounded up all of them years ago."

At the time I didn't understand what he meant, though I later learned the seaport town of Innsmouth had a *very* unsavory reputation—let's just say for activities of a distinctly un-American kind—and had largely been destroyed and its population resettled in 1927, following a joint FBI/US Navy raid to close down a major bootlegging operation.

And that was it. I never again saw any of the caretakers, and a few months later the banks ordered the demolition of Beacon Towers.

Charles Christian

The Ghost Hunter's Story

Pleased to meet you all. I'm the author of *Long Island's Ghosts & Other New England Hauntings* and a whole host of other great books. Is it all right to mention that?

Normally I always conduct my own personal investigations of any reports of paranormal activity, but in the case of Beacon Towers I've obviously got to make a big exception, what with the place being demolished so long ago. Why, it was gone and turned to rubble before I was even born! However, I have done some desk research, and I think you'll agree that what I found out is fascinating.

It is true that some of the Gold Ghost hauntings were entirely specious. At least three I know of were invented during the 1920s to disguise the activities of Prohibition bootleggers who used to land their hooch on the private quays on the North Shore before trucking them to the speakeasies in New York City.

The first reference to a ghostly manifestation at Beacon Towers was during Alva Belmont's day; however, she was way too much of a blue-stocking and suffragette to ever have anything to do with illicit liquor. It seems several guests and some of the housemaids all reported a creepy, cold sensation when they were near the big fireplace in the Great Hall. What is weird is that they all felt the chill even when there was a log fire burning in the hearth!

Now what I find especially interesting is that this fireplace was originally shipped from London, England, where it had been moved from the ruins of a Knights Templar preceptory at Dunwich. That's Dunwich, England, not that awful place on the Miskatonic Valley up in Massachusetts.

I don't know if you've heard of Dunwich, England. It was a once-thriving seaport town that in mediaeval times had twelve churches, but they've all now been washed away by the sea. They say on a clear night you can still hear the church bells chiming from beneath the waves. Isn't that cute? There are still some monastic ruins left on the cliff edge, and sometimes human bones from the old graveyards can be found on the shore. Pretty gross, huh? But I'd still love to visit there one day; it sounds like a perfect place to conduct a ghost hunt!

So what I hear you say is: what is the connection between a Templar fireplace and Beacon Towers?

Quite simply, this is what we call a residual or imprint haunting. These are the most frequent type of ghost sighting, where the spirit is oblivious to its surroundings or anyone present and just keeps living out the same set of past events over and over again. You can't communicate with this type of ghost. In fact, there is a theory that they are not so much spectral beings as a playback, like a video recording or an audiotape, of an event in the ghost's past life that was so powerfully emotional or traumatic it left an imprint in the surrounding fabric of a building or the landscape.

And let's be honest: as life events go, the fate of the Knights Templar—being arrested, thrown in prison, tortured, and finally burnt at the stake—don't come much more traumatic.

3
The Lighthouse Keeper's Story

Yeah, I guess it is kinda ironic. After spending all my working life with the U.S. Coast Guard service manning their lighthouses, I'm now spending my retirement with the U.S. Lighthouse Society, helping them to preserve and promote this great country's lighthouse heritage—as well as trying to undo some of the harm the Coast Guard causes when they decommission old lighthouses. Okay, that last remark was personal.

Why Long Island? Because it has one of the greatest collections of lighthouses in the country. Over 30 have been built here since 1796 and they include some of the most iconic lighthouses ever designed.

How the Coast Guard ever got away with knocking down such a fabulously beautiful and historically important light as the Shinnecock Bay Lighthouse in 1948 we'll never know. It's weird; it could have been saved by public support, which is one of the reasons why the Lighthouse Society was established. It was the same story a year previously, in 1947, when the original Lloyd Harbor Lighthouse was apparently accidentally destroyed by fire. Had there been a local group caring for it, it would probably still be standing today.

4
The FBI Agent's Story

As the Supervisory Senior Resident Agent with the Federal Bureau of Investigation for this area, I am authorized to supply you with the information you requested under the Freedom of Information Act 1966, save only where information has been redacted or is otherwise deemed exempt from disclosure and to remain secret on the grounds of national defense and law enforcement.

And if it is any consolation to you, some of this stuff is so weird I don't even know what it refers to or why it still must remain secret after all these years.

I can tell you it is incorrect to say the Beacon Towers residence was demolished in 1945 on the instructions of the bank that owned the property. It was actually destroyed by a company of the Fighting Seabees; that's right, members of the U.S.

Charles Christian

Navy Construction Battalion, acting under a direct executive order of President Harry S. Truman. It is interesting to note this was one of the first orders President Truman gave when he succeeded Franklin Delano Roosevelt in the White House.

You have to remember that the Seabees are not only good at building things; they also understand how to knock them down again. As you can see from the parts of this document that have not been redacted, the Seabees were to pay particular attention *to the destruction of any cellars, subterranean passages, crypts, vaults, catacombs, bunkers and concrete pens* lying beneath the building. Given the location of Beacon Towers on the shore, I can only assume that some of these underground chambers were either below sea level or provided access to the ocean.

You will also notice the records report the Seabees encountered *fierce armed resistance* that was only overcome following a sustained firefight involving the use of *pistols, carbines, axes, machetes, sub-machine guns, heavy machine guns, flamethrowers, grenade launchers and bazookas.* All of which seems a little excessive, since the Seabees were just dealing with a group of caretakers.

I confess I'm also at a loss to explain the heavy casualties sustained by the Seabees, including seven dead or who subsequently died from their wounds, four missing in action, and five who spent the rest of their days in the secure psychiatric wing of the U.S. Naval Hospital at Portsmouth, Virginia.

I am also permitted to inform you that the same company of Seabees was subsequently involved in the destruction by fire of the old Lloyd Harbor Lighthouse in 1947 and the demolition of the Shinnecock Bay Lighthouse the following year. Both these events were also authorized by executive order of the President.

The documents reveal no reference to any fighting or casualties; however, there is a cryptic comment which reads *Throughout history, lighthouses have been erected to guide mariners away from harm and towards safe waters. However, sometimes they attract that which is unwelcome.*

5

The Cryptozoologist's Story

Now don't you go all surprised that I'm a woman of color. Cryptozoology is not just a game for old white men. I've been the Professor of Cryptozoology and Teratology at the University of Miskatonic, Arkham, for the past three years now.

For the record, cryptozoology literally means the study of hidden animals. This includes looking for living examples of animals considered extinct, such as dinosaurs; animals whose existence lacks physical evidence but which regularly appear in myths and legends, such as Bigfoot and Chupacabra; and wild animals dramatically outside their normal geographic ranges, such as big cats, like cougars and panthers, being reported in urban areas. Teratology is the study of abnormalities in physiological development, such as two-headed calves. It was the preponderance of such creatures being born in this part of Massachusetts in the mid-1920s that first led to the establishment of my department. It was expanded to include cryptozoology in the 1950s.

Because Long Island Sound is an estuary running into the Atlantic Ocean, it is not unknown for deep-sea creatures to find themselves trapped or beached in the Sound. You therefore get far more unusual carcasses washing up along the shores of Long Island and Connecticut than in many other parts of the United States.

You've probably read in newspapers or seen on TV those reports of the bodies of sea-monsters and mysterious creatures being found on beaches by horrified holiday-makers? And then the remains are removed by scientists and that is the last you hear of the story. A cover-up? No; it is because there is no story.

When a large sea creature decomposes, it can frequently result in weird shapes. For example, when the blubber has rotted off or been eaten away from a whale's carcass, you are left with an oddly shaped skull, a long neck and four big flippers. What does that sound like? Exactly: a sea-serpent or the Loch Ness Monster, perhaps even a plesiosaur that somehow survived from the Jurassic era.

It's the same with giant squid. Huge tentacles lined with sharp-toothed suckers, truly enormous eyes, a mouth with a parrot's beak and a barrel-like mantle, or torso, ending in a couple of angular fins. When anyone but a squid specialist finds the decayed remains of one of these on the shore, of course they are going to think it is the body of some kind of alien monster previously unknown to science.

Hey, have you ever read any of those stories by H. P. Lovecraft? He's a local hero around here. In one of his tales he has what he calls "Elder Things." His description of them almost exactly matches what a partially decomposed giant squid looks like. He must have seen a squid washed up on a New England beach and drawn his inspiration from there.

That said, sometimes these mysterious sea-monsters are just that. Mysterious monsters from the depths of the ocean.

6

The Naval Historian's Story

The U-857, you say? Yup, that's one of Hitler's missing U-boats. There are about 50 U-boats still unaccounted for out of a total of nearly 1200 that sailed with the *Kriegsmarine* during World War Two. 'Unaccounted for' is not really the right term; most of those 50 were sunk by Allied ships and planes or struck mines, but there remains confusion over precisely when and where they were sunk—and who by.

Charles Christian

That said, the U-857 has developed its own cult following. There are plenty of signed-up members of the Nazi weird-science fan club who are better qualified than me—well, the use of the word 'qualified' in this context is moot—to tell you about the crazy theories surrounding the fate of the U-857.

Let's just say there have been reports of its wreck being spotted at the bottom of the Churchill River in Labrador, over 60 miles from the Atlantic Ocean. There's another report that it sailed down to South America and then up the Amazon River on a secret mission to locate the lost city of El Dorado, and is now marooned somewhere in the rain forest. And there are reports that it was one of the submarines that fled to a secret base the Nazis built in Antarctica.

The truth is rather more prosaic.

During the summer of 1944, Allied intelligence picked up reports that the Germans were experimenting with launching rockets from U-boats. This rumor gained more credence in early December 1944 when the Nazi spies William Curtis Colepaugh and Erich Gimpel, who'd been captured in New York City after being landed in Maine from a U-boat, told their interrogators Germany was preparing a flotilla of rocket-equipped submarines. The following month, Herr Albert Speer, the German Minister of Armaments & War Production, made a propaganda broadcast from Berlin in which he claimed long-range V-1 and V-2 rockets would soon be falling on New York City.

The U.S. Navy took these threats very seriously, particularly reports of a Nazi secret weapons project involving U-boats towing V-2 rockets in submersible transport containers across the Atlantic to within range of their targets and then launching them at U.S. cities and factories. To counter such a threat, the Navy set up a special carrier and destroyer taskforce, called *Operation Teardrop*, to intercept and destroy Nazi submarines before they could come within range of the United States.

The result was that during mid-April and early May, in the very final days of the war against the Third Reich, the U.S. Navy conducted a major campaign off the East Coast that saw a total of five U-boats, belonging to a submarine wolf pack code-named *Gruppe Seewolf*, intercepted and sunk. Happily for the citizens of the United States, the subsequent interrogation of the surviving members of these U-boat crews revealed that none of *Gruppe Seewolf* were fitted with missile launching equipment. Indeed, after the war, an examination of *Kriegsmarine* records revealed that despite some successful trials earlier in the war, the rocket U-boat plan never made it off the drawing board.

This brings us neatly back to the U-857. Although not part of *Gruppe Seewolf*, it had the misfortune to be caught up in the *Operation Teardrop* U-boat interdiction sweep.

On Friday 6th April, a German U-boat was sighted on the surface near Devil's Reef off the Massachusetts town of Innsmouth.

The following day, a Cannon Class destroyer escort ship, the *USS Gustafson*, fired a hedgehog of anti-submarine mortars at a target, believed to be the U-857, off Cape Cod. A glutinous oil-like slick was subsequently spotted on the surface; however, a postwar assessment by the Navy concluded that the *Gustafson* didn't hit a U-boat, but some other underwater non-sub target, possibly a whale or a giant squid.

Just over a week later, on Wednesday 18th April, a U.S. Navy blimp airship dropped a homing torpedo on a submarine spotted at the entrance to Long Island Sound, midway between Newport, Rhode Island and New Haven, Connecticut. *Kriegsmarine* records indicate the last contact with the U-857 was in early April, and the assumption is that the sub was lost with all hands and that its wreck now lies somewhere off the East Coast of the United States between Boston and Long Island.

So what were *Kapitanleutnant* Rudolf Premauer and the crew of the U-857 doing on their mission?

One suggestion was that the U-857 was making its way up Long Island Sound to make contact with Nazi sympathizers. There were rumors at the time that one of the Gold Coast mansions, shuttered up by its owners for the duration of the war, had been taken over by fifth columnists. Maybe the U-boat's mission was to drop off supplies of weapons, gold bullion, secret agents or even senior Nazis to help keep the cause alive through sabotage and subversion in a North American version of the *Werwolf* guerrilla movement in Germany?

Another suggestion was that the U-857 was on a kamikaze-style suicide mission carrying a Nazi secret weapon—perhaps an atomic bomb—and was trying to sneak up the Sound before detonating it as close to New York City as possible in one final act of terror and vengeance against the American people. We know the Nazis had their *Uranverein* heavy-water nuclear-energy project; maybe they had made more progress than the Western Allies realized?

And then there is the mystery of the original Devil's Reef sighting. Why did the submarine need to visit Innsmouth, a town that had never been of any strategic significance? Besides which, the place was pretty much abandoned and derelict after that incident in 1927. If we could ever accurately locate the wreck of the U-857—and some Long Island fishermen have hinted they know where it is but are keeping quiet because the surrounding waters are providing an unusually rich catch in lobsters—we might have a definitive answer to these questions one way or another!

Charles Christian

7

The Nazi Conspiracy-Theory Blogger's Story

Dude! If you want to hear weird stories about weird Nazi science, have you come to the right place. You've seen the website, I take it. It's the global clearing house, portal, forum, whatever for conspiracy theories about Third Reich mysticism and occultism, no matter how wacko they might seem. And, the biggest joke of all is that it's being run by me, a Jewish geek, operating from a small office over a diner in Roswell, New Mexico. Ooh, spooky coincidence; cue somebody playing a few chords on a theremin!

So anyhow, here's your inside skinny on Nazis in Antarctica 101, which will hopefully give you some kosher fat to chew over.

As you no doubt already know, the Nazis had this belief in an ancient Aryan master race that the present Nordic people of Europe, including the Germans but definitely excluding anyone of a Jewish persuasion, were all descended from. But where did the Aryans come from, and what subsequently happened to them? During the 1920s and 1930s, there were a raft of theories being discussed by esoteric societies with strong Nazi links, such as the Thule Society, the Vril Society, the *Ahnenerbe* SS division, and Himmler's Wewelsburg Castle Black Sun outfit, which is where the SS played at being Knights of the Roundtable and were sent off on expeditions to Tibet to look for the Holy Grail and the Spear of Destiny.

Somewhere along the way, the Nazis also picked up the idea that the foundations of the Aryan race could be found at *Ultima Thule*—or *Hyperborea*, as the Ancient Greeks and, coincidentally, Conan the Barbarian referred to it—a remote island located at the ends of the Earth surrounded by ice and snow.

The next thing you find is the Nazis have blended the Thule legend with the *holweltiehre* Hollow Earth theory, which is another idea that goes back to the Ancient Greeks but crops up in mythologies from all across the world. Remember those Nazi expeditions to Tibet in the 1930s? They were also trying to find an entrance in the Himalayas that would lead into the Hollow Earth. You can see where we are going here, can't you? We just need to toss in Indiana Jones and have Led Zeppelin on the sound system cranking out *Kashmir* and the *Immigrant Song*, then turn up the dials to number 11 to feel properly at home!

Eventually, so the rumors go, the Nazis *did* find the entrance to the Hollow Earth. Seems it was in Antarctica all along, which is why you have so much U-boat activity taking place in the Southern Ocean during World War Two. But, and get this, not only did they find the way into the Hollow Earth, but they also found the home of the Aryan master race who, believe it or not, turn out to be a species of giant space aliens—called the Elder Race—who are prepared to help the Nazis save the Fatherland. Yes, we've even got a taster of the *Ancient Astronauts* myth in here, much favored by Erich von Daniken and others in the post-war years.

These aliens arrived on Earth from the Aldebaran system about 500 million years ago and initially settled on the now-lost continents of Lemuria and Atlantis. When they sank beneath the seas, the Elders moved to Mesopotamia and became the gods of the Sumerians, in the process jump-starting Mankind's first civilizations. They spent most of their time dwelling in temples, pyramids and ziggurats (I love the *dwelling* bit; mere mortals like thee and me only get to *live* in places) pausing only to break the monotony by doing the wild thing with Earth women. The progeny of these couplings would become the original Aryans. After a time of living on the surface of the Earth, the Elders became worried that our Sun's rays were causing them to age prematurely, so some of them flew off to a base they already had on Jupiter's moon Europa, while the remainder moved to the South Pole to build the legendary city of Kadath in the Cold Waste. It was some time after this that the Elder Race began tunneling beneath the Earth's surface to create the huge subterranean complexes in which they now live.

Now we fast-forward to 1943, where we find the U-boat supreme *Grossadmiral* Doenitz—and he was one of the saner members of the Nazi elite—claiming that the German submarine fleet had built "in another part of the world, a Shangri-La land, an impregnable fortress." Later still, during the Nuremburg war-crimes trials, when you maybe would have thought he had more serious things to worry about, Doenitz spoke of "an invincible fortification in the midst of the eternal ice."

Within conspiracy-theory circles, this has become synonymous with the legendary Base 211, the Nazi's own Antarctic equivalent of Area 51.

This is also why from the late 1940s onwards you get a surge in reports of UFO sightings. These flying saucers were not visitors from the stars but Nazi craft built using the alien technology helpfully provided by the Fourth Reich's new allies! There is even a suggestion that by using one of the Elder Race's many tunnels beneath the Earth, they were able to burrow into Hitler's Berlin bunker in April 1945, so that he, Eva Braun, Martin Bormann and the rest of the senior Nazis hierarchy could escape to their Antarctic redoubt.

Perhaps they are still there, with Hitler having lived out his days painting watercolors of snow scenes and icebergs? Maybe they've all gone off in flying saucers back to Aldebaran? Perhaps the place is like those old Doug McClure movies *The Land that Time Forgot* and *Warlords of Atlantis?* You know, populated by improbable dinosaurs, cavemen, and hot chicks like Caroline Munro? Or

Charles Christian

maybe the Elder Race just got fed up with Hitler's rantings and turned him and all the surviving Nazis into a bunch of penguins?

Right, my friend, I don't know about you, but *I* think it's Margarita o'clock.

8

The Antarctic Explorer's Story

Oh, the Nazis in Antarctica! That's a myth that is never going to go away, despite the fact there is not one shred of evidence to suggest they built a secret base there during World War Two. And I can also assure you that if there were a gateway to some underground civilization or the ruins of the lost city of Kadath, the number of ground-based expeditions, aerial photography missions and, more recently, satellite mapping activities over the past 100 years would have most certainly found them.

The bald facts are these: in 1938, Nazi Germany sent an expedition to Antarctica, where they laid claim to an area they called *Neuschwabenland*— or New Swabia—although most of the territory was already administered by Norway under the name of Queen Maud Land. But (here the *but* is a big but) after 1939 the Nazis didn't take the venture any further, and to this day the area continues to be known to the wider world as Queen Maud Land and is still run by Norway. In point of fact, Germany had no permanent presence in Antarctica until 1981, when it established a research facility.

The one contribution the Nazis *did* make to Antarctic exploration was to take over 16,000 aerial photographs of the region and in the process identify and name a number of geographic features, including peaks, valleys and mountain ranges. Most of these names are still in use today, and quite rightly so, as some of the older informal names were really rather silly.

For example, what the Nazis christened the Penck Trough had previously been known as the Plateau of Leng. And the adjoining Muhlig-Hofmann Mountains used to be called the Crazy Mountains, and before that, the Mountains of Madness, which just sounds like something out of a Victorian melodrama. Seriously, we shouldn't laugh, as those mountains are where the ill-fated Pabodie Expedition from Miskatonic University came to a sticky end in 1931.

One thing the Germans didn't spot in 1938, not altogether surprisingly, since nobody had the technology to detect such phenomena—in the 1930s anyway— was that part of New Swabia included what is now called Lake Vostok, the largest sub-glacial lake in Antarctica.

Over 160 miles long and 30 miles wide, the lake lies beneath 13,000 feet of ice and its waters are believed to have been isolated from the rest of the Earth for

20 million years. The Russians are only just starting to get probes down through the ice and into the lake water itself but the theory is that the environment could be similar to that of the ice-covered oceans of Jupiter's moon Europa.

9

The Landlady's Story

He's a lovely man. Never caused me any trouble. Keeps himself to himself in the cottage he rents at the bottom of the yard. Always pays his rent on time, and if he sees me, he is always friendly and happy to talk a while—I'm a widow, you know—or come in for a cup of coffee.

Researching a history book he is, about the Gold Coast houses during World War Two. Last time I saw him, he was really excited. Said he was on the trail of a conspiracy involving the Nazis and some secret society. He didn't tell me the full details but said he'd met a fisherman down from Kingsport way who knew the location of a U-boat wreck and was planning to scuba-dive the site.

I know he often works late into the night, typing up his notes and doing online research, so he often sleeps in late on a morning, and sometimes you won't see the curtains pulled back till the afternoon.

However, I grew concerned when I realized there'd been no signs of life at the cottage for the best part of three days, yet his car hadn't been moved from the driveway. When I went over to investigate, I found the front door partially open. What tipped me off that something was wrong, which is why I dialed 911, is that not only was he missing but all his research notes and manuscript printout notes had gone, along with his computers and tech equipment.

He was meticulous about his files and, while it isn't unusual for him to be away on a trip for a night or two, he was in New Mexico recently; he'd always leave his stuff here. But now … it's all gone, yet his clothes and personal possessions are still here.

It's not like him to do this. He's a considerate young man. I'm worried about him.

10

The Medical Examiner's Story

The deceased John Doe is a white non-Hispanic male, found wearing the remnants of a neoprene diver's wetsuit. I'd estimate his age at the time of death to be somewhere in his mid-thirties, but a more precise figure is impossible, given the damaged and decomposed state in which the remains were delivered to the autopsy rooms.

Positive identification of the body is not yet possible, as most of the flesh on the face has been either eaten or dissolved away. The impression is that the skin and muscle tissue has been sucked clean from the skull. I have been able to obtain a partial fingerprint, so there is a chance that a search of the IAFIS fingerprint identification database may produce a match.

The other striking feature of the corpse is that the limbs and abdomen were punctured by a series of circular wounds that have left raised welts and rings of teethmarks.

This is not the first time I have had the misfortune to encounter a corpse in such a condition and suffering wounds of this nature. Regrettably, I am not alone in my experiences.

From the records available at this office and from my conversations with my colleagues in neighboring counties, it would seem corpses like my latest John Doe have been washing up along the shores of the Long Island Sound since at least the 1920s, when my illustrious, but nowadays much-maligned predecessor Herbert West conducted the autopsies in this county. As well as here on Long Island, medical examiners and coroners in Connecticut, Rhode Island and Massachusetts have all reported similarly mutilated human remains turning up at their morgues.

Today's corpse was found on the Gold Coast shore, just down the beach from the site of the old Beacon Towers mansion. Coincidentally, this was where a cluster of human remains were recovered during the war years of the 1940s.

Over at Arkham, the Professor of Cryptozoology and Teratology at the University of Miskatonic is of the opinion that the culprit is an as-yet unidentified sea creature, possibly an unknown form of giant squid, that haunts the shores of the East Coast of the United States. I'd like to think she is right, and that this is the explanation.

THE YOTH PROTOCOLS

BY JOSH REYNOLDS

Sarlowe sat on the Ford's hood, dribbling cigarette ash onto the ground below as the Oklahoma sun beat a tattoo on his head and shoulders. The heat pierced his fedora with ease, making his scalp feel like a cooked lobster. He sucked smoke into his lungs and expelled it slowly through his mouth and nose. His suit was rumpled and felt grimy, thanks to two days on the road and a motel shower that had put more dirt on than it had taken off. Damp patches formed under his arms and on his chest, soaking right through the regulation white shirt.

"You almost done?" he said, sucking the last bit of life out of the cigarette and dropping it to join the small pyramid of its brethren between his feet. He pulled the distressingly light pack out of his coat and extracted another coffin nail. He stuffed it between his lips with mechanical precision and fished for his lighter. "Only, it's hot and my stomach thinks my throat's been cut." Right on cue, his stomach gurgled.

His partner didn't reply.

Sarlowe lit his cigarette. It wasn't a substitute for greasy eggs and overcooked bacon, but it was all he had, other than a half-ounce of turgid coffee-flavored sludge in the bottom of a thermos; nicotine and caffeine, the G-man's best friends. Sarlowe looked around. They were a few miles from a no-nothing town called Binger, parked near the mound. The mound didn't have a colorful name, and it wasn't on any maps, not anymore. No one but the Boys in Binger knew it was there, and they were paid to make sure it stayed that way.

When you first saw it, it looked like any other lump of dirt. Slightly square and oddly angled and shorn of vegetation. It was only when you were on top and looked closer that you saw the stairs. Stairs in odd places, going down into the deep dark, taking everything you thought was true and real with them. There were hidden places, tumors in the earth, stinking of blood and old, wild things. Not just in Oklahoma … everywhere. The Warren site in the Big Cypress, the Martense molehills, certain secret cellars where a certain artist had painted certain pictures and almost certainly been eaten. Poor old Inspector Craig and his Special Detail in the subway tunnels beneath New York....

Worms in the goddamned earth, Sarlowe thought and chewed on the cigarette, trying not to think about dark places and tight corners and *things crouching just out of sight.* Or in plain sight, as the case might be. He eyed his partner through the initial expulsion of smoke and couldn't repress the old, instinctive shudder.

The man who called himself Indrid Cold stood some distance from the Ford, long arms spread above his head, speaking old words in his oddly-pitched voice. Unlike Sarlowe, who had a Carolina drawl, Cold affected Massachusetts vowels, though he sounded like a nest of wasps stuck in a tin can most of the time. Cold was dressed in Hoover's best, black on white, tie and shiny shoes, black gloves, but it looked *wrong,* like a wrapper on a rotten fish.

As if he'd heard Sarlowe's thoughts, Cold dropped his arms and turned. Sarlowe flinched. "Did you say something?" Cold said. His face was like wax and stretched in an unnatural grin. Cold never stopped grinning, that was what the boys in DC said. They also said that if he ever did stop, Sarlowe was to shoot him, and then burn what came out. Sometimes he wondered if that was a standing order. Sarlowe wasn't Cold's first partner, nor would he be his last. He outlived them, mostly, though if what Cold did could be called living rather than just … persisting, Sarlowe didn't know.

The water-cooler gossip back at the spook show was that Cold had met Thomas Jefferson once, and that there were a number of the latter's letters which had been excised from public record because of that. Hoover was right when he said that the rot went deep, though even the Director wasn't aware of the true extent of said rot or the yawning, cosmic abysses it spread from. Sarlowe knew, though he wished to God he didn't. "Not a damn thing," he said to Cold. "Are you done?"

The locals in Binger had sighted lights in the sky and heard strange noises which could have been earthquakes, and since nothing had been scheduled with the involved parties, the Director had concluded that it needed to be checked out. It wasn't often that it was something, but when it was, it had to be handled. The flying fungi liked to play rough with hillbillies and dairy farmers, but there were worse things in Heaven and Earth than dreamt of in Alhazred's philosophy, things that were interested in human affairs and liked to *take sides.*

The local 'old ones,' the Shonokins, the *K'n-Yani*, whatever you wanted to call them, were like a crowd at a boxing match, yelling and placing bets on the hairless monkeys with their quaint intercontinental sling-stones and primitive ideologies.

To keep them happy and friendly, a regular coffee klatsch had been authorized. If you stayed on a first-name basis with a species, they were less likely to start chatting with the Kremlin. That was the theory, anyway. Keep them happy and keep them out of human affairs. Sometimes Sarlowe wondered if there was a hill chieftain in whereverthefuckistan who was thinking the same thing about the Good Ol' US of A.

"They haven't replied," Cold said. His cheek twitched and for a moment, Sarlowe couldn't help but imagine what was under there. He sucked in a shaky lungful of smoke and expelled it with a cough when he processed what Cold had said. The K'n-Yani were telepathic, on top of everything else. They didn't like coming aboveground, and nobody particularly wanted them to, so someone from the spook show, usually from the Binger brigade, would come out once a year to chat about how Spain was doing in the Finals to the empty air. They always replied; had always replied.

"That's not good," Sarlowe wheezed.

"No," Cold said.

They were only out here because of the lights, because somebody had seen something where nobody was supposed to see anything on account of the ancient and decadent pre-human civilization liking its privacy. Sarlowe took a shuddery breath. "So what do we do?"

Cold looked at him, his eyes as wide and as black as the lenses of Sarlowe's sunglasses. "We go down."

"That's not SOP," Sarlowe said quickly, his heart sputtering like a jackhammer from too much coffee and nicotine. "The Yoth Protocols state that we don't go down if they don't go up." Standard operating procedure was to call for backup if they failed to establish peaceful contact, and to set up a cordon.

Cold looked at him.

"They didn't reply."

"I'm not going down there," Sarlowe snapped and crushed his cigarette and flung it down.

"Then stay up here," Cold said, starting towards the mound. Of course he knew where the stairs were, curling down into the dark.

Ladies' lingerie, housewares, Sarlowe thought, releasing a bitter chuckle. With a grunt, he dropped off of the Ford and hurried after Cold. Standard procedure after the Frenchman's Flat incident was to not let Cold go anywhere

Josh Reynolds

without a human handler. Bad things might happen otherwise.

"We should let Binger know," he said, as they reached the top. He coughed and wheezed as he caught up with Cold. Too many cigarettes, not enough time on the obstacle course. He bent forward, palms pressed to his knees, and spit up something foul-tasting.

"There is no need. We will investigate," Cold said, dropping to his haunches. The stairs were hidden beneath a circular stone, like a well cap. It had been placed after the Zamacona Cylinder had been unearthed. Tentative, quiet contact with the indigenous inhabitants had been established not long after the cylinder had been unearthed. Every alphabet-soup agency existent in the Twenties had tried to get a hand in. Cold had led the delegation, because Cold led every delegation of that sort. Had done, always would do.

Sarlowe had been down into the blue-lit caverns only once, and that had been enough to last him a lifetime. There were things man ought not to know, not if he wanted a functioning liver and an easy conscience. It was easy to understand why it was considered important to maintain good relations with their ground-floor neighbors, besides the obvious: with the Reds getting twitchier by the year, they might all need a few miles of topsoil between them and a dose of nuclear sunshine sooner rather than later. But you couldn't very well just move in. Not down there, where things walked that ought to crawl. You had to know somebody in the building to get an apartment.

Cold lifted the stone easily. He was stronger than he looked. The stench that rose out of the aperture was like that of a cellar in summer, and Sarlowe waved a hand in front of his face. Cold didn't appear to notice. He rose to his feet and started down without turning to check that his partner was following him. Sarlowe tensed as they descended, expecting to be confronted at any moment by the mutilated guardians that normally haunted the passage.

But no one greeted them, living, dead or otherwise. There wasn't even a hint of the weird wind that normally accompanied a descent. Cold stopped on the stairs, head cocked, gloved fingers twitching idly as he examined the great basalt blocks that made up the tunnel around them. Sarlowe touched the automatic holstered beneath his arm, looking for reassurance as the darkness seemed to press down on him. The K'n-Yani could move through solid rock like it was fog, and he imagined them moving around him and Cold, giggling silently in the darkness.

Higher mathematics, Sarlowe knew. That was what the think tanks said, at any rate. It was all mathematics and 'extraplanar matter.' That's why bullets didn't bother them, and why they couldn't stick a nuke down a chute and fumigate the basement. It might work on the kissing cousins, like those things under the subways in New York or the batrachian hillbillies in Massachusetts, but the old ones weren't from around these parts. The only crap that worried them was stuff in the vaults in Yoth and those *things* in N'kai. Both of which worried everybody else as well, which was why nobody had made too much fuss about the K'n-Yani being between them and those other things.

The dark gave way to a bluish light that seemed to seep from the stones and the stairs slabbed smooth near an arched aperture. "No guards," Sarlowe murmured.

Cold's head twitched in reply.

"Do you have your amulet?" he said.

Sarlowe's hand went automatically to his neck. Hidden beneath his collar and tie, pressed close to his skin was the round amulet every agent on the spook detail was issued. It was shaped like a face, but one not even a mother could love. It was like the lovechild of a bat and a toad, and it had a grin like Cold's carved on its bloated face. The amulet was made out of some soft green stone that no geologist had ever been able to identify. Like too many other things, they'd been provided to the federal government by Cold.

Sarlowe tapped the amulet. "Yeah, I got it," he said.

"Good," Cold said.

You needed an amulet if you wanted to get through the archway to K'n-Yan, either coming or going. Water-cooler gossip had it that it was a gesture of good faith from the downstairs neighbors, and that they could get out any time they wanted. Sarlowe didn't know whether that was true or not, but he knew that the archway wasn't just for them. There were worse things down in the dark, things that the K'n-Yani had fought so often that they'd stopped worrying about them, but that could do a lot of damage if they got topside. He and Cold stopped in front of the archway. There was a familiar smell on the air, and Sarlowe had flashbacks to red, wet rooms and black lumps on concrete floors.

"We should go back," he said. "Something has gone wrong." He felt a tingle in his spine, a bit of Carolina hoodoo that warned him when it was all about to go sour. That was why he was on the spook detail, though no one had ever said as much. Family history had a lot of weight with the Director.

Cold looked at him. "All the more reason to investigate," he said.

Sarlowe closed his eyes and took a breath. He wanted a cigarette, but resisted the urge. "You first," he said hoarsely. Cold's thin lips twitched in a smile.

They stepped through the aperture and Sarlowe's spine seemed to burn and freeze at the same time, and the amulet around his neck became as hot as a pan pulled fresh from the stove before the heat drained away a moment

Josh Reynolds

later. "Oh sweet Jesus," he whispered, as they stepped out onto the great stone balcony that overlooked the infinite cavern beyond.

The first time he'd seen it, he'd gotten a bad case of temporary agoraphobia. There was too much space in the darkness. The void was too big, the scale of it too vast for him to comprehend. He'd been down in the dark before, in other deep places, but this was the deepest place in the world. A yammering abyss where cities did not sit idle on the solid ground but coiled about massive encrustations of rock and rose like serpents from the deep wells of darkness that was Yoth, and below that, forbidden N'kai.

The thought of the latter made him shudder unconsciously. No one knew what was in N'kai. The K'n-Yani weren't saying, and official policy was 'we're better off not knowing.' Cold probably knew; but then, Cold was the only one who'd ever used the Voormithadreth Corridor and hadn't rotted from the inside out. The Corridor was a minute-past-midnight contingency plan due to the weird chromatic radiation that permeated it. They thought it came out somewhere in Mongolia, but no one was certain, not even the Reds.

There were a dozen cities in the cavern, occupying the spaces between titanic stalagmites and stalactites, like urban moths pinned between stone fangs. Or there had been. Once, they'd have been lit up like Christmas trees, with billions of lights piercing the gloom in all directions. Now, there were lights, but they were different, and far, far fewer.

Sarlowe looked out across the great stone bridge which connected where they stood to the nearest of the cities—Yath, he thought, though he wasn't sure of the pronunciation. The last time he'd visited, there'd been two enormous statues, glaring at one another from nitre-encrusted niches set to either side of the undulating cavern wall, guarding the approach to the bridge. Both of those statues now looked as if they'd lost an argument with an artillery division. Eerie-hued witch-fires danced on their cracked and oddly blistered forms. The glowing pinpricks made his skin crawl, the way the lights-out at Frenchman's Flats had, after the nuclear test.

Cold extended a hand, and the witch-fires were pulled from their perches to swarm about his spread fingers like fireflies. He made a fist, snuffing the fires all at once. "Valusian spectrum radiation," Cold said. Rather than echoing, his voice was swallowed by the sheer enormity of the space before them.

"Valusian—," Sarlowe began. The prickling sensation on his skin got stronger as he realized what Cold was talking about. "Oh, oh no, no, no, no, we have to report this, Cold. We have to get Binger on the horn, get the Bureau." His heart was pounding in his chest, not from exertion now, but from fear. Not the casual fear that being around Cold engendered, but something more crippling. He looked out at Yath, and saw more witch-fires, curling up from the shattered husks of distant buildings. *Earthquakes and lights in the sky*, he thought, and stifled a sudden giggle. Something had happened down here, and God alone knew how long ago it had been. It was something much worse than any unplanned nuclear detonation or lateral troop deployment. The amulet suddenly felt like it weighed a ton, and he hoped it was only his imagination that was making it seem as if it were getting warmer.

"Someone has entered Yoth," Cold said, as if Sarlowe hadn't spoken. The grin wavered, and Sarlowe's fingers crept towards his automatic instinctively. "Can you smell it?"

"Smell what?"

"War," Cold said. He froze, as still as one of the crumbled statues that loomed over them. "Something is coming."

"The old ones," Sarlowe said. He looked around, expecting to see smiling devils bleeding out of the walls, chuckling and smiling. The amulet was hot on his chest, and he half-thought about taking it off, but didn't.

"No," Cold said, "Something hungry. I can feel it, reverberating through the dark." His head twitched, like a cat that'd caught the chirp of a bird, just out of its line of vision. "The vaults of Yoth were sealed from this side. Whoever did it would have had to come from below."

"N'kai," Sarlowe whispered. The darkness felt stifling all of a sudden. The agoraphobia was replaced by increasing claustrophobia, as if the unseen walls of the cavern were closing in. He blinked and stepped back from the edge. He heard something, a soft, wet sound, an insistent susurrus that echoed from all over the cavern. "Is that—that's smoke, right? Cold, that's smoke moving out there in the darkness, isn't it? It's just smoke," he said, trying to convince himself.

"No," Cold said. His head oscillated. "No, it's not smoke."

"It sounds like the ocean," Sarlowe said quietly.

"It's not that either," Cold said. He sounded amused.

Sarlowe's hand found the amulet and despite its warmth, he clutched it tight. He didn't ask the obvious question. Whatever had come up out of N'kai, the K'n-Yani had bombed their own cities into oblivion to kill it, from the looks of things; a millennia-old Cold War gone suddenly hot. If they hadn't done the job, that didn't bode well for those of them in the penthouse. "We have to go. Protocol—" he began.

"I am well aware of the Yoth Protocols," Cold said softly. He turned towards Sarlowe. "I devised them myself. No one in, or out, if they have been exposed," he said. He reached out and tapped the amulet beneath Sarlowe's shirt. "As long as you wear this, you will be fine."

"And what about you?" Sarlowe said.

"What about me?" Cold said. "But you are correct. We must leave. I—"

Whatever he'd been about to say was lost in the sudden roar of a pistol. Sarlowe jerked back as Cold was knocked backwards, over the lip of the balcony. He didn't bother to stretch out a hand. Instead, he turned and sprinted for the archway.

He didn't reach it. Two shapes, clad in fatigues, glided forward and the blows came hard and fast. They were trained, and better than him. The stock of a PPS-43 machine gun smashed into his stomach. He hit the ground hard, his body aching. He scrambled to his feet as they circled him. As he stood, a third shape materialized before him, and the heavy weight of a revolver crashed down across the side of his head. Sarlowe went down again. This time he decided not to get up.

"Get his gun," someone croaked, in accented English. The world spun, and he thought his nose might be broken. Rough hands clawed open his coat and jerked his automatic from its holster. He looked up into a face that had seen the wrong end of a punishment baton more than once, with small eyes and steel-capped teeth that glinted in the weirdling light of the cavern. The teeth flashed as their owner said something; *Russian*, Sarlowe thought as if the teeth hadn't been a dead giveaway. "Yes, leave the amulet. They are not as foolish as all that are they, American? Only you can use it, yes?"

Sarlowe blinked, trying to clear his vision. He didn't reply.

Someone sighed. "I am speaking English for your benefit, my friend. Please do me the courtesy of replying," the voice said.

Sarlowe pushed himself onto his hands and knees and then rocked back onto his rear.

"Who are you?" he said.

"My name is Grigori Petrov. Maybe you have heard of me?" He said it expectantly, as if he expected Sarlowe to gasp or sit up straight. He was a thin, scary-looking old man, with strange tattoos on his face and neck and hands, and wearing a greatcoat that was two sizes too big for his shrunken frame. His goons had the same look—their fatigues hung off them. They'd been big men, once. Now they looked like concentration-camp survivors.

"No," Sarlowe said.

"Ah, well, such are the fortunes of war. Look at me, please." Sarlowe did.

"Waste is a great sin, according to the little red book," Petrov said harshly. He looked old in the weird light of K'n-Yan, all skin and bones and bent under the weight of invisible chains. Sarlowe fancied he'd been a big man, and wolfish looking, when he'd been younger. Now he was a scarecrow of flesh and bone. The automatic in his hand didn't waver despite the seeming fragility of the hand that clutched it. "I would hate to kill you, if it were not necessary."

"Especially since I'm the only one who can get you past those wards, isn't that right?" Sarlowe said, brushing blood out of the corner of his mouth with the heel of his palm. "You need me alive if you want to get out of here."

Petrov inclined his head. "Your summation is accurate, if unnecessary."

"Russians," Sarlowe said, trying to play for the time he needed to think, "What the hell are Russians doing down here? Don't you have a fucking plateau to play with, or are the Chinese being selfish?"

Petrov didn't reply. He looked at steel-tooth. "Get him to his feet. It is long past time to climb to a healthier atmosphere."

Steel-tooth dragged Sarlowe to his feet while his buddy watched the stairway warily, the PPS-43 cradled in his hands like a talisman. Sarlowe wondered if Cold were really dead. Petrov looked like a Siberian shaman playing dress-up as a communist commissar, which he might well have been. Uncle Sam wasn't the only one with pet necromancers. He might have had a clip full of blessed bullets for all Sarlowe knew. That'd explain Cold going down like a sack of potatoes. The goon shoved him forward. Sarlowe staggered. His head was still jangling. Petrov was strong for a senior citizen.

"You have an automobile aboveground," Petrov said as he took hold of Sarlowe's lapel and dragged him along towards the archway. It wasn't a question. "We will leave you to walk back. That way you will not alert your comrades to our presence until we have a—how do you say—'head start'?"

"You're not going to kill me?"

"Why waste a bullet, when what may yet follow us up into the light will do the job just as well?" Petrov said, with a shrug. "If you would not see it before your time, I would walk faster, yes?"

Sarlowe stumbled along, brain trying to catch up to his feet. "What the hell were you even looking for down there?" he said. He heard something scrape, somewhere in the darkness. "You couldn't have come through K'n-Yan. That means you had to have come through ..." he trailed off.

"N'kai," Petrov said. His voice wasn't as steady as it had been. Sarlowe glanced at him. The old man looked even more skeletal than before, and his flesh had a washed-out, waxy look in the faint glow radiating from the archway. His goons had similar washed-out looks to them, as if they'd flown a glider

Josh Reynolds

over hell, and gotten the smoke in their lungs. He wondered how many of them there'd been when they'd started out; probably not just the three of them.

Sarlowe licked his lips. "The Voormithadreth Corridor," he said. He caught sight of something, out of the corner of his eye. He wanted to turn, but didn't. The shadows were alive with movement. He heard the ocean again, and louder. He wasn't the only one to hear it either—Petrov paled. "There are doctors—quarantine—we can help," he began. If he could dart through the archway first, they'd be trapped. Granted, they could still shoot him. There was a downside to every plan. But they couldn't be allowed to get out.

God knew what they'd been exposed to, let alone what they'd done, especially if they'd opened the vaults of Yoth. That was why there were protocols in place—there were too many colors, too many unknown radiations, too many chemicals unknown to science. If you didn't have quarantine protocols, you started getting malformed deer and invisible, elephant-sized twins. Or worse, you got *squatters*.

Petrov cackled. "We have been down here for four months," he said. The goon with the machine gun scratched at his cheek. His skin looked dry and flaky and gray in the weird light of the archway. As he scratched, flakes fell away. Sarlowe felt a thrill of disgust. He'd seen men die of Gardner Syndrome before. Better a bullet than that. The darkness closed around the goon, as something caught his attention, and he stepped out of the light.

Sarlowe fell silent. There was no help for them, and both he and Petrov knew it. Petrov gave a ghastly smile. "I warned them. Untenable, I said, to take men and machines through—and for what? To annex a territory of horrors, just so you Americans couldn't have it." He jabbed Sarlowe with the automatic. "But that is the game our masters play, is it not? Check and mate, round and round we go. That is why your government wastes money on lucid dreamers and trying to recover the Zann Concerto. That is why my masters spend men like bullets, feeding them into the maw of Leng, or on ventures like this. Check and—"

"Mate," Cold said.

Cold stepped out of the darkness, holding the PPS-43 casually. Sarlowe hadn't heard or seen a whiff of him taking down Petrov's man. *Maybe he didn't,* he thought, *maybe something else did and he just took advantage.* He pushed the thought aside and lunged for Petrov's gun, as the latter swung around, face stretched in shock.

Steel-tooth whipped around, a pistol coming up, but too slow. The PPS burped and steel-tooth did a little dance and fell down. Sarlowe caught hold of Petrov's wrist and jabbed the old man a quick one in the kidney. Petrov backhanded him. Had he been twenty years younger, Sarlowe thought the blow might've snapped his neck. As it was, it dropped him hard to the floor. Petrov turned, firing. Cold ducked back, vanishing into the creeping dark.

"Hello, Grigori," Cold said, from somewhere out of sight. "It's been quite the while, hasn't it? When was the last time we saw each other? Was it '44, perhaps? It was Berlin, I know that. You'd finally made peace with the Party, and come out of the cold. I was pleased for you."

"Quiet, you reeking sack of maggots," Petrov growled. He kicked Sarlowe in the gut. "Come out so I can blow a hole in that thing you call a face." The old man stepped back, catching Sarlowe's hand beneath his boot heel. Sarlowe yelped. Petrov sank to his haunches, his eyes still on the dark where Cold had vanished. There was definitely something moving in it, though whether it was Cold or something else, Sarlowe couldn't say. Petrov snatched the amulet from around his neck. "My apologies, but I require this just now," he hissed.

"I'm the only one who can use it," Sarlowe gasped, trying to shove Petrov's foot off of his hand. Petrov brought the gun down on his head.

"At the moment, I am willing to hope that is not the case," he said, glaring at the darkness. "You hear me, Indrid, yes? You hear me, maggot-man? I go. If you follow, I kill him. Maybe I kill you too."

"Oh, Grigori, you know the old saying...'that which is not dead' and all that," Cold said. Rocks clattered somewhere close. Cold's voice seemed to come from everywhere and nowhere all at once. "Just as you know that I cannot let you leave. You've been exposed to some terrible things, and we simply cannot have you carrying the contagion upstairs. Gardner Syndrome, Grigori," Cold said. "How many little piles of gray dust did you and your men leave in your wake, as you trudged through those lightless abysses, pursued by the things you freed?"

Petrov's face had lost all of its color. He swept the automatic back and forth as he rose to his feet, Sarlowe's amulet dangling from his free hand. "I will not stay down here," he snarled.

"Afraid of what you've let out of its cage, are you?" Cold said. "Understandable. Only those amulets around your neck are keeping them from your throat. How long has it been since they polished off the indigenous population? A month or two, I'd wager. There never were very many of the K'n-Yani down here, their claims to the contrary. And the formless spawn of the depths are ever hungry."

"Then you stay down here and take the edge off of their hunger," Petrov said as he backed towards the archway. Sarlowe rolled away as soon as Petrov's foot left his hand, but the Russian gestured with the gun, stopping him before he got to his feet. "You as well," Petrov said. Sarlowe tensed. He didn't think he was quick enough to beat a bullet, but some deaths were preferable to others. Rocks clattered down from above the archway. Petrov froze and then turned. Sarlowe looked up.

Cold clung to the wall above the archway like an enormous spider, limbs bent at impossible angles, the machine gun dangling from his neck by its sling. His grin was still as fixed as ever. Petrov cursed and raised his weapon. Even as he fired, Cold was pushing himself away from his perch. He dropped onto the old man like a hawk striking a field mouse. Sarlowe flinched away, as the sound of bones snapping, and Petrov's scream, filled his ears. He'd heard the stories, but until you saw it up close, it was hard to credit them.

When Cold rose to his feet, he was holding a handful of amulets, including Sarlowe's. Petrov was babbling and cursing in Russian as he tried to crawl towards the archway. His legs and his spine were bent wrong and he left a smear of red in his wake. Cold turned his grin towards Sarlowe. "Good thinking. Keeping them distracted like that."

"I couldn't let them get out, could I?" Sarlowe coughed.

"No, we couldn't have that." Cold looked down at Petrov. "What was the plan then, Grigori? Let Tsathoggua's children loose to leap and play and do your work for you? Only you discovered that you couldn't escape the way you'd come, or this way, and so you were caught. How long you and your men must have sat here, waiting for someone to come down, to investigate. How long you must have huddled, your numbers decreasing with every day until…" Cold trailed off. He turned and looked out at the cavern. The distant, ruined cities were barely visible in the dark. He slumped slightly, as if in exhaustion.

"They were among the last, you know. Of the truly old ones," he said, to no one in particular. "And now they're gone." For a moment, Sarlowe thought that Cold had forgotten him. Then Cold looked at him and said, "But I'm still here." The grin never wavered, but his cheek twitched and jumped as he spoke.

Cold dumped the whole lot of amulets, save for the one Petrov had taken from Sarlowe, into the latter's lap. Sarlowe looked up at Cold, and made to speak. Cold tapped his lips with a forefinger, and Sarlowe fell silent. Cold looked at Petrov. "And you, Grigori. You were always quite troublesome. But not for much longer, I think."

The darkness moved. The shadows bubbled and boiled like hot tar and polyps of obsidian stabbed from every direction at once. Petrov's howls grew in volume and rose in register as each polyp struck home, hooking itself into him. Then, he was tugged up and back into the dark, like a fish hooked from the sea. His howls ceased abruptly, as he vanished. Cold waited a beat, then two and then sighed and said, "Poor Grigori. Then, I always knew he'd come to a bad end." He looked at Sarlowe. "I'm sorry."

"For what?" Sarlowe coughed, getting to his feet. He still held the amulets. After seeing what had happened to Petrov without them, he didn't want to risk it. "What the hell are those things?"

"Hungry. But lazy," Cold said. His smile twitched. "In a few decades, they'll slither back down into the depths from which Petrov inadvertently freed them, and someone will come back down and replace the seals."

"You, you mean," Sarlowe said.

"Maybe," Cold said. He fingered the bullet hole in his shirt-front. Petrov's bullet had connected after all. Something white and squirming was visible for just a moment, before he prodded it back into place.

"Evil the mind that is held by no head," Sarlowe muttered.

Cold looked at him.

"What?"

"Nothing/ Can we get out of here now, please?"

"Yes," Cold said. He turned towards the archway.

Sarlowe saw that Cold still had his amulet dangling from his grip. He tossed the others aside and hurried to catch up with him. "Hey, aren't you forgetting something?" he said, reaching for him. He felt the tingle again, his hoodoo senses doing a dance up and down his spine.

"No," Cold said.

Sarlowe grabbed his arm. "My amulet, I can't get out without it."

"I know," Cold said. His grin twitched and stretched as he stiff-armed Sarlowe backwards. Sarlowe staggered back, and wiped his hands on his coat. He felt things moving beneath Cold's sleeves. "I cannot return it, Sarlowe. I'm sorry."

"What are you talking about?" Sarlowe said. But even as he said it, he knew. His stomach lurched. The Valusian radiation, Gardner Syndrome … but he'd only been exposed for a few minutes. "No. I'm fine. If you get me to Binger..."

"The protocols say that no one who's been exposed comes in or out," Cold said. "It's SOP, Sarlowe," he added, echoing Sarlowe's earlier words. "You know that." He stepped through the archway. Sarlowe took a step after him, hesitated, and stopped. If he tried the archway, he'd be dead.

"You can't leave me here," he said. He looked around. The darkness seemed to shiver in anticipation. Cold was watching him from the other side of the archway, his grin still in place. "Cold, please … I didn't even want to come down here!" he shouted.

"I know," Cold said. "I'm sorry. I was too curious—a failing of mine. You were right."

"Don't leave me here alone!"

"I won't," Cold said. He tossed the PPS-43 through the archway to land with a clatter at Sarlowe's feet. Sarlowe looked down at it, and then up. Cold was gone. He could hear his shoes clicking, as he ascended. Then, he heard nothing at all, as the darkness closed in. It obscured the archway and the statues. He snatched up the machine gun. He wished he'd kept hold of Petrov's amulets. He wished Petrov had killed him.

The last lights of distant Yath went out, one by one, like candles being snuffed.

The darkness padded forward on a hundred paws.

He'd been wrong.

Up close, it didn't sound like the ocean at all.

A Feast of Death

BY Lee Clark Zumpe

1

stood atop the glassy plateau at the summit of a grim, narrow peak rising above the dense forest. After only a few moments, I trembled and sank to my knees beneath the mind-bending panoply spread before me. Such vistas, I thought, were not meant for the eyes of men. Of the count-less atrocities I had witnessed over the last ten months, nothing rivaled this lurid tableau—nothing I had experienced since landing at the mouth of the Shatt-el-Arab gnawed at my sanity like this unbearable spectacle.

How like reality this uncanny fever dream had been, how like an omen whispered from the deepest shadows of twilight.

—Nathan Longcroft, *Interned by the Turks*

2

"They're coming down the lane now, Lieutenant Macready." Corporal Guy Blacklock of the 6th Division stood beside a barred window that looked out across a little courtyard where two pear trees and an acacia offered small patches of shaded ground. "It's the commandant, his interpreter and a German officer. Can't say I recognize the Hun."

"I warned him there would be hell to pay," Lieutenant Cyril Macready said, his voice somber and anxious. "Best wake him if his fever has broken. He'll need a moment to compose himself."

Blacklock hastened into one of the small chambers where a dozen British prisoners slept on dirty sheets speckled with the carcasses of lice.

"Sir," he said, gripping a slumbering man's shoulder. "Lieutenant Colonel Longcroft, you'd best get your wits about you. Best prepare for the worst, sir."

Throughout the siege of Kut Al Amara, Lieutenant Colonel Nathan Longcroft had habitually beseeched God to let him live another day. By the time he had reached Afion Kara Hissar as a prisoner of the Turk, he—like many others who shared his fate—sometimes prayed not for life but for a quick and painless death. Only thoughts of returning home to his walled garden in Madras kept him from desperate measures. Thoughts of his beloved Clarissa made survival a necessity.

In the days that followed his arrival in the spring of 1916, Longcroft faced an endless string of inquiries from other captives of the Ottoman Army. He continually recounted the fall of Kut and the long, intolerable trek through Baghdad, Samarra, Shilgat and Mosul. He spoke of standing knee-deep in muddy trenches as the Tigris swelled with rain, of snipers inflicting heavy casualties upon the Anglo-Indian defenders in the redoubts, and of dwindling rations and nauseating meals of horse, mule and camel meat. Longcroft admitted a certain sense of relief when Major-General Charles Townshend finally surrendered Kut Al Amara, and two Turkish battalions entered the city unopposed. By then, disease, fatigue and the ravages of malnutrition had become endemic among the worn and weary fighters.

As desperate as the defense of the British-Indian garrison in the town had become in those final months, the subsequent forced march northward proved an even harsher trial.

The Turkish victors, finding themselves the grudging custodians of thousands of war prisoners, employed one simple tactic: to drive their enemies mercilessly on and on, cruelly on, until almost all were dead, or withered and weakened so that they could not muster any form of resistance. The bones of many of Longcroft's countrymen rested along that damnable Mesopotamian route, picked clean by the lynx, the fox and the hooded crow—and other monstrous scavengers he could not readily identify.

Some things Longcroft had witnessed on that nightmarish trek he did not dare divulge. Exhaustion, dehydration and starvation coupled with hopelessness provoked one's mind to dwell upon morbid fancy and evoke gruesome hallucinations—visions of faceless, vague winged entities congregating among corpses, slight as shadow but hungry as vultures. He dismissed the haggard horrors as consequences of delirium, yet the fluttering of the membranous wings sometimes woke him at night even now.

The ordeal seemed singularly malevolent, and the Kut prisoners wondered what had prompted such harsh treatment by the soldiers of the Ottoman Army. As it turned out, their systematic callousness during the campaign was not limited to this one incident: Longcroft learned later that certain Turks had shown even greater malice to the Armenians in 1915, as stories of organized, state-sponsored massacres began to circulate.

In fact, the structure that now served as a detention center for hundreds formerly had been an Armenian church. It sat beneath the massive, solitary rock that squatted like an ancient slumbering pagan god in the middle of Afion Kara Hissar. The Armenians who once worshipped here had been forcibly displaced—some slaughtered, some banished into the most forbidding and desolate provinces of Asia Minor.

Longcroft shambled out of the vestry into the basilica, yawning and rubbing the sleep from his eyes. He had anticipated a confrontation. Two days earlier, one of the Turkish sentries had chanced upon the bundle of foodstuffs he had stashed behind an Armenian tomb in preparation for an escape. Some capricious prisoner had named him as the ringleader, possibly under threat of torture. Longcroft did not know his accuser, but doubted he was British. The camp held an assortment of Frenchmen, Russians, Ukrainians, Greeks and Jews along with various people of Baltic and Eastern European derivation.

"This should be quite the spectacle," Longcroft said, joining Macready. Had he not been afflicted by some digestive malady which he initially mistook for cholera, he and his co-conspirators might well have been traversing the Turkish countryside on this crisp November morning, eluding Ottoman and German patrols. "No need for us all to suffer the consequences of this folly. I'm willing to face retribution alone. The rest of you should disappear into the sea of faces. Take refuge in anonymity."

"No, sir," Macready said bluntly. Co-conspirators Blacklock and Corporal Wyndham Hutchison had joined them, prepared for the inevitable penalties. "If we're in for a penny, we're in for a pound."

A moment later, the massive iron door of the church swung wide and a small entourage entered the church. Each man bore a solemn expression and an air of palpable antipathy.

The commandant, Ali Fuat Bey, was customarily inclined to be obligingly apathetic. Though criminally negligent in terms of providing basic human needs—and blind to the frequent brutality of the Turkish guards—he seemed disinterested in carrying out his duties. During his reign, he had shown a reluctance to harass his prisoners and had only on rare occasions implemented harsh punishment for even the most grievous transgressions.

Lee Clark Zumpe

As he approached, his eyes divulged a conspicuous shift in attitude: For the first time, he appeared genuinely enraged. His interpreter—a short, fat Turk with a persistent scowl—muttered something unintelligible to his colleagues before addressing the prisoners.

"You," the interpreter finally barked, pointing at Longcroft. He eyed the assembled British soldiers with contempt. "You have again dishonored your most gracious host. Because this is not the first time you have attempted to escape and because you involved others in your efforts, his Excellency has no choice but to seek other accommodations for you until the hostilities between our two countries have been resolved."

"You don't suggest that there is a venue even less agreeable than this one," Longcroft said, smirking. "Are the guards even more vicious than the ones here?"

"Our German friends have generously offered to transport you and your countrymen to one of their camps in the Taurus Mountains," the interpreter said, nodding obediently to the German officer. His lips curled with a strange, wicked smile. His dark, malevolent eyes revealed a chilling impression of delight, as though he felt immense gratification at the knowledge of Longcroft's fate. "Permit me to introduce *Oberstleutnant* Waldemar von Edelsheim."

"I am delighted to make your acquaintance." Edelsheim looked sly and amused. Tall and broad-shouldered, the fair features of the young German officer's handsome face had been furrowed by a great scar running down the left side, from his eye to his chin. "It is most unfortunate that our first encounter should be under such regrettable circumstances."

"*Fritz sprechen Sie Englisch!*" Blacklock's poorly timed slight could have earned him a mighty beating, but the commandant restrained himself. He nudged his speaker, evidently eager to rid himself of four troublesome British prisoners.

"By edict of his Excellency Ali Fuat Bey, Lieutenant Colonel Nathan Longcroft, Lieutenant Cyril Macready, Corporal Guy Blacklock and Corporal Wyndham Hutchison will have the great privilege of helping our German allies complete the Berlin-Baghdad Railway at Akdurak."

Though the men had expected to be reprimanded, the stark decree came as a blow. More so than any other internment camp in Asia Minor, Akdurak evoked thoughts of misery and malevolence. Longcroft had only been at Afion Kara Hissar for a few months, but he had heard more than one wary Tommy muttering this unsettling refrain:

"Should the Sultan send you to a labor camp in the Taurus Mountains, expect death. Should the Kaiser send you to Akdurak, embrace death."

"Apparently, gentlemen, we have arrived." Nathan Longcroft felt the bitter cold as he stepped off the Büssing Lastwagen transport truck. Dozens of circular tents sat clustered alongside a steep cliff, its sheer face dropping dramatically to a riverbed far below. Above them, the snow-capped, wind-swept heights of some inhospitable summit towered darkly. Even at midday, patches of frost accumulated in the shaded hollows of the camp and a fierce, glacial wind howled. "Quite a charming little mountain retreat, is it not?"

"At least it doesn't reek like Afion Kara Hissar," said Cyril Macready. As he scanned the ridge line toward the western horizon, he caught his first glimpse of the Berlin-Baghdad Railway several hundred feet below the camp. The track skirted the mountain upon a slender shelf carved from the precipice. Despite the squally weather and the severe landscape, Macready felt more at ease than he had in months. "Nice to breathe fresh air for a change. That old church was ill-lit, airless and strewn with litter and filth."

"*Seien Sie still!*" A boyish German soldier leered at the prisoners impatiently. He clutched his Gast gun confidently as he inspected the British captives. The twin-barreled machine gun buttressed his bravado and gave him a tyrannical brashness that seemed inappropriate for such a young lad. "*Kommen Sie mit!*"

The Ottoman Empire had established and maintained an extensive portfolio of prison camps since aligning itself with Kaiser Wilhelm and entering the fray in 1914. Many prisoners of war found themselves involved in railroad construction projects. A few lucky soldiers held cozy supervisory positions. Most found themselves toiling in labor detachments, working in perilous conditions on track beds and tunnel construction. The Turks oversaw most of the working camps such as Aleppo, Belemedik, Bozanti, Entelli and Bagtche.

The Boche ran Akdurak. *Oberstleutnant* Waldemar von Edelsheim made that fact abundantly clear within moments of their arrival as he addressed them at an oddly informal orientation in his office.

"Akdurak is in German hands," he explained, addressing his newest laborers in one of four low, flat mud-brick buildings occupied by administrative quarters, a kitchen and refectory. "The Turks, I am told, want nothing to do with this section of the railroad. They are a superstitious people, and they look upon this spur of the Taurus Mountains as being cursed or some such nonsense." Edelsheim's exasperated expression betrayed his cynicism. "Nevertheless, this work must be completed. It is a logistical necessity. I will not insult you by pretending that ours will be a pleasant relationship, gentlemen. You are here to do dangerous work, understand?"

"Yes, sir, commandant." As ranking officer, Longcroft answered for the group. His response lacked enthusiasm but it carried a suitable degree of respect.

"However," Edelsheim began, his eyes lifting from a blizzard of paperwork. "I wish to assure you the horror stories you have undoubtedly heard are far more bleak and forbidding than reality, gentlemen." The commandant's oily voice seemed chillingly placid. His impeccable English—coupled with the accent of the London aristocracy—suggested he had spent a great deal of time in England before the war, possibly as a member of the diplomatic corps. "Do as you are told, and your chances of survival are surprisingly good. Regrettably, those who choose a different path—that of defiance and insubordination—are, in due course, eliminated."

Edelsheim's office was Spartan in its simplicity: The chamber boasted a simple Austrian Empire mahogany pedestal desk, a walnut desk chair, a washstand and a baroque bureau cabinet. Longcroft, an incurable bibliophile, could not help but notice a number of ponderous books stacked on the desk's cherry-veneered writing surface. Though the age and superior quality of the tomes captured his attention, he did not recognize a single title. The collection included cryptically-named editions such as *De Vermis Mysteriis*, *Unaussprechlichen Kulten* and *Andere Götter*.

"Finally, since the four of you were placed in my charge following recurring attempts at flight, you should relinquish all thoughts of escape now." Edelsheim stood and beckoned one of the guards. "The geography of this country makes it quite impossible. Those who are foolish enough to run never get very far in this wilderness. By the time my patrols track them down, in most instances they are already dead."

Edelsheim dismissed them, instructing one of his subordinates to fetch them "standard issue dress." Each prisoner received two pairs of rough work clothes, a single pair of well-worn boots and a black waistcoat. The men had an opportunity to wash themselves—a luxury none of them had enjoyed in months—and then collected a ration of bread and cheese.

An hour later, the four British officers found themselves sharing a single, cramped tent. Each man had a crudely constructed cot topped by a straw mattress, a single fur sleeping bag and a woolen blanket. A wirework cupboard, situated awkwardly between their beds, provided storage space. A sheet-iron tent stove, its pipe extending up through the roof, kept the cold at bay.

"Seems a crime to help Fritz finish a railroad that will take supplies down into Mesopotamia," Cyril Macready said, breaking the silence. Macready was sturdy, honest and dependable. He always kept his suffering to himself and went out of his way to lift the spirits of his mates. "Where do you suppose all the other prisoners might be?"

"This time of day? Tunneling through that mountain, I would think. Shhh—" Longcroft put a finger to his lips to silence his comrades. When the howling wind subsided for a moment, the sound of rocks tumbling from the ledge echoed through the camp. "They probably do their blasting early in the morning, then spend the afternoon clearing debris. We'll know soon enough."

"That must be where all the guards are," said Corporal Guy Blacklock. Blacklock—the youngest of the group—smiled like a hyena. His once-fetching features had been diminished in captivity. Hunger and maltreatment had left his cheeks hollow, his eyes sunken and his raven locks gray and thinning. "Since we arrived, I've only seen three Huns other than Edelsheim."

"Now that you mention it," Macready said, "the camp does seem understaffed. Hardly anyone here to notice if we were to slip away before the rest of the prisoners return."

"No," Longcroft said, putting a stop to any further conjecture. "Edelsheim might have been exaggerating about the chances of survival in these mountains, but I don't think he's lax enough to leave the camp unguarded. There's a single watchtower at the east end of the camp, and I'll wager he's got half a dozen snipers posted on the ridge."

"For someone who had such ambitious plans at Afion Kara Hissar, you seem awfully pessimistic all of the sudden, sir." Blacklock regretted his denigrating tone of voice more than the criticism he had uttered. He had been just as keen on escape as the others. "Sorry, sir," he continued. "I meant no offense. Do you think escape is out of the question?"

"No," Longcroft said. "I just think it would be wise to get our bearings before doing anything rash. I would like to know more about our host, for one thing. From what I have seen, Edelsheim is no ordinary German officer."

"I can assure you, he is not." Corporal Wyndham Hutchison laughed nervously as his fingers fidgeted with the flap of his waistcoat. Generally quiet and subdued in his ways, he glanced nervously over his shoulder as though he expected someone to drag him out of the tent at any moment. "What he is even doing here I cannot imagine. He is a distant relative of the Kaiser. He is quite wealthy, and he lived in London before the war."

"How do you know all this?" Macready asked. "Why didn't you say something before?"

"Until we stood before him in his office, I wasn't certain. My father …" Hutchison hesitated as though struggling with his conscience. "In his last years, my father became fascinated with mysticism and the occult. He fell in with one of those brotherhoods—a secret society, you might say. After a few months, he insisted that I join him at one of their assemblies. After attending a few of their gatherings, I refused to go back. The ideas they espouse, the concepts they present … are terrifying."

"Edelsheim was a member of this group?" Longcroft wanted to know more about the order's principles and teachings, but he could see the memories haunted Hutchison. "Do you think Edelsheim recognized you?"

"Edelsheim was no mere member," Hutchison said. "He founded the Uruk-Choronzon Temple of Fraternitas Argenteus Crepusculum." He shuddered as he spoke the name of the organization. "I don't believe Edelsheim would recognize or even remember me. I'll not soon forget that voice, though. I'll not soon forget the blasphemous proclamations he uttered. Do not let his intellect and civility deceive you: The man is truly a monster at heart."

At that very moment, the sound of shuffling feet distracted the men from their conversation. Longcroft extended a hand to silence his companions as he moved toward the slit in the tent. Single-file, barefoot and in rags, the first prisoners came streaming listlessly into camp. Starving and half dead, those at the front of the line appeared to all be from the Indian Corps. Behind them, a sizable contingent of British and French soldiers trailed, equally overstretched though better outfitted. Longcroft winced as these desperate, exhausted, emaciated skeletons staggered through the labyrinth of tents.

Their hollow eyes swarmed with shadows of subjugation. Underneath the dirt on their faces, their vacant expressions revealed perpetual anguish. The Huns channeled them through the camp, gleefully striking any individual who happened to stumble and falter. They marched resignedly toward a mud-brick building where some paltry meal awaited them.

"So much for Edelsheim's claims of benevolence," Longcroft muttered, careful not to draw attention. "Conditions here may well make Afion Kara Hissar seem like holiday by the sea."

Still peering through the opening in the tent, Longcroft witnessed the final stragglers trudge down the path. Behind them, two German officers held on leashes two additional laborers—things that *were not quite human.* Standing no more than four feet tall on their naked soles, these wretched creatures had olive-colored skin, thin lips and obtruding and jagged teeth. Though as sluggish and depleted as the other detainees, their luminous, sunken eyes moved continually, scrutinizing every aspect of their surroundings.

Hairless and scrawny, the two had been beaten bloody by their German captors. Despite their hideousness, Longcroft felt as sorry for the creatures as he did for the other prisoners.

4

Prior to military service and before I accepted an appointment
as assistant superintendent at the Madras Government Museum,

I worked briefly under the direction of D. G. Hogarth excavating outlying sites related to Carchemish in Southeastern Anatolia. The expedition catalogued significant remains of various ancient cultures, including temple complexes, fortresses, basalt statues and reliefs bearing hieroglyphic inscriptions.

Despite published material indicating otherwise, excavations at sites neighboring Carchemish reveal a civilization there extending back to about 3000 B.C.—and perhaps much earlier—which may not have been Hittite in its beginnings. Among the best-preserved artifacts recovered, I recall a small assortment of grotesque idols formed from some porraceous rock not common to the region. These icons depicted imaginative monstrosities of varying unpleasantness, including one with a winged anthropoid frame supporting an oversized head shaped something like a marine mollusk of the cephalopod family.

Mr. Lapham, an ingenious anthropologist from a noted university in Massachusetts, surveyed the objects found in tombs at these older sites and suggested the ancient stone statuettes— fetishes, teraphim, or whatever those abominations may have been—originated from some unknown Bronze Age civilization deeply obsessed with preternatural and occult knowledge.

I now know that civilization's borders stretched at least as far as the Taurus Mountains.

—Nathan Longcroft, *Interned by the Turks*

5

The first night at Akdurak held a macabre pageant of fresh horrors for Lieutenant Colonel Nathan Longcroft and his friends.

Outside their tent, the groans of the wounded, the weak and the famished filled the night air. The woeful howls of suffering and pain reminded Longcroft of the death pangs and final convulsions of dying animals. All trace of decorum and poise lost, these once-noble gentlemen had been subjected to something far worse than mere slave labor—their exploitation had been thorough and severe, but the Boche subjected them to more than poor working conditions.

Around midnight, the sounds of torture became evident: the harsh cracks of the whip, interspersed with muffled screams; merciless beatings, punctuated by the breaking of bones; and less obvious—but equally gruesome—signs, including

Lee Clark Zumpe

pounding hammers, bone saws and the pulpy contents of buckets being emptied onto the ground. Shrieks gradually settled into quiet cries which soon gave way to sporadic whimpers.

Sleep offered no reprieve as nightmarish visions assailed them all. In their dreadful dreams they imagined unspeakable scenes of wanton carnage. Longcroft's own outré reveries rendered scenes of corpses piled high in huddled heaps, layered in the blood and the mud and the slime of the trenches—corpses with dead eyes that saw in spite of death. Soaring overhead, circling in the lurid twilight, a clutch of faceless, vague winged entities—like black angels from some subverted heaven—surveyed the endless massacre with ever-intensifying appetites.

The men's disconcerted slumber led to collective silence in the morning.

The first full day at Akdurak began before dawn. The prisoners were mustered alongside the edge of the cliff, more than a few barely able to stand. They segregated themselves tidily, splitting into distinct groupings determined by nationality and ethnicity. Longcroft wordlessly led Lieutenant Cyril Macready, Corporal Guy Blacklock and Corporal Wyndham Hutchison down the line of laborers until he found a clique of wiry, keen-eyed Tommies. The Englishmen welcomed the new arrivals with more pity than cordiality.

The Boche distributed moldy bread and canteens filled with water from a nearby mountain stream. The laborers took their wretched breakfast standing, and in little time began the hike down a crudely blazed switchback trail to the railroad bed.

Throughout the morning hours, the Taurus Mountains thundered as dynamite shattered the stony face of the near-vertical cliff, each blast dislodging innumerable bits of rock and sending debris careening down into the valley. A dozen Huns oversaw the operation, sending teams of laborers out to place the explosives. The prisoners scampered over the mountainside supported only by a flimsy network of unsound ropes. After each detonation, the men would rush in to clear the rubble and chip away at the rock, slowly leveling the bed where the tracks would soon be laid.

It was midmorning before anyone found the courage to speak.

"What news, my boy?" A scraggy gentlemen, thin and somnolent, spoke softly as he addressed Longcroft. Both men continued working, filling up a wheelbarrow with pieces of rock. "How fares it with the war effort?"

"Can't rightfully say," Longcroft replied. "We were transferred, from Afion Kara Hissar. Our hosts were neither communicative nor reliable."

"Pity," he said. "Would do the fellows good to hear heartening news." The man paused, a sudden look of bewilderment enveloping his face. "Brownlow; that is my name," the man said, his eyes displaying a flicker of disbelief as if he thought he had forgotten what others once called him. "David Brownlow."

"Nathan Longcroft."

"Good to know you, sir." Brownlow wrestled with a large rock, wincing with pain as he lifted it into the wheelbarrow. "It is December, is it not?"

"The 20th of November, 1916," Longcroft said. "How long have you been a prisoner here?"

"Six weeks," Brownlow said, his voice revealing disappointment. "Time passes slowly here, you see—as slowly as in a sick-house. Days and nights blur. Death does not come as quickly as one would wish it."

"I have no intention of dying here."

"Everyone thinks they're invincible for the first few days, lad." Brownlow said. "Bitter truth will come to stare at you in the face soon enough. If hunger and the mercilessness of the Huns aren't enough to do you in, the mountain itself will kill you."

"*Geh zur Seite!*" A German soldier beckoned the laborers to fall back as another wave of charges were prepared. "*Beweg dich!*"

Soon followed a series of deafening explosions in quick succession. The mountain trembled and masses of rock tumbled down the slopes. As they had done a dozen times already that morning, the men promptly moved back into position, preparing to clear the debris—but this time, Longcroft noticed something different. The tremors from the detonation seemed to be reverberating much too long. The ground beneath his feet refused to settle.

A harrowing, unforgettable cacophony arose from deep within the mountain. The disconcerting sound froze Longcroft in his tracks. It was as if the wounded earth growled in misery and resentment.

The unquiet mountain began claiming the day's victims one by one. One of the Russian prisoners screamed as he plunged over the ledge. Another man fell wordlessly, his silent resignation confessed by the awful tranquility of his countenance. A quartet of Indian laborers who had too quickly clambered back onto the rope ladders doggedly gripped their holds until the mountain, uncompromising in its search for vengeance, shook them off like puny parasites and dropped them down into the valley.

The tremors finally subsided, but not before the Taurus Mountains could claim one last victim. Corporal Guy Blacklock had taken refuge in a recess along the cliff wall. He cowered there, squatting, his arms protecting his head from falling rocks. Longcroft moved toward him to see if he had been injured. Before he could reach him, a slender, sinewy black whip-like appendage wrapped itself around Blacklock's abdomen and drew him down into a narrow fissure. The fracture vanished as soon as the corporal disappeared into the darkness.

Brownlow read the astonishment in Longcroft's eyes.

Lee Clark Zumpe

"I told you," he said. "The mountain won't tolerate much more of this abuse." Brownlow grinned maniacally, his tone expressing equal measures of hopelessness and madness. "In the next few days, the Huns will haul the boring machine into place to start tunneling through that outcropping up ahead," Brownlow said. "Mark my words, Longcroft—the mountain won't stand for it. It'll send us all over the cliff and down into that ravine, or worse, sure as you were born."

6

The recent discovery of the habitations of lost races of men in remote regions of Asia Minor, and of remains of various articles which those people once used—tools, religious icons, weapons, adornments, bones of animals they fed upon, seeds of plants they cultivated and consumed—has inspired a new impetus to delve deeper into the antiquity of the human race. To date, the most curious trait of these habitations comes in the form of cave paintings: Not crude renderings of hunters stalking prehistoric beasts, but strange, cryptic designs employing peculiar lines and angles. These primitive efforts at geometry possess a certain hypnotic quality that captivates the novice and causes learned mathematicians much consternation.

Few researchers trouble themselves fretting about the possibility of uncovering Promethean knowledge best left to the obscurity of the ages.

—Nathan Longcroft, *Interned by the Turks*

7

"I do not often interact with the prisoners, you understand." *Oberstleutnant* Waldemar von Edelsheim sat at his desk, his nose buried in one of those cryptically named tomes. "Aside from orientation, the only time I generally wish to face my prisoners is at an execution. A man should never condemn another man to death unless he is willing to see it through himself."

"Yes, sir, commandant."

Edelsheim had appeared vexed when Lieutenant Colonel Nathan Longcroft first appeared at his office door requesting an audience. The commandant's second-in-command, *Hauptmann* Gerhard Fangohr, had grudgingly made the request. A burly great red-faced fellow, the Hun spoke only a smattering of English. He evidently latched on to enough of Longcroft's story to justify disturbing Edelsheim. "I apologize for interrupting your study."

"Considering you are, at present, the ranking British officer at Akdurak and that you suffered the loss of one of your close comrades today, I will make an exception—this time." Edelsheim tried to mask his lingering displeasure with a forced smile and an invitation. "Perhaps you would join me for dinner?"

"I would be honored," Longcroft said, choking on his own artificial tactfulness. He doubted the commandant's offer was genuine but treated it as such nonetheless. "But I would prefer to eat with my men—or to forfeit a meal entirely for the opportunity to discuss something with you."

"Suit yourself," the commandant said. "*Hauptmann* Fangohr mentioned that you experienced something, well … unsettling."

"Yes, sir, commandant." Longcroft's muscles ached from his 15-hour workday. He knew Edelsheim had no intention of asking him to take a seat. "Corporal Guy Blacklock was one of the day's casualties. I wish to notify his family, with your consent."

"No need," Edelsheim said abruptly, his gaze still fixed upon the text he scrutinized. The corner of his mouth opposite his scar curled in a sardonic grin. "It is my policy at Akdurak to send death notices the day a new prisoner arrives. As far as the 6th Division of the British Indian Army is concerned, all you chaps are—what's that quaint euphemism you Englishmen use?—'pushing up the daisies.'"

"Yes sir, commandant," Longcroft muttered. Edelsheim's admission struck a blow as excruciating as any physical torture could be. The knowledge that in the coming weeks, his family would be advised of his premature death nearly brought him to tears. Longcroft remained outwardly indifferent and compliant, denying Edelsheim the gratification of seeing the anguish he wreaked. "There is something more, however."

"Yes, yes, get on with it," Edelsheim said. "Your friend—Blacklock, wasn't it?—didn't just stumble over the side of the cliff, did he?" Finally, the German officer lifted his eyes from the page and glared at his prisoner. Edelsheim looked at him with growing indignation, a cauldron of self-righteousness bubbling just beneath his autocratic exterior. "Pulled into the mountain, was he not? Disappeared into the darkness through some unseen crevice?"

"Yes," the corporal said, his voice sounding suddenly small and insignificant in the small room. Like his friend Corporal Wyndham Hutchison, Longcroft suspected Edelsheim had ulterior motives. "What are you looking for here? What's in the mountain?"

"What makes you think I am not as confounded by this enigma as you, Corporal Longcroft?"

Lee Clark Zumpe

"Something brought you here," Longcroft said. "A German nobleman and relative of Kaiser Wilhelm would never agree to an assignment as chief officer of a far-flung labor camp, not when comfortable appointments are readily available."

"A logical assumption," Edelsheim said. "Either you are exceptionally perceptive or you are a learned man with some credentials. Tell me, Corporal Longcroft, what profession did you follow before the war?"

"I was assigned to the Madras National Museum," Longcroft offered, "I studied archeology."

"Fascinating." Edelsheim shuffled through a stack of tattered old documents and scrolls, searching for something. "I must remember to commend Kaiser Wilhelm's intelligence gatherers. They uncovered your background and managed to locate you in Afion Kara Hissar. It was a matter of convenience for me that your recent escape attempt made Ali Fuat Bey eager to divest himself of you and your associates. I also was advised that you had field experience in this region."

"It was several years ago," Longcroft said. "I was part of Professor Hogarth's expedition. I worked mainly in the Şehitkamil district, near a small village. If I remember correctly, it was called Doliche."

"Yes, I am quite familiar with it," Edelsheim said. "And, if you have been to that place, you should be familiar with these."

Edelsheim beckoned him to his desk as he opened a scroll, smoothing its many creases judiciously. The yellowed parchment featured unsophisticated drawings seemingly illustrating some eccentric form of geometry. The byzantine sketch embraced atypical curves, unconventional lines and weird spirals which, when combined, appeared to contradict the laws of traditional mathematics.

"I have drawings like this," Longcroft admitted reluctantly. "In a cave not far from the village."

"A cave the villagers refused to enter."

"Yes."

"Let me tell you something, Lieutenant Colonel Longcroft," Edelsheim said. "The Turks claim there is an ancient city in this range of the Taurus. Historical narratives mention it in passing, a place of wicked worship and pagan deities, equated to Sodom and Gomorrah. Its name—assuming it ever had one—is never mentioned and its precise location is never recorded. I've spoken with Turkish academics who assure me it is nothing more than a fable, yet I believe it exists. I believe the world is cluttered with secreted enclaves, hidden from the present by a veil which only thickens as time passes."

"And if you find this ancient deserted city, do you suppose acclaim and admiration will follow?" Longcroft's question undoubtedly irked the commandant. He felt it necessary to press the man into revealing his true objective. "After word of

Akdurak's atrocities spread, no one would praise you even if you claim to have dug up the Ark of the Covenant."

"I think you realize I do not seek notoriety," he said. "In fact, I have found the city." The gaze of his devouring eyes grew infinitely more intense. "It is deep inside this mountain—and it is not deserted. If I could just find a door, I would gladly show you. My patrols have even managed to apprehend a few of the creatures that dwell within the rock. They were found in caves filled with drawings like this," he said, tapping the scroll. "Drawings like the ones we have both seen on the cave walls near Doliche. These are doorways, Lieutenant Colonel Longcroft. These are doorways that lead not only to some forgotten metropolis but to undiscovered and unfathomable spheres of superfluous dimensions and worlds outside the perceptible space-time continuum."

"That is absurd."

Longcroft wished he had more faith in his allegation. In his mind, logic clashed with recent experience: He had seen wholesale butchery on a scale he would never have dreamed humanity capable of in his youth; he had witnessed battlefield horrors indistinguishable from his most vivid nightmares; he had experienced events that made him question his own sanity. Longcroft recalled the two beings he had observed the previous evening. The creatures—the things that were *not quite human*—might well have descended from some isolated branch of primitive hunter-gatherers. Other Stone Age cultures had been discovered in remote parts of the world.

Perhaps the creatures retained arcane knowledge lost to civilization.

"Most people doubt the validity of my theories, Lieutenant Colonel Longcroft." Edelsheim chuckled as he began rolling up the scroll.

The German failed to notice Longcroft's clever sleight of hand—he had handily nicked one of the commandant's fancy pens from the corner of the desk, quickly concealing it in the fold of his coat sleeve.

"Sadly, none of our attempts to communicate with the creatures have been successful. They do not seem to comprehend the purpose of torture."

"Let me speak to one of them," Longcroft said. "Maybe I can find a way to communicate."

"I had hoped you might offer your services," Edelsheim said. "If you are successful, I will see what arrangements can be made to have you returned to the 6th Division of the British Indian Army."

"And my colleagues?"

"Very well," Edelsheim said, though Longcroft doubted his veracity. "You and your friends will be liberated—if you manage to get that thing to lead us into the mountain."

Edelsheim summoned *Hauptmann* Gerhard Fangohr and barked an extensive

Lee Clark Zumpe

set of instructions. Fangohr grasped Longcroft by his shoulder and escorted him toward the door. "And, Longcroft? You have two days. A boring machine is due to arrive and, when it does, I will make my own door into this mountain."

8

Hauptmann Gerhard Fangohr conducted Lieutenant Colonel Nathan Longcroft through the maze of circular tents nestled atop the bluff overlooking the valley. Darkness in the Taurus Mountains brought colder temperatures, despair and new terrors. Once again, the moribund prisoners whimpered and wailed, and the night absorbed a doleful expression of grief in a varied chorus of heartbreaking lamentation.

They finally arrived at a cage housing the only surviving creature. Longcroft surmised that the second individual had been subjected to torture the previous evening. The Germans had likely brutalized it maliciously until death mercifully claimed it. The survivor cowered in a far corner of the enclosure; its abnormally long and scrawny arms concealed much of its face, though its luminous, sunken eyes remained visible.

Longcroft noticed immediately that the cage had been left unguarded. He did not know whether the Germans assigned to the task had deserted their post, or if *Oberstleutnant* Waldemar von Edelsheim was so lacking in experience as an officer that he would fail to allocate manpower to watch over his valuable prisoner. Either way, the lack of security emboldened him: He knew he had to act quickly, and he saw no better opportunity on the horizon.

Longcroft waited patiently as Fangohr unlocked the cage. The moment the door swung open, he attacked with a fury that instantly overwhelmed the larger man, pitching his full weight into the German's side and stabbing madly at his jugular. An instant later, Longcroft found himself straddling the Hun, blood surging from the spot in his neck. A few inches of Edelsheim's pen jutted out of the gushing wound.

Longcroft signaled the creature, urging him to escape. The thing needed no further prompting. It jumped to its feet and shambled across the cage, speeding through the door as it picked up momentum. It brushed past Longcroft at breakneck speed, leaving him struggling to regain his footing.

Longcroft followed, racing into the hostile wilderness of the Taurus Mountains. He hoped the creature would be appreciative of his efforts and would lead him to safety. He wanted to retrieve his friends—he wanted to liberate the entire labor camp. He knew neither scenario would be successful. For the moment, he did not even know if he would survive the night. Right now, he did not even know if the creature intended to repay his kindness.

For an hour, he pursued the creature as it scampered along narrow trails carved into the face of the mountain—paths not appropriate for human passage. But each time Longcroft believed he had lost sight of the beast, it reappeared, waiting patiently for its rescuer. By dawn, Longcroft was convinced it was leading him to some route that would take him back to civilization—or to some cave that would lead to a very different destination.

The sun had reached its zenith when Longcroft felt the creature's knotty digits clamp down on his left arm. He did not dare fight against it as it dragged him down into a dark grotto. Deep inside the cave, a virescent radiance glimmered off lustrous, polished stone. Intricate geometric designs covered the walls, teeming with anomalous lines, aberrant inclines, and shockingly slanted perspectives. The patterns and structures portrayed had parallels both in textbooks on higher mathematics and in forbidden medieval grimoires. Longcroft found himself losing consciousness of time and place while maintaining a fixed discernment and rapt mindset.

Gradually, a sense of disequilibrium overtook Longcroft. He felt momentary lightheadedness and a rush of giddiness. He felt the creature tugging on his shirt, and he shuffled his feet across the floor of the cave though he knew his mind had issued no such command. As they approached one of the renderings, its pattern gradually realigned his faculties, revealing a hidden aperture in the wall of the cave—an opening little more than a crevice.

As they slipped into the twilit realm beyond, Longcroft saw only an indigo blur crowded with formless things. A rush of blackness soon overwhelmed him.

When Longcroft regained his bearings, the creature led him along a cobblestone path through a bizarre jungle populated by towering trees with thick, purple trunks. Countless ebon vines dangled from the distant crimson canopy far overhead, and faceless winged beings perched on small outcroppings of rock along the steep cliffs that encircled the forest. Dwellings had been cut into the face of the stone, too—an ancient city hidden inside the mountain, inhabited by some offshoot of *Homo sapiens*.

The creature directed Longcroft to the center jungle and to the base of a freestanding stone. A series of steps spiraled toward the pinnacle. He looked down at the hairless, gaunt entity and, for the first time, saw a delicacy and splendor in its form. It tapped its chest gently and pointed to the dwellings on the cliff. Next, it patted Longcroft's chest and pointed toward the top of the escarpment.

Home.

The word seemed to form in Longcroft's mind. He nodded and began his ascent.

Scaling the lofty stone might have taken minutes or it might have taken weeks—for Longcroft, time had ceased to exist. He felt no pangs of hunger and not a single muscle complained as he climbed step after step, his gaze ever fixed on the stone path he traversed. Not once did he look down to see how far from the floor his journey had taken him. Not once did he stare up toward the distant peak.

He did not even notice when a rumbling swept through the mountain at the very moment when some trifling machine of human construct began to burrow into the rock. That final nuisance caused a swift and unforgiving response as the tentacle-like vines stretched across time and space and emerged from narrow fissures, scouring the landscape for each and every human on the mountain. Germans, British and Indians found themselves picked off one by one as slender, sinewy, black, whip-like appendages coiled about them and drew them down into subterranean darkness. Their screams echoed through the enclosed jungle, but Longcroft paid no attention.

Finally he found himself standing atop a glassy plateau at the summit of that forbidding crag rising far above a dense forest.

Slowly, Longcroft lifted his eyes and let them rest upon the excruciating panorama. From the crest he could see endless fields of corpses, buckled towers, deteriorated monuments, disintegrated cities, vanquished civilizations, fragmented empires, charred worlds, extinct races, dead stars and lifeless galaxies. Even the horrid cosmic entities who seemed to benefit from this eternal feast of death suffered casualties, as the bloated carcass of more than one self-proclaimed god rotted amongst the boundless transdimensional graveyard.

Longcroft trembled as his sanity faded. As he sank to his knees, he thought only of his walled garden in Madras and his beloved Clarissa.

9

I have never been able to explain adequately how I managed to find my way back to Madras. My daughter, Clarissa, age 7, found me in the garden one morning. When questioned by the authorities, I was at a loss to account for my miraculous return from the Ottoman Empire. Most of my superiors eventually settled upon a heroic narrative that detailed my escape from the Hun at Akdurak and a lengthy cross-country trek in which I outsmarted the Turks and their allies as I made my way across Asia.

Somewhere along the journey, they conclude, I suffered a form of traumatic amnesia.

Many years have passed, and as I write this memoir I discern the portents of war once more. It is an interminable cycle from which there is no escape—and yet it is utterly purposeless, as is our very existence.

I still spend a great deal of time in my garden. No one else has noticed the cryptic pattern inscribed upon the wall near the very spot where Clarissa discovered me all those years ago.

—Nathan Longcroft, *Interned by the Turks*

THE ITHILIAD

BY CHRISTINE MORGAN

1
The Priestess

"Father Dagon, hear my prayer. Hear and help your faithful daughters, taken from our homes.

We have seen our kinsmen slaughtered and our cities sacked by these Achaeans, these men of Greece.

We are apportioned out to them in the dividing of the spoils, Chryseis and I. Now, through us, O Dagon, punish them for their offenses. Weaken their alliances. Sow dissension amid their noble ranks."

Briseis, kneeling, dipped her cupped hands into a basin and lifted them, brimming with sea-water. It trickled through her fingers, not yet webbed by more than the finest silvery film, and ran down her slender arms.

"Breathe down upon their camp a plague-miasma," she said. "Let them fall sick and ill. Let them suffer and despair. With oracles and omens, show them that they have offended you, god of the deep trenches."

She closed her wide eyes and poured the sea-water over her upturned face. It wetted the length of her bronze-hued hair, lending a greenish cast. It flowed the lines and hollows of her throat, past small and delicate shell-like ears, past the faint white folds where gills would one day be, along the glistening fish-scale iridescence that traced the nape of her neck and supple spine.

"Show them that it is with Agamemnon, kingly leader of these armies, where their greatest grievance lies. He claims fair-cheeked Chryseis for his own. He has known her touch, O Dagon. He has known the salt-nectar of her palm, and lips, and all those moist and tender places that men do so covet."

The sea-water, far more than her cupped hands should have held, continued spilling from them. It coursed along the naked curves of her lush and youthful body as she knelt there, lit by lamplight in the well-appointed shelter. As the water reached the mat of woven kelp-grass, it became absorbed and spread no further.

"He has refused the offered ransom," Briseis went on. "Greatly he desires her, to have and keep her in his house and bed. He would not be parted from her, or return her to her family. That which is his, he will not willingly give up, and despite all that he has, his greed for gain is strong. Strong too is his pride, this son of Atreus, stronger even than that of Menelaus his brother, on whose behalf these ships were gathered and this war begun."

From beyond the shelter's walls came the evening-sounds of camp, the meals being made, the watches being set. Her time for prayer and privacy had, she knew, almost come to an end. She opened her hands so that the sea-water rained from them.

"Send sickness to them, Father Dagon, until all other kings of the Achaeans agree that mighty Agamemnon must bend. He has already risked defying the gods of Olympus, who would not send him wind to sail until he made sacrifice even of his own child. Let him now make sacrifice also to you, lord of the deep and far vastness. Let Chryseis be released from him, so that, in his anger and shame he demands just compensation."

Briseis smiled, revealing tiny teeth like smooth white pearls. Then she rose from the mat of kelp-grass, drew on her chiton and girdle and sandals, and made ready for the return of the man whose shelter this was, famed Achilles, to whom she had been given.

So it would be, her plea granted, and so it soon was. For nine days, death and misery beset the Greek armies, and the corpse-fires burned. On the tenth day, an assembly of the leaders was called. To die in battle, beneath the swords and spears of their enemies, these men expected, and promised to deliver the same. To die like this, like sick dogs, plague-struck and wretched, was far from the glory of war.

As she had expected, Achilles returned from that assembly in a black and furious mood. He and Agamemnon had exchanged many words of contention. In the end, Agamemnon agreed to return Chryseis of the fair cheeks, but he would, he said, have Briseis instead.

"When I," Achilles told her in aggrieved wroth, "fight as hard, if not harder, than any other man! Yet they would take from me my reward? I am come here as favor to them; the warriors of Ithilium, however strange their blood, are not *my* sworn foes. They have done me no wrong. Against venerable Priam, tamer of shoggoths, I hold no animosity. It is for the sake of Menelaus, whose wife was led astray, that I am here. See how he and his brother thank me!"

Briseis went to him, Achilles, Peleus' son, lord of the Myrmidons. She took his face, strong-jawed and handsome, in her hands, cradling it. Her eyes, so wide and round, gazed into his. From the soft, tender flesh of her palms was the salt-nectar secreted. It passed into his skin, more intoxicating than wine, more pervasive than the fruit of the lotus. With a groan, he pulled her to him and kissed her, drinking deeply of its briny sweetness from the font of her lips.

"I would have slain him on the spot," said Achilles when the kiss ended, "but Athena in her terrible wisdom held me back. That I must give you up, my dearest Briseis, leaves me stricken! And to that man-shaped dog, Agamemnon, who sends his people to die while he stays safely far from the ambuscade? He will regret this insult ... all of them shall ... for I am *done* with fighting freely on their behalf!"

"Yes," Briseis said, as she caressed him. "How thankless they are, how they mistreat you!"

"What chance do they have against the great walls of Troy without *me*? Who else would stand against Hector, slaughterer of men and Ithilium's defender? Agamemnon himself? Bah! I think not! They *need* me!"

"They may need, but they do not deserve," she said. "Let them be sorry; let them eat out their own hearts, that they did no honor to the best of the Achaeans."

"I will sit by my ships," Achilles declared, "and stay well away from all battle, until proud Agamemnon sees the error of his ways."

This he vowed, and this he soon did. Chryseis was sent home, with sufficient sacrifice made that the plague was swept from the camp. But Agamemnon also did as *he* had vowed, dispatching his most loyal heralds to fetch Briseis to him from the shelter of Achilles. They went unwilling, in much fear of his anger. He told them that they had no blame in his sight, obedient servants to their king as they were.

Then Achilles bade his own most-trusted friend, Patroclus, to bring the girl forth to be taken away. Patroclus alone was not unhappy to see Briseis go; he had been the closest of companions to Achilles before then, and from jealousy despised her.

Away she went, looking back to see Achilles sitting by his ships as he had said. Without him, all the armies of the Achaeans amounted to little, she knew, and most were already dispirited by the bitterness between the two powerful men.

That night, in the grand pavilion of Agamemnon, Briseis curled herself

Christine Morgan

around the king as he slept. As he'd known the touch of Chryseis, and the sweet salt-nectar secreted, now too did he know hers, and it had its effect.

She pressed her mouth close to his ear. Hair-fine tendrils, like wavering sea-fronds, slid from beneath her tongue to whisper into his mind.

To attack, these whispers urged ... attack high-walled Ithilium with full force and fury, strike the Trojans, Priam's city ... to conquer it at last, after so many years ... avenge the wrong done to his brother, yes, but, more, to win the decisive victory ... and to do it *without* boastful, arrogant Achilles ... how satisfying it would be!

Then, upon awakening to rosy-fingered Dawn, this very thing did Agamemnon at once set out to do. He summoned his fellow kings and leaders, and told them how, in dreams, the gods had bespoken him with good and urgent purpose, that Troy must fall. For a full day, they held war-counsel, which Achilles did not attend. There were those among them who felt bitterly for how Agamemnon had cheated the son of Peleus, yet, in the end, all were agreed.

They rallied their armies, those strong-greaved Achaeans. The ground shook beneath the multitudes, countless warriors taking their battle positions. At their backs were their ships, beached upon that wide Hellespont joining to the sea. Before them stretched the field of life and death, and beyond that, the walls of Troy.

Fear did dwell within many of their breasts. Nine long years now had this war been waged, and the bronze-armored Greeks knew well their foes. They knew of the cities and neighbors who'd answered Troy's call for aid, and those wilder folk from far lands whose swords and spears were for hire. They had much cause to dread the slaughtering Hector as well, first among the Trojan princes, first and best of the fifty sons of Priam.

They knew that Priam's line and the noble houses of Ithilium ran rich with the deep-blood and star-blood of those strange immortal races against whose gods the high Olympians vied. They feared the very names of Azathoth, Hastur, Dagon and Yog-Sothoth ... cruel Yidhra and Nyarlathotep ... Yhagni, Shub-Niggurath ... those dwellers out of the farthest darkness.

Yet, despite their fears, the Achaeans made their readiness. Whatever lofty reasons men might give for war—such as, this cause of betrayed Menelaus—in the end, they fought for simple reasons. They fought for the glory of their deeds, that their names would live on in song and history. They fought for the plunder of the fallen. They fought for the treasures of Troy itself: gold and conquered women, however strange their blood.

All their preparations wide-eyed Briseis watched. So, too, from where he sat darkly brooding, did Achilles.

Yearn though he might for the clash of arms and battle, he would not stir from his spot. The cleverest entreaties of Odysseus fell on deaf ears, as did the good counsel of old Nestor, wisest of them all. Achilles' men, the Myrmidons, amused themselves with games of the discus. Their horses stood idle beside their chariots, and they did no fighting as the rest went forward onto the plain.

Paris, son of Priam, strutted forth draped in a leopard-skin, to give challenge to the Greeks. But when that challenge was answered by Menelaus of the loud war-cry, whose wife Paris had stolen, the prince of Troy fled back green-pallored, until his own brother, Hector, shamed him into doing his part.

It was agreed that the two, Menelaus and Paris, would meet in single combat, the winner to claim Helen and her possessions. Then the Trojans and Achaeans would make peace as friends, to let end the long hostilities at last.

So it might have been, had not the gods of both sides interfered. Weapons were glanced aside, armor straps snapped at crucial moments. When all else seemed failed, Paris was whisked away to safety by Shub-Niggurath's intervention.

The truce was thus broken, and terrible battle ensued.

Bronze spear-points thrust through shields and corselets, into chests and bellies and bowels. Arrows sang from bowstrings. Great sword-blades slashed, splitting torsos open, hewing arms at the shoulder. Flung stones cracked apart skulls and smashed hip-bones in their cup-sockets. Guts spilled, ichor spattered and blood spouted in the air.

The dark mists descended over many warriors' eyes. Their armor clattered around them as they fell. Foes sprang swift upon them to strip their corpses. Some men flung themselves down in surrender, begging to be made captive and held for rich ransom; sometimes these pleas were granted, and other times they were met with a killing blow.

The men greatest at warcraft made themselves well-known that day. Hector of the shining helm, mighty Ajax, strongest of the Greeks, godlike Sarpedon, brilliant Aeneas, as deadly as if accompanied by Hastur himself, and Diomedes, inspired by grey-eyed Athena.

Bodies piled and sprawled face-down in the dust, the sons of Ithilium and the Achaeans alike. The tides turned this way and that as gods bickered and men fought for their lives.

Through it all, in his torment of wroth, Achilles would not relent. He kept his men by the ships, their spears un-bloodied, their horses idle. When Agamemnon, humbled and regretting the madness of his pride, offered such a generous wealth of presents that no man could think of its equal, Achilles still spurned the gifts with harsh words.

Christine Morgan

Sooner, he said, would he gather his ships and set homeward sail, and would urge the rest of the Greeks to do the same rather than have them follow Agamemnon, who would lead them only to further disaster. He even refused to take back Briseis, feeling the insult he'd suffered was not yet appeased.

At that, spite bristled in Briseis, and she determined to find yet another way to bring sorrows upon Achilles.

One night as the watch-fires burned around the camp and atop the high walls of Troy, she sent for Patroclus, his longtime most intimate of companions. This, she did under the guise of settling their differences, for their shared love of Peleus' son.

"Let us no more be at odds," she told him, fixing him with the gaze of her wide, round eyes. She held out her hands to him. "Let us be friends, and I will give you good counsel."

Patroclus submitted to having his hands clasped in hers, and as the salt-nectar from her pale, tender palms permeated his skin to suffuse him, he listened.

She suggested that he don the armor and take up the shield of Achilles, going forth in his stead. This would, she said, give great heart to the Achaeans, who would fight with renewed vigor. It would lessen the ignominy of Achilles' sulking. It would bring the Myrmidons, and Patroclus himself, much glory.

And Patroclus, swayed by her words, and Dagon's influence behind them, agreed.

2

The Princess

She had gone in great speed to the great bastion of Ithilium upon hearing that the battle was so fiercely joined. A nurse went with her, attending to the baby, their child, Hector's son, Astyanax, their young shining treasure and future lord of the city.

Oh, her poor little one, her poor dearest boy, and what would become of him if the city should fall? If he be left an orphan, and she, Andromache, a widow? No mercy would there be for the wife and child of Hector, who brought such slaughter to the enemy.

Yet, no mercy for herself did Andromache crave. She had no desire to live without her beloved husband. It was for Astyanax her heart tore at itself with terror's anxious teeth.

Hector found her there at a lull in the battle. She ran to meet him, uttering a glad cry that turned into tears as he held her. He had come, he told her, to urge his mother and sisters, and the noble ladies of Troy, to heed a message of the augurs delivered to him. They must go to the temples sacred to Yhagni, and Yidhra, and make sacrifice so that those fearful elder-goddesses might protect from the Greeks the Trojan wives and innocent children.

That done, he had sought out Andromache at their own house, then asked of the servants where she had gone; he wished to visit her before he must return to the field where men win glory.

"For I do not know," he said, "if ever again I shall come back this way."

She beseeched him to stay there safe upon the ramparts. "They will kill you," wept Andromache. "Your own strength and courage will be your death. And oh, my dear husband, have I not already lost my own father and seven brothers to the spear of Achilles? Must I lose you, as well?"

But, of course, Hector's valiant spirit would not let him shrink from the fighting; he could not be a coward, shamed in the many eyes of Ithilium. He embraced little Astyanax, then placed the child in Andromache's arms and enfolded the both of them in his. They stood there as the wind blew skyward in spirals the sacrificial smoke from the temples.

Then Andromache asked of him a different boon. "If you will not stay, and I know already you would not have me take up the war-weapons like some Amazon instead of the good loom and distaff, at least open to me Yog-Sothoth's way. Do not leave me waiting for word of your fate. Let me, in this manner, go with you, so that we are not parted."

Hector nodded his assent. He drew off his helm of glinting bronze to be set aside. His brow opened outward in a fleshy star, its tapering points like uncurling fingers of a fist or a flower's thick petals blossoming. Ridged with thin ribs of bone, edged with hooked slivers, the segments fanned out and splayed wide. Exposed tissues and pulsating veins gleamed there, wetly, sheened in colors for which the Achaeans would have had no words. At the center, a membranous orifice shone with unspeakable light.

Astyanax screamed in terror upon seeing his own father in such aspect, and screamed again as Andromache's fair brow did the same. The nurse stepped quickly forward to pluck the crying child from his parents' arms.

The two, Andromache and Hector, tilted their heads the one toward the other. With a slick sound, the star's-ray segments of their brows interlaced—again, like fingers, those of two hands brought together.

They met at the threshold, and then he drew her into him. His senses were hers, she a rider in the chariot of his body. Not a driver; the reins were beyond her reach, the horses not hers to control. A passenger, one who could but hold on and observe.

Her own body, of which she remained dimly aware, stepped back as if

Christine Morgan

sleep-walking or under some trance. She watched herself through Hector's eyes, saw her brow close and the fair skin mend seamlessly. The nurse guided that figure of Andromache away, taking her and the child back to their house.

And Hector, bold Hector, his brow also shut and his shining helm once more in place upon his head, went on toward the gates of Ithilium. Andromache felt the vigor and power of him, a man's strong limbs and sinews, a man above all other men of Troy.

He encountered along the way his brother, Paris, that wretched bringer of troubles who had caused the city's misfortune. Paris, rescued by Shub-Niggurath from single combat against Menelaus, where he otherwise surely would have died ... sent in safety to his bedchamber to dally with Helen while other Trojans fought his battles for him.

Now Paris *did* go, and fight, and fared well in the violent encounters. And Hector fared better still, between them destroying a number of their foes. Andromache shared in his senses. She heard the clangor and shouts, smelled the sweat and blood-spray. She felt the hard impact of bronze, the weight of armor and shield. She saw Greek faces, flowing-haired or bearded, twisted in fury, contorted with the agonies of their wounds.

With losses so heavy upon both sides, the gods again intervened, this time to encourage another meeting in single combat, man against man. Hector issued the challenge to save lives of his countrymen, and it was gigantic Ajax, immense among the Achaeans, to accept.

Andromache, silent passenger that she was, rode out that dreadful duel, which proved so evenly matched that dusk came with both Ajax and Hector scarcely scratched. They resolved to give way to the night-time, resuming their struggle by daylight, when one must eventually gain victory over the other.

Yet it was not to be so. Animosities were stirred, hatreds rekindled. Paris, despite the urgings of his fellow Trojans, refused to return Helen. His stubbornness fanned the flames of anger burning in the bosom of Agamemnon and Menelaus.

War raged on again.

Arrows tore into thigh-muscles, and shoulders, and punctured throats like wine-skins gushing generously their contents. Bronze spear-heads drove through shields and corselets and broad war-belts. The clamor was incessant. Several sons of kingly Priam and bright princes of the Achaeans were cut down by sword-blades in the close confines. War-cries rang forth. It was horses and fire, the nodding of crests atop helms, the frenzy of multitudes. Like lions and like ravening dogs, they fought. Like wild oxen, they stampeded. Bodies dropped with the clatter of armor and the life fleeing from their eyes as the dark mists descended.

Unwilling to leave her beloved Hector, Andromache endured with him those full horrors and furies.

Word came, a rumor, that the Myrmidons had joined the field. Led, it was said, by Achilles, who had relented his wrathful brooding at last. The first proved true; the Myrmidons came fiercely to battle. As for the second, it was not Achilles himself but his true companion Patroclus, wearing the very armor of Achilles, fighting in his stead.

In Achilles' stead, but not with his skill, which was unmatched. The bravery, luck, and foolishness of Patroclus killed many men, but could not sustain him for long. A thrown javelin struck him a sore wound, and, as he sought desperate escape, it was there that Hector found him. He stabbed his spear into the depth of Patroclus' belly and pushed the sharp bronze clear through to emerge between the bony knobs of the spine.

He stripped Patroclus naked of the armor of Achilles, and would have severed the head from his neck and dragged off his body to feed the dogs of Troy, but for the vengeful arrival of huge Ajax and Menelaus of the loud war-cry. Hector fell back with his victorious prize. The armies of the Greeks, at the loss of Patroclus, lost their weariness as well and came back with a roaring thunder. They fought to defend the body of Patroclus, and the Trojans fought with equal fervor to claim it.

More brutally than ever, the war continued raging on.

Some swift-footed messenger, or winged words of the gods, must have brought the news to the ears of Achilles where he sat darkly brooding by his ships. For, in a suddenness, he was among them.

The fine armor which Patroclus had donned and Hector had taken was replaced now by even finer, by bright and brilliant god-forged stuff more beautiful than any man had ever seen. He sprang upon the Trojans with a ghastly cry. The first of them he slew, he struck down the middle so that the corpse fell in two pieces, writhing with tentacles and the ichor flew in a high arc.

Hector saw this, and through his eyes Andromache saw it too. They saw also the youngest and fairest of Priam's sons, Polydorus, most beloved, the marks of his strange blood nowhere near yet upon him and ageless lifespans stretching out before. Priam had forbidden him to go to battle, but to stay instead within Ithilium's strong walls. Yet here he was, having disobeyed their kingly father in youthful excitement, and it would cost him dearly.

Achilles hurled the spear far-shadowing, crafted by Hephaestus, smith of the gods. It took Polydorus at the small of the back, where the war-belt's golden clasps joined, and carried straight on through to push his bowels out at the navel. Polydorus dropped to one knee, groaning, catching at his entrails with his hands as the mists closed over him, when he should have lived long centuries before following his ancestors to the eternal palaces beneath the seas.

Giving such a cry that he might have borne the fatal wound himself, Hector ran to face Achilles, hefting his bronze spear like a blazing flame.

Andromache, also, would have voiced a cry, but could not, not with her body resting senseless within their house in Troy. She would have implored her dear husband with every persuasion to turn him from this course, fearing that the time of Hector's death loomed near, but neither could she do this.

They clashed with great violence as the battle swirled and stormed around them, as countless men went dying to the earth. Thrice, Hector broke from the combat and thrice Achilles pursued him with hard-minded tenacity. Each time, Andromache wished he might retreat within the walls. Each time, he did not.

Then, at the very gates of Ithilium, the two met again … and there, full within sight of those looking on in dismay from the ramparts, Olympian-armed Achilles struck his bronze-tipped spear above the collarbones, into the soft part of Hector's neck.

The rending stroke drove the life from his body. Andromache, still having the lend of his senses, felt both the bright pain and its swift surcease, and perceived how the dark mists came over her husband.

Yet she could not withdraw. Some power, some spell of the god-forged weapon, held her there, beyond the threshold, bound to her husband's dead flesh, entrapped as pine-tar might entrap a hapless fly.

Hector, gone now, spirit flown to the eternal blackness between stars, knew nothing of the indignities next inflicted upon his sorrowful remains. But she was less fortunate. Voiceless, she wailed as Hector's armor and tunic were stripped away. The Achaeans, slinking dogs in their boldness, jabbed at the corpse with their own spears. They laughed. They mocked his nakedness, and how much less fearsome this prince of Troy was than they had thought.

Next, to her even greater horror and humiliation and pain, Achilles tied oxhide ropes tight around Hector's bare ankles. Peleus' son sprang into his chariot, lashed the fast horses, and set off at full speed around the walls of the city. He dragged behind him the once-proud Hector, bouncing and twisting and rolling in the rough dirt, and over brambles and rocky places. A seething dust-cloud arose in the chariot's wake.

Each scrape of the sand, each cut of the stone, each bone-rattling thud, Andromache felt. She saw the land and sky jolting, veering, swapping places. The taste of grit filled her mouth. She could not break free. She could not close Yog-Sothoth's way and return to her own body, her own senses.

A shrieking madness consumed her, and she went with it gladly.

Some unknown time later, her wits seemed to return. She became aware of the cold, stiff weight of Hector's limbs … lungs unmoved by breath … the vital fluids sunk and pooled thick. His eyes had been shut, showing her nothing through them. One ear had been mangled, half-torn and clogged with dirt. With the other, she heard someone speaking suppliant words.

It was Priam, wise old Priam, Ithilium's king, tamer of shoggoths, Hector's father. How he had come here, to the camp of the enemy, she could not guess. Yet, come he had, and by the sounds of it he bent himself at Achilles' knee, clasping and kissing the very hands that had killed so many of his sons, to implore that the body of this one, the best and dearest of them, be given back to his people.

"Remember your own aged father," said Priam, with the deep tides rushing in his voice. "Think of your own children; would you have them so dishonored? Left naked, left filthy, a feast for the crows? His wife lies stricken, like one near death herself. Their son cries, inconsolable. Let me take him home. Let his mother weep over him, let his sisters wash him and anoint him with oil. Let us mourn him, and bury him properly. In that, above all else, your gods and ours must agree."

"You have stirred my pity, old one," grim Achilles finally said. "I will consent. Take your princely son home. He fought like a lion. Honor him with a good funeral. I shall do the same for my much-loved companion Patroclus, who went to battle and died in my stead. Let us celebrate them with feasts, games and races."

Strong men of the Myrmidons, at Achilles' bidding, lifted the corpse of Hector from where it had been left by their lord's shelter. Andromache noted well how they were now treating the body with care and respect. They placed it into a cart and draped it with fair cloth.

She heard Priam's sorrowful sigh when his gaze fell upon his son. She felt the cloth turned down from Hector's face, and the touch of the ancient king's hand—trembling, damp, and web-fingered—settling onto Hector's brow.

And that touch released her, so that she was drawn back into herself. She sat up, gasping, startling Astyanax's good nurse who had watched over both mother and child since that day of the battle.

"Give me my son," Andromache said, extending her white arms. "We have a funeral to prepare."

3

The Prize

Oh, that she had never seen him!

Oh, that he had never come to Sparta, led there by his goatish lust and the promise of the fecund goddess who spewed forth her teeming brood!

Christine Morgan

Paris … Paris of the divine countenance and the flowing locks … handsome Paris, golden-skinned Paris of the sea-green eyes … the muskiness and manliness of him … a look and she'd been lost.

Never mind her marriage oaths, the honor of her family, the insult to her husband. Never mind her home, her friends, her country, her precious half-grown daughter.

A look, and she'd been lost.

Even now, the thought of him sent desire melting in her loins.

Even now, as the city hung banners of mourning for his brother, as his mother and sisters harrowed their cheeks with grief.

Even now, as she loved him.

Even now, as she hated and despised him.

Paris. Paris the vain, Paris the glorious. Paris, who preened and strutted and made much boasting, but whose skills at the craft of war were much less so than at the arts of love.

Paris, shameful coward! Whiner! Bleater! Forever suckling, indulged and plump, at Shub-Niggurath's greasy teats!

Paris, said to be almost her own equal in beauty, Helen, peerless among women.

Helen, who oftentimes hated and despised herself as well.

Oh, that curse of her face and form! Since girlhood it was her prison and her destiny. Now it was her doom.

Her doom, and that of the Achaeans. Her kindred and countrymen, her people.

The fierce competition by her suitors had been only the beginning. There would have been bitter strife then, had not clever Odysseus suggested that those whose suit did not succeed swear a pledge to defend the rights of whichever of them won her. Yet it was that selfsame pledge causing these years of wretched violence.

The doom of the Achaeans.

And of the Trojans. Who blamed her, the cause of all these their troubles, bringer of war to their shores.

She was Helen, doom of men.

Doom of men, bane of widows, orphan-maker.

For Paris. All for Paris, and her own weak-willed desires.

How many deaths to be laid at her silver-sandaled feet? How large a basin to hold the tears of wives and children, and mothers weeping for their sons?

Whenever she tried to leave, Paris always somehow stopped her. Never by force, always with reason and persuasion. What would she do, he'd ask, caressing her lovely hair, her cheek. Return to Menelaus, in humble contrition, and beg his forgiveness? If not that, where would she go? The pride of Sparta and its king had been so stung, Menelaus would follow her to the ends of the earth. Or beyond it, should she do something so foolish as to drink of poison, or hurl herself from a high tower ... did she think Tartarus itself would be far enough to escape? Would death stop her embittered husband from pursuing her even there, past the River Styx's shores?

And she, Paris inevitably told her, was made for life, which was for the living, for the pleasures of the mortal world. For love-making and luxury, and basking in drowsing passion's warm after-glow. Not for the gloomy Underworld, not to be a bleak, unhappy shade.

He would say these things, and, next she knew, they'd be once more in his great carven wood bed together. Only later, long after the heat-sweat cooled and Helen was alone again, did the dark thoughts return.

She was often alone, when Paris was not with her. The men of Troy admired or desired her, their women were envious and resentful, and while she was never shunned or sneered at, in all, they avoided her.

This was not her city. This was not her home. These were not her people.

The gods worshiped and offered sacrifice in the temples of Ithilium were *not* her familiar gods. Within these walls, there was no place for Zeus, gatherer of clouds, or Hera, Olympus' queen. Apollo, the striker from afar, was not welcome here. Grey-eyed Athena and Aphrodite of the milk-white shoulders received no wind-borne smoke and savor, no libations of wine and oil.

No.

Not here.

Here were darker offerings made, black beasts cut and eaten raw. Here were unspeakable rituals held when strange stars wheeled in moon-dark skies. Here were guttural chants raised to Dagon of the deep trenches, to Azathoth the blind and idiot lord of all things, to yellow-robed Hastur and that she-goat of the greasy teats, Shub-Niggurath with her thousand young.

And what blood ran in their veins, these people of Troy, these sons and daughters of Ithilium?

Helen shuddered to think of it.

She had heard but not heeded, known but not believed. Not until Paris brought her to his father's palace and she'd seen the aged Trojans in their grotesque varieties. Some families seemed untouched. In others, the changes came only with advancing years. They spoke of minglings, and immortality, and chaos all-consuming, and gifts of glistening gold from great cities in the dark depths.

Christine Morgan

Chief among them were the king and queen, Priam, tamer of shoggoths, and Hecuba, his wife. She, fierce devourer of livers, went with her brow opened into a bony, thorny crown and her bent legs cloven-hoofed beneath the hem of her rich and trailing garments. Priam himself was hunched of stature, thick of body, and scaled of skin, his broad mouth almost lipless and eyes bulging.

It was Priam who, led cloaked in deception by crawling Nyarlathotep, ventured by stealth into the camp of the Achaeans to sway the heart and mind of Achilles, begging that Hector's body be returned.

So it was done, and the days allotted for funeral games and feasts were to be let to pass in truce. The dead of both sides were fetched back from the fields of battle, where they lay dirt-covered and thick with dried blood, so that it had to be washed from them and their identities be known. Throughout high-walled Ithilium, corpse-pyres smoldered, and likewise did they smolder beside the beach-drawn ships.

And, those days, Helen, alone but for a handmaiden, walked here and there about the city. She thought of Menelaus, whom she had not loved but who was the better man than Paris by far ... Paris, shrinking in doglike cowardice from strong confrontations.

She thought of the half-grown daughter she'd left behind with barely a backward glance, pretty Hermione, who would be by now a woman in her own right, of marriageable age. She thought of her sister, Clytemnestra, Agamemnon's wife. And their brave brothers, Castor and Pollux of the twin likenesses ... had they come to the war? She had not seen them from the high walls, with her friends and kinsmen.

She thought of these things as she walked, and her heart was heavy.

Truce though there was, amid the games and feasting, fear held thick in the streets of Troy. The walls stood, but with brilliant Hector gone, Ithilium's defender, how long could those walls withhold the onslaught of the Greeks?

Helen found herself wishing that the gods let it somehow fall soon. If only, in some or any way, she could hasten it along! Just to let this suffering trial at long last be at an end!

Then it was, in her wanderings, she glimpsed a face and form oddly familiar, and saw that it was crafty Odysseus, going in disguise to spy among the Trojans. She secretly approached him, and addressed him in winged words.

"Son of Laertes, equal to the gods in cleverness, are you come on behalf of Menelaus of the loud war-cry, my wedded husband, to retrieve me?"

He looked on her with kind sorrow and replied, "Fair Helen, loveliest of women, it is no longer for your lamentation that the Greek armies seek to destroy Ithilium. Menelaus, once your lord, would rather now bring you death with his own hands."

She, tearful, inclined her head. "Then let him come and do it. I will part my robe for him and bare my breast, that he does not ruin the fine cloth with sharp bronze."

The shaggy brows of Odysseus rose at that, and a wry smile curved his lips. "Such might, if nothing else, give him cause to reconsider. But, first of all, we must find some way to breach the high walls without much more loss of life. Too many good sons of the Achaeans have gone already to the dark houses of Hades."

Helen caught at the mantle he wore. "Hear me, then, Odysseus of the devious mind."

They spoke a while in hushed urgency, devising between them a plan. Then did Odysseus, wiliest of men, go back to the hollow ships, where he would call together an assembly and present that plan to them.

And then did Helen return to Priam's palace, where she found golden-skinned Paris waiting with desire much upon him. She went again to his bed, surrendering to his eager lusts.

The alloted truce-days passed, twelve of them in all. On the morning of the thirteenth, when rosy-fingered Dawn scattered light across the sky, she revealed not the armies of the enemy standing shield-ranked and bristling with spears. The far-flung plains were empty, the swift ships gone from the beach-strands of the Hellespont.

And there, in their place, stood a most majestic offering. Great and tall and wide it was, a massive thing, immense and hulking, built of wood and tar-covered, dotted with myriad pustules of eyes, limbs protruding in profusion. The Trojans, seeing their foes absent and this great shoggoth they had left, marveled.

"Is it trick, or tribute?" they wondered.

"It is a gift," Helen said. "A gift from the Greeks to honor their valiant foes, to placate the gods of Ithilium, and to beg that Dagon of the deep-sea trenches grant them safe passage home."

This overjoyed them. They brought the shoggoth through the gates, and garland-bedecked it. The maidens of the city danced in rings around it. The wine flowed all that day in revelry and celebration.

That night, as they slept and dreamed their wine-sodden dreams, the belly of the shoggoth opened. Hidden within it, as Helen and Odysseus had planned, were thirty of the best Achaean warriors. Unstoppable Diomedes emerged,

Christine Morgan

and Philoctetes of the stinging arrows, and Idomeneus, and Anticlus, and Neoptolemus, the young son of famed Achilles.

They sprung the gates, admitting the full strength of their armies, who'd sailed their ships only beyond the headland to wait in hiding out of sight.

The Greeks fell upon the Trojans, slaughtering them in their beds. The sons of Priam were cut down. Their wives were seized as concubines, their children hurled howling to their deaths. Priam himself, Neoptolemus killed at the very altar of Azathoth. Paris, from a safe distance, slew Achilles with an arrow to the heel, laced with poison given him by the Black Goat of the Woods. But Paris was himself in turn shot by the bow of Philoctetes.

In the panic, Helen waited for her fate to be decided. Menelaus, wrathful, found her in the courtyard by Priam's palace. He drew his bronze blade to stab her through the heart. So Helen, as she had told Odysseus she would, parted her robe, baring her fair breasts to him.

"Strike quickly, if ever you loved me," she said to Menelaus.

The sight of her beauty so stunned him that his sword fell from his hand. He forgave, and spared her.

But, for the people of the city, no such mercy was to be had. The streets ran thick with their strange blood.

And Ithilium burned.

THE SINKING CITY

BY KONSTANTINE PARADIAS

T he tiny, hard-limbed thing that I am using as a vessel is paddling in its wooden craft, beating furiously at the churning, frothing waters. It moves with the terrified speed of a creature that knows it is about to die, its thoughts churning in red-black fear.

My name is Robert Bendis, it keeps babbling in its mind. *And this is all a dream, nothing but a dream....*

It fights me even now, as we reach the shores of R'lyeh, kicking and clawing against my grip on its mind. Its struggles have become fiercer now, more feral. The monkey that is its lower brain snarls and claws, screeching at me.

I have a wife, Denise it drones on. *Two children: Randolf and Millward. Randolf is six, Millward is eight* ... it goes on, repeating names and numbers like a mantra. It has become the core of its thought-process, the center of its being.

No matter. It will be dead soon, after all. I will probably follow it into oblivion.

The vessel I am possessing reaches out its stocky, hairy arms as we reach the shores of R'lyeh and attempts to focus its eyes into a single coherent point. The shore is a mass of fused obsidian, the stone blossoming outward into dimensions that its brain cannot comprehend. To me, the rock-face appears like the roots of some strange plant-form, radiating from the shore in every possible direction, each branch festooned with wicked barbs. To the vessel, it seems like a whirling vortex without shape, beginning or end. It does not know in which direction it should steer the wooden craft that has led us here.

This is a dream it whimpers; *I'm not seeing this. There is no shore, there is no sea. I am lying in my bed and no one will wake me.* ...

I keep trying to shift its perceptions, to make it see a fraction of what I see by tapping into its higher-brain functions. Its fight-or-flight instinct flares up, throwing me off. It is only moments before I reach down through its brain, deciding to risk a full lobotomy, that the vessel is finally distracted by the trail of blue-green fire above us, smashing its way past the invisible barrier of R'lyeh and setting its obsidian face ablaze.

To the vessel, the fire means divinity. To me, it is the sign that the Hierarchy has abandoned me and opted for the standard approach. The full frontal bombardment of R'lyeh, despite all indications toward the futility of this plan.

And I saw fire descend from the Heavens and a third of the trees and the crops were reduced to ash, it prays, thinking itself caught in the throes of some apocalyptic vision. *And the damned, which dwelt upon the forsaken Earth, bore witness to it and suffered.*

Jolting the movement centers of the vessel's brain, I assume control of its arms, making it pick up the length of twined hemp with the knotted end in its arms. Before it has a chance to stop me, I move its arms in a clumsy fashion and toss it almost blindly. It latches on to a protrusion that appears to me like a polyp-claw. The vessel's struggling helps to fasten the knot. We have reached the shores of R'lyeh.

Above us, the monolithic face of Cthulhu's citadel turns at a downward-inward angle. The intricate murals (invisible to the vessel's eyes) begin to flow like mercury, shifting their forms into long protruding spirals, many miles across. I hear the steady humming of unseen faith-generators as they begin to gather power through the collective prayer of the citadel's denizens. Knowing what is about to follow, I force the vessel to jump into the waters. They burn like the heart of Cthugha himself, the heat affecting even my thought-form.

In the reaches above, the spirals begin to heat up, their brightness reaching the intensity of the furnace-heart of stars, before releasing their charge in a moment of quiet pandemonium. The sea around us parts. The super-heated air blisters the vessel's skin and propels its body over the beach and to the shore. I feel its skin blister, its bones cracking as it crashes against (what appears to it) empty space. The bundle strapped on its back remains unharmed in its metal casing. Behind us, the charge has been released, its trajectories visible in the ultraviolet spectrum. I needn't look out for the crashing cacophony of its impact to know that the city of Ponape (the frontal line of our assault) has been wiped from the face of the planet.

I am not hurt, this is not true pain. I am not in Hell, I'm only dreaming. I'm only dreaming and no one will wake me ... it whimpers; then, looks at the white-red jagged edge protruding through the skin of its arm.

The vessel screams its hoarse cry as it looks at the bone protruding from the skin of its arm. Its terror and shock are too much for me to overcome, so I excite areas of its brain that stimulate fear. The vessel soils itself, but it is now more malleable. Before it has a chance to inspect its surroundings, I reach out into its remaining arm and make it slide the bone back into place. The vessel's pain is too much for it to handle, so it blacks out. I shut off its higher-brain functions and assume command, forcing it to get up on its feet and lurch up the hewn obsidian staircase upon the face of R'lyeh.

We move through unknown corridors that exist in the direction known as *vur-mat,* which is the direction of inside, radiating outward. Scaling the angles and branches of the fractal architecture of Cthulhu's citadel, I move in the manner that the oceanic vertebrates do through coral, although in a far less graceful manner. Around us, the slave-soldiers of Cthulhu, children of Dagon and Hydra, spill out from the parapets, riding on their writhing, hissing mounts. The mounts swim across the air by extending pseudopods from their bodies, latching onto spaces in the direction of *vur-fal,* which is the direction of outside, radiating inward.

We remain unseen by the growth-like probes that constitute the defenses of R'lyeh. Within this vessel, I am invisible to them, my anatomy a riddle that is designated as mammalian-vertebrate but, most importantly, *non-intelligent.* To the defense systems, I am little more than a desperate trilobite, scaling the unknowable heights in search of food. Finding the fruits of my labors to my liking, I move upward a few meters further, closer to one of the flyers' parapets. Somewhere in the distance, the children of Dagon are swarming, scaling the reaches of the atmosphere to dive down into the ruins of Ponape and eliminate any stragglers of my race.

I have been a sinner, an unclean man. I am suffering now for my doubt and for my violence. I am cast into Hell, my soul ridden by a devil. I am asleep and no one will wake me....

The vessel begins to stir and waken, as I force it to climb up the parapet. Its conscious brain restores itself to function as I am hauling us upward, the interior of R'lyeh coming into view. In my eyes, I am looking into the beating heart of the city of my enemy. In the vessel's eyes, however, it is a sight that crushes its mind. I temporarily cease the function of its lungs, to stop the scream that is escaping its lips and the vessel collapses, soundlessly. Looking through its eyes, I can see the expanding, terrible geometry of it

Konstantine Paradias

all: the churning, tar-black depths that have been tapped by the machines devised by Cthulhu and his kin to tap into the core of the planet; the cathedral-factories, where the sons and daughters of Dagon and Hydra are sacrificed in great meat-grinders, their screams drowned out by the babbling prayers of the priesthood to power the faith-generators. I see the sprawling, screaming factories that churn out the war-machines which Cthulhu will unleash on my kin across the star-system, manned by creatures whose form does not wholly exist within the current Universe. I see pathways that seem like malignant growths, interconnecting the abodes of the mad-eyed zealot-warriors of R'lyeh.

And in the absolute center of it all, I see the kelp-choked fortress of Cthulhu himself, to which all pathways lead and from which all things in R'lyeh radiate, where the arch-priest of the nuclear Sultan Azathoth himself sits on a throne hewn from granite, himself tall as a mountain, his voice booming in the speech of its birthplace of Xoth.

No angles or turns, no reason or design. Only nightmare, nightmare hewn in black rock, in the heart of the world, and I am stuck in this place, where reason comes to die surrounded by monstrosities. This is Hell and I am the least among the damned it whimpers and cries in the confines of its own mind, even as it is slowly asphyxiating.

My vessel struggles and finally ceases. I wait until it is on the brink of death (moments before serious brain damage occurs) and then restore the function of its lungs, to ensure it is broken. Its willpower is considerable but I will only need a very short amount of time to achieve my goal. Removing the package from its back, I tap a series of hidden buttons. A *click-clacking* noise begins to sound from the interior of the package. The displacement-bomb is primed. One of the automated defense-probes crawls into my line of sight and turns its solitary eye to look at the hunched form, examining the package. It ponders on it, cross-referencing the simple cubic design in the knowledge-base it shares with its kin. Finding it harmless after a few moments of careful deliberation, it skitters away. My plan is working, for now.

ᒻᕰᒉᑊ

To infiltrate the domain of Cthulhu, to cross into Mu itself, was considered by the Hierarchy impossible. Braver Yithians than I had, after all, been killed the moment they set foot within Cthulhu's domain, their presence revealed either via the scrutiny of automated probes or by Xothian sorcery. Any attempts to bombard or directly assault R'lyeh were catastrophic failures, wave after wave of our forces decimated before reaching even a few kilometers close to its shores. *The Xothians were winning by virtue of their occult superiority. And no manner of ballistic advancement or even the greatest weapons available to our kind could give us an edge.*

ᕮᛁᛚᚱᛐ

I lead the vessel across what appears to be thin air, its feet stepping on a trail of opaque stones invisible to its eyes. We move in the heights above R'lyeh, too small to be picked up by the eye of its citizens, too alien to be acknowledged by its defense systems. When a spawn of Dagon passes by, we hide in the shadow of great basalt pillars that reach up from the core of the planet into the heights above and continue, unseen.

ᕮᛁᛚᚱᛐ

It was baffling how the Hierarchy had not noticed the dent in R'lyeh defenses beforehand: when a group of captured polyps was translocated into the borders of Mu in the hope that the beasts would wreak some havoc in Cthulhu's domain, the beasts were ignored by the defense systems, attacked only by waves of Dagon-Spawn and the lowliest servitors. The polyps killed many before they were finally driven back or destroyed, but the flaw had been made apparent:

R'lyeh's most powerful defenses could not acknowledge what was not known to them.

ᕮᛁᛚᚱᛐ

Jumping onto a ledge set up above one of the factory-cathedrals, I check our surroundings. The distance to the fortress of Cthulhu is still considerable, but the displacement-bomb's radius is great enough to achieve the desired effect without having to be set at ground zero. All we would have to do was make sure we remained unseen. Then I could escape from the vessel to safety moments before I was captured. The vessel would be sacrificed for the glory of the Race of Yith. It pained me how I could not make it understand the magnitude of the achievement it was about to perform.

My name is Robert Bendis, and I am to be Hell's assassin, to deliver a blow to the Devil for the sake of his upstart kin it babbles on, perhaps abandoning itself to some primeval fantasy.

Ⲭⲗⲟⲓ

I proposed my plan to the Hierarchy: the idea of sending one of our kind within a vessel from the distant future of the planet, one that would be unknown to the Xothians. A creature whose anatomy and structure would place it among the vertebrate species, possessing some intelligence (though not fully aware, so as not to unintentionally notify the defense systems) and a limited capacity for handling Yithian interfaces. I volunteered to capture this creature myself, snatching it from the abode it had dwelt in, set in the middle of a green field infested with grass, beneath a blue sky. Its form had been frail, yet well-kept. It possessed opposable digits. Its brain immediately shut down as I assumed control and returned to my time.

Ⲭⲗⲟⲓ

Outside, something crashes against R'lyeh and the fortress shudders. Perhaps my people have mounted some sort of counter-attack, perhaps even using some of the higher-yield destructive weapons to breach the walls. It is possible they could have repelled the Dagon-spawn and set up some sort of counter-attack. I know that it is futile and I bet that the Hierarchy is aware of this as well. I am certain that, even now, they are abandoning their thought-forms, leaving the simple-minded beasts that are their vessels to perish in the bale-fire of R'lyeh's retaliation. They are wise in their decision to flee. Where I am standing, all of R'lyeh is reverberating with the sound of collecting prayer, the droning of Cthulhu himself as he musters his faith-energy. The vessel's hairs stand on end, agitated by the sensation of gathering power.

Satan is roaring from his Pit, rumbling and turning, roused from his place of rest. He speaks in tongues; perhaps he has caught a whiff of me. Hell wakens it says. *The blow must be struck now* it urges me on, perhaps driven by newfound courage born from desperation.

Ⲭⲗⲟⲓ

When I returned, I found that the war between Ponape and R'lyeh had progressed. In my days of absence, following the massive quake that had smashed the planet's supercontinents into a gestalt, the cities of the Elder Things had been reduced to ruin. In the oceans of the Magnetic North, the world had spilled its bubbling life-blood and cooked the creatures in the confines of their own homes. Cthulhu had mobilized his forces, once the southern front of his war had been dealt with. Now, only Yith stood in the way of his absolute domination. This war had suddenly evolved from a millennia-long territorial dispute into full-fledged genocide.

ﾌ:ﾙﾀﾞ

We move, the vessel and I, in perfect harmony. It is spurred on by terror; I am driven by a desire to end this before my homeland is completely deci-mated. Halfway through our jump on a ledge, a spawn of Dagon screams its guttural cry and reaches out a taloned hand to grab us, taking a chunk of the vessel's flesh with it. We crash onto the stone face of a building, grab on at the last minute and try to get up, only to find that the vessel's right leg has ceased to function. A quick examination reveals that a tendon has been severed. The next jump will be impossible. Around and above us, the spawn of Dagon howl in alarm. From the balcony of a factory-cathedral, a Xothian flexes it tentacles and beats its wings, noticing us.

The craft which had transported us from the borders of Mu into R'lyeh itself was built according to the exact specifications taken from the vessel's knowledge-base. It was a crude craft that required muscle power to move, but it had reached its target without incident. The vessel fought against me, of course, as fiercely as it does at this very moment, looking into the terrifying form of the Xothian that jumps from the balcony and flies toward us. We roll aside as the Xothian crashes into the stone, reducing it to powder. When the dust dies down, it roars and reaches out with its claws. The vessel strikes it with its fist and its arm comes clean off from the shoulder.

I am too weak, too frail, too little ... it cries in its own head back at me, as it looks at the severed mess that has become its arm. It is paralyzed in fear, soiling itself, useless now, its fight-or-flight instincts clashing uselessly in the presence of the Xothian.

With its remaining hand, I remove the displacement-bomb. It won't be anywhere near enough, but I can't risk coming any closer. The vessel howls and screams, and I fight back, assuming control of its arm, pressing a sequence of buttons. I am jerked away moments before detonation. As I look down, I see the Xothian chewing on the vessel's legs, crushing bone and rending flesh with its teeth. The defense-drones swarm around me.

I have a wife, Denise it drones on. *Two children: Randolf and Millward. Randolf is six, Millward is eight* ... the vessel retreats back to its mantra, its own defense, blocking out the terror somewhat by weaving for itself a mental cocoon.

There is no chance to escape, so I fling the displacement-bomb down the parapet and into the depths. I see Cthulhu, turning its eyes to look down into me. The shock of witnessing his countenance kills my vessel, and I am trapped inside it, as the Xothian takes its final bite.

This is all a dream. I am lying on my bed and no one will wake me ... I am safe, unhurt. I will open my eyes and won't remember a thing.

Thankfully, I am aware in those final moments of the *hum* of the displacement-bomb as it goes off, collapsing space around it, ripping a chunk of R'lyeh's life-sustaining machinery and a half-dozen of its factory cathedrals, sending them hurtling through Time and Space to destinations unknown. The gathering power dissipates. The city quakes, shudders, its walls and building covered in spider-web cracks. A torrent of obsidian rolls down into the impenetrable darkness. Something crashes through the obsidian face of R'lyeh and pours inside it, burning red-blue, as soon as its defenses collapse.

I perish, smiling.

THE SHAPE OF A SNAKE

BY CODY GOODFELLOW

I chanced to serve in war under one who later became president of your country, although I came to no great understanding of his essential humanity. For, while our association in the field of battle was brief and unremarkable in itself, it is because of a brief and elsewhere unrecorded episode that I cannot recall the grinning face of the father of our regiment, but only an ecstatic, blind berserker hewing down friend and foe like so many saplings, his broad, rugged face a scarlet mask gleaming darkly with our blood.

In the hot, malarial week after the flag of truce had been delivered and terms were being discussed for the surrender of the city of Santiago, the lieutenant colonel of our regiment was forced on several occasions to hitch up a pack train and set out the coast to forage for such food and medicine as the US military failed to procure for her own soldiers. After his "crowded hour" atop San Juan Hill, he was jubilant and most energetic, even as the portion of his regiment not killed in the fighting succumbed to hunger and malaria.

So it was that eight officers, including Lt. DeVore and myself, accompanied Lt. Col. Roosevelt to the Hotel Cibola outside of Siboney, and the conspiracy of the Eternal Serpent.

The sergeant who led us there was a silver-haired, earless half-Comanche, a former cavalry scout and now bounty hunter, as far as one could get from the decorated polo players and tennis champions who crowded the upper echelons of our unit—the lieutenant colonel's game but green friends from the Oyster Bay polo club and the Daniel Boone Society in New York. They looked at Sgt. Hull as if expecting a magic trick. Instead, he had offered them a beached freighter of unknown registry and an abandoned Spanish hotel, which was, despite its dilapidated state, lit up like Christmas and entertaining guests.

Stranded in the sweltering jungle hills above besieged Santiago, our only action since the battle atop El Caney had been to raid abandoned Spanish positions for supplies. Our principal adversary had not been the Spanish Empire, but the United States Army. The torturous crossing aboard the *Yucatan*, the catastrophe of poor planning, had reduced the Rough Riders from an elite cavalry regiment to a volunteer infantry unit and cut our numbers by more than the Spaniards ever would.

Alongside Lt. Col. Roosevelt, Sgt. Hull and myself, our foraging party included Captain Homer Helps, a former Texas Ranger; Captain Peter Kiesling, a crack shot and former Pony Express rider; Lt. Barnard Scovill, a polo champion, boxer and big game hunter; Lt. Truman Van Patten, a celebrated yachtsman and horse racer; and Sgt. Tom Heslop, a lifelong cavalry officer and veteran of the Indian Wars; and Lt. Hamilton DeVore, a veteran of countless Manhattan society scandals. Only our officers had kept their horses in the crossing, and so our pack train was a motley string of native mules and nags abandoned by the Spaniards.

Due to a contract I need not elaborate upon here, I was charged with the personal protection of young DeVore by his father, who had procured my contract in the usual way. I had accompanied him from New York to San Antonio to enlist in the volunteer cavalry regiment popularly known soon afterward as the Rough Riders. The same strings that insured the scion of the famously warlike DeVore clan a commission despite his inexperience in all things but sports and debauchery had also been pulled to speedily outfit the newly minted regiment so it could get to Cuba in time to see fighting, and likewise found no difficulty in placing me as Lieutenant DeVore's Master Sergeant.

"Not a hair on his head shall come to harm," the elder DeVore had commanded. "Do not," his mother added, "allow those Spanish bastards to touch him." I could have advised them that the heartfelt yet vague idiomatic terms of the contract would lead to grief later on, if ordered to do so.

Roosevelt knew DeVore's older brother tolerably well from philanthropic jaunts and hunting expeditions in the wilds of upstate New York and Canada. It stung young Hamilton that he hadn't ranked high enough to sit in a staff tent and toast a map with planter's punch, but neither the tropics nor life as a troop commander had suited him so far, though he was loath to desecrate the family name. There was no shame in defeat and death in such families; only in failing duty.

Roosevelt cut a fine figure, almost crackling with the sound of history bending to his will. While half the regiment was down with malaria, and yellow fever hysteria ran rampant, he'd shed twenty pounds and was a picture of obscenely robust vigor. He suffered a few splinters in his eyebrow and a welt on his wrist the size of a robin's egg from an ingot of artillery shrapnel. Two enlisted men close beside him were filleted by the same shell. When McKinley had finally acceded to Hearst's hounding and declared war on Spain, his masthead crowed HOW DO YOU LIKE THE *JOURNAL*'S WAR? But no one who knew anything about it could argue but that destiny and Mr. Roosevelt had fought with equal fervor to meet here, in this place, for *his* war.

I strenuously avoided such men, unless contractually compelled to serve. Though I shrank from his notice at every turn, he seemed to seek out in the men of violence with which he'd surrounded himself—some mirror of his own imminent transformation.

Fortunately, he fastened upon Sgt. Hull. At some point in their lopsided conversation, Roosevelt said, "I have bested men in athletic competition, and I have stalked and killed all manner of wild game. I find it quite difficult not to look to those experiences when reflecting on the excitement of the battlefield."

"I think you've just found the reason for sports," DeVore interjected, but a snapping glance from the Colonel shut him off.

"Killing men is nothing," Hull said. "Any cornered man or beast can kill. But to send men into battle ..."

"I ask nothing of any man I would not myself undertake, Sergeant." The soft brevity of his tone was the only hint of his fraying temper.

"A man who can send others to their death without feeling it is a monster...."

"But a man who would balk at saving millions for the sake of a few able young men who know the wages of the game ..."

"The *game*," Hull growled, "is what men like you call other people's lives."

Roosevelt tensed so that his horse balked on the trail. "Indeed, and millions of lives, indeed the whole world, in the balance. The Spaniard must be driven from the Western World. The days of his empire are over."

And ours have only begun, I didn't say, for it wasn't my place.

Roosevelt ordered Hull to return to camp and report to Col. Wood, then impatiently rode ahead to the water.

The ship was as Hull had described it. It looked unlikely to have sailed to Cuba under its own power, and less likely ever to leave. Beached, scuttled

Cody Goodfellow

and rusted through, her superstructure was encrusted with barnacles and stranger things that had burst with the rigor of being lifted from the ocean bottom.

And yet the name of the vessel stood out in white paint upon its broken prow—*Nykøbing*. Roosevelt was ignorant of its derivation. A Danish clipper ship, I whispered to DeVore, lost in the North Atlantic between Godthab in Greenland and Copenhagen ten years before. He repeated this to garner an appreciative glance from the Colonel. We could only conclude that it was not here at all when our convoy landed near Daiquiri.

Not far from the lagoon, we crossed a broad, overgrown lawn decorated with strutting peacocks and headless statuary, and soon came within sight of the sprawling ruin of the Hotel Cibola.

The scabrous whitewash and brick façade of the hotel had all but returned to the jungle, but the saloon within was brightly lit, and two rows of fine carriages were lined up before the stables. Roosevelt dismounted from Little Texas beneath a tree a hundred yards from the wide front porch. Heslop was ordered to remain on guard and ready to ride at a moment's notice. Hitching up his Sam Browne belt and kicking his cavalry saber in its cumbersome scabbard out from between his legs, he strolled up the front steps and threw wide the doors.

The vast expanse of marble floor was furnished with scattered tables and chairs. The gambling tables were shrouded, but a small crowd was gathered in the vestibule as if awaiting some terribly urgent message. A quartet of musicians played in tandem on an enormous marimba in an alcove, oblivious, for they were all blindfolded in order not to see their clientele.

Roosevelt grinned broadly and raised his hands to signal his peaceful intent. "Gentleman and dear ladies, I implore you not to panic. I know not where your sympathies lie in the current conflict, but I most emphatically assure you that our attentions are peaceful...."

Eleven men and two women studied us with varying degrees of fear, loathing and longing. I had seen similar faces in opium dens and on murderer's row in any number of jails. Three Celestials with braided queues that reached the floor smiled inscrutably over steepled hands; a Hindoo fakir swaddled in the seemingly endless length of his own beard sat opposite them, chewing betel nuts and staring fixedly and unblinkingly at our commander. A tonsured scholar in the robes of some disavowed Catholic order glared at elaborate cabalistic calculations in chalk upon his tablecloth. A fair-haired identical twin brother and sister stood at the bar, decked out like antebellum plantation owners awaiting a slave auction. An ancient Prussian officer in a uniform festooned with every conceivable military honor quivered in a wheelchair pushed by a dead-eyed bulldog with a long scar running from his scalp to his jaw through one white, unseeing eye. A blind man in an undertaker's black worsted wool suit sat against the wall with one hand cupped against the mahogany wall clock, nodding approvingly in time with the music. And on the edge of the gathering, a pale, worried young woman in the uniform of an American Gibson Girl gnawed at her thumb and blinked some desperate telegraphic message.

"No Spaniards, at least," DeVore said too loudly.

As Roosevelt held forth, a hunchback wearing a fez and caftan shuffled past and bumped into him, making a most exotic variation of the Evil Eye at him before he scooted away. An older man in a stained white suit and string tie rose to interrupt Roosevelt, bearing a cage of wire mesh and shaking it to agitate something sleeping within. "The hour is upon us!" he shouted. His accent was of the Alabama piney woods, his booming tone that of an apostate tent preacher. "Unbelievers are welcome among us, for they will be crushed in the coils of the Eternal Serpent!"

"Then I suppose we're entitled to an apéritif," DeVore said, which set the officers to laughing.

Roosevelt, polishing his spectacles, drew us into a circle. "No drinking. We must tread lightly here, until we know what manner of conspiracy we've blundered into."

Looking about the room, Lieutenant Van Patten said, "This isn't a conspiracy, it's another World's Fair."

"Look around you, gentlemen," Roosevelt said. "The flotsam of every decadent, bygone empire haunts this place, but for what fell purpose....?"

The troopers encamped at a table nearest the door. DeVore ambled over to the American lady's table.

Once she'd complimented his uniform and his bravery, she covered her mouth with a fan as she hissed, "You men must leave while you can! They're choosing the last of their inner circle tonight! After that, I fear the rest of us will be ... Oh, it's too horrible!"

DeVore smiled. "Rest easy, Miss, the cavalry is here. Meet Sgt. Cameron. He has to do whatever I tell him...."

"Privilege of rank," I hastily added, using DeVore's pause to recharge his flask to question the lady. "You're here to cover the war...?"

She offered her ungloved hand, pickled in sweet ladysweat. "Elizabeth Arnesen, Sergeant, of the *New Orleans Picayune*. I did come here on my own initiative to cover the war, but that … *man* …" She pointed at the gentleman in the white suit, who sat with one hand in his cage and an eerily vacant expression. "He's a fugitive wanted in Louisiana for burning down his church with the congregation locked up inside…."

"How awful!" DeVore said.

"Indeed! And what's worse, he's come here with these others of the same notorious cloth to be chosen to receive some prize or to share some secret … None of them will say what it is. But they'll kill to get it. And none of those who have received this all-important blessing have deigned to shed any light upon the mystery." She waved a hand at the Chinese scholars and the Hindoo, who regarded the rest of the gathering with an unsettling arrogance.

"Oh, come now," DeVore said, sliding a cup of fortified coffee across the small table, "*we're* the only story, my dear. They're eating dogs in Santiago. The war's all but in the bag. Surely you've heard of Teddy's Texas Tarantulas…?" He pointed to Roosevelt, who was orating dramatically with his billfold out at a sleepwalking servant, attempting to buy supplies.

"These men all appear to be of a metaphysical bent," I said. "And you say they're all after some secret. Is the prize whatever came in that derelict ship in the lagoon?"

Her eyes widened. "They were beside themselves when it appeared! They despise each other, yet they all carry snakes, or trinkets or idols or fetishes, and whatever it is they found down there, they've been quite keen to get their hands on it." Looking about defiantly as if at war with herself, Arnesen sipped DeVore's coffee. "There was another man the first day; he died right here in the lobby. They say the Kiss of Wisdom rejected him…."

"What the devil is this Kiss of Wisdom?" DeVore asked. "Are you perchance qualified to administer it?"

Silence fell over the room like a wet shroud. Some stood and sat down again or wrung their hands. All eyes fixed on the front doors, standing open to let the smoke from cigars and the stifling humidity waft out into the night. From somewhere outside came the ominous sound of drums.

Roosevelt clapped his dusty gloved hands. "Gentlemen! Rally and retreat!" We all of us picked up, swiftly stubbing out cigars and downing rum drinks before donning our campaign hats and mustering near the door….

Then *she* walked in.

At the first glimpse of her, the room collectively sucked in its breath and held it.

She wore layers of crepe and lace that obscured all but the vaguest outline of her form. She glided like a jellyfish into the center of the room, then twisted round and ripped away a veil. Underneath, glossy black hair, dusky brown skin and the sheen of scales ...

We drew together with our backs to the door, but not one of us, not even our stalwart and famously married commander could take a step closer to it.

The drums seemed to draw nearer and to throb faster.

Another veil was torn away and lofted over the transfixed mob.

Lieutenant DeVore was lost to us. Her arm clutching at mine, Miss Arnesen stared into my eyes with a searching, probing intensity. "Are you familiar with Haitian vodun, Sgt. Cameron?"

To such an odd question, at such a strange time, I could only give a discreet nod. I'd had occasion to observe such rituals. "This woman is being ridden by a *loa*?"

"Exactly so! But she is only a messenger. These people have come seeking congress with the gods! And yet ..." She pinched the bridge of her nose. "I must speak to Mr. Roosevelt...."

"That'll be a tough one," DeVore said, chuckling. "If there's one thing he likes more than talking to reporters ..."

Lt. Col. Roosevelt stood with arms akimbo and head straight forward as if held in place by an old-time photographer's brace. The veiled dancer now wore only one diaphanous lace veil and the long coil of an enormous snake that clung to her modesty in a way far more lewd than mere nudity. She circled him and doubled back, her intent unmistakable. An angry murmur flowed through the assembled occultists. The Egyptian drew a short, cruelly curved blade and stabbed the darkly gleaming mahogany table.

Miss Arnesen let go my arm and reached out to Lieutenant DeVore, who stood much like Roosevelt, utterly absent. Much as every man in the place save myself, for whom such charms have little appeal, and several of the guests.

So we all stood by when the dancer threw out an arm to rip away the last veil, and dispelled the illusion that we had been watching a human woman at all. A column of serpents entwined in the crude likeness of a human body, they sprang and spilled out at the still-hypnotized soldiers. Rearing up almost as tall as a man, an enormous viper with fangs longer than fingers slithered up close enough to Roosevelt's naked face that a mist of aerosolized venom condensed upon and dripped from his spectacles.

In spite of my relative alertness, it was almost like moving underwater, shoving others aside to throw out an arm and knock Roosevelt down and at the same time duck under the striking head of the gigantic snake.

Cody Goodfellow

Before either of them had fallen, the spell broke. Our party circled the lieutenant colonel and drew revolvers. The guests erupted from their seats. The snake lashed out at the fugitive preacher, fastening upon his neck. The others seemed to freeze, abruptly robbed of their urgency, indeed of all hope.

A torrent of bodies poured in the doors and windows, dropped from the ceiling and sprouted from the floor. Some among the guests resisted as strenuously as I, but even when my revolver was empty and most of the bodies crushed against me were growing cold, the mob carried us inexorably out of the hotel and into the night toward the swampy lagoon, where the drums gradually grew ever louder....

ꝥꞁꝯꞇꞁ

A compound of mud and reeds in the feverish swamp, where a massive pit had been dug in the sand. The flooded bottom of the pit writhed with an assortment of imported vipers. High on a rampart of sand overlooking the pit stood a rude stone altar, and upon it a globe of black glass the diameter of a wagon wheel, which emitted a sinister, syrupy green vapor. The noxious steam from the globe seemed to vent synchronously with the wild rhythm of the primal ceremony and to deepen the acrid, reptilian stench. A ragged crowd of glassy-eyed Cuban blacks pounded drums and chanted and danced wildly about the pit. Beside the rampart, a close knot of people stood silent and still beside the altar—the Oriental delegation, the monk and the bearded Hindoo all appeared to have passed.

I have seen such things and come away unmoved. But my fellow troopers remained quite oblivious of our imminent peril. One of the hotel's staff broke free of the mob and tried to flee but went down in a hurricane of machetes.

I abruptly found Miss Arnesen beside me. Her eyes gleamed with lascivious zeal as she pressed the tip of a most ladylike stiletto to my back.

Presuming she was magnanimous enough not to kill me outright, I asked her if she might not elaborate upon her earlier warning.

"The true masters of this world have returned to claim it, little half-man. They lay at the bottom of the ocean for only ten years, but were imprisoned by human treachery in the summer of lost Mhu Thulan, three million years ago ... and yet within, scarcely a score of seasons have turned...."

The nature of the globe was suddenly quite transparent to me. Seeing the weird disconnect between her seeming and her sense, I observed that her demons might have come from the distant past, but they caught on fast, now able to pass among us.

Far from showing dismay at being discovered, she positively beamed with supercilious glee. Compliments must be scarce, among her kind. "Oh, my unworthy self is as unlike them, as you are unlike the great apes. Our kind has been devolved and debased, our blood polluted by hiding among you scavenging brutes that stole from our ancestors all the knowledge that raised you up from the slime. Stole our birthright! Hating in silence, striking out in secrecy to bring you ever closer to chaos and ruin. But no longer! Your pretty, petty wars, your parades of filth and empty noise, your defilement and misrule of this perfect world … it begins to end tonight!"

I wiped her venomous spittle from my cheek, but offered no reply.

As the ritual escalated, many of the hotel's sinister guests were manhandled to the edge of the pit, struck with clubs or machetes and dropped, wailing and grievously wounded, into the snake-choked pit. The circle of favored guests began to chant in low, hissing tones that became a slurred, savage roar as the careening peasants took it up. It was no sound for human ears, any more than it was for human tongues to say, yet it was unmistakably a name. Green clouds whistled out of the black orb like steam from a teapot.

The snake-bitten preacher was escorted up the slope to kneel before the sphere. He seemed to vanish within a cloud of green steam that rolled out to envelop us all.

I know that what happened next was not a product of my sleeping imagination, for I do not dream.

The sky, a soup of seething green clouds—pyramidal towers of mossy black basalt—a triangle of iridescent orichalcum etched around a circle that glowed and crackled with the strain of containing the black lightning sweating off a red metallic orb that snorted and exhaled fumes as our reflections twisted …

I raised my age-knurled forelimbs high as my brother acolytes intoned the song of the Eternal Serpent in time with the throbbing rhythm that shivered the earth beneath our coiled tails.… We raised our voices higher and basked in the cascade of little lives pouring into the confines of our prison. Drawing power from our own captive daemon to force wider the door, to speed the stuck calendar wheel and reverse the singular pull of the gravity that kept us from escaping …

At a gesture from the Eldest among us, I stepped over the orichalcum border of the outer threshold.

And suddenly, the red orb became a mirror showing us a world choked with fire and smoke and overrun with grunting, vulgar hominids.

We raised our voices higher and fed our daemon handfuls of souls.

The mirror became a door.

The door yawned wide and a host of pale, soft bodies lay prone and open for me to choose. ...

Fading as abruptly as it came, the vision left me confused, but seemed to leave my fellow troopers unfazed and oblivious to their peril.

When the noxious green mist dissipated, the preacher stood on his own, shaky but somehow imbued with a strange new vitality, though he walked down from the altar as if unfamiliar with the workings of a human body.

"Now, the most fit among you must be selected," Arnesen raved, "to bear the Eldest. The offerings will fight to the death for the privilege of receiving the kiss of his wisdom."

I told her we would do no such thing, albeit without much faith behind it. No doubt we could be induced to fight, but I could see little point in it. If the invaders desired a superior body to host their supreme eminence, then none on offer could compare with the pedigree and natural assets of our commander.

Almost before I thought it, Miss Arnesen reached the same conclusion. "That one!" she shrieked in Spanish and then in that hissing, gargling language that seemed to call for two tongues. She pointed at Lt. Col. Roosevelt. "Our master will have *their* master's form! Kill the others...."

I saw little point in letting her continue. Her knife was easier to reach than my own, so I took it from her and tried to secure her silence.

Even under such straits, I could not bring myself to stab a woman unless so ordered, but as I took her in my hands, the body in my grip twisted and squirmed out of my hands as no human form possibly could. Instead of throwing up her arms to protect herself as any man or woman would do under such an assault, she lurched at my face with her mouth wide and a venomous mist fizzing out over bared fangs.

The moment the blade penetrated her heart, the glamour was broken, though none seemed to notice except myself. The creature had brown scales like brittle autumn leaves wherever its stunted, gnarled limbs protruded from its Gibson Girl disguise. Its head was almost more crocodilian than serpentine, the tapered, underslung jaw with its outgrown and recursive fangs a sad travesty of a once-mighty species whose empire on earth had seen the rise and fall of the dinosaurs. She had walked among humans for a lifetime, despising us and dreaming of our extinction. She almost lived to see the return of her ancestors from out of the mists of pre-history. She almost insured that one of them would inhabit the body of the most famous man in America.

Before I could let her fall, Lt. Col. Roosevelt stepped forward and drew his cavalry saber. We rallied round him and drew our own weapons, awaiting his order. But Roosevelt said nothing as he chopped Captain Helps' hand cleanly off just above the wrist.

None of the others seemed to take notice as he pivoted and chopped at Helps' neck. The wild blow had every ounce of the bull-necked officer's weight behind it, yet the blade still lodged in the captain's vertebrae. Roosevelt staggered over the falling body as he wrenched his blade free. The rest of us spread out into a circle with our knives or machetes given to us by the hissing, growling crowd.

One of the dubious gifts of my condition is that I am immune to hypnosis. But I was alone in a circle of sleepwalkers.

What went through each man's mind as he turned on his comrades was impossible to guess, yet each used his natural skills to defend himself or eliminate the competition as if in a dream of battle. Scovill lunged into Kiesling and Van Patten with a knife in each fist. Van Patten fell with a blade lodged in his cheek, machete waving. Kiesling fumbled at his empty holster, but his other hand windmilled crazily with a bowie knife, keeping Scovill, the champion boxer, at bay until Van Patten waded into it, taking the knife to the chest and burying his machete in Kiesling's forehead.

Scovill turned to seek another enemy and walked into Heslop's knife, which sheathed up to its hilt just below his navel. Scovill struggled and came unzipped, stumbling on the seemingly endless stream of his own viscera as he strangled Heslop to death.

Roosevelt slewed across the improvised arena with his saber up, clearly crossing the floor to me. I was looking at him and sizing him up when DeVore showed more initiative than I gave him credit for and stabbed me in the back.

The knife skated across my right shoulder blade and snagged in my woolen outer blouse. Taking as much care as I could, I struck him in the belly to break his resolve, then buffeted him about the head until he went down.

In the meantime, Roosevelt had executed Scovill, running him through just below the sternum. Incredibly, he had discovered a natural aptitude with the cumbersome ceremonial sword, a butcher's easy confidence with meat and steel.

What did he see, as he waded through us with his saber flashing and jets of blood splashing in his face like hot red rain? Did he see his hated, cowardly Spaniards with their green coats and detestable smokeless powder? Did he see monsters, phantoms of the demons who manipulated us, or loathsome apparitions of his sickly childhood? Or did he see us as we were, as men entrusted to his care in the brotherhood of arms, men whom some whispering forked-tongued voice had told him were obstacles in his path to greatness?

No others stood between us, the rest insensate, dead or dying at our feet. The savage mob pressed closer. I took up a machete and weighed the possibilities of stopping this dreadful charade. None of those who had bathed in the vapors from the orb were close enough, and they seemed not to be the prime movers, in any case. It was the unguessably ancient black orb which held sway now, as it had wielded influence to have itself dragged across the ocean floor and delivered to this benighted backwater on the eve of a great upheaval, where their alien nature would attract little attention until they could seize power. And yet they were bottled up within the sphere, just as those I had glimpsed in that fleeting vision kept some presence of enormous power as an engine for their experiments in alchemy and magic. The spherical prison was so charged with energy by the souls of those sacrificed to it that those trapped within were able to escape in immaterial form to somehow take possession of a fit human body.

It was to win this dubious prize that the assembled snake-worshippers and deluded occultists had come from around the globe; and it was for the sake of this privilege that Lt. Col. Roosevelt came charging at me with his saber upraised and a barbaric Knickerbocker roar on his blood-flecked lips.

Just then, I heard a moan, and a familiar voice called my name. I turned to see DeVore lift himself up on one arm and peer blearily about him through blood from his lacerated scalp.

The distraction left me vulnerable when Roosevelt hit me. I feinted to my left to draw his swing away from his body and tackle him, but with a dexterity that belied his empty, impassioned gaze, he anticipated me and swung for my head. The stroke would have split my skull if I had not deflected it. The knife in my hand was inadequate for such a maneuver, so I threw out my arm at such an angle that the saber pierced my forearm and sheathed itself neatly between the radius and ulna.

Before shock could overwhelm me, I let my arm absorb the swing and twisted it to wrench the saber from Roosevelt's hands. Overextended, he stumbled into me as I turned and brought up my knee so that his own weight drove him into it hard enough to inflict a concussion. A twist of the leg and his neck could've easily broken before he hit the ground, but DeVore cried out, "No!"

I nearly lost my lights from the pain of removing the sword. Hefting it in my other hand, I moved to protect DeVore. He ordered me to stop, to protect Roosevelt from the thugs skulking forward to drag him away. The other dead men were already gone into the pit. "You save me, you're just saving trash. I hate him the way nothing hates everything, but Teddy, he's got to survive this. You carry him out of here, or I'll make you sorry...."

His rank aside, he could order me to take any action that did not violate the letter of the terms of my contract. Roosevelt lay at my feet. He would presumably regain his wits when he awoke, but what DeVore said about Roosevelt also made this entire contest an empty, deadly charade.

I could not protect both men. There could be only one way to derail the serpents' plan. The circle of the elect stood vapidly, not quite in possession of the alien faculties they had usurped. Swinging the cavalry saber to clear a path, I advanced on the altar. They began to chant another name, but made no move to stop me. There was no need.

As I drew close enough to touch them with steel, I heard DeVore shout my name, and turned back in time to see him hurled into the snake pit. I could not have saved him even if I had thrown myself after him. Falling, he convulsed and went limp as if snuffed out by a seizure, so that what struck the floor of the pit to be attacked by maddened vipers was only untenanted flesh.

Before me lay the altar, and the sphere. Its surface was like deeply grooved obsidian, hot enough to raise blisters on my palms. Its heat beneath my hands, however—indeed, my hands themselves—vanished in a torrent of green vapor.

As before, the vapors seemed to draw me downward into a whirlpool, at the bottom of which I sensed another sphere that glowed deep, dull red. To pull against that gravity would have been impossible, if I was a stranger to travel outside the body. As it was, I could barely resist the current of magical force which transmitted the naked, flaming souls of those sacrificed into the red sphere which the serpent mages kept within their own prison. Entombed by their own wizardry, they hoped to escape and leave behind the captive abomination that had fueled their eternal research.

I fought free of the current and sought out the one location familiar to me in this strange place—the body I had momentarily contacted when first exposed to the exhalations of the sphere.

It was suddenly *there*, suddenly and completely *me*, and this time it was no hallucination, for the mind, the spirit, the soul, of the creature which had been born into this body had departed just as I entered. To the disorientation of entering a body and a brain and seizing its organic processes to serve, indeed, to *be*, oneself was added the horror indescribable of suddenly finding oneself unmanned and utterly inhuman. It is a tribulation I would not wish upon many of my enemies.

My time was short, for even as I took possession of this strange form, my own memories and sense of self were disintegrating and blowing away like so much smoke. Fighting to hold on to something of myself, I had at the same time no choice but to ransack the cold, strangely chambered brain for memories, for the key to the prison before me lay somewhere within. I have never studied nor practiced black magic, but this much I have learned from bitter experience: that some entities which may not be destroyed or contained may yet be bound utterly if the spell of containment includes the true name of the prisoner.

Somewhere within that fever-swamp of a reptilian brain, somewhere inches short of believing myself a serpent, I found that name.

Opening my eyes, I beheld my brethren, those who yet awaited evacuation. The rest lay spent and empty around the perimeter of the triangle, the sphere within it glowing a sullen, brooding red, yet in its insatiable hunger the entity encased within could not escape for devouring those sacrifices which the foolish hominids had seen fit to feed them. I looked about me at the citadel of basalt spires, once the highest seat of knowledge in all of the northern supercontinent that humans called Laurasia. And I beheld with a surge of venom in my glands the empty, false green sky of the demesne that had entombed the citadel of the Ouroboros in the earliest days of shaggy, devious, thieving proto-humanity.

I looked down at the gnarled scales on my forelimbs, etched with incunabula and alchemical formulae, and at my slippered nether limbs and the luminous border of orichalcum dust circumscribing the seething red sphere which contained a larval Outer God.

I closed cloudy nictitating membranes over my cataract-pitted eyes and chanted the name, even as I stretched out my slippered foot and scratched a break in the line around the red sphere.

In the space of that naming, the red sphere ceased to exist and its contents materialized and crushed us. The citadel was suddenly and completely flattened, every cubic inch of the prison which was a world to us filled to bursting with the body of a god.

And I?

I was cast out of my body and there was only the one I had set free and all of us within it forever, until someone called my name.

And the vapors took me away and suddenly I lay in the arms of Lt. Col. Roosevelt, and the world was on fire.

I sat up and touched my face and closed my eyes and searched myself inside and out and found no one else ... The one who had presumably come to usurp my body was nowhere to be found, much as I expected. Under even the best of circumstances, my body is not a pleasant place to be.

Roosevelt sheepishly offered me a canteen. "So glad one of you survived, or no one would believe me...."

"I'll never tell," I said.

Looking around him with pinched fear and bewilderment on his face, he finally, gratefully nodded.

We lay on a sandbar in the marshy lagoon near the snake-worshippers' compound, now ablaze and thoroughly demolished by our dynamite gun. A full troop circulated between the swamp and the hotel at the far end of the lagoon, lit up in ghastly red-orange relief by the blazing wreck of the *Nykøbing*. Sgt. Hull went down a line of prisoners, forcing them to repeat some quickly whispered test. "*Ka nama kaa lajerama,*" he urgently whispered and a moment later, the one who failed to repeat it was executed.

As he meditated upon what little of the event he remembered, the lieutenant colonel's characteristic lusty grin became a sour mask of utter dejection. All his life, he had craved action and adventure and risked all to decisively prove himself a man by defending his life under fire. Now, he looked upon his hands with a headless but galloping horror of something they had done that he could not, and must never, remember.

"Those degenerate bastards won't live to regret it," he finally said, "but I certainly will...."

He did not elaborate, and it did not occur to me until much later that no one subjected Lt. Col. Roosevelt to Sgt. Hull's test.

I thanked him and turned to make my way back into the swamp when I was ambushed and assaulted by a naked black Cuban who threw himself at me and screamed a mad jumble of Spanish while waving his arms high over his head. I was unarmed but in no serious danger, a shot rang out and the man fell at my feet, gasping out insanity to the last breath.

I thanked Roosevelt again and made my way to the ruined compound where, with much risk and sacrifice, I was able to secure the portion of my charge demanded by the letter of the contract. It pained me then, and pains me still, to fail in my task, for I am not allowed to fail. But I was yet able to return every last hair upon the head of Master DeVore in much the same condition they were in when they left New York.

As to the first order ... The official records show that Lt. Hamilton DeVore served with distinction at Las Guasimas and San Juan Hill, but succumbed to and died from malaria during the siege of Santiago. Let the official record show that he was never touched by a Spaniard.

Though Lt. Col. Roosevelt was fluent in French and no doubt could command a horse in German and follow the thread of an Italian opera, he apparently knew not a word of Spanish, or he might have had a moment's pause before he shot the black who accosted me on the sandbar.

Amid the desperate babbling, which seemed to come from two mouths at once, I heard the Negro say, "Thank God it's you, Cameron ... It's like a nightmare ... Please wake me up! Don't look at me like that, old man; you've got to believe it's me, I'm *Hamilton DeVore....*"

MYSTERIOUS WAYS

BY C.J. HENDERSON

"God moves in a mysterious way
His wonders to perform."
—William Cowper

SEVERAL MILLENNIA AGO

T he centurion could not believe his eyes. His men, hardened Roman troops that had survived a score of campaigns, being defeated by bare-assed savages. Roman armor, covered in blood, bodies of the Empire being trampled in the mud. The rain coming in endless torrents, blinding the troops, shielding the naked enemy. The horror of it was almost beyond his comprehension.

As he strained to gain some measure of control, his soldier's brain pieced together what must have happened. The savages had been clever—far more clever than they had even been given credit for. Their attack could not have been a thing of luck. The world did not work by coincidence. No—they had studied their enemy, figured out when the Roman days of festival and worship were. They had watched for a changing of leaders—his arrival signifying someone new in charge, possibly untested, not yet familiar with his men or the land and its people, ignorant of the situation—and then …

All they had needed to do was wait for the rain.

As his mind roared against the insanity of what he was seeing, the damnable natives continued to move like ghosts behind the drenching sheets. The walls had been breached before anyone had known there was anything wrong. And now, the hordes poured over them, screeching their heathen blather—

"Stop thinking about *how* it happened," the back of the centurion's mind snapped at him. "Think about what you're going to do *now*."

Turning his head from side to side, the soldier glanced about himself, turning his attention from the reality of the battle, looking for … something. Something overlooked, something extra, something beyond, something that could possible turn the tide. And then, a whisper from the back of his brain focused his attention on the thin strands of incense smoke rising from the fort's simple temple.

Instantly the centurion began to sprint for the home of the gods. Dodging his way through the battle as if his life were charmed, he slammed the doors open and threw himself inside. Racing to the altar in the center of the structure, he dropped onto his knees before it, intoning as loudly as he could:

"Save us! Turn this battle to your children. Do not allow these blue-painted savages to drive the might of Rome from this wretched isle."

The soldier stopped to catch his breath, his mind exploding, wondering at what game he thought he was playing. Did he really expect his weak prayers to be answered? He had no sacrifice. He knew not the proper entreaties. He was no priest. His place was with his men—

But then, before he could do further, a voice sounded within his brain in all the languages he knew.

You would decide who lives and dies?

The centurion did not understand the question. Surely what he heard within his mind, unless he had gone mad, was indeed the voice of one god or another. Not knowing what else to do, he answered as best he could.

"I would see my men spared, and the honor of Rome spared. I care not what happens to me."

There was silence for a long moment, a time filled with the sounds of further screams from without. Then, suddenly there was silence. Even the rain seemed to evaporate, not daring to interrupt the suddenly commanded quiet. As the soldier blinked, wondering at what was happening, the voice spoke again.

Your men are spared. The honor of Rome is saved. And you …

As the centurion pressed a hand against his scalp, forcing the water from his hair, the voice concluded in a grinning tone—

You care not what happens to you.

NOW

Harold peered out of his kitchen window, staring out over his garden. Doing so always lifted his spirits. Over the years, he decided as he studied his handiwork, he had become quite the talented gardener. Not fancy, not wildly original, not creating the kind of landscapes that made people pull out their cameras. But still—good.

His was a quiet style. Strong, but understated. Full, but uncluttered. He knew where to put color, which plants to place in direct sunlight, where and how to utilize shade, when to crowd and when to display—

"Face it, Harry," he said quietly, allowing himself the smallest of satisfied grins, "you know what you're doing."

There were birds in the garden that morning. Seeing them utilize the three separate water spots he had created always pleased him. Of course, they were only the usual little brown balls of personality-less feathers. Never a blue jay or a cardinal. Not anymore. There had been a time he would see something colorful splashing about or feeding in his garden every day. But it had been, oh, so many years since all the beautiful species had been driven out by the hundred-and-seven look-alike browns. Dull. Common. Ordinary—

Still, better than nothing, he supposed. Even when beauty flees, life goes on.

As he lifted his coffee cup to his lips once more, Harold found he had already drained it. The event was no surprise. He had done such before. He had been retired for so long that simply staring out the window at his garden could make an entire day pass. What else is there to do, really?

He knew many could find much to complain about in their lives, but to do so was not in his nature. Harold knew his strengths and he knew his weaknesses. He had lost any trace of notions such as amassing wealth or any kind of power long ago. He was past the age where sexual conquests held any attraction for him. Certainly he still enjoyed women—their company on occasion; staring at this or that one that might revive some long-ago memory. But bothering with the idea of pursuit, all the games needed to arrive at the final intimacy, well … frankly … the idea bored him. Too much effort. Too little return. He had plenty of memories. Any more, looking was just fine.

Just like his garden.

Not that he would not put effort forth for his garden. There, he was still a workhorse. There, he could bring to the fore a reserve of effort as he could for nothing else. His well-groomed half-acre was his chance to still give something to the world. He had no inflated ideas about his contribution, of course. There was no denying his garden was small, and unknown to the overwhelming majority of human beings. But it was beauty that he gave to all who cared to view it. It was quiet and peace and at the very least oxygen which he gave to all freely—

C. J. Henderson

Even the usual little brown balls of personality-less feathers.

Harold chuckled at the thought. He must not be a very terrible person, he told himself, if he was willing to tolerate even—

And then, his mind froze. Every thought drained from him, his blood freezing within his veins. A dread anticipation flashed across his mind. Time split in uncountable fragments. He saw his coffee cup slip from his fingers, saw himself clutching it so tightly he broke its handle, watched himself hurl it against the window—more.

Far more.

Harold knew, with the certainty of a man watching losing dice roll toward the end of the table, that there was about to be a knock at his door. His body felt the wood of his floor scream as memory of its life as trees flooded through it, the recall of its savage reduction to planks and sawdust filling his home with agony. The smell of shattering eggshells flooded his mind, their uncomprehending failure to protect the life within them screaming about the unfairness of the universe. Outside, his garden fell into shadow, an utterly alien blanket of purple and hissing green that burned his grass and left all the brown birds choking.

And then, as the walls began to close in, sliding toward him, chanting in the low voices of all the world's forgotten structures, as Harold's eyes ran with tears, after some five seconds of agonizing anticipation … the knock he was expecting came at his door.

Two sharp raps of his door-knocker.

Both of exactly the same volume and intensity. Perfectly separated by the exactly correct amount of time. Distinct. Memorable. Unmistakable.

Harold did not answer the summons. He knew there was no need. His visitor would show himself in. It always did. His spirit drained, the colors of his vision reduced to nothing but grays, he collapsed into one of his kitchen chairs. Waiting.

"Harry, my dear boy, you're looking absolutely splendid."

The Crawling Chaos had returned.

"I love what you've done with the outside, so neatly cultivated, so orderly, so above question—"

Harold hung his head, unable to look up. He could not wonder at why such was happening to him again. He knew. It was his fault. Everything that happened to every man was their own fault. That was the problem with being born; it was just asking for trouble.

"Harry, Harry, Harry," said the tall, rake-thin shadow making its way into the kitchen, "such negativity. One would think you weren't happy to see me."

"It is … a mixed blessing."

The shape still several feet from Harold's table grinned with smug satisfaction. Extending a part of itself stable enough to pull the chair opposite Harold's out from the table, the thousand-faced horror curdled its way around and onto the seat, positioning the amount of it which it had oozed into that particular dimension neatly across from its host.

"So, Harry, old top, how have you been? Tell me everything. I simply *have* to know."

Harold sat, silent, eyes still downcast, his hand still holding his empty coffee cup. *It wasn't fair*, he thought. *It had been so long ... I was so certain it was over. It has to be over—how can it not be over ...*

"Harry," answered the slightly out-of-phase form across the table from him, "really, now. You know it's never over, or, more correctly, I supposed, that it's never *going* to be over. That's not the way it works."

There was no anger within Harold, no possibility of resistance or even some form of cynical contempt. What could he do? He was, after all, merely a man, a finite sack of sinew and bone and various fluids, more helpless against the thing in his kitchen than a three-legged ant that he might discover on his counter would be against him.

"Is it?"

Like it always did, his mind went back to the horrible night in Britain, the storm all about, the smell of blood strong enough to mask that of the rain and mud and sweat. He remembered every detail, every minute fragment of word and scent and noise. He remembered his prayers, so heartfelt, so sincere, and honest enough that they touched the gods. Or at least, whatever his guest that morning actually was.

"You know what I am, Harry," said the thing so comfortably entwined within his brain, "I am that to which you prayed so long ago. I am the only voice in all the universe that was willing to answer your ever-so-noble plea. I am that to which you pledged yourself. That to which you owe your existence. I am all, my dear little Harry, all you shall ever need, and all you shall ever know."

"Wraps it up neatly, doesn't it?"

"He speaks!" Nyarlathotep clapped its hands with joy, a seemingly honest reaction to Harold's words. A wide smile breaking open the deeply tanned face the Crawling Chaos had finally chosen, it said, "Wonderful. Oh, my dear little Harry. You are ever so kind to me in my eternal loneliness."

"What do you want from me?"

For a moment, the thousand-faced god went silent, head held high, body pulling back slightly, mouth now a grim straight line. Tilting its head slightly, the thing across the table from him told Harold:

C. J. Henderson

"I suppose I want ... well, Harry, what I always want."

"But ... it's been so long. So long, this time ... I thought, I mean ... you—"

"Ohhhhhh," came a noise one not familiar with the thing there at the table might mistake for sympathy, "I understand. You thought your days of service were over. That you had done *enough* ... is that it?"

"It's been more than three-quarters of a century," shouted Harold, his spine stiffening ever so slightly—ever so recklessly. "How long does this service last? What's more, when ... what ... what do you want?"

Harold's retort had started out strong, his voice level and growling. By the end, however, it was not much more than a frightened whine. He had thrown all the defiance he had been able to build up over the decades, and it had petered out on him in less than fifteen words. The reality of his weakness washed over him, was felt by his guest as well.

"Oh, my poor, poor Harry. First, you had to know you were still in my service. Look at yourself, not a day older since last we saw each other. Not a wrinkle, not an ounce of fat, not a worry in the world. You knew I would return, didn't you?"

"Yes ..." admitted the near-sobbing man in a low and pitiful whisper.

"Fine, since we've established that much, let us go all the way. Tell me, Harry, the answers to all your questions. Prove to me that you're a clever monkey. Why am I here? What do I want?" Nyarlathotep went silent for a moment, then a hiss that came from all directions demanded, "Tell me, Harry."

The frightened man, knowing the inevitable conclusion of their meeting, bowed his head, breaking eye contact with the Crawling Chaos so as to be able to speak at all. Grinding his teeth together for a moment, finally he said, "I'm your connection to this world.... I mean, one, one of your connections. You can't—can't do more than influence things here—"

"Yet," corrected the boiling mass steaming on the other side of the table. Harold nodded in agreement, echoing:

"Yes, yet. Of course. Someday, but for now, you need ... agents ... here. Those to make your decisions."

"Oohhhhh, so long my fingers reach inside your skull, and still ..." Nyarlathotep shook what appeared to be its head at the moment, then whispered, "you do not make *my* decisions, Harry. You make your own. I give you choices, and you make your own decisions."

Harold felt waves of conflicting emotion creeping across his brain, urges to scream, to beg, to cry. One by one, he asked himself—what would he scream? For what would he beg? As the tears he could not argue away began to wash his cheeks, he nodded in agreement and continued.

"I called out for someone to help me, my men ... so long ago. You came to our aid. Now ... since I ... took it upon myself to decide who would live, and who would die ... I have become the eternal referee. Whenever you want to ... I don't know what to call it ... play, perhaps, with humanity ... you work through me. You appear—"

"As I have now ..."

"Yes ... you're here," Harold said, as if just suddenly at that moment realizing what the appearance of Nyarlathotep actually meant. "You're *here* ..."

The weeping man shuddered, his body pulling in on itself until it seemed to have lost a third of its mass. Pitifully, he asked, "There's a war somewhere, isn't there?"

"Harry, you're a human being. There is always a war going on somewhere in your miserable little world. Most of them don't interest me. Look at how long it's been since I was last here. If I needed you to make a decision about every war your planet spawned, why ... you'd be asking for overtime."

As the Crawling Chaos chuckled to itself, Harold shuddered in horror. It was coming again. He would be shown combatants along with their battlefields, and he would be expected to choose the winners and the losers. Mountains of bodies, lakes of blood, all his responsibility. And he would be kept alive, eternally young and fit, to wait for the next time he would be needed.

Most of the time he could ignore the terrible truth of his longevity, the price he paid for every breath. But, he asked himself, what else could he do? It had not been his doing. He had not asked for anything but the lives of his soldiers—

"And why did you do that?"

Nyarlathotep's question dug beneath his skin, stinging Harold, making him squirm. He could lie to himself, decade after century after millennia, but he could not lie to the thing across the table from him. How, after all, do you lie to something within your own brain?

He had not been lying to himself. He had been begging for the lives of his men so long ago in the rain ... but his visitor knew the truth. He had done so out of shame—out of fear. Their deaths would have meant embarrassment for him, his family. To lose his first command, to have them slaughtered out from under him, only weeks after he arrived on the cursed British shore—

Harold shuddered. He thought on what would have happened to his family. All they would have lost. Of course, he would have been long dead by the time anyone in Rome heard of what had happened, which, when he was honest, was what had actually terrified him. Death—

C. J. Henderson

Death—

"Oh, my poor little Harry, perhaps I've kept you at this for too long. Maybe I've been cruel, keeping your tiny human mind and soul functioning for so long."

As Harold looked up, the thing across from him was completely unstable. Swirls of orange vapor revolved around a floating golden and black striped central oval of flesh, one covered in a hair of tiny eight-fingered arms, all of them clutching and unclutching without rhythm. Small shards of burning ice dripped from the impossible shape, hissing as they shattered against Harold's kitchen floor.

"Maybe you were not built for a service so extensive," the mass emitted, a tone of giggling concern coating its words. "Perhaps it would be compassionate of me to allow you to finally expire. Tell me—"

Harold trembled at the notion. Never did he think his duties would ever be fulfilled. There had never before been such a hint. "Would you like to die?"

So many hundreds upon hundreds of years. So many wars. So many peoples delivered into that which waited beyond the veil. By his hand. By his choice. Decisions made without malice, without prejudice. This one or that one. One from column A or one from column B. The e'ne, me'ne, mi'ne, moe of uncaring destruction.

Billions of lives over the millennia. Billions.

"Would you, Harry?"

Like the last time. World War II. His choice had been about how Hitler would deal with the Jews. The Führer himself, during *Kristallnacht*, had made certain those of the Hebrew faith were driven into the streets—ruined. But not killed. What came later, the camps, the gas, the ovens, the gold teeth harvested, the lamp shades made of human skin, the soap made of human fat—

"Would you?"

That had been Harold's choice. When asked, without hesitation, knowing he was sending millions to their deaths, he had not stopped to weigh their coming horror and pain against his own passing.

"No …" Harold answered weakly. "No … I wouldn't."

He had picked the Jews for death, adding in the gypsies and all the rest on his own, because he thought it rounded things out nicely.

"Excellent," whispered the Crawling Chaos, its tone one well-pleased. Without hesitation, Nyarlathotep unfolded the current conflict which interested it so. And, as always, Harold listened attentively, preparing to make his choice, all the while thinking of his garden, wishing that someday the cardinals might return.

MAGNA MATER

BY EDWARD MORRIS

1
"THEN ON YOUR NAME SHALL WRETCHED MORTALS CALL …"

wo hours' drive from the Front by Jeep, the dark French hills rise wild with barbed wire, and thin grows the veil between Earth and the godless Deep. Five geologic points ring the black flame-tip of a veritable esoteric iceberg, shadowy woods full of fragments of a vaster tapestry as the bloody battles it memorializes are retold with its remains as audience.…

On this cold, snowy morning past, at ten sharp, my employer's empty coffin was laid to rest here in the frosty, pre-dug ground of our own churchyard. We paid well to do it this way, and there were no hitches whatsoever. All of Rennes-le-Chateau breathed a sigh of relief, and went about its other affairs.

There have been much bigger headlines, of late, even sixty-five kilometers from the Front. Both sides are trying to dig in and not actually wipe out the other. That's not why they're here. Not yet, anyway. Things have to get a little more insane.

And they will. I know that my blood knows that. But not just now.

My dear, dead mother taught me that the secret to keeping any form of employment is to make oneself utterly indispensable at it. For years, I have done so. I have sacrificed. And I have become the position.

Those German deserters came sucking and grinning around here again, leaving their tracks in the mud and their dog-end cigarettes everywhere. Nothing escapes my notice, on these grounds. I saw the map sticking out of their tail-end Charlie's pocket, the feeble-minded one who picks his nose. The X on every map marked a different spot. It would have been funny. Truly. Truly.

Truly. Not much goes on for miles that escapes my ears, my eyes, my scrying.

Pride, I know. An old woman's pride in her co-collection: the ancient paper books with their bright colors we kept below stairs, with covers which were sometimes recopied in calligraphy or woodblock-press where the old typeface might have occasionally fallen away. *De Vermis Mysteriis. The Pnakotic Manuscripts. Biblia Titanica.*

And the eldest, the special one, bound in human skin. The so-called *Book of Nicetas*, the Lost Book of the Cathars, written by a madman somewhere in the Fertile Crescent. The book that Father and Brother Alfred both said could only be opened on Judgment Day. The Bishop of Carcassone, the Abbé's immediate superior, had taken that one off the hands of a Diabolist named Alphonse-Louis Constant, who called it "beyond control."

All the old books, buried against the final fall of darkest Night. I will miss the fun we had, all we did. But now we have built our Dream, and I must follow my Teacher soon.

Je me souviens. So many memories, in and out of those old books. The cellar we dug for them was quite a team effort. That other priest helped, and his occasional dashing Mystery Guest.

Abbé Boudet, tall and distractible, had been a miner or some such awful thing when he was a boy, and really knew how to swing a pickaxe. He was different when he worked, more hard-put than the lanky, distractible bookworm who came stork-walking over here about every third or fifth sunset with his nose buried in some old phantasy or philosophy as he made the trek from Rennes-les-Bains for their little nightly chats.

Sometimes he did not come alone, or on shank's mare. Sometimes the mare was in fact a pair of geldings coal-black as night, hooked to a phaeton driven by a fellow of Eastern extraction for the Aegyptian fellow … or was he Somali? My memories of that scholar are somewhat cloudy. Perhaps with good reason.

I loved Nyarlah, as the black man graciously pronounced his name for me. It was like having a seven-foot *djinn* in our own parlor, muttering and croaking about hollow pillars and pentagonal geometry and the way that Westerners will believe anything you tell them. It was grand to listen to him talk in that accent, *mais bien!* But that courtly ifrit exterior masked something I only saw once:

╤9ᘓᗅ9

We had another irregularly regular guest who was often far less than regular, or welcome. The Abbé's twin brother Alfred, who'd went to seminary school in other parts, who could have been Berenger … Father, excuse me, Father's twin, but for the lighter hair and the different lines about his face. (Most of the lines in Father's face are laugh-lines; his brother's, the opposite, and burst capillaries in the cheeks and nose. *Très chic.* Good riddance to the sot.)

Father Alfred … for I respect the ordination, if not the individual … was over even more often than Boudet. At most social matters outside of the duties of his calling, the man was a cock-up. If he didn't write it down, he forgot it. Drove me up the wall, half the time he was around. It was like trying to have a conversation with a child.

His brother told me once in confidence over tea that he could count on his twin for about four or five things, constantly. "Mostly matters of *realpolitik* between dioceses, the kind we deal with now as the Pharisees try to drum me out of my collar," was how he put it. Which certainly explained Alfred's constant presence in the past few weeks. That silver-tongued devil was always underfoot, sucking up the fine Charteuse liqueur, and worse.

But there was a line Alfred crossed, and he did it to himself. I remember the day the good Father came home at ten in the morning to the rectory, with graveyard dirt and blood under his nails and tombstone chips in his hair.

꞊9ͼ꓾9

The kitchen door in the rectory tended to bang loudly shut. It was badly hung. I thought I'd left it open. When I came out into the kitchen, Alfred was standing there with his hair gone mostly white and fingernail-tracks in his cheeks, laughing and crying at the same time. I waited, my plain black apron covered in flour. Behind my back, the marble rolling-pin also awaited its orders. I had none for it.

"The keys," he moaned to no one in particular, across the parlor sunbeams where he saw no one stand at first, just the tall shadow that made me wince where I stood over in the kitchen doorway. "I can't find one of the damned keys. This is all wrong."

He was too worldly for his brother's work. He got too out of control. Nyarlah slithered through the parlor, and cocked a leathery arm around Alfred's broad shoulders.

"You went downstairs," he said in that voice that had nothing wrong with it and everything wrong at the same time. That rich upright bass of beauty and abomination measure for measure and equal. He sat himAlfred down like a baby on the divan, the way a minder would in a tavern with someone who didn't need any more down their neck.

Alfred's eyes were fogged, vacant. Nyarlah snapped two bony pink-brown fingers in front of his eyes and barked something in a language I didn't know.

"*Allons-y!*" he continued, more jokingly. "You found the stairway down. Down to the squared circle."

Alfred grimaced, eyes at the toes of his plain black brogans, looking like he was swimming up from a black and poisoned tarn. "Knew about that.... Try not to go near. Try to stay out of ..." He essayed at an ironic smile in the direction of the black man's smooth, round pate. "Your hair. Sir." The smile was all gone. "I. I. I. Ha. You. Work for the Germans, too. You're ... the Devil. You work for ... everyone."

Nyarlah smiled. It just made my skin crackle. "What else?" he said, in a voice that poured water over Father Alfred's mouth and nose, and made him sit up.

Alfred was looking into Nyarlah's strange eyes. It made me a bit weak in the knees. But to Alfred, it was doing something else.

Something else indeed.

"I ... don't remember. I don't ... The way down. I found all sorts of ... other rooms, and other ... stones, the more I tried to dig up. But there weren't ... keys in any of them, not the way I heard my idiot brother ... on about ..." He sighed long and heavily. "It made sense. I thought it did. If I followed the five most prominent headstones, the way he hinted at in his journal, then ..."

I had to butt in. "Idiot. Who taught you to read Latin? And you went to seminary school."

Both of them looked at me. "*Claviculae* is a metaphor in that usage. First of all, you had no business looking in the Abbé's own diary; for shame. But ..." I took a breath. "If you had any understanding of the nuances in the language, what he was saying was that the only things *like* keys he can find are in the five oldest books here in the house. The ... special books. How did you get ..."

I had to stop and think. I was shuffling Latinate roots in my head, trying to imagine how even Alfred could have gone off on such a tangent. But Nyarlah was shushing me with those eyes, bidding me to fade back.

"Unimportant," he began, as I moved back toward the kitchen door like a good housekeeper, trying to go find something to pretend to do.

When I came back in, Alfred was screaming. Nyarlah had those gigantic hands on both sides of Alfred's pale, bloated face and he was sucking, sucking, *sucking* something out of his mouth and nose that looked like snot at first, then black smoke, then wavering snow. Snow made of light, sparks, Impressionist sparks that all stayed one muted, drunken color.

We had the walking remains committed in Paris. It cost the Earth, but better to keep it out of the papers. The Abbé and I had several little 'come-to-Jesus meetings' about the matter, you may rest assured.

Father worked right up to the bell, as the schoolchildren used to say. Even while stripped of his duties, there was a need for priests, with a war on. Father continuing to say masses for the troops kept up our own front. It kept many different sorts of eyes away from what we were really doing. What we've just finished, and I can finish up for myself with my own Change....

"What I found were brought here by Arab spice-traders after the fall of Atlantis. Dear Marie, my contemporary, my friend, my hands and eyes, they are the sigils of the very goddess who lives beneath these hills ... Tsathoggua. *La mère des crapauds.*"

But I was nodding at every little godlet in the glass case. "I have seen these before, *Père*. My family in this valley predate the Roman colonials' discovery of the Old People in the caves. I know my history ..."

I think those words again. Ecclesiastes tells us that there is nothing new under the sun, and that there are a time, season and purpose to all things. Even, perhaps, the gravest annoyances.

This is not the first time treasure-hunters ... or Beasts ... have come to the Abbey. When I drew the curtain in the rectory, of course they came up to the front door and knocked, pretending to have just arrived.

"Ah, the good housekeeper greets us. Marie-*chère*!" Colonel Rauffenstein oozed at me in execrable French from behind the latch chain. The white officer's gloves he wore were not stained with the blood of the hart. He was out of breath. A vein stood out in the side of his pasty, stubbly head, snaking out from under his cap like the tentacle of some sea-beast. "*Mlle*. Denarnaud—"

"Call me Miss again and this old toad tears your throat out," I said softly but clearly in High German. Rauffenstein winced. His two toadies hung back, muttering at each other in Slovak, which they probably thought I couldn't understand.

(It was not God who gave me the gift of tongues. That came more recently, with the memorization of certain verses, the sacrifice of certain kinds of blood, the walking of certain Dreams. As it says in the Book of Hebrews, the substance of the Future, and the evidence behind the Present ...)

"*Cowboy her and let's search the grounds.*"

"This is a house of God, pig. Be silent and listen."

"Oh, God, my foot. Have you heard of some of the—"

"SHUT IT AND LISTEN! Pardonnez-moi, Madame. Je … uhhh, je m'excuse. Continuez …"

I continued at his partner, in Slovak. *"I could kill you where you stand, capon,"* then at the colonel, before the moon-faced lad in his too-large greatcoat had time to gape, "My good Colonel, my dear employer and friend and Father Confessor the Abbé is newly dead, and I fear I am not far behind. He left us last night. His nerves, you see. He worked himself right into a great big heart-attack."

I feigned weariness, letting them see that aspect of my face. Lighting it up, in the ways I could light up other aspects.

It comes from the eyes. It is a gift and a sigil and a telling from the eyes. They began to listen a little more. It wouldn't last, but there is a dance in the old dame yet. I try. They listened while it lasted

"Be reasonable, *meinen herren.* There was no Priory of Sion, no treasure of the Cathars or whatever the version is this week. Every schoolchild knows this hereabouts. We are in mourning, however, and that is quite real enough. Please, show us some respect. I beg. No more. As your wise adjutant points out, this is a house of God."

I spoke the truth. There was going to be quite a Requiem for Abbé Saunière. Quite a Requiem indeed. Those Kraut barbarians needed to keep this abbey clear of their poking noses, and every other part of them. They needed to get back to the front and stay out of our business. *Les Anglais, aussi.* Barbarians on both sides.

There are not very many townsfolk. We all have our common way, when the moon is high, no matter the views we hold. Many have helped us fake this funeral for photographs and the eyes of any outsiders that may stumble in and be eaten at the Wake.

Perhaps, I thought, I would pre-empt that, with those three. Presently, the adjutant gaped at what he thought was my command of Slovak (I'd pulled the meanings from their breath, their minds, the vibrations of their words,) and the colonel blushed to the center of his vast, luminescent pate, which I saw when he removed his hat and stammered apologies. "We come merely to pay our respects, having just in fact heard that—"

My answer, though lengthy, was not in fact ladylike, and does not bear repetition. I made myself understood, and in so doing shooed the big bald jackanapes and his other two stooges from the front porch of the rectory as my peasant mother did with men when she was my age.

While I did, I used some of the same curse words as *Memère*, and that made me marvel at the passage of time and the telling of blood. Blood that will soon change, but is still me. And her. More than I foresaw, that bittersweet mark, so like the kiss of the Sleeper of N'Kai, which all may receive but few in this life even partially undertake.

The Sleeper's kiss that touches the very groundwater in our town, the plants and the soil and the air, and makes us all come together after our own fashion. The way we do out here, particularly Out Here. Not like a church, or a hive of bees, or a squadron of soldiers marching as to war. But like neighbors.

The Bishopric tried to reconsecrate the grounds out here, in the spring. When the toads were out. The Abbé humored their little wishes. They've hauled my employer into court off and on for years, the Bishopric and the schoolmaster and the bill-collectors and the whole lot of them, always trying to get more money, though the gold never ran out and the payments were always on time.

"What of this stairway, beneath the Abbey?" their seconds always sniped, *"The one that goes down, and down, and down, to the vault? The vault full of gold?"*

'Twas not a vault, ever, but only several pieces of a white-gold metal that has no name. Those metal pieces call the gold, never the Ark of the Covenant or Templar nonsense. Only some items found on a ship. Sealed in a cask of mortar in the hold of a ship that sank off the coast of Corsica, and travelled to Rennes.

Sometimes, Father Saunière calls the little godlets Babylonian, sometimes Sumerian. The one that looks almost human, with the same face repeating twice in number, the one with legs and wings and a mouth full of tentacles, calls fish from the rivers and … all sorts of things … from the sea, and blind-robins and eels from the freshwater springs and limestone caves that catacomb this beautiful old Abbey on all sides, into the water table and further toward the center of the Earth. Eels … and trout, trout for days, swimming upstream toward the sound of their Mother's voice.

The other two godlets repeat in the architecture around here with much more frequency. They are twins of the same form, one a reflection of the thing in formless black shadow-shape, and one the thing itself, crouching. Squatting. Croaking.

Father would touch both of them at the same time. In that case, they called more gold, when the right words were said over them, the right obeisances made and powders burnt. The gold showed up in the squared circle, down the stairway they couldn't find. Floating in the freshwater spring in the squared circle of stones. Sometimes it was Spanish doubloons, or Dutch guilders. Sometimes it was melted down. But it always came, when he said that particular rite.

Enough gold has come from that rite to sink the plots of three mansions, one in my name until the public outcry forced a change just as work on the Tour Magdala began in earnest.

At the end of the day, his fellow priests thought he was selling Masses short at twice the price. They called us Communards, and progressives, and anti-government, and everything but a priest and his housekeeper.

But we needed to draw in new parishioners, you see. For the real church, the heresy, the schism which could not manifest. Yet.

Not then. Everyone is distracted now, though. It feels like the Last Times, though I know better. The imaginary countries of the world pour out their hatred down shell-holes through the corpus of their young men. Europe gnaws at its own entrails. Things look outwardly dire.

Every country in the world seems to have forgotten what War meant, going into this one. There hadn't been one of consequence for a century and a half, I dare say. The Fiddler must always be paid.

The August Madness was carefully planned and orchestrated. We turned a regional conflict in the Balkans into the bloodiest, most needless war in human history. But Triple Entente or Triple Alliance, the last thing those great houses want is the dissolution of big countries. Heavens, no.

Humans are worse than any Elder God in our inventiveness. We discovered poison gas, barbed wire and machine-guns, sub-marine and trench warfare and the Bombardier tank, fulfilling the darkest nightmares of Leonardo da Vinci and Jules Verne in blood.

Millions have died. But I know one who cannot. Not now. And I'm next in line....

≠9©∩9

I must have nodded off, just then. I dreamed those damned deserters were camped in the yard, circling, looking for holes in the wall. They more than likely are. My dreams are rarely wrong.

It is night now. The long night after the Working. I must spend a few such long nights here alone. And while I do, I must feed this forward, and be fed in turn.

It will take more wars to wake the Elders with blood. But they stir. And this morning, my employer went to join them. So may I, too. Though tonight will be very long, and this room feels very empty, so may I, too.

The good Father told me that enough sacrifice to Tsathoggua guarantees a return, just as it was done when they called her the Magna Mater and burned peat and sea-coal to her in bronze braziers...

Enough blood, and the land will wake. Enough sacrifice and, like Abbé Saunière, I, too, may change form, and travel far under the earth, to our ancestral home. To the great Mother at the Central Fire ...

I can feel a unit of fresh young *Anglais*, four or five in number, stumbling back to their barracks through the woods. There are a few such units locally. They'll be shipping out soon. Father is gone. I must feed the altar. They'll do.

They'll do.

Now I must begin to call the toads …

In nomine Mater et Fili, et Signum Crocus

In Tsathoggua's name, eternal swampy wellspring

between the circle of five peaks, beneath,

deep. Deep beneath.

Thirteenth. From your eggs of earth and frost,

Make it snow.

Ask your Mother. Ask your Mother.

Make it snow …

Sauvons la caisse, père,

     frère, maître … Ami.

       Chacun pour soi.

Pour toi …

2

AND OFFERED VICTIMS AT YOUR ALTARS FALL

It snowed it snowed it snowed. Like yesteryear. Like home. Like Hope.

On a dark and snowy night on a windswept hillside in northern Gaul where hot springs boiled to the surface through thousands of feet of limestone, a long-in-the-tooth lieutenant named Hodgson teetered on the brink of the nearest steaming pool, plunging his grazed hand in up to the wrist.

The water. The primal water. When can I ever get away from the sea? Every time I get near it, my heart starts to pound. They all love the sea-stories, but they don't understand the impetus.…

Out of turn, out of sequence, he remembered the tentacle snagging his hand with infernal rapidity, forming into a webbed, three-fingered claw of the same perilous stuff, soft as a bog and sharp as edged metal.

Hodgson's scream made rippling echoes for a mile or more, mostly unimpeded. It was more than a little cold. The eyes in the forest may have been wolves. It didn't matter now. He'd saved a round for himself. And the left hand still worked.

It snowed. It snowed. It snowed. Time grayed out for him for a little while

Something had made his brain go foggy. Something he had seen while in his cups. They were just coming back to kip. In their cups. Not even shipped out yet. Then the thing. That fragmented everything like stained glass. Happened.

Happened. The absinthe had numbed him to it at first. He didn't want to

        Edward Morris

remember how. It was … Germans. Deserters, probably. A ragtag and bobtail band of deserters. Had to be.

Had to be. They could have been surrounded. They were a long f-----g way from their CO. And now he was lost.

Lost. The ravine below ate at his eyes. There was a cave, far back there. He was trying to find something to wrap the wound with, knowing it was clean enough now.

Breathing through the pain. From the wound that came from a webbed, swiping claw, and no gun. The webbed swiping claw of something that walked on two legs, lurching up out of the fog, forming from formless ooze.

The perimeter was clear. He withdrew his hand slowly, reaching at his belt for the entrenching-tool that could club, and chop, and most importantly stab, quite handily in field combat. The lieutenant preferred to box, but all was fair tonight. Oh, yes, tonight.

He thought of his Bessie, sitting by the window in the cold morning light before work, the cold January light of home, Merrie Olde England regular as treacle and tap water and nothing … ever … like what he was seeing now.

The fragile meniscus of the hot spring was stirring like bubbles in yeast, tearing into a stump on a neck. Black yeast, undulant, ophidian. Black stump.

Eyes, turning to blip-blip-blink. Gold-ringed eyes with diamond pupils, staring at him with primal malignity. The black spawn reached for him with opposable thumbs and anthropophagic intentions. Terror stole the lieutenant's speech.

But not his boots. When he stopped bolting pell-mell through the woods, he nearly tripped over a tiny stone fountain with some kind of frog sitting in the middle, protruding from the roots of a century oak.

You hallucinated that, the survivor part of his brain told him, the skeptic part that had once tightened the cuffs on the greatest skeptic of them all, Harry Houdini. He'd only started writing fiction because it was what sold. But the fiction was nothing compared to the life that spawned it.

He made himself not let the side down. The sun finished sinking in a welter of blood, and the great shouting, gibbering Dark reared up and whacked him like a hand. He was conscious first of every star overhead; so many, in bands and charts burnt into his eyes from an early age. He was conscious of his place within that Infinite darkness, too, a secret vessel alive and hunting and hunted.

Hunted. He'd breasted that hill and come out in a little stand of trees, and done no more than stand still for a second behind a tree when the … thing … clipped his hand.

His dumb right hand. He made the left one work. He had a copy of the *Roman Ritual* in that pocket. This valley was supposed to be a strange place.

His right hand sure didn't know what his left hand was doing. The bleeding had stopped.

≂9౿ഩᎩ

Out of tune. Out of true. Out of time. The last voice he held in his ears was Private Pegg from their company, grousing about needing a ball of string just to get through two miles of woods. Pegg was so pissed on midnight-requisition Scotch he couldn't have lain down on the ground if one instructed him how, and most of the men weren't much better off.

This was War. These things … happened, no matter what form in which anyone was prepared to accept their coming. But this felt different than Jerry. Worse. Local. Old.

≂9౿ഩᎩ

After a time, he bound the wound again and continued, stumbling on hailstones that were still coming down and headstones that looked too old to be patching the path, at parts, splintered sections of them showing pale knights and pale kings, or complicated Latin poems.

He was thirty-*six*, his brain babbled at him in the extremity of his terror. Too old for the 117th, though he'd passed the Medical Boards on Boxing Day and they were getting ready to ship out to Belgium.…

Out of sequence. His aquiline nose twitched toward the smell of blood. Blood on the leaves. A human handprint. Someone stumbling. *One of them came this way.…* Even as his mind came apart, he kept tracking his comrades, and whatever had taken them. He was an Army lifer. That was just how his kind were made.

There was another handprint up ahead, and lying in the brush … No, not a hand and arm. Yet. Wooden stock … gleam of metal … *Enfield.* The lieutenant crossed himself, and slapped his pocket full of reloads.

Bending down to grab it, the lieutenant reckoned it would have to be broken and cleaned soon. The blood on it stunk of brains, and worse. This did not bode well, but he didn't think about it until there was another end placed on it. At the moment, there was a rifle. And by the reassuring clack-clack, it still worked.

He couldn't stop ruminating. Getting ready to ship out. God d--- it to H---, they weren't even in *combat* yet! He and three of his mates had been coming back to barracks from the *pub!* They saw no one in the woods, and no one met them on the road.

He remembered bits of field-chatter, before that long hour when they walked

259   Edward Morris

through the ring of stones and the fog quit all at once.

"How the Hell far are we from Rheins, sir? We good and noble Knights of Templar appear to have uh beaten back the marauding Visigoth in the immediate uh vicinity, unless the Colonel plans on saving B Company some Kraut snipers to keep things interestin'."

"This valley ain't on any maps, sir, at least not the way the mountains—"

"Shut your noise, Sarge, it bally well is.."

"No, the town is, but the valley … See, look, I …"

But he'd not seen that. He'd seen three of his mates, men he'd trained with, done his Basic with, drank and fought and gotten wounded with, *whisked* up out of the fog by something that squirmed. Something taller than that kind of squirming should support.

No more blood. No more blood to track. When had he lost the trail? It kept starting and stopping.

There were black slime-trails *everywhere*. When Hodgson attempted to make sense of them, his head hurt and he grew sleepy. And he had to sit down.

The black slime, however, began to move. Again. As it had. As it would. Before he touched it. With or without him. When he thought it could not grow any shinier, or thicker, it did, it would.

It grew behind him when he turned his head. It watched him without eyes. The formless spawn of the forest never rested. No matter where he wasn't looking.

It could eat him, if it wanted to. He knew that. It didn't. It had touched him. The formless spawn of the forest touched his skin. It didn't take his flesh. But his mind was changing. Through the tiniest of cracks.

Changing. The forest was talking to him from inside. His brain was squirming. Like a toad. He fought. And fought again. The woods grew thicker and more rampant. Trees had rooted themselves in the road.

He could see a light up ahead, up a low hill in the woods, before a taller hill that was almost a mountain began. There was a cave below the tall building up on the cliff, and blue light poured from it, visible for miles in the slowly-falling snow.

It made the lieutenant tired to look at that light, all of a sudden. Like he wanted to get to that cave, and just lie down. Lie down in the mud. Deep in the mud, and then … swim further down. Too tired to stand, he got on his hands and knees and began to slither, almost hop, to the place where the trees would hide, and the hole in the rock give something like shelter.

But he paused and dared to look back. Of course, there was nothing. As he made his way up the side entrance to the Abbey from the road, the squirming forms showed up everywhere he looked. In the windows. In the cave. Come to pay respects. To welcome him home.

Some of the neighbors wore robes, and masks that looked like wax. He fell into line behind a queue of these, trying not to breathe until he could slink away. As he passed closer to the cave, he saw what looked like a vast and central stairway, museum-like. Temple-like. But the pyramidal steps led down.

He looked at his left hand. Where there'd been a scab, there was now viscous white stuff, almost green, leaking at every knucklebone and joint. The raw bits between the fingers were almost trying to web.

Somewhere, an owl began to hoot. Lt. Hodgson blearily watched the shadows wake and snarl and snap in the strange fungi and undergrowth that crawled up the hill toward the back end of the Abbey. Every shadow seemed to want to lurch forward. The cave whistled with chill breeze, spilling … *Light, a fire that burned pale green, then red, then changing color—*

But as he approached the light in the woods, his vision began to clear, and what he saw was both more and less dire.

᛽ᛉᚳᚩᛁᛁ

I can still hear those *Boche* scum behaving like cuckoos out in the yard. The screams and hooting and wailing and whatnot have mostly stopped, but none of it ever sounded like interpretable language. Not after a while.

The adjutant is eating part of what looks like someone else, and I don't hear the Colonel's other toady carrying on any more.

I can hear the Colonel's nails on the middle parlor window. (There is very little left of those white gloves.) I can see his eyes trying to turn yellow, the skin turning gray. I can hear his labored breathing in the rosebushes.

It is precious to watch him struggle under bufotenine, to watch the life slide down through the veins in his pinched face, thinking it is leaving when it is merely cycling endlessly through the same resistor. Cooking the fear-hot flesh to a turn.

Then: Checkmate. Watching him throw those ruined gloves in the air and wave them around like white flags. In the clearing stands a man only a little taller than Napoleon, a boxer by his stance, a sailor by his equilibrium, a fighter by his eyes that burn from that pretty face as pale as Death. They are assassin's eyes. His hands are nimble white spiders.

"I SURRENDER!" Rauffenstein screams in perfectly accentless English, not that it would have done much good by that point. He's squinting without his monocle, peering off into the woods to the west. I see *my* last toady reflected in the Colonel's eyes, the English looey pale as Death, who takes the higher ground …

POP. POP-POP. POP.

POP. POP. POP.

Edward Morris

POP.

The two remaining deserters buck and slide to a fall, twitch and generally take their time expiring.

Rauffenstein is already feeding the roses in quarts. (I should mulch the one who got eaten, but in the zinnias or the lupines, never the chard.)

The shadow in the woods lowers the Enfield rifle to port arms, and stepped into the light, archaic, ashamed, a pale Britisher with dark hair and spindly hands and eyes that never could be called human. Not inside. Before he ever left Blighty.

As he comes into the yard, I let him see me some more. He looks like a good altar boy, saving an old lady in distress hiding in her house from the awful Teutonic horde. Until I come out from behind the window. And he sees what my eyes look like when this kind of work is afoot.

That I am old, but not remotely in distress. I *am* Distress. And I am no lady, but acolyte and priestess with dirty, callused hands.

I go out into the yard, and bow. And I let him see me call the toads. I let him see me put my head down and make that subaudible sound in the back of my throat.

The lads come quickly. The lieutenant comes no closer, as I permit him to see the lads feeding, then burying their scut in the flowerbeds. It is over very quickly, even the sounds.

I raise my left hand, whose fingers have fused now to but three, and croak a single word. The lads disperse back into the woods.

"Welcome to the black fane, Lieutenant," I call out amiably. "Welcome to the fold." (I can smell where one of the lads bit him.) "Join us?"

When he throws the rifle at me and runs, making an inchoate scream, I know he thinks it is the bravest thing he's ever done. No big loss. I got three. The shell at Ypres will do for Lieutenant Hodgson next year.

He was marked before. The toads are fed for a while. The Work moves on....

᚛ᚕᚌᚔᚏ᚜

It was days before a farmer found him, washed up on a creek bed in Rennes-les-Bains, babbling and unblinking and in severe shock. The locals, long used to such things, said nothing to anyone. There was a new priest in town, and things were as back to normal as they ever got. No need to question another local casualty.

Part of Lt. William Hope Hodgson never made it back from France.

᚛ᚕᚌᚔᚏ᚜

FOR RICHARD STANLEY, CLARK ASHTON SMITH, AND WILLIAM HOPE HODGSON.

DARK CELL

BY BRIAN M. SAMMONS
& GLYNN OWEN BARRASS

1
Prison

In a dog-eat-dog world, Jacob kept to himself for the most part. He didn't fraternize with the other prisoners much, unless it involved getting cigarettes, or sometimes, more intoxicating substances. He had money— correction; he'd *had* money—and now he was in hock to a dealer, and keeping to himself was no longer an option.

John Grout, the man who controlled the drugs in Chapelmoor Maximum Security Prison, stared at Jacob from across the exercise yard, as he had done for the last ten minutes of recreation time. Jacob thought it high time he did something about it.

He stood up from where he had been slouched against the yard wall and approached Grout, placing his hands in his coat pockets as he approached the enemy. After ten years in Army Intelligence, Jacob knew what to do with the enemy, which is why in his left pocket he gripped a headless toothbrush with a sharpened tip.

Grout's two bodyguards, a fat black man and a tall white fellow with heavy, bony features, stepped forward with menace at Jacob's advance.

"Step away, geezer," the black man said in a surprisingly light voice. He clenched his hands menacingly.

"Let him be, boys," Grout said, crossing his tattooed arms over a not-insubstantial chest. "Fella, you come to pay up?" Grout's head was shaved bald, his scalp crisscrossed with scars. Small, mean blue eyes glared at Jacob as he paused before him.

"I got your threats, your messages," Jacob said. "I've come to pay my dues, right now."

Grout dropped his arms. He sneered, revealing a row of gold teeth.

In a split second, Jacob ripped his hands from his pockets and was on him, making three stabs to the left side of Grout's flabby chest in quick succession. Not too deep, he didn't want to snap the blade yet, but beneath Grout's jacket bright red blood blossomed. Jacob next went for his throat, and blood sprayed from the man with abandon.

Then, a blow from behind staggered Jacob from attacking further, a jab to his kidneys sent him to the ground. He saw boots coming for his head, felt pain accompanied by sparks of fireworks, then darkness.

2

Jordan

Jacob was growing used to his own space in solitary confinement, a week there so far, when the guard arrived saying that he had a visitor. Jacob assumed it was his solicitor, come with bad news. He had almost killed a man, so was expecting that, but when he was ushered into the Interview Room and found himself face to face with a casually dressed stranger, he was puzzled, to say the least.

"Be careful of this one, he's a nutter," the guard said, and to Jacob's further surprise, the plain, nondescript stranger in a leather jacket replied with an American accent.

"You're not going to hurt me, are you, Jacob?" He waved his hand toward the empty seat facing his at the table. "You can leave us to it," he continued to the guard.

The man grimaced, said, "It's your funeral," and left the room.

Jacob looked at the chair like it was some offensive object, the poker-faced man likewise, then sat. "You're a brave man, whoever you are. Don't you know I'm public enemy number one in this prison?"

The American nodded, tapped his fingers on the table's aluminum surface. "In answer to your first question, my name is Jordan. And yeah, I know you half-killed some rival scumbag and I know that once you've finished your stint in solitary, you're a dead man, and that's without your fellow prisoners even knowing what you're actually here for."

Jacob snorted. "The powers that be want me to suffer every minute of my confinement after selling weapons to the IRA. I'd be dead already if people knew."

"Well then you're up shit creek, regardless," the man calling himself

Jordan said. "Unless you're ready to make a deal."

Jacob's eyebrows rose. He didn't know the man's motives, but was intrigued. "I'm interested."

3

Freedom

Jacob faced the motel room's wall mirror and grimaced. A bruised face scowled back in return. Wearing the civilian clothes Jordan had given him felt strange—he was that unused to it. Green combat pants, black boots, a blue navy jumper and black parka; Jacob guessed his companion and guard had shopped at an Army Surplus store before coming to release him from prison.

His ankle itched where Jordan had the prison doctor administer an injection after his physical. It was a tag, apparently, not of the ankle-bracelet variety but something high-tech that would inform Jordan and his superiors exactly where Jacob was at all times. The American told him they did the same things to pets now, in case they got lost. That had made Jacob laugh a little, until he saw that Jordan wasn't joking. So, unless he could find something to remove the damn thing, there was no escaping for Jacob.

Still. the deal was a good one: introduce this American to his old IRA contacts, and Jacob would be placed in another lockup, a minimum-security prison, which would have the added bonus of stopping his murder back at Chapelmoor. A reduction in sentence? That had been too much to hope for. If he could remove the tag and escape, however, the sentence wouldn't be a problem.

꒪ᴥ꒪

Jordan paused at the motel room door and composed himself. This man, this Jacob, was the lowest of the low, scum that would sell out his own people for money. Wasn't there a treason law in this country, meaning he could be hanged for his crimes? Jordan didn't trust him, and there was a lot he wasn't telling him.

He had no intention of telling Jacob that he wanted his 'in' with the terrorists not to sell them arms, but rather to see how entrenched the group was in a certain book, an ancient tome of druidic evil called The Black Goat in Ireland. The thought of the most militant and diehard IRA holdouts being involved with the beings that had been such a bane to Jordan's life ... he looked forward to nipping this group in the bud, permanently. He opened the door and found himself face to face with the scum in question.

"Let's go to work," Jordan said.

Contact

Jacob made the call. He had two numbers for the terrorists memorized, and thankfully one of them was still in service. He made it from a call box, with Jordan stuffed in the small cubicle beside him watching his every move, while their breaths plumed out into the confined space. The man was watching for a double-cross. The man was wise.

Three rings and someone on the other end answered.

"What?" the Irish accented voice said abruptly. It was Patrick Birkett, the cell leader.

"This is Jake, at the dry cleaners; your suit is ready," Jacob said. He turned to Jordan and placed his hand on the mouthpiece a moment. "The codeword, just as I said."

"I didn't think that suit was coming," the voice replied. "Especially considering your current circumstances."

"Things change, and I got out. This suit, it's a really good fit."

The line went quiet for a few moments, then, "Delivery tomorrow, nine p.m. Spitalfields."

Jacob placed the phone back in its cradle. "It's done. Now what?"

"Now we go back to the motel," Jordan said and left the telephone booth.

"So now I've done what you've asked, how about you tell me something?" Jacob asked.

"Like what?"

"Like what's an American like you doing here mucking about with the IRA?"

Having reached the rental car, Jordan removed the keys from his pocket and switched off the alarm. "That's need-to-know and you don't. Now get in the car before we freeze out here."

ꓘ𝖂𝖈𝖈

The meet was at the old docklands, one of the places Jacob had used in the past when dealing with his clients. The Spitalfields docks: halfway to regeneration with the skeletal shapes of partially constructed apartment blocks facing a Thames that looked black and sluggish in the light from a spatter of dull stars. Jordan had parked the car near a row of shipping containers, blue but chipped and rusty. The pair stood side by side, staring at the Thames, Jordan not happy with the river's brackish odor and Jacob quite enjoying it.

"Used to come catching eels here when I was a brat." Jacob said. "Lying in the undergrowth with a cheap fishing rod in hand." He took a drag from his cigarette and tossed it into the weeds. "They tasted good with mash."

There was a sound of footsteps, multiple footfalls, and both men stood straight and turned to the source. Four shadowy figures, approaching the shipping containers, they paused about ten feet away. All four men wore casual clothes and black balaclavas.

"Remember, keep it simple and let me speak for myself." Jordan whispered out the side of his mouth as the quartet approached. "And should anything go wrong, you'll be the first one to die."

ᛑᛠᛣᛣ

The face masks didn't bother Jordan; the telltale bulges in the men's jackets did. He was glad he had his own, better-concealed bulge from his firearm of choice; a H&K USP .45 loaded with the now-discontinued Black Talon hollow-points. He was also happy that the turncoat traitor beside him wasn't armed.

"Jacob," a strong, Irish-accented voice said. It was the man at the forefront of the group. "What on earth are you doing breathing the same good clean air as the rest of us?"

"You call the air around here clean?" Jordan said, speaking with an impressive Irish accent of his own. He felt Jacob staring at him, but he quickly recovered.

"Ignore my new friend, boys," Jacob said. "He's not good with the conversation but very good at dry-cleaning."

The leader stepped forward, his men followed suit. "There's a lot of factors to dry-cleaning, though. isn't there? Quality and quantity, and a bargain price." He walked until he was just a few feet from Jacob. "Then of course there's—" Quick as a flash the man pulled a 9mm Berretta from his jacket and aimed it at Jacob's head.

"You think we're stupid, boy?" He ripped off his mask, revealing a red scowling face with a shaved head and a full, black beard. "You just walk out of prison and come straight to us. You fucking fool!"

Jacob raised his hands. Jordan, keeping his cool, stepped forward to intervene. One of the bearded man's companions grabbed him. A tussle ensued where Jordan struck the man in the face to knock him back and pulled off his mask, revealing a shaved head, brown goatee, and surprised eyes. Then like a magic trick, Jordan was pointing the business end of his .45 at the terrorist's face.

"Fuck you," the man said as blood trickled from his broken nose.

"Simon, you arsehole," said the leader. "You let him get the drop." The other two men now had their guns pointed at Jordan. He turned and looked from the leader to Jacob. Jacob's hands were shaking. Jordan felt death only moments away, for him and his companion. It wasn't the first time he had that sensation, but this could be the last.

"This standoff, most of us die," Jordan said, trying weigh up options with those two guns pointed at him. There weren't many.

"You reckon?" the leader said. "Thing is we didn't need your guns in the first place, boy. We have just what we need already. I just kinda wanted to meet and kill this moron after he sold out a bunch of my mates."

"He doesn't die; I still need him." Jordan said, his authentic-sounding Irish accent still in play.

"Oh, he dies," the leader said. "You too, whoever the fuck you are."

Jordan pressed his gun hard to his man's right temple. Beads of sweat were forming there. Jordan then slid around behind him, making sure his meat shield was between him and the other two shooters.

"Please, Patrick," Jacob said weakly.

"How about we all just back off, consider our attempt at business a failure, and you," Jordan looked the leader, Patrick, straight in the eye, "if you really want to murder Jacob, I'm sure your chance will come again."

The leader raised an eyebrow. "We all live? Sounds like a plan. But if I see you again, boy, you may not like what happens."

"Ditto," Jordan said, and took a step away from the man called Simon.

"Okay boys, back away." The leader raised his free hand and tapped Jacob on the cheek. "Later, or maybe sooner than you think." He took a few steps back and his men followed suit. Both sides stepped away, guns still aimed, in a choreographed retreat. Jordan didn't start breathing easy until the IRA men were out of sight as he and Jacob had backed around a shipping container.

"What a fucking bust," Jacob said and rubbed his face.

In an instant of red rage Jordan found himself pinning the man to the container with his gun leveled against his jaw.

"Friends of yours, huh?" Jordan spat. "So what good are you to me alive?"

To Jordan's surprise, Jacob grinned.

"Well, I have this for a start." He raised his left hand and revealed a cellphone.

He thought it a neat trick, lifting the phone from Patrick's pocket, and the act seemed to have placated Jordan, who sat beside him in the car now, looking through the contents.

"So," Jacob said. "How does an American like you have the juice to get me sprung from Chapelmoor to go on this little holiday? Let me guess; you're CIA?"

That got the man's attention, who stopped going through the stolen phone and looked at him with a mask of practiced indifference on his face.

"Yeah, I thought so," Jacob said, grinning, "That still doesn't explain why America is here, mucking about with something that is obviously a British problem."

He wasn't expecting an answer. He got one.

Jordan went back to examining the phone. "Nationality has got nothing to do with it. It's bigger than that. I have a friend in MI6 that does the same specialty work I do. Counter-terrorism against a kind of threat I'm not at liberty to disclose. He uncovered a cell of idealistic Irish hardliners with tangential links to the IRA, headed up by some of your old friends."

"Patrick."

Jordan nodded. "They got their hands on a certain rare book; you could call it a guide to creating biological weapons, and so he called me in take care of it."

Is that what Patrick meant when he said he didn't need guns anymore? Are they crazy enough to go messing around with killer germs and stuff? "So you came all the way from the US to do this? If he's MI6, why can't he handle it?"

"My friend is bedridden with cancer, and I owe him to see this through. Not everything that kills you in this line of work is a bullet or ... something else."

The man's words were cryptic, but Jacob didn't press further as Jordan looked up from the phone with something approaching excitement in his usually cold eyes.

"I might have something here. A text. 'Loughton, Epping, Dark Young, Rush Hour—Monday.' Loughton? Epping? Do you know those names, Jacob?" Jordan passed him the phone and he read the screen message.

Jacob thought for a moment then replied. "Epping is probably Epping Forest; Loughton I don't know, but it could well be somewhere near there. But what on earth is a 'Dark Young'?

A living, moving, and very angry bio-weapon, Jordan thought, *and in the middle of London? That would be quite the terrorist attack.* If the ultimate goal of terrorism was to spread fear, Jordan could think of few things more horrifying than that. "I have no idea," he lied, "but since tomorrow is Monday, we had better find out fast."

He removed his own cellphone from his jacket pocket and tried a web search for the name 'Loughton.' Lots of hits came up, too many, so he retried along with the words 'London' and 'Epping.'

Loughton Tube Station. Paydirt.

"All right, there's a subway station called Loughton. Whatever your friends are planning, I'm betting that's part of it."

"One, they're not my friends, as you now no doubt know, and two, what do you think they're going to do? A gas attack like what happened in Tokyo back in '95, but with a virus or something?"

"No; something worse."

"Well, okay then, it seems like you know where they'll be and at what time, so I take it we'll be parting company, yeah?" the Brit asked with saccharin hopefulness in his voice.

"Wrong," Jordan said as he put the car into gear. "I'll let you know when I no longer need you. You're mine until then."

"Shit. What can I help you with when it comes to diseases or whatever the hell 'something worse' is? Call the government, let them send in the SAS, and have done with it."

Jordan stepped on the brake and looked at the man across from him. "The SAS, or anyone else for that matter, wouldn't know how to deal with this threat."

"That is complete and utter shit. I knew some SAS killers from back in my army days. They're all hard men with—"

"And I've trained with them," Jordan interrupted. His mask of calm reserve slipping the slightest bit. "They are first-rate soldiers, but sending them into this, unprepared for what might happen, would just get them killed. Only a handful of people in the world have had experience in dealing with this kind of threat, and I'm the only one here that's not slowly dying from cancer."

"Then why the hell are you dragging me into this?" Jacob shouted, his face going red as his hands balled into fists.

"Those madmen are planning on killing lord knows how many innocent people. Your people, by the way. Women, children; they don't care. Hell, for them women and kids are prime targets. The more terror they can create, the better. Doesn't that mean anything to you?"

"Well, yes … maybe … I suppose. But I'm just a onetime poor excuse for a soldier, now prisoner. What the hell can I do?" Jacob fumed.

"If worse comes to worse, I might need you, that's all, so you're coming with me. End of discussion."

Jordan was well-trained to read a person and anticipate their actions before they made them. He saw that the convict was weighing his options between making a run for it, attacking him, or biding his time for a better opportunity to present itself later. Jordan tried to remain outwardly calm, but he readied a punch to Jacob's throat should the man twitch either toward him or the car door. The strike was sure to disable, and only had the off chance of killing the man. What Jordan had said was true: he still needed the former British soldier alive and with him. For now.

Jacob looked to have picked Option C and bide his time as he un-balled his fists, turned to look out of the front windshield, and said, "Anything for Queen and country and all that."

"Good man." Jordan said as he took his foot off the brake and had to consciously remind himself to stay on the left side of the road. "We'll go back to the motel and get a few hours of shuteye, as we could both use it and might need it tomorrow." *Plus I've got to gather a few things I'm afraid I may need,* he thought.

"How do you know I won't make a run for it while you're tucked up in bed?" Jacob asked.

"My buddies from MI6 who still think of you as a terrorist-loving traitor. I asked them to keep an eye on both of us, and they would stop you. Of course, only after they kicked your face in." Jordan looked over at the other man and smiled a shit-eating grin. Often the best way to sell a lie was cockiness. "What, do you honestly think I'd have you on the outside with just myself to keep tabs on you? Come on; you're too smart for that."

Jordan could see doubt in Jacob's eyes, and he hoped that doubt would continue to keep the man in check.

5

Woods dark and deep.

From the outside, the Loughton Tube Station was less than impressive. Jordan had seen bigger public bathrooms. A square brown brick building with a large half-circle-shaped window above its entrance, it had a hair salon on one side and a florist on the other. Seemed hardly the place for hardened men to meet up and plan the murder of innocents. Then again, he was here, and that was exactly what Jordan had on his mind, minus the innocent part.

He turned to Jacob. The man was asleep, or at least doing a passable job of faking it. "Hey, Jacob? Hey?" He said as he shook his companion.

"What?" the Englishman said, sitting up, alert.

"Over there."

Jacob looked to where Jordan indicated. Beneath the red circled 'Underground' sign to the right of the station, stood a man they both recognized. Shaved head, goatee, and now with tape on a broken nose. Simon, he was called. He stood there, well-wrapped in a long black coat and scarf, blowing into gloved hands. He wore a large rucksack over his shoulders.

"He been there long?" Jacob asked.

"A few minutes," Jordan said absently. "A cab dropped him off."

"Any sign of the rest?"

"Not yet—wait, look." Jordan said as a man he didn't recognize walked up to where Simon stood. The two looked at each other briefly and tried not to acknowledge one another. The pair weren't very good at being covert. Gun thugs, nothing more.

"They're arriving separately. Smart." Jacob said.

Jordan reached around to the car's back seat and picked up a leather attaché case to check its contents. Inside was an H&K MP5 submachine gun with attached suppressor and green laser sight. Two extra magazines, a trio of flashbangs, and a pair of M67 fragmentation grenades, for those just-in-case moments, completed the gear.

"I guess I'm still not getting a weapon, then?" Jacob asked.

"You guessed right."

Jacob cursed under his breath loud enough to make sure that Jordan heard him and sat back in brooding silence. They both watched out the windshield until two more men appeared, one of them being the leader of the group, the bearded Patrick. The four men then began walking together, heading toward the northeast, where Epping Forest was located.

"OK, out of the car. It's easier to shadow someone on foot," Jordan said as he stepped out of the rental, his attaché case in hand.

"I've never done anything like that before. I was just a humble squaddie in the army, so I'll wait here, yeah?"

Jordan said nothing, he just turned and looked at Jacob with a withering stare.

"I didn't think so, but it was worth a shot. Oh and don't you go blaming me if they see us, then."

"Stick close to me and do what I do; you'll be fine." Jordan said.

The pair followed the quartet of terrorists from the Loughton Tube Station for a few miles to the border of the forest, and the transition was startling to Jordan. One minute there was the gray concrete and red bricks of the city all around them, and the next moment there was a wall of trees dressed in yellow, orange, and red as autumn settled in over London. A road and a footpath led into the forest, but the IRA men didn't take it. Instead they walked for another quarter of a mile before cutting into the woods, and after a brief wait, Jordan and Jacob did likewise.

The forest was thick with the scent of rotting leaves. A dampness clung to a chilly breeze, and the rest of the world seemed to melt away as the American and the Englishman followed their Irish quarry deeper into the ancient trees. Epping had been a Royal forest for centuries before Queen Victoria declared it "The People's Forest" in the 1880s. It contained thousands of acres of woodland, grassland, rivers, bogs, and ponds. It was as primal as anything found on this old island. The raw beauty and power of nature seemed to make the very air within it hum with potent power.

As a boy growing up in Michigan who learned to hunt in and love the woods found there, the man called Jordan admired and respected the old forest. But never once did he take his eyes off of the group of killers he followed.

The IRA diehards stopped in a little clearing near a small pile of stones and fallen trees. They began to talk to each other in low voices. Jordan started to circle around to their flank to get a good firing position, when he heard a twig snap behind him and Jacob. His heart sank when he heard someone say "Don't you fuckers move" in a thick Irish brogue.

Jordan put his hands up and saw Jacob following suit while uttering another curse. Patrick obviously had more than just three men in on this plan, and not all of them were without skill in being covert.

Turning around, Jordan saw a young and slight man with curly red hair, dull green eyes, a smile on his freckled face, and an old Webley revolver in his hand. "I got 'em," Freckle face shouted.

"Good; bring their arses out here." Patrick yelled back.

"Move," the redhead said, motioning with his gun. Much to Jordan's disappointment, the kid knew to keep far enough back to keep him from trying to make a go for his revolver.

Once in the clearing, and with a sixth Irish thug that had joined them from the opposite side of the woods, Patrick took Jordan's case and had both him and Jacob patted down for weapons. The IRA vet whistled at the attaché case's contents, then passed it to broken-nosed Simon, who stood grinning to his left.

"I knew you would be tailing us once I discovered my phone was missing. You looked the type to not let things go." Patrick said. "This cowardly piece of shit," and he nodded with his bearded chin toward Jacob, "I'm surprised to see here. But that's fine. We've got two for the price of one."

As the terrorist leader spoke, two of his cronies moved around behind Jordan and Jacob. Both drew knives as they walked, and that made Jordan's stomach sink. Knives were never a good sign; they usually meant things were going from showing off to deadly real, and on some primal level, he always feared blades more than bullets.

ﾌﾙﾞﾞﾞ

"What's the plan, then?" Jacob asked. He figured the longer he could keep Patrick talking, the longer he lived, and he liked that idea. "This guy won't tell me anything, so what's with the hike through the woods?"

"You two really don't know?" Patrick said and then turned a scrutinizing gaze onto the American. If Jordan knew anything, his stone-faced expression didn't betray it to Jacob. Patrick must have thought so too, as he snorted and said, "Well, wrong place, wrong time for you two, I guess."

The terrorist holstered his gun in a shoulder rig, then knelt down to unzip a rucksack at his feet and retrieved an old, leather-bound book. Standing up, one of the last of the IRA hardliners carefully held the book as if it was a newborn baby.

"You see, boys, me and my mates have gone back to our roots. To the ancient ways of my people before invaders shat all over that and changed things. Here," at that Patrick showed off the book like it was a treasure, "is true power. Here is ancient wisdom long forgotten by most, but not by all. Not by the true sons and daughters of Ireland. Not by those that reject the martyr on the cross and remember what came before him."

He's gone completely mad, Jacob thought as he saw the gleam in Patrick's eyes. The man turned the book back toward himself, used one hand to hold it up, and the other to open it to a marked passage. The two knife-men were now behind him and Jordan, so the redhead youth now walked around to the front to join his mates.

Patrick continued on. "We don't need to buy explosives or guns no more, nor run the risk of getting caught with them or blow ourselves to hell when trying to set them up, thanks to some stupid mistake. All we need is this old book, and we can take a book anywhere, over any border and through any checkpoint without raising questions. It is the ultimate, undetectable weapon.

"Unfortunately it does require one thing to work; a sacrifice. It's the old ways, remember? The old ways were bloody ways, and the Old Gods always demanded sacrifice. So we were gonna grab one of the homeless from the underground and lure the poor sod out here. It's got to take place in the woods, you see? That's where the gateways can still be found, according to this book. Then after some chanting and the cutting of a throat, boom: instant weapon of mass destruction that the fucking English pigs will never forget."

"You're crazy, talking that black-magic shit." Jacob said as the ice-cold hand of fear tightened its grip on his heart.

"You'll see soon, and it will be the last damn thing you *do* see, boy. You and this asshole here," Patrick nodded at Jordan, "will give us two of the Shub-Niggurath's Dark Young to let loose on London. The children of the Black Goat, She Who is Life and Death, are none too pretty, but they are mighty and they ever thirst for slaughter. And in all the chaos and death that comes from that, we'll drop our weapons and just melt away, with nothing but an old book in our possession."

Patrick stepped closer to Jacob to gloat, "Crazy, you say? It's fucking brilliant, and—"

There was a flurry of motion to Jacob's left where Jordan was, but he didn't turn to look. Instead he brought a knee crashing up into Patrick's balls. In the moment of surprise that followed, he turned and head-butted the man behind him. Smashing the IRA man's nose flat. Jacob then pulled the knife easily from the man's hand and rammed it three times in fast, prison-shank-style thrusts, into his gut. He turned to do the same to Patrick, but saw him hobbling backward with one hand holding his precious book, and the other his aching jewels.

"Move, damn it." Jordan hissed to his left, and Jacob turned to see the American had disarmed his man, pulled the terrorist's pistol from his belt, had it against the other man's head, and was walking backwards, using his hostage as a shield. Jacob didn't know if Jordan had spoken to him, or his trembling human barrier, but he thought moving right now was a great idea.

As he turned and ran, he heard the Irish lads start shooting, soon followed by Patrick shouting, "Don't kill 'em, wound 'em. We need them alive for the sacrifice. And someone drag Kellen over here."

The Irish got behind cover while two of them ran out and dragged back their stomach-stabbed comrade. Jacob saw Jordan pull the gun from his hostage's head and return fire at the IRA, just as one of their shots hit their own man the American was hiding behind, in the chest. The sudden impact, combined with not looking where they were going, caused Jordan and his now-screaming living shield to tumble over a dead log and down into a shallow depression behind it. Jacob, seeing only thin trees around him to hide behind, also dove into the ditch for cover as bullets whistled past him.

Jordan was up against the side of the embankment, looking over its edge toward the terrorists. The man he had dragged with him lay at the bottom of the ditch, crying and coughing up blood. "See if he has any more magazines or weapons on him," the American ordered, and Jacob obeyed without question. He found two more clips for the automatic, but nothing else of use.

An unexpected silence settled over the woods that was soon broken by hushed voices coming from the terrorists' side of the clearing. Jacob strained to listen and heard someone say, "No, Patrick, we can't do it. Not to one of our own," to which the bearded man said, "Look, he's dead already. Some good might as well come from it." There were frantic, wet-sounding pleas, followed by Patrick saying, "Sorry, Kellen, but it's for the cause. Now, you two, hold him down."

"Shit." Jordan said next to him.

"What's going on?" Jacob said, still not wanting to poke his head out of the hole for a look and risk getting it blown off.

Jacob heard Patrick chanting in some bizarre tongue. He could not make sense of it, as it just sounded like nonsense words, gibberish, grunts and deep, throaty bellows, to him. But as Patrick chanted, Jacob saw Jordan's face blanch, and that greatly worried him. When the American pressed the automatic into his hand, it only added to Jacob's unease, not lessened it.

"Here, in case they try to flank us. Keep your eyes open and don't let them stop me once I start," Jordan said as he reached into his leather jacket and tore out the sewn-in lining. He revealed an envelope hidden within, which he opened and pulled a sheet of paper out of.

"Wait, what? And what's that?" Jacob said, with fear giving way to confusion.

"A last-chance backup plan. Those bastards aren't the only ones with old books." Jordan said, as he looked around and then picked up a fist-sized rock.

Then Jacob heard a shriek come from the man he had shanked, followed by a gurgling sound and an end to Patrick's chanting. Jacob recognized a death rattle when he heard one and he knew that poor Kellen had just been sacrificed "for the cause."

The moment the Irishman expired, something ugly, uglier than death, started up around them. Everything seemed to freeze and hold its breath as if waiting. An electric hum filled the air, followed by a vibration that made his hair stand on end and the fillings shake in his teeth. This was what Jacob felt, as the American next to him said in a hollow whisper: "It's coming."

The colored leaves that still clung to life on the trees around them all fell at once in brown, shriveling clouds. They didn't reach the ground, but flew in a storm of movement as howling winds picked up around them. This was disturbing enough; worse was the sinister creaking issuing from one of the trees behind Jacob. He shared a look with Jordan, and turned. One of the larger trees, with a thick trunk and an even thicker tangle of dry, brown branches, shifted unnaturally.

Jacob gasped, someone in Patrick's group shrieked, and the branches twisted. Bark flaked off in huge chunks to reveal glistening red, raw flesh. Boles exploded with black ichor, revealing gaping maws of rotted brown teeth that gnashed. Jacob fought hard not to scream, as the things that had been branches broke free of earthly wood to become squirming, snaking tentacles. Mouths spat and gibbered, and lapping, vein-filled blue tongues drooled out between bleeding lips. What once was a tree lumbered from the cracked base of a trunk on three huge, tumor-covered, elephantine legs terminating in yellow, scabby hooves bigger than dustbins.

Jacob stared at the obscenity, and found himself swatting absently at a dried leaf stuck to his face.

"Trees are bastards," he said, and fought back an insane giggle.

A smack to the face from Jordan brought him back from the brink of madness, if only temporarily. "Snap out of it!" the man barked at him. "And keep those bastards away from me until I finish, or else we're both dead."

Jacob, not understanding, nodded and looked over the edge of the embankment toward the terrorist side. He saw one of the IRA toughs stand up and run screaming into the woods in the opposite direction of the huge horror that shambled toward them. He then heard a bang and saw the curly-haired redhead kid fall out from behind a tree. The barrel of his revolver was still in his mouth and blood poured out of his nose like a faucet. Mixed in with all that, there was Patrick's maniacal laughter and shouts of "Isn't it amazing? Isn't it so damn beautiful! Iä! Iä! the Mother of the Death and Rebirth, she who sows and reaps."

In the ditch, Jordan began to chant his own insane words as he crouched low, next to where the terrorist was shuddering and bleeding out. At once, the giant, tree-like abomination stopped its march toward the Irish. Instead the behemoth swayed and let out ghastly keening sounds from all of its many mouths.

"What? No! Stop him! Stop that son of a bitch!" Jacob heard Patrick scream, then saw the man stand up from behind a large rock. Jacob fired a shot at him, missed, and struck the boulder, but it caused Patrick to crouch back down.

"Go on, damn it. Get them. Kill them!" Patrick shouted.

One IRA gunman still had some wits about him, so he made a dash from tree to tree, looking to close the distance between himself and their hollow. Jacob fired at the man as he went, ignoring the return fire from Patrick, and on his fourth shot, hit his target, sending the man sprawling with a yelp.

"Damn it!" Patrick howled and once again stood up and ran forward.

Jacob fired once, missed, then the automatic's slide came back and locked into place, telling him that it was empty. He hit the button on the side of the grip to eject the empty magazine while reaching for another, then stopped in his tracks as he looked over at Jordan.

The American's chant had reached a chaotic crescendo as Jordan raised the hand holding the rock over the bleeding terrorist. The IRA man raised a hand of feeble protection and was trying to stammer out a plea, but Jordan brought the rock crashing into the side of the wounded man's head. Again and again, Jordan bludgeoned the man as he chanted, cracking the Irishman's skull open, spilling blood and exposing brain. The memory of Patrick's voice came to Jacob's mind as he watched the American bludgeon the helpless man to death: *The old ways were bloody ways, and the Old Gods always demanded sacrifice.*

Then Jordan stood up in the trench, extended a hand at where Patrick now sat slumped and weeping in defeat. "Kill him. Kill them all," the American said with his own mad gleam in his eye.

The monstrosity reacted at once. It thundered toward the terrorist leader, trumpeting like an elephant and roaring like a lion. One of its many tentacles snapped up Patrick, who was now shrieking uncontrollably, and shoved him head-first into one of its drooling mouths. When the tentacle drew back, it still held what was left of the IRA true believer, but everything from his chest on up was missing. In three more bites, nothing was left of Patrick but a bad memory.

However, the horror was not done.

It uprooted a nearby tree to expose broken-nosed Simon crouching behind it, hands over his eyes like a child trying to hide from the nightmare he had helped unleash. Simon was not devoured like his friend; instead, he was trampled to death under the thing's massive hooves. Another man stood up out of the brush and fired six shots into the monster as it came toward him, but none of the bullets seem to have an effect on the creature. Before the thing could reach him, the man put the barrel of his pistol under his chin and pulled the trigger. This seemed to enrage the horrible thing, as it next went for the runner Jacob had wounded. That poor soul was grasped on opposite ends by two of the thing's mighty tentacles, and then slowly pulled apart like a well-cooked chicken.

When the monster went crashing through the trees in the direction of where the last IRA man had fled, Jordan yelled out, "Stop!" and the beast, much to Jacob's stunned disbelief, halted in its tracks.

"Go, return whence you came." Jordan said, and Jacob saw the American shudder sway on his feet, and that a trickle of blood was running from his nose.

The abomination roared in protest, but Jordan repeated the command, and the beast almost seemed to sulk back into the thicker woods behind it. For several long minutes, Jacob heard the huge thing crashing through the forest as it stomped away and then … nothing. All sounds of its passage ceased. It was gone.

Then Jordan collapsed to his knees, vomited, fell over on his side, and curled up in a foetal position.

Jacob remembered the empty gun in his hand. He looked at the trembling American, the man who was sure to put him back into prison, and loaded a fresh clip into the weapon.

"So what was all that crazy shit, then?" Jacob asked as he walked over to Jordan and looked down at him.

"I … bound the … Dark … Young." The man wheezed out.

"What?"

"They summoned it … but I … I bound it before they could, so it was mine to command."

"You had that, what, spell ready from the beginning? You just needed to find out where they were doing their thing to take control of it, right?"

"No, I wanted to stop them. This … this was a last ditch effort. Too … too damn costly." Jordan coughed and shook.

"Yeah, I guess so, but not just for you, huh? You caved that man's skull in, for a sacrifice, right? There's always got to be a sacrifice. Well what if you hadn't grabbed that guy? What would you have done then?"

Jordan stopped trembling, looked up, and the two men locked eyes. "I thought one less con in the world would be a small price to pay to stop that thing."

Jacob's fingers flexed open and close on the pistol's grip. His jaw clenched. He then pocketed the automatic, turned, and walked away.

"Hey," Jordan yelled out behind him, "there is no chip in your ankle. I lied. And there are no MI6 Agents watching, either."

Jacob shook his head, smiled despite himself, whispered, "Bastard," and continued walking into the growing gloom of approaching night.

COLD WAR, YELLOW FEVER

BY PETE RAWLIK

October 18, 1962

or the last few days Mitchell Peel had not slept well, Guantanamo Base was on high alert and the activity associated with such a state included roving search lights, planes coming and going, and the constant sound of men and equipment moving about. The food had been surprisingly good, as was the coffee. He hadn't yet finished his first cup of the morning when word came that he was wanted for a briefing. Peel hated Cuba. It wasn't that it was too hot or humid; he was used to that. The real problem was the mosquitos, which were the size of small bees. There was a stiff breeze coming off the ocean, but that didn't help at all. He hated the island, and resented that his vacation had been interrupted. Still, being flexible was one of the things that the Joint Advisory Committee on Korea paid him for. The fact that he hadn't ever been to Korea—and that the war was ostensibly over—wasn't really important. He worked for JACK; they paid well, and if it was one thing he had learned was that he should always expect the unexpected. If that meant being called during your vacation to an island military base surrounded by soldiers intent on killing you, so be it.

There had been security at the door, but one look at his identification, and they parted like the Red Sea, even escorted him to a seat. His boss sat at the head of the table. Actually, Peaslee wasn't his boss; if he remembered the chain of command correctly, there were five layers of management between the two of them. Peel had only seen the TOM once before, at a program realignment meeting. Officially he was Colonel Doctor Wingate Peaslee, but everyone in JACK called him the TOM, the Terrible Old Man. He had a reputation: mostly for being ruthlessly efficient, but also for getting the job done no matter what the cost. God help you if you were in his way or even just standing nearby. Collateral damage was not only acceptable, but expected; Peel's own equations suggested that it was at times even necessary.

There were three others in the room, men about his age, but in significantly better shape. Rough men, dangerous men, capable men; they all carried side arms. Peel suspected that they weren't analysts, and that his years of study in Sydney and Tokyo would be less than impressive to this company. He thought of making small talk, but then decided against it.

Peaslee took a drink and then spoke in the thick New England accent he was famous for, "Mitchell Peel, twenty-six, born and raised in Sydney, Australia. You have degrees in Mathematics and Statistical Theory. Last month you had a breakthrough on some equations associated with the Yellow Sine. You have Omega Blue clearance." His voice was firm and direct, like an instructor at some private school. Peel tried to speak but the TOM cut him off. "As of right now your clearance level is Pi White. Do you understand what that means?"

"It means that I can be terminated without cause. I'll place a letter of resignation in my file."

"Son, that is not what we mean by 'terminate.'"

Peel's eyes grew wide as he realized he had made a terrible mistake.

"It means that if I think you've been compromised, if I think it's necessary, I can shoot you in the head. No questions asked." Peaslee wasn't smiling, and that made Peel nervous. "Relax, son. Major Millward will attest that I've never shot anyone."

The largest man, whose uniform bore no insignia, smiled and in a deep Texan drawl confirmed what Peaslee had said. "The Colonel doesn't shoot people." Peel let out a breath. "He has me do it for him. Eight times in the last two years."

As the young statistician choked, one of the other men laughed. "Welcome to the big leagues, Mr. Peel." The others, excepting Peaslee joined in.

Once the laughter subsided, Peaslee rose and began the briefing. "Following the debacle of the Bay of Pigs, the CIA inserted several dozen operatives into Cuba to carry out a variety of sabotage and terrorist acts in the hope of undermining Fidel Castro. This project was known as Operation Mongoose. Amongst the operatives deployed was this man," he raised a grainy photo of a bearded man with glasses and a scar across his left eye. "Esteban Zamarano, a fervent member of the anti-Castro movement. His family had extensive holdings in the city of Banes, in the Northeast area of the island. It was to this area that Zamarano was deployed in the hopes that he could enlist family connections." Peaslee paused and took a drink. "The Zamarano family of Banes was on the JACK watch list in 1958. According to the sales records of Pent and Serenade, they bought six volumes from the sale of the Church of the Starry Wisdom Library, including what appears to be a Spanish-language edition of *The King in Yellow*. How this bit of information was overlooked during his recruitment process is being investigated, but is not a subject of our mission. For three weeks Zamarano kept to all required schedules. However, his last daily report is now nine hours overdue. This in itself is not unusual, but two other operatives sent to Banes have also failed to report. A third, Joseph Gamboa reported reaching Banes and sent a brief message before we lost contact. Gamboa's message was '*Donde esta el signo amarillo?*' In English, 'Where is the Yellow Sign?'"

A murmur ran through the men, who obviously knew more than Peel did. Peaslee ignored it. "We aren't the only ones with eyes on this. Banes has gone silent, but reports from the Cuban military flights suggest that there are bodies in the streets. The Soviets are most assuredly aware of what is going on, and they have been sensitive about *The King in Yellow* since the Romanovs. Analysis suggests that the Kremlin would be willing to neutralize the situation with a first strike. Washington does not want to see another Gizhinsk, particularly so close to the US borders. Thankfully, the Soviet missiles already in place are not yet armed. This gives us a window of opportunity to find another solution. Operation Yellow Fever will determine if this is an incursion, which given Gamboa's message seems likely, find the cause, and neutralize it as best we can. Any questions?" Peel started but then stopped himself. "I have copies of these files for all of you. Remember our motto."

With that, he handed out the files to everyone and slumped back in his chair. Peel turned to the man nearest him, a thick-necked bruiser with a cauliflower ear. "We have a motto?"

His accent betrayed his New York origin. "Be nimble. Be quick. Be saucy."

Peel smiled, almost laughing. "I get it Jack be nimble, Jack be quick, but I've never heard of 'Jack be saucy.' Is that from an American version of the rhyme?"

The man called Millward slapped him on the back, "Naw," he said in his deep Southern drawl, "it's British, like you. You ain't ever heard of Saucy Jack?"

"I'm Australian." He quipped. "Saucy Jack—you mean Jack the Ripper?" Both men nodded, which explained nothing to Peel, who still looked puzzled

Major Millward finally offered a translation, "Be flexible, be fast, and kill if you have to, but don't get caught."

Pete Rawlik

Peel slide back into his chair and repeated what Peaslee had said, "Welcome to the big leagues."

CHULHU

October 19

If you could get around the batteries of guns, the navy warships and the constant air traffic, the beach inside the base was quite beautiful. The sand was soft, white and clean. The water was a crystal-clear blue that showed the vibrant tropical fish that darted beneath. The breeze cut the humidity and made the heat tolerable. In the distance there was a small boat moving toward the beach. A man waved at them. Peaslee waved back.

Peaslee sat down on a large rock and took off his shoes and socks. Peel did the same as the man briefed him about what was about to happen. "In a few moments, Major Romero of the Cuban Security Forces is going to show up; he'll be accompanied by agent Romanova, of Soviet Army Intelligence. Romero will do most of the talking, but make no mistake: despite her appearance, Romanova is in charge. Do not tell them anything unless I tell you to. They are here to discuss how our team will get to Banes, and how many soldiers we will need to get us there."

Peel looked around. "Shouldn't we all be here? Where's the rest of our men?"

Peaslee looked at his watch, "They left the base yesterday; they should be half way to Banes by now."

It was just then that the small boat beached itself and the Cuban and Russian leapt into the shallow water and came ashore. Romero was typically Cuban, dressed in white linen shorts and a nearly translucent shirt. Beneath a thick mustache the remnants of a cigar were still smoldering. Romanova was wearing a sundress, which accentuated her wavy hair, allowing it to flow down around her shoulders and bare arms. It was hard to believe this woman was a spy, but perhaps that was why she had been recruited to begin with. She moved daintily through the shallows while Romero simply forced his way to shore, grinning all the way.

"*Hola*, Professor," he bellowed. "It is good to see you again." He wrapped two beefy arms around Peaslee in a kind of loose hug. Peaslee smiled and whispered a greeting back. Romero laughed and with an open arm introduced his companion. She didn't smile, and barely made eye contact. "We have updates if you need them, Professor." The old man nodded and Romero knelt down and with a piece of driftwood sketched out a crude map. "Banes is 100 miles north of here, on the coast between the sea and the bay, with mountains to the west and south. The main road runs south into the mountains. The terrain is covered with jungle, and is too treacherous for most people to traverse. We have forces on the main road, about ten miles away from town, and smaller units along the mountain road to make sure no one comes through the jungle. Aerial reconnaissance reports that the roads are littered with the dead. There are signs of movement, but visual contact with the source hasn't been achieved. Whatever has happened down there it is *muy malo*, very bad."

"There is still no radio contact?" asked the professor.

Romero and Romanova exchanged looks, knowing looks. There was a pregnant pause that Romanova finally broke. "We have had no contact with anyone in the affected area. There is a signal, however; really three intertwined signals. They are simple sinusoidal oscillations. As far as we can tell they aren't coding any information, but they all originate from Banes."

"Mr. Peel will investigate. He has a way with such things." Peaslee was staring out at the ocean. "How soon do we leave?"

Romero was suddenly very serious. "We will leave in the boat after sunset, and head out into the ocean. A ship will pick us up and take us round the island to Barnes. We plan to land our forces just before dawn. That should give Mr. Peel plenty of time to analyze the radio signals."

Romanova was equally frigid, a state that seemed at odds with the beautiful beach, the sun, and the light cotton dress she was wearing. "Mr. Peel, Colonel Peaslee says you might be able to find a solution. I hope he is right. I am willing to give you time to prove why he has such faith in you, but make no mistake, if you fail, I will do what is necessary to protect the peoples of Cuba and the Soviet Union."

"Let us hope it does not come to that," Peaslee suggested, and with that he pulled Peel off the beach and back toward the base. Peel's head was spinning, but even so he couldn't help but notice the American soldiers who were making sure that Romero and Romanova were staying on the beach.

October 20

The morning wind was gentle and cool; flying fish would occasionally scatter as the ship cut through the calm sea. Earlier, a pod of porpoise had decided to ride the bow wake of the fast moving warship as she sped toward Banes. The ship was late—Peaslee called it "Latin Time"—and the sun was already rising as they came into the harbor. Peaslee, Romanova and Romero were still asleep in the cabin, but Peel couldn't get comfortable and had crawled out onto the deck. Some of the crew, a mix of Soviets and Cubans found it amusing and had whipped out fat, greasy cigars that stank and turned him a different shade of green. The odd thing was that despite being sick he couldn't stop thinking about the signal waves.

Once he knew they were there, they were easy to find and then isolate. One was quite strong, while the other two were relatively weak, and as he continued to monitor them seemed to be fading in strength. Meanwhile the third one seemed to be growing, gaining strength and dominance. What bothered him the most was that he recognized all three waves, well at least their visual complements. The weak ones he identified as belonging to the colors of red and blue. It was as if someone was transmitting an analog of these colors on a radio frequency, which was slowly fading away. In the meantime, the remaining wave corresponded to an entirely predictable color, one that was gaining strength and overriding the other two.

As he clung to the railing on the port side, he watched the first rays of sunlight break over the horizon and play out over the bay and the town beyond. At first he thought it was a trick of the tropical light, that something in the air was acting as a filter, but he knew that was simply impossible. The crew came up beside him, mouths agape in awe and fear. One of them dug into his shirt and pulled out a small rosary that hung around his neck and whispered, "*Madre de Dios*."

The commotion served to rouse Peaslee and the others, who filtered through the hatch and clung to the side of the boat. The captain had apparently seen the horror as well, and decided quite on his own that he would stay as far away as possible. The ship changed course and headed back toward the welcoming blue-green ocean and the orange and pink clouds that framed the sun. As they turned from shore Peel threw up again, but he didn't mind. Anything was better than what lay behind them, for the village of Banes had been transformed, altered, drained of all life and vitality, of all color, save for one. It was the color that Peel associated with the radio signal, the one that was growing stronger and eclipsing the others.

Romanova swore in Russian something that sounded like "Zhol-tee!"

Romero shook his head in despair and muttered, "*Amarillo*." I swear there was a tear in his eye.

It was Peaslee that put a better name to it than Peel ever could, for while it was a shade of yellow, it was not warm; rather, it was pale and sickly. It crawled into the eyes and squirmed into the brain, infecting those who had seen it with a sense of loathing and dread. Even from this distance, it had damaged those who had looked at it. Peaslee seemed to spit as he said the word, as if it was an effort to name the foul hue that now stained the town and shoreline. He called it *"Giallo,"* and that seemed oddly appropriate.

ᏩᏞᏃᎿᏗ

October 21

The captain had moored more than two miles off shore, and he steadfastly refused to move any closer. No matter what Romero said, no matter how he threatened or cajoled, the captain would go no closer. Romanova tried to pull rank, and for a brief moment there were the sounds of Russian guns being brought to bear, but it was met with the sound of Cuban guns, and the standoff was brief. Romanova lost face, but nobody was shot.

It took the rest of the day for Peaslee and Romero to negotiate the use of a launch. The captain refused to order any of his men to go ashore, and none of them volunteered. The Soviets were more accommodating; two of them agreed to follow Romanova. She warned the others that they would be disciplined, but they still refused. Consequently, when Peaslee and Peel finally went ashore they went only with Romero, Romanova, and two Soviet soldiers who barely spoke Spanish, let alone English.

The trip aboard the launch was rife with anxiety. Romero was at the helm, while Romanova and her soldiers took up positions with their guns, Kalashnikovs that they were constantly touching, as if they were some sort of talisman. It reminded Peel of the man with the rosary, and he wondered which one was more valuable in this situation. The ocean gave way to the bay, and the bay to the harbor, and the harbor succumbed to *giallo*. As they approached the yellow line the anxiety built, for they all expected something to happen when they finally crossed that threshold and left normalcy behind, and entered the queerly stained realm that had succumbed to the infection. It was therefore somewhat anticlimactic when they finally crossed the line and absolutely nothing at all occurred.

"The water feels wrong" said Peel as he caught some of the yellow spray in his hand. "It reminds me of kerosene: it's oily." He shook his hand, but instead of flying off, the stuff just seeped off of his hand in thick, viscous drops. "I thought maybe it was a contaminant, a dye, an alga, maybe even spores or pollen, but it's not, is it? It's an actual physical change to the water itself."

"I think it's more sinister than that," offered Peaslee. "I think perhaps it is a fundamental alteration to the *matter* itself. I think that whatever has happened here is changing the very nature of the building blocks of our universe, making our world into something else."

Pete Rawlik

"An interesting theory, Colonel Peaslee," yelled Romanova over the sound of the engine. "Care to explain further?"

"I have an idea," suggested Peaslee, "but I'm not ready to share. Not just yet."

They made several passes across the water front searching for signs of life, trying to draw out some kind of attack, but there was no response. Eventually they picked a sturdy-looking dock that was sitting low to the water and cautiously tied up to it. Like the water, the wood, nails, steel and concrete that made up the harbor had all turned a sickly shade of yellow, with only shadows and texture providing any real sort of contrast.

They weren't even off the waterfront when they found the first bodies: a cluster of middle-aged women who had been stabbed repeatedly in their abdomens and lower backs. There were defensive wounds on their hands. Blood ran from their bodies and mingled into crusty pools that dotted the street. The blood was yellow. The soldiers spoke rapidly in Russian, and Romanova responded angrily. The team pressed on, but every few steps there was another body. Some stabbed, some bludgeoned, some simply dead. One man had been decapitated by a hand trowel. A woman had been strangled by a silk scarf. An elderly couple had been pierced through their heads by a length of rebar. It made Peel and everyone else nervous as they moved through a silent city of the dead.

Only Peaslee seemed calm enough to make notes, which after about an hour he handed to Peel. "Do you see a problem with this, Mr. Peel?"

Peel looked at the numbers Peaslee had been writing down and the bar graph he had sketched out, a bar graph that hinted at something terrible. "Romero, is there a school nearby?"

Romero looked at his map, and then at the street signs. He pointed westward. "One block that way."

Peel took off at a brisk pace with Peaslee following closely behind him. The others were momentarily confused but decided it was better not to argue, and fell in line as the two Americans suddenly took control of the team.

The school was as quiet as the rest of the town. It was small; a single-story building that sprawled around a simple playground. There were three bodies on the steps, all women. Peel leapt over them and ran inside. Peaslee stopped at the door and held the others back. They could hear Peel inside throwing open doors and pounding down hallways. He was crying, moaning in denial, really, and with each passing moment his cries grew louder and louder and louder.

Without warning he burst through the door, startling the others. One of the soldiers jumped and brought his weapon to bear. Romero pushed the barrel to the side as the man pulled the trigger and let off a single shot. They all stood there in silence in a dead yellow city as the man who had fired the shot tried to compose himself, and Peel tried to catch his breath.

"They're all dead," he panted. "There are six more inside. Four teachers, one administrator and an older man who I think was a janitor. No one else." He put his hands on his knees and then crumpled to the ground. "There is no one else."

Romero cast a confused look in Peaslee's direction. Peaslee raised a finger and then with his foot rolled one of the teachers over. There was a pencil embedded in her gut. Several other holes suggested that she had been stabbed with it multiple times. "These wounds, most of them are to legs, or the abdomen, some to the hands; very few are to the head or neck. All of them are upward thrusts."

Romanova bent down and examined another body, and then cursed in Russian. She seemed to be thinking about something and then suddenly made a decision. "We need to find shelter, someplace we can use as a base, someplace defensible."

"What have you learned, my friends?" Romero was on the verge of panicking because he hadn't figured out what Peel, Peaslee and Romanova already had.

It fell to Peaslee to explain. "How many bodies have we seen? How many men? How many women?"

Romero's face grew more confused, "Over a hundred, maybe a few more men than women. Why do you ask?"

Peaslee flipped his notebook in the air. "Not counting these people here, I've counted one hundred and six dead. Sixty-eight are men; thirty-eight are women."

"So there are more men than women. The area we passed through was waterfront and warehouses, places men work. No place for women."

"We didn't come to the school to look for women," Peaslee finally admitted. "We came to look for children. Tell me, Romero, where are the children?"

Romero was about to speak when there was a very unexpected sound. Out across the bay there came the undeniable boom of heavy gun fire. Just a single shot, but it made them all pause and turn back toward its origin. In the sky over the ocean a flare had been launched, and it was slowly falling back down through the sky.

Romero was cursing out the ship's captain, "He was not supposed to launch that flare until we were late to report at 1800 hours. The man is a son of a dog."

The Russians were scrambling to get their radio out and establish contact with the ship, but Peaslee was looking at the sky. "How long since we left the boat?" he asked.

Peel looked at his watch, "About two hours and ten minutes. Why?"

"I think we should leave this place now, while we still can."

"What? Why?"

Peaslee grabbed one of the backpacks and started loading the equipment back inside. "We need to maintain radio silence. The captain didn't make a mistake with the flare. Look to the west. The sun is going down. Apparently it is not only matter that is being rewritten, but time as well."

They turned to head back down the hill toward the waterfront, and the avenue gave them a clear view of the harbor below, the bay and the shoreline beyond it. There was a city on the far shore where no city had been before, and it was unlike any human city any of them had ever seen. It froze them in their tracks for none wanted to approach it or its terrible beauty, or the thing that rose up out of the waters before it. It rose out of the yellow bay like a nightmare, a great globular thing that cast a pale light across the waters, replacing the sunlight, which was rapidly retreating. It rose out of the waters and into the sky, impossibly huge, and impossibly passing in front of the distant towers, instead of behind them. It was a hideously luminescent sphere, covered with a murky mist that hid whatever it was that was the source of the light.

"Please tell me that's the moon," begged Peel.

Peaslee shook his head. "Not our moon, I think."

"*Demhe*," spat Romanova. "The bay is no longer safe. There is a barracks not far from here. It should supply us with a more defensible position. We should go there, now."

No one argued.

ᏩᏈᎿᎵ

The Russian soldiers were dead. Nightfall had brought heat, and with it came a kind of lethargy. It seemed that they had drowsed for hours, but their watches no longer agreed. Some were off by minutes, others by hours—but that was the least of their worries. At night the dead city came to life. It had been unnerving, listening to the sounds of children running wild through the streets, their macabre laughter echoing off of the walls and windows. That children could play among the dead, that they were likely the murderers themselves, instilled an unsettling sense of dread within Peel, one that he felt sure had found a home in the others as well. In an attempt to remain calm he had begun listing the digits of pi. Unfortunately, his recitation had little effect on the others. Panic took hold of the two young soldiers, and against reason and orders they had left the security of the concrete barracks. Where they had planned on going hadn't been an issue. They wanted out, no matter what. The shooting started just moments after the door slammed shut. It stopped not long after.

Later, when the noise had stopped, Peaslee and the others had ventured out into the morning light, or what passed for it in the transformed town. They had found the bodies, dismembered. Their guns had been left behind, the barrels bent beyond repair. The bodies and the guns had turned yellow.

It left the team with Romanova's Kalashnikov, her sidearm, and Romero's as well. Peaslee wasn't comfortable with their lack of firepower and suggested that they rectify the situation by raiding the local police station.

"What about our team, Colonel," Peel blurted out, "when will they get here?"

Romero and Romanova stared at Peaslee, waiting for an answer and an explanation. The old man sighed and glared at Peel. "Millward, McCoy and Peterson penetrated the quarantine zone several hours before we ourselves arrived. If they were still alive they would have made contact by now."

Romero was suddenly outraged. "You disappoint me, Colonel Peaslee. Yes, I am disappointed, but I am not surprised. We trusted you and you betray that trust. You bring armed Americans into our country without telling us, and then you wonder why we ally ourselves with the Soviets?"

"Calm yourself, Romero," suggested Romanova. "It is typical American imperialism. Their greed blinds them, makes them think they can do whatever they wish." There was a knowing smile across her face. "Is that what happened here? Did one of your attempts to meddle backfire? Did *you* do this, Colonel Peaslee?"

"Does it matter?"

Romanova chuckled. "No, Colonel, I suppose at this point it doesn't."

It took an hour for the four of them to make it to the police station, but the place had been ransacked already. The guns were gone; all that remained were a few batons and some canisters of tear gas. The radio was gone, but the connection to the antenna remained. Romero unpacked the radio from the backpack and began hooking it up.

Peaslee went to stop him, but Romanova shook her head. "The time for radio silence is over, Colonel. We need to know what is going on. We need to know what our governments are thinking. We need orders."

Peaslee started to protest but thought better of it, and then, simply nodded. He and Peel watched as Romero worked and coaxed the machine to life. It sputtered static, and Romero swiped at the volume knob, before playing with the frequency. There was a screeching pulse that burned their ears for an instant as Romero dialed through it. He settled on a station with an official-sounding voice that was doing its best to hide the fear that was trying to break through. The accent was heavy, and even Romanova was straining to understand what was being said, until a familiar voice—President Kennedy's voice—was suddenly speaking.

Pete Rawlik

All ships of any kind bound for Cuba, from whatever nation or port, will, if found to contain cargoes of offensive weapons, be turned back. This quarantine will be extended, if needed, to other types of cargo and carriers.

Peaslee looked at his watch and cursed. "We've lost more time. That speech was scheduled for the evening of the twenty-second, and only if we had failed. Things are escalating."

"My government won't tolerate the situation much longer." Romanova was stating the obvious, and creating an impasse.

Peel stepped in and moved toward Romero. "Let me try something." He turned the volume down as far as it would go, and then dialed the frequency back to the frequency with the pulse that burned; the one which he knew was carrying the Yellow Sine. The all-too-familiar wave form jumped to life on the oscilloscope. The strength of the signal was immense, almost unbelievable, and from what Peel could tell, incredibly close. "Can we use this to find the source of the signal?"

Romanova dug through the bag and pulled out a coil of metal and electronics. There were plugs that attached the contraption to the radio. "This should work," she said and then gasped suddenly and pulled back from Romero. His hands had begun to turn yellow.

He stared at them in horror, holding them out for all to see. "You did this," he spat at Peaslee. "You find a way to fix it." He brought out his sidearm. Romanova reached for hers but then relaxed as he laid the weapon on the table. "You'll need this more than I will." He took off running and was out of the door before anyone could stop him. Peel started after him, but Peaslee grabbed him and pulled him back.

"You can't go out there, son!"

"Let me go!"

Romanova shut the door and threw the bolt. The city had appeared on the far shore, and the moon had risen from the bay. Soon the children would be coming.

ᏨᏗᎩᏫᏝᎭ

"Why the children?" Peel asked as he held the radio and tried to find a stronger signal. "Why aren't they dead like everyone else?"

It was Romanova who spoke up. "The human mind is like clay, Mister Peel. It must be molded, taught, indoctrinated. This not only applies to languages and culture, but to the laws of the universe as well. There have been events, inexplicable cases like this one, that suggest that the rules of the universe may vary from place to place. That matter, time, gravity may be different, may actually change. The adult mind rebels at these changes, crumbles, shatters. It is too well-trained and set in its view of the universe to accept any changes. The mind of a child isn't so rigid; it learns, and can change when it needs too. If properly stimulated it can see the universe in ways that adults cannot. There are documented cases in the West. The Paradine children. That village in Winshire. There are other cases we could discuss. I am surprised that you do not know these. Colonel Peaslee, do you not properly educate your agents in JACK?"

But Peaslee wasn't listening; he was staring at his hands. His fingertips were yellow, and he was shaking.

Peel grabbed him by the shoulder and pulled him forward. "If we find the source, maybe we can reverse the effects."

They wandered through the town, picking their way through the sickly yellow wreckage and the dead. Peel thought that there should have been a smell, a stench of rot, but there wasn't, and as far as he could tell there were no animals either. No dogs, no cats, or birds. He hadn't seen a rat or a roach or a spider. The bodies did not draw flies. They just sat there waiting, as if they had been painted into place as scenery.

"You're good with that thing," said Romanova, talking about the radio.

Peel nodded. "My younger brother is an electrician in Sydney. When we were kids he was always building things like this. Radios, metal detectors, electric eyes."

She nodded. "That is respectable work."

He looked at her and made a decision. "My name is Mitchell. My friends call me Mitch."

Her eyes were full of suspicion, but only for an instant. It was the first time they had spoken of something that didn't concern the mission. "Tanya; they call me Tanya."

"And my name is Wingate. I don't have any friends, but my employees call me TOM." He marched passed them. "In case you've forgotten, I'm dying here." The yellow had engulfed his forearms, and there was a patch of something that was working its way through his hair.

"You need to stop, Colonel," said Peel.

"We don't have time to stop. I don't have time. The world doesn't have time. We have to find the transmitter."

"No, Colonel, you don't understand. The transmitter is here; we've found it."

The three looked up at the cathedral that loomed over them, casting a dark shadow in a landscape of endless yellow. The windows were boarded shut, and the doors chained. Some of the glass was broken and there were pockmarks in the stone walls, tell-tale signs of gunfire. Romanova shrugged. "The revolution was not bloodless."

Pete Rawlik

They worked their way around the back and found a door that had been pried open. They crawled inside. They had thought the place would have been dark, but it wasn't. There was light everywhere, electric lights being driven by a generator that had been set up in a hallway. They followed the cables into a small room and approached what they found there with caution.

There was a man—or what had once been a man. He was yellow, and where his head had once been there was an empty space, a void of yellow nothingness that seemed to pulse and seethe. He was slumped in a chair in front of a radio transmitter, with the microphone nearly embedded into the mass of yellow where his head once was. The transmitter was still on, and Peel could see the Yellow Sine as it danced on the oscilloscope. All around him there were pages from a book. The ink had gone yellow, as had the pages.

Peel reached for a random page, but a single touch from Peaslee stopped him. He nodded, realizing the danger, but then suddenly chuckled. "All because of this. All these people dead. Three nations on the brink of war. Soldiers mobilizing, ships with guns pointed at each other, missiles ready to launch. It's a strange new world we've built for ourselves. War used to be about men being commanded on the battlefield. Now it's come to this. Oh, there are still forces to manipulate, but the real battles of the future will be fought by just a few men who know what buttons to press and what knobs to turn." He reached out and clicked the transmitter off. "And just like that, the crisis is averted."

But it wasn't.

Nothing had changed. The oscilloscope on the handheld radio they had used to find their way here was still showing the Yellow Sine marching across its screen.

Peel's eyes grew wide. He pulled the plug on the transmitter, and then threw the machine to the floor. The plastic and bits of metal shattered, but the world didn't change. He took his gun and fired into the headless body, but with no response.

"We're too late," whispered Tanya. "The reaction is self-sustaining. It can't be stopped."

Peaslee grabbed the handheld radio and spun the dial, searching for a particular frequency. "Maybe, but maybe not. Perhaps now that we have cut off the origin signal the manifestation is vulnerable."

"What?" said both Peel and Romanova.

"Perhaps we can change the wave form now. But we're going to need a very large explosion." He found the frequency he was looking for and grabbed the microphone. "Aquatone actual to Oilstone unit, respond. Aquatone actual to Oilstone unit, repond. This is a pi utility command. Over."

There was a static filled pause, and then the radio burst to life. "Oilstone to Aquatone, acknowledged. Awaiting orders."

Peaslee was smiling. "Oilstone, you are to proceed to the following coordinates." He grabbed the map and found a position just west of Banes. "You are to then proceed low over the city until you reach the bay. In the bay you will see a large yellow sphere. That is a target. Do you understand?"

The radio crackled back. "Acknowledged, Aquatone. Please confirm that you are aware that I am light. Repeat: this is an Oilstone light mission."

Peaslee and Romanova exchanged a glance and then he spoke once more. "Understood, Oilstone. You have your orders."

"We should get to the bell tower," said Romanova. "We should be able to see from there."

They were running, and then climbing the stairs. Romanova first, and then Peel who had taken the radio, and then finally Peaslee. As they climbed the sun went down, and in the distance they could see the waters of the bay begin to stir. It was Romanova who first saw the plane. An ungainly black thing silhouted against the dying sun. It was quiet in the sky above the village, but only for a moment. For as the moon bubbled up out of the cloudy depths, the children came out of hiding.

"Is this going to work, Colonel?"

"I hope so, son. I haven't got anything else to try, do you?"

Something in the church below them crashed. The front doors had given way and children were suddenly inside the church. They were breaking things, slowly working their way through the building. Heading toward the tower.

Peel pulled on Tanya's jacket. "The pilot said he was 'light': what did he mean?"

Tanya Romanova gestured at the slowly arcing plane. "He's a spy plane, strictly reconnaissance. Built for speed and taking pictures. He's not armed. The only way he has to attack the target is by hitting it with the plane itself."

"But that's suicide!"

Tanya nodded and said nothing more.

The plane had finished its arc and had become little more than a thin black line in the distance that was slowly growing larger as they watched it get closer. Below them, the children had reached the door to the tower but were having problems breaking through. Others had given up trying to get in and were busy climbing up the side of the structure, clinging to vines and loose boards. Their tiny fingers and feet seemed perfect for the task, for they were making significant progress. Tanya handed Romero's gun to Peel and motioned toward the horde of frenzied kids that were crawling toward them.

As he looked back, he saw Peaslee's head suddenly shake and turn yellow. He reached out to the transforming man, but was pushed away. The Terrible Old Man lunged for the window, but Peel caught his jacket and swung him to the floor.

Pete Rawlik

The plane roared overhead. The children reached the belfrey.

Romanova fired her handgun, covering Peel as he dragged Peaslee to the corner. The TOM was screaming in agony. Together Peel and Romanova rose up and began firing as a wave of small bodies poured through the window. They were yellow, twisted, and covered in filth. In the distance the plane flew on. Body after body fell as Romanova switched to the Kalashnikov. Blood, still yellow, sprayed through the air.

The black plane grew small against the moon, and then plunged into it. The milky surface shuddered and then exploded in a geyser of color that swirled back into being. On the distant shore, the alien city wavered and then faded into nothingness. The moon that Tanya had called Demhe shrank as it vomited forth the stolen colors of the world. It collapsed in on itself until there was nothing more than a small glowing speck. Then the speck began to fade and Romanova could see the wreckage of the spy plane fall to the earth.

The children halted their advance, and Romanova stopped shooting them. Some of them, caught by the surprise of their location, fell to their deaths. Others began to cry. Romanova took the radio and sent an all-clear message. Cuban and Soviet soldiers would be leaving the line, coming as fast as they could to help. Tanya and Peel did what they could while they waited.

ᒉᗡᓄᕓᕽᕁᕽᕐ

It took two days for Peel and Peaslee to be returned to Guantanamo, and another day before they were stateside. Peel was briefed, debriefed, examined, questioned, interrogated and forced to sign certain documents that suggested he could be punished very badly. He later learned that Agent Romanova returned to the Soviet Union and was promoted and reassigned. In late December he flew home to Sydney for Christmas and took a job with the Australian government.

Colonel Doctor Wingate Peaslee stayed in a military hospital for six weeks. There was scaring on his hands and neck where the yellow was particularly bad, but the greatest damage was to his mind. The doctors diagnosed him with dementia. Security forces interviewed him extensively but found that he had no memory of his work with JACK. He was found unfit for duty and medically discharged. He was retired to a minimum security facility near Arkham, Massachusetts, where he developed a collection of rocks and glass bottles. He was prone to rages and tends to mutter incoherently to himself and his collection. On occasion he cried out before going into convulsions, during which he screamed the same word over and over again. The seizures never lasted for more than a minute. The word was *"Giallo."*

STRAGGLERS FROM CARRHAE

BY DARRELL SCHWEITZER

aybe it was just madness, or the delirium of wounds—maybe the entire experience was no more than that—but when Marcus Vibius suddenly said, "I'm thinking of leaving the army," his words seemed so strange, so impossible, that I just had to laugh, loudly, hysterically, madly and, yes, dangerously. Dangerously because it might invite the Parthians in to share the joke.

There we were in the glorious Year of Rome Six Hundred Ninety-something-or-other, in the stinking butt-hole end of Asia minor (aka Carrhae), lying in a ditch among piles of corpses, our heads kicked in, blood on our faces, blood pouring out of a hundred wounds as out of a hundred fountains—I exaggerate but slightly, for rhetorical effect—as the sun set and the triumphant foe settled down to dinner and a nap before resuming the slaughter of our comrades in the morning. *There.* Utter annihilation. The biggest upset since the days of Hannibal. Our imperious leader Crassus and his generals were all dead, the truce negotiations having turned out rather badly. The Parthians had supposedly poured molten gold down Crassus's throat on account of his boundless avarice—for this had been a completely pointless war brought on by the richest man in the world's desire for more loot—and *then*, under *those* circumstances, my friend said he was thinking of leaving the army.

I caught my breath, gasping. I glanced over at the Parthian campfires, at the smoke and dust staining the darkening sky. There were no Roman formations visible. All the golden eagles had fallen.

"I think the army is leaving us."

He heaved himself onto his elbows, trying to sit up, wincing. "No, seriously. I think the wisest course would be for us to just slip away. To the south, I suppose, into Arabia or one of those places. I'm sure some barbarian chief would be ready enough to hire a couple of slightly dented ex-legionary swords. We could make a good living. Become robbers if we have to."

I shook my head. This was still too crazy for words. "That's desertion. You remember what Centurion Macro said about desertion."

"No I don't. Tell me." He smiled, like a child about to hear a favorite story again.

Imitating the Centurion's high-pitched, almost feminine voice as best I could, and his ridiculous hand-gestures, I said. "The penalty for desertion is crucifixion—and loss of pay."

Now he was the one to find this uncontrollably funny. Under such circumstances the perspective on humor, madness, sanity, righteous action, whatever, tends to dribble away like sand through your fingers when you're trying to drink and there is nothing *to* drink. Speaking of which, we were both desperately thirsty from a hard day's getting slaughtered, and our voices were no more than rasping croaks. I began to argue that unless we gave the impression that we were a pair of cackling demons up from the underworld, all this impromptu merriment just might attract the attention of Parthian patrols or looters, and maybe we'd best remove ourselves hither, or thither, or words to that effect; and Marcus Vibius agreed, and added, "We're not deserters after all. If we run into a Roman unit, we join them and say we're stragglers from Carrhae, which we are, and then we straggle on with them, and I guess we don't get to be robbers in Arabia after all, but otherwise we just keep on straggling all the way to fucking Arabia ..."

"Time to straggle," I said.

"Follow me."

Now there was a time in my life when I would have followed Marcus Vibius anywhere. I had followed him *into* the army when I was a poor boy shoved out of the family farm (to make room for heroic veterans, who had been promised farms!). He was a clever wastrel on the run from I didn't know what, and the prospect of twenty years of legionary chow looked better to both of us than immediate starvation. I had followed him through marches, battles. I admit I looked up to him as a brother, a father even, the one steady anchor in my otherwise randomly drifting life. He always seemed the wiser, cleverer, stronger, more experienced one—or at least he talked a good line—and I, quite naturally followed, like when he'd grabbed me by the collar and hauled me out of the way as the Parthians, covered all over with metal scales like enormous lizards, rode down our formation. Vibius hauled me into a ditch while the tide of battle washed over us and smeared the landscape with bodies and broken weapons, stray limbs, shit, and Roman blood. Yes, he seemed to know what he was doing. He straggled. I followed. And so on through the night until we truly could not go on any longer, and he dropped to his knees, and remained kneeling on top of one of the numberless brown, barren hills, until he couldn't anymore and tumbled down into a ravine.

I climbed down beside him and lay against him, my head on his chest, my tongue so parched I tried to lick the sweat off my own arm for relief before I passed out. And what dreams I dreamed that night! Great vistas of the black, yet burning world of the damned, over which I soared as if I were a bird, caught on an inexorable wind and blown helplessly before the very throne of King Hades himself. The wind howled and almost screamed, then died down to a whisper as the dark god leaned forward on his onyx throne and demanded of me my name, and how I came hence, and how I happened to have died, and what sort of presumptuous fool did I think I was if I didn't know my name and was still claiming to be alive just because my friend Vibius talked a good line?

But then the wind carried me on further, out of the throne room and into a darkness filled with stars—stars like foam glowing on the beach at night, stars swirling and racing around me, the waves of them breaking around my legs, hot and cold at the same time, as I stood among them—and then the dark sky was filled with wings, not those of birds, but great, featherless, flapping things like ragged tent-cloth in a desert storm; and in the darkness, all around me, so close that I could feel it everywhere, against every part of my body as if I were forcing my way through dense, dry underbrush, the air itself was thick with hard, wriggling claws.

When I awoke, Vibius was awake and sitting beside me, and next to him was none other than everybody's favorite officer, Centurion Macro.

"He can't be real," I said sitting up, poking Macro with my finger. He was solid enough, though dry and hollow, it seemed, like a husk; and the reason I had doubted his reality was that half of his skull had been sheared away, and one of his arms was missing, and where blood should have been pouring out of these grievous wounds, there was only a foul-smelling, tarry mass.

I poked him again, and his single remaining eye blinked.

"This is ridiculous," I said, although the hilarity of the previous evening had definitely begun to fade. "He can't … I mean, nobody could … I mean, *just look at him!* Poor Macro. He was a bastard, but I wouldn't have wished this on him—"

"Shut *up!*" said Vibius. "This is serious. It is a sign from the infernal gods. Nobody comes back from the dead without the express permission of a god."

"He is dead, then? Not just a bit banged up? I mean, you never know;

Darryl Schweitzer

some people have survived the most remarkable wounds; there was that guy we heard about in Gaul with the spear that went in one ear and out the other –"

Vibius slapped me on the side of the head, hard, and said, "You're babbling. Shut *the fuck* up."

My friend was in charge again. Yes, definitely. I would follow him anywhere.

To Centurion Macro, Vibius said, in a muted, respectful tone, "Sir, can you hear me?"

Macro turned his one eye toward Vibius. He opened his mouth. At first there was only a whispering, hissing sound, like the wind in my dream, and a foulness so thick you could almost see it. The air rippled.

"Sir," said Vibius again. "What message do you bring from the land of the dead? What god has sent you back us?"

And the Centurion replied, quite plainly, *"Nyarlathotep."*

Somehow, for once, both of us had the good sense to say nothing.

"Nyarlathotep," the Centurion repeated.

We stared at one another, and at the Centurion, both of us amazed and stunned, and beginning to be very much afraid, which was itself frightening. I mean, we were soldiers, Roman soldiers, who are quite used to imminent death, destruction, mangled bodies, and gaping wounds. But this was turning theological. We were out of our depth. The only thing I could think of, inasmuch as I could think at all, was that this was some new, unknown god of darkness, first revealed to mankind through *us two*, which made us prophets or sages or something—not bad work; you can get used to the benefits, gold offerings, buxom priestesses, the whole bit—but somehow, *somehow* I really doubted any of that was coming our way, any more than our lives would ever be what we wanted again. We weren't going to get to pillage Arabia, I didn't think, no, not a bit.

"Can we straggle now?" I whimpered.

"Yeah. Straggle."

Vibius hauled himself to his feet, then me. We climbed out of the ravine, looking this way and that for Parthians, but saw no one. Overhead, the sky still seemed to swirl with smoke and dust, and it was filled with cawing, black birds all streaming toward the battlefield to feast on our late comrades. You didn't have to be an augur to know *that* was an unpromising omen.

I tried to formulate a prayer to someone. To Mars, god of warriors. Yeah, we were still warriors, weren't we? To Mercury, god of thieves. We'd need him if we ever got to Arabia.

"To the unknown god, whose name is—"

"Just shut up and straggle," Vibius said. Good advice.

You want to talk about omens? Portents? How about this? The ruined corpse of Centurion Macro *followed us.* We couldn't get rid of him, as much as we had the strength to try. He, being dead, did not tire as we did. He, being entirely dead, was not half-dead with thirst. He, admittedly, stood by patiently later that afternoon when we finally came to a stream, and Vibius and I dropped down to frantically refresh ourselves.

Overhead, some of the black birds cawed and began to circle.

Not good.

Somehow we survived the day, Vibius and I who were alive, and the dead thing that followed us. That night, when we camped in another ravine between two more dry, jagged hills, I think it was Vibius who had the truly terrible dreams. I dreamed only of an abyss, and I had a sense that something terrible sat there in the darkness, waiting patiently, but it did not stir and it did not speak.

But it must have been Vibius who dreamed the great dreams that night, because when I awoke just at dawn—and the sky was still mostly dark, just beginning to lighten in the east, yet with cawing black birds circling overhead—*his* dream was still going on. He lay on his back, his eyes wide open, staring at the sky. He was still asleep or at least not awake in the usual sense; I could tell that—and he called out in a loud voice in a language I did not know—all clicks and coughs and grunts, and it seemed as if he were conversing with something out there in the fading darkness, something he was calling down out of the sky. Something huge and winged; not the black birds, but something I thought I glimpsed myself. I must have still been dreaming too, then, for in one instant the sky was thick with bat-winged monstrosities with too many limbs, slightly resembling enormous wasps in their shape, or maybe winged crabs or lobsters— absurd as that sounds—part of the joke, the joke, the *joke,* remember? The one we were still laughing at.

Gradually I became aware that, all around us, the late Centurion Macro had been joined by more of his kind. A least two dozen corpses in varying degrees of mutilation stood or sat or crawled among the sand and stones on every side, rustling slowly, turning toward Vibius as he spoke in his dream or trance or whatever it was. There were even a couple of dead Parthians among them, although the enemy had taken but few casualties in the recent battle.

I crawled over to Marcus Vibius and shook him. "Wake up! This has to stop! Stop what you're doing!"

Slowly, he did wake up, but it was as if his spirit was returning to his body after a very long journey. His voice was hollow and distant, and raspy, like the wind, and it seemed to be coming from some greater depth than merely within his body.

"Nyarlathotep," he said. "I come at the bidding of my lord Nyarlathotep."

Darryl Schweitzer

And the dead men around us all cried out, or made such noises as they could, to echo the name of the god Nyarlathotep, for I did not doubt it *was* a god, some strange god of darkness unknown even to Pluto or Dis or Mors or any other god of the Romans or the Parthians—they've got a Lord of Darkness too, I forget his name, but it's not *Nyarlathotep*, I am sure –

"You're babbling, my friend," Marcus Vibius said to me, in a voice that almost sounded like his old self again. "I can hear your thoughts. Even in your thoughts you are babbling."

I looked around at the corpses, who were staring at us intently, but, I felt, waiting for some signal or command before springing into action.

"What the *fuck* is going on, Marcus?" I was almost weeping then. Yes, we were the fearless, manly, allegedly invincible legionaries of Rome, but at this moment—

"Oh, if you could see what I have seen already—"

"Yes?"

He began that mad laugh of his once more.

"Yes?" I demanded.

"You wouldn't understand a damned thing!"

I shook him once more, and slapped his face to bring him to his senses.

But he only went on as if it were all a big joke.

"And if you saw what I am *about* to see, well, forget it."

A wind seemed to whirl around him, like invisible wings beating. Sand and grit swirled up, into my face. The wind blew me away, tumbling over backward, as if a whirlwind were forming around Vibius, and then he *rose up into the air.* Something lifted him. I could *almost* see it. There was something wrong with the light. The air rippled. It was as if my eyes saw something but my brain could not make sense out of it. And for a moment, as the dawn broke and the sun rose, I *could* see clearly against the paling sky. I *saw* him dangling in their grasp, as he was carried off into the sky by two of the winged things with too many limbs and impossible shapes, which I have learned from subsequent adventures and dreams and revelations are called *Mi-Go.*

꓾ꟿꚙꚙꚖꛓꛕ

Now the only *rational* explanation for any of this, for this entire gibbering tirade, is that I, your humble narrator, am insane, that it is all an insane joke conceived in the heat and dust and the stink of the battlefield of Carrhae, when the Roman formation broke and the Parthians in their scale armor rode us down and Marcus Vibius *didn't* pull me aside before some axe or mace split my skull like a melon, and as my brains went splattering hither and yon, little hurtling lumps of gore and gray matter, on their own initiative, began to ask the question *What the fuck is going on? They* invented this more-than-slightly incoherent story about walking corpses and unknown gods and Marcus Vibius being hauled off into the sky by *Mi-Go—*

But then I am not always one for rational explanations. But let me try. Please. Just listen.

As I got up that day and staggered about the landscape, straggling, straggling, I asked myself over and over *What the fuck is going on?* a phrase foreign to the elegant Latin of learned men—I mean, can you just imagine the famous Cicero writing a treatise called *On What The Fuck is Going On?* Maybe he should have. The phrase is familiar enough in the argot of rough and semi-literate soldiers. Maybe he should have joined us in the muck as we all asked: *What the fuck is going on?* A question worthy of the greatest minds of our age, or the most profound of long-winded philosophers who blather for a living in all the great cities of our world, even in Athens. I was in Athens once. Didn't like it much. The food was greasy and terrible and so were the whores. And I didn't know enough Greek to ask one of the philosophers who abounded there, *What the fuck is going on?* I could have, should have, might yet, because I have *my theory* as to *What the fuck is going on?* which says that I marched that whole day without food or water throughout the landscape, trying to find my way south to Arabia where the food and the whores and the loot might be better and there would be no philosophers asking *What the fuck is going on?* In my delirium and weakness—for I'd had a little water, but not eaten in … however long since our last feast on much-vaunted army chow before the battle … with the result that I entirely lost count of *how many* resurrected dead men were inexplicably following me and whispering the name of Nyarlathotep.

I got no answer to my quite reasonable question until Marcus Vibius *returned.*

Did I say he returned to me? No, I did not. But he did. I am not making this up, any more than I am insanely babbling my way in the vaguely general direction of the conclusion of a joke to which I don't know the punch line.

It was dark again. Another night? Did I but dream the day? Had the sun ever risen? Was I really accompanied now by a virtual army of mangled corpses, with black birds swirling and cawing and swooping down to eat their faces and peck out their eyes, which did not even slow them in their progress?

Well, maybe. In the darkness, then, as the air vibrated with the nearness

Darryl Schweitzer

of great wings—not the birds, something far, far larger and stranger—and there was also, everywhere, a buzzing like the sound of a million bees—in this darkness, out of this darkness, the voice of my lifelong companion Vibius spoke to me, descending from the air, drawing ever nearer, until he was again sitting beside me on a shelf of stone, as we two looked down over the battlefield where the Parthians had pitched their tents to more conveniently loot the adjacent slain—for it seemed that our long meandering march had been more or less circular, and we'd come right back to where we'd started, only now we had an army of dead men at our backs and the unsuspecting Parthians below.

He put his hand on my arm, as if to calm and comfort me, but his touch was cold and dry, like a lizard's or an insect's. His voice was not his own. It was as if some *other* spoke through him. And his eyes were not his own. They were just hollows of blackness.

But still he spoke to me, and he said that I could not imagine or hope to describe what he had seen and felt until I *gave myself over wholly* to Nyarlathotep as he had in his dreams. He explained a great deal to me, yes, because, he said, I deserved an explanation and an answer to the very reasonable question of *What the fuck is going on?* He was proud of me. Here I had gathered his army for him, and waited for his return. He would make me his first tribune, he said, and together we would serve Nyarlathotep, who was, indeed, a dark god from beyond any realms known to mankind or human priests or augurs, a god for whom the gods of Earth and the underworld were as insects. And this god was but a *messenger* of even stranger gods, who sometimes, for their own inexplicable reasons, meddled in human history even as Nyarlathotep proposed that one good historical upset deserves another and wouldn't the Parthian general Surena be surprised when we two led an army of invincible corpses and winged *Mi-Go* against his supposedly victorious men and conquered the whole world and ruled it in the name of Nyarlathotep and Nyarlathotep's masters in an endless epoch of darkness and horror?

"Yeah, I bet he would be surprised," said Vibius, and he laughed, and for just that moment his laugh was his own and there seemed something human left in him, and to prolong that moment *just long enough* I repeated a mixture of an old army joke and a mutual recollection, something about greasy whores in Athens, and again he laughed, and I knew that for that instant, whatever transformation he had undergone, he was still human enough to be mortal, and so in that instant I was able to slide my sword out of my scabbard and up under his ribs, into his heart, so that he died, weeping for the grandeur of his visions, his head in my lap, spitting out honest, red blood, not black slime, and in my very last moment of sanity I told myself that the Parthians at least were human, and it was better to let them have their victory now—Rome could always defeat them later. Better Parthians than let the darkness win, after which there would be no more victories.

𝕵𝕾𝕵𝕵𝕵𝕽𝕾𝕸

So, the rational explanation is that I, your humble narrator, who probably had a name once, Somethingus Somethingus Something, am *completely mad*, and a despicable scoundrel who, having deserted the Roman army after the catastrophic defeat at Carrhae, murdered his dearest companion in the desert and very likely ate the corpse—for where is it? What proof is there of any of this? It is impossible to believe, of course, that the sun came up that day and I found myself sitting alone on that rock ledge, with my old friend dead in my lap, the Parthians spread out on the plain before me, and *no* sign of the late Centurion Macro or any of his fellow corpses anywhere, as if they had evaporated with the first rays of the wholesome sun, which, I am told, the Parthians quite sensibly worship as the principle of goodness, cleansing the universe of all evil contagion.

That must be the truth. The sunlight cleansed the world of my evil dream, and that's the end of it. We must not believe that I, the murderer and madman, arose and straggled off, into darkness that does not end, while Nyarlathotep walks beside me always in my dreams. I can almost see him, the hollow eyes, the air rippling about him like a black cloak. I can almost see the *Mi-Go* who worship him, and the beasts of the desert that lick his hands.

But we mustn't believe any of that. No.

We mustn't believe that Nyarlathotep and the rest, the unknown, dark gods, seek to return to our world, but aren't quite material, and so must come into focus in the dreams of some great dreamer, some visionary, someone considerably more imaginative and intelligent than myself, like Marcus Vibius, for instance, who died before his dreams quite came to fruition.

We must expressly deny that Nyarlathotep walks beside me, not angry or vengeful, for his kind are far beyond such petty human emotions; but he still finds me a bit of a disappointment.

I do not expect to be telling this story much longer. The air around me is filled with flapping wings, with buzzing.

I call upon King Hades to welcome me, soon, into the comforts of his

311

Darryl Schweitzer

kingdom. I sacrifice to him, because there are far worse places where I, where all of us, could end up.

We are all stragglers, with nowhere to go in the end.

That is, if you believe any of this. Which is the punch line of the joke, at last.

THE PROCYON PROJECT

BY TIM CURRAN

t was an easy gig and Finn pulled it because he was a real, bonafide small-town hero. When he got back to Caneberry Creek from the Pacific, people couldn't do enough for him. They all wanted to hear how he'd given it to the Japs on Guadalcanal as if he had taken them down single-handedly. Sometimes he almost believed it himself … at least until he woke sweating and shaking at four in the morning from nightmares of Japanese soldiers rushing by the dozens from low cave mouths, blood-smeared and fanatical.

Regardless, he did his best to sell himself as the hard-bitten, tough Marine and defender of freedom. It got him free lunches, dates with pretty girls, and even tickets to the latest flicks at the Rialto on Main. If they wanted to believe he was some hard-charging, bullet-eating, lean mean killing machine, so be it. He wasn't stupid enough to look a gift horse in the mouth. He played the part and they ate it up. And all it had cost him was his nerves and his left leg.

He wasn't back two weeks when he was offered the job at Blue Hills, which was a former pesticide plant that had been tricked out—as part of the war effort and something called the Procyon Project—as a weapons-research facility for the Defense Department. What went on there was classified, strictly hush-hush, but it paid well and all Finn had to do was check IDs when the workers and eggheads showed. It paid well and gave him plenty of time to read his magazines.

It was strictly creampuff stuff, and after Guadalcanal, he was more than ready for a life of leisure.

Just after Halloween in '43, he was pulling midnights because two of the guards had been drafted. He drove out to Blue Hills, clocked in, grabbed a cup of joe at the cafeteria, then made his way out to the guard shack. He was in luck. Manpower was in such short supply that they had called in a couple retirees to fill out the ranks. One of them was Chester DeYoung, another old jarhead from the old days. He'd seen his share of action with the Marine Corps during the Philippine Insurrection forty years before.

"Well, look what we got here," Chester said when he saw him. "Old blood-and-guts himself. What's a good-looking grunt like you doing in a place like this?"

Finn giggled. Chester always gave it to him and he liked that. He was about the only one in town who treated him like an ordinary human being. Everyone else acted like he was made out of glass. And he'd told Chester that more than once.

"Guilt," was Chester's answer. "They ration gas, collect metal, can't get panty hose or good beef, but you *really* sacrificed and they know it. You gave a limb to keep the flag flying. But don't worry, son. You give it a year or two, they won't give a damn. You won't be able to pay them to listen to the stories of an old leatherneck. Take my word for it."

Finn found that both liberating *and* disturbing.

But that's what he liked about Chester. He had a way of putting things into perspective. Every time Finn told him about something that bothered him, Chester would sort it out for him and give him a new way of looking at things. Unlike his own father, who got up every day and stared at his son's medals on the mantelpiece like he was gazing upon the Ark of the Covenant itself. Finn was pretty certain old Dad liked the medals better than the guy who'd won them.

"How's it tonight?"

Chester shrugged, stretched. "Same, same, same. Check 'em in and check 'em out. I'm so good at it I ought to bag groceries at the A & P. How you holding up, son?"

"Good, pretty good."

"Still getting the nightmares?"

Finn thought about lying, then he just nodded his head. "They've been bad lately. Real bad."

"They get that way. I know I had my fill and now and again, I still get them. You can't go through combat and walk away from it pure as snow. Something in you forever changes. You just have to accept that and plod on."

Chester told him that the heavy fighting for the Sohoton cliffs in 1901 still came back to him in his dreams. The ground was wet with blood. He'd never forget the men he mowed down during the assault.

"Sometimes it seems like a lifetime ago, and sometimes it seems like last week."

But, Christ, that was forty years ago, Finn got to thinking. *Am I still going to be dreaming about this shit in the 1980s?*

A sudden rumbling sound broke up the talk. It was coming from one of the main research complexes. The entire ground seemed to shake, then vibrate. Finn felt suddenly lightheaded, his guts clenching like a fist. He teetered uneasily on his artificial leg.

"Been hearing that off and on all night," Chester admitted. "Hell if I know what they're doing up there. Hopefully they won't blow us up."

Finn stepped out of the shack and leaned against it, sucking in lungfuls of cool, clean air. Crazy. That's what it was. The rumbling made him tense up like when the shells were incoming on Guadalcanal. It felt as if his guts pulled up into his chest. That was bad enough. But the weird vibration made his head spin, his eyesight blur, and his skin feel like it wanted to crawl off his bones. There was something wrong about that.

"My neck gets sore when it does that," Chester said. "Goddamn old ticker skips a beat."

Finn worked his jaw. The fillings in his teeth made his molars ache like the metal was expanding.

"What the hell kinds of things are they doing up there?"

But Chester just shook his head. "Don't know and maybe I don't want to know. Can't say that I care for it much."

Finn lit a cigarette to calm his nerves and steel himself. There was something very strange about this whole business. Suddenly, his scalp prickled and it came again—that low rumbling that made the ground shake. It was followed by something like a high electronic squealing, then the vibrations. His head spun again. When he opened his eyes … it seemed as if the world was moving, the trees writhing in the woods though there was no wind. And the stars overhead had changed. Instead of looking like tiny white pinpricks, they looked much closer, like glowing, pulsating marbles.

Then all returned to normal.

"It gets you inside, don't it?" Chester told him. "I thought I was going to throw up the first time. I called up to Building A to see if something happened, but Doc Westly said they were just having some generator problems."

Generator problems, Finn thought. *That wasn't no goddamn generator. Felt like the fucking world was about to split its pants.*

He didn't really know what the Procyon Project was, but he was pretty certain it had nothing to do with generators.

Chester snapped his lunchbox closed. "Well, I best get going. The old woman waits up for me. Keeps the soup hot." He dropped a wink to Finn. "Worries about me heading into town and catting around with the girls."

"Sure," Finn told him, forcing a laugh.

Chester waved and then he was outside the gate, moving pretty fast across the lot to his old Ford. He looked like he couldn't get away from Blue Hills fast enough.

Shivering, Finn didn't blame him one bit.

TRAINING

The first hour was easy. Finn sat around in the shack and listened to Kay Kyser live from the Aragon Ballroom in Chicago and paged through one of his mystery magazines. It was quiet, low-key, and boring. Just the way he liked it.

Around 1:30, he started making his rounds of the facility, keying in at the various watch clocks. Buildings A and B was where the research was going on, but there were a dozen other sheds and storage Quonsets that had to be checked. There were two guards on as always: Finn and Jack Coye. Finn had the gate sector and Jack had the western sector, which included Buildings A and B. They had it all timed out. They'd start their rounds at 1:30 and by 2:15 they'd meet up over at the dispatch office, which was unmanned at night.

Ever since that weird stuff earlier—the rumblings and vibrations—Finn was feeling more than a little on edge. He was looking forward to running into Jack and having a smoke with him. Not only for the company, but because Jack always seemed to know about things he wasn't supposed to know.

Jack usually made it to dispatch before Finn did. You could only go so fast with a wooden leg.

Although the various drives and parking lots of Blue Hills were strategically lit, it was still a damn dark night. The black forest seemed to be pressing up closer to the fence than usual. A crescent moon hung above the dark thickets and fields of tangled yellow grasses.

Finn felt like he was the last person on earth.

The damp seemed to be reaching up under his coat and crawling along his spine. He couldn't shake the chill that encompassed him. He was even getting the phantom stiffness in his missing leg again. Of all things.

He moved along the outer road, *gimping along,* as he liked to refer to it, checking the fence because they were real particular about their fence at Blue Hills. There was nothing to see as usual, just lots of weeds and shadows and that awful encroaching darkness that Finn simply could not tolerate tonight. Maybe it reminded him too much of those black nights on Alligator Creek during the Battle of Tenaru when the Japs assaulted their positions all night long … or maybe it reminded him of the pooling shadows that seemed to ooze out of his closet door at night when he was a kid.

Whatever it was, it was really doing a job on him.

He patrolled along the outer road, scanning the fence with his flashlight, almost afraid of what the light might reveal in the long grasses. He felt tense inside, his heartbeat fluttery.

It should have lessened after he got back on the main road and made his way up to the boiler house, but it increased. Nothing felt right tonight. Everything was out of whack somehow and he couldn't put a finger on what it was. When he got up near the dark hulk of the boiler house, he thought he heard a noise. A sort of *fssst! fssst!* sort of sound. The first time he paused briefly, but the second time it came he stopped dead.

Hell is that?

He waited there, looking from the cars of the night crew parked in the grass to the boiler house itself.

Fssst! Fssst! Fssst!

It seemed more insistent now and it was coming from over near the cars themselves. Finn approached them cautiously, ever aware of the .38 at his hip. His hand eased down toward the gun, fingers wrapping around the butt. As he withdrew it, a dew of sweat speckling his forehead, he panned the cars with his light. They were all dark and empty.

He saw something scamper behind a coupe.

It was large, too large to be a woodchuck or even a bobcat. In the back of his mind, he thought it had been a man scampering away on all fours. Swallowing, he looked around. What he would have given for some backup just about then. There were always the boys in the boiler house … but what was he supposed to tell them? That some night animal had him scared white?

Shit, Finn, we didn't think Marines were scared of anything.

Yeah, he could hear it now. Whatever this was, he would have to handle it on his own. He heard the *fssst! fssst!* sound again and by then, he was shaking. His nerves weren't good since the Pacific. He had a habit of starting at the slightest sound. Even his sleep was thin, so thin it could barely be called sleep. A twig scraping against the roof or a dog barking three streets away brought him fully awake, eyes staring, muscles bunched and ready for action.

The .38 was shaking in his hand.

"Hey!" he called out, his voice scratchy and weak. "Hey! Who's over there?"

There was no response but that same *fssst! fssst!* which sounded a little too

Tim Curran

much like the call of a night grasshopper ... except it would have taken about 10,000 of them to reach the kind of volume he was hearing.

Carefully, he edged around the cars, keeping the light in front of him. He had heard some very weird sounds in the Pacific at night, animals and insects that were truly disturbing, but this was beyond that. Now he was hearing something else. It almost sounded like a soft, meaty chewing.

"Hey!" he said with more volume now.

The chewing stopped. It was replaced by an almost throaty purring sound, then that *fssst! fssst!* noise, but louder now. Almost like a warning. It was coming from behind the Chevy in the back. Finn tried to swallow as he made his way over there, but there was no spit left in his mouth. The gun was shaking in one hand and the flashlight in the other, its beam bobbing frantically.

He moved around the Chevy, smelling a sweet, almost decayed sort of odor that stirred his guts. Then he moved around the back of the car and saw ... he didn't know what he saw ... only that it was enough to make him take two or three awkward steps back that put him firmly on his ass.

The light glanced off something.

Something that went *fssst! fssst!* and then rose up into the air on membranous wings that made a whirring sound like the prop of an airplane. It flew right over him and off into the darkness. He sat there, his breath barely coming, his heart pounding in his chest. Whatever it had been, it was nearly the size of a man but looked almost like an insect, a wasp maybe, except that it was set with sharp spiky hairs like needles and had three globular yellow eyes. *And* it had a mouth filled with backward-curving fangs like those of a rattlesnake.

When he pulled himself to his feet, his light picked out the remains of what must have been a raccoon that was split right open, its entrails cast about like bloody clocksprings.

That thing ... that bug ... it had been eating it.

He stumbled back toward the boiler shack, bound and determined to tell the night crew what he had just seen, but then he stopped, knowing he couldn't. They would think he was nuts. Another crazy shell-shocked gyrene. They might not laugh to his face, but after he left they would be doing just that.

No, he wasn't going to say a thing.

Maybe he *had* hallucinated it. Maybe his nerves were more shot than he realized. Maybe the war had unscrewed something in his head.

But he didn't believe that for a minute.

ᛏᛟᛉᚾᛁᛉᚷ

He was late getting over to dispatch and he knew it, but things weren't exactly easy after the big bug. Maybe outside he was no longer shaking, but inside he was still trembling, his guts coiled white. He had to key in at four different watch clocks before he got to dispatch and his hand was shaking so badly at the first two that he could barely hang onto the key.

Finally, he just stopped, breathing in and out, forcing himself to calm down.

You survived a war, meathead, and now an overgrown hornet is giving you the heebie-jeebies?

He thought that sounded real, real good, but it didn't hold water. He had seen the teeth on that thing and since when did insects have teeth? And the wings … now that he thought about it, there hadn't been a single pair, but maybe two or three pairs. No, it was wrong in every conceivable way. Bugs did not get that big and they did not have fucking teeth.

He keyed in at his last station and breathed a sigh of relief.

He couldn't wait to see Jack.

Jack would have some good gossip about all this weirdness, and he knew it.

Finn walked down the lonely moonlit road, getting closer and closer to Building A, and dispatch, which was housed in a Quonset just down the way from it. A cup of coffee and a cigarette, and he would start feeling human again. Things would make sense then.

The rumbling came again.

Oh shit, not again.

The rumbling noise grew louder and louder, sounding suddenly like huge waves crashing into a pier. The ground was moving and again Finn found himself on his ass. The vibrations began right away. He could feel them in his bones, in his blood, in his tissues. It felt like the very stuff he was made of was going to fly apart at any moment. The nausea moved in waves through his belly; his head spun like a top. When he blinked it away, he saw the world as he had never seen it before. It was grotesque and twisted, the trees like wriggling black fingers reaching up to luminous clouds in the sky, the buildings like leaning monoliths, the stars above incredibly bright and incredibly close, each of them pulsating and fleshy, like beating hearts, and each of them opening like eyes in livid blood-swollen sockets.

Finn screamed.

Then screamed again as he saw a flock of those horrible insects pass over the face of the moon, which was unpleasantly close and unpleasantly bloated, like a slice of moist rotting fruit.

Then it ended.

He got to his feet and hobbled the rest of the way to the dispatch Quonset. When he got there, he leaned against it trying to catch his breath. He could not seem to find

Tim Curran

his center. He held onto the outer metal shell because he was literally afraid that it would happen again and this time he really *would* fly apart.

After about five minutes, he was calm.

As calm as he was going to get anyway. He went through the door and found Jack Coye waiting for him. He was sitting by the radio, monitoring the air traffic out there. A cigarette dangled from his mouth. His usually robust face looked pale and pouchy. There were brown circles under his eyes.

"Crazy night," he said. "One hell of a crazy night."

Finn dropped himself into a swivel chair, pressing his hands flat against his legs so they would not shake. Jack poured him a cup of hot black coffee and he sipped it slowly, dragging off a Chesterfield.

"You look like you seen a ghost," Jack said.

"Seen more than one," Finn told him.

"It's that … whatever they're doing over there. Some kind of generator, word has it. Some kind of energy source or something. Lots of weird stories making the rounds. I almost pissed my pants the last time they fired it up." He turned from the radio and looked at Finn. "Been getting to you, too?"

"Oh, yeah," Finn said.

"Feel it in your guts?"

"Yeah."

"Your head?"

"Yeah."

"Makes you want to vomit out your stomach?"

"Yes. What's it about?"

Jack shook his head and lit another cigarette. He sat there smoking it. A long gray ash fell from the end onto his uniform coat. He didn't seem to notice. "Every time that machine up there kicks in, radio goes crazy. Everything cuts out. Nothing but static. But you should hear the traffic out there when it comes back on. Planes stalling out in the sky. Police losing their frequencies. Trouble over at the power plant. Maybe it's not related; I don't know."

Oh, it was related. Finn was certain of that. Whatever kind of machine they were developing or testing up there, it was like no machine the world had ever seen. He had no idea what it could be, but he was starting to be very afraid of its potential. Every time they kicked on, things went insane. The world changed, the sky changed. And each time it seemed to be a little worse.

And what about that creature eating the raccoon? He asked himself with a slight involuntary shiver. *What in the hell was that about?*

Again, he didn't know. All he knew for sure was that it looked like some kind of horrible insect, but like no insect of this world. He wanted to tell himself it was unrelated to what they were fooling around with up there, but he wasn't buying it. And particularly after he saw that swarm of them when the machine kicked on just a few minutes before.

They were related, but in what way he did not know. It was simply beyond his comprehension.

"I don't know what they're doing, Jack, but they're putting out a lot of power. Power or energy like we never seen before."

Jack nodded, pulling off his cigarette. "The only scuttlebutt slipping out is something about a generator, a power source. That's the core of Procyon, I guess. Gotta be something big, though. I pulled day shift last week. We had brass from the Defense Department coming through, and a general from Army Intelligence. I hear they had admirals from ONI and ONR here on Monday. This is big, Finn, real big. You know what else?"

Finn looked at him. "I'm afraid to ask."

"Way I hear it, it won't be just us handling security come next week. They're bringing in soldiers to man the fence."

Finn was liking all of this less and less. They already had MPs guarding the main buildings, but now the fence, too? "Well, I hope they don't blow us off the fucking planet."

Jack looked around conspiratorially as if he was trying to see if anyone was listening. "Now, I don't claim to know what they got up there, but get this," he said in a whisper. "I got a cousin over in Puxley. He works at a meatpacking house. Apparently, they've been doing business here at Blue Hills."

"A meatpacking house?"

Jack nodded. "For the past month they've been bringing over truckloads of meat and blood."

"Blood?"

"Yeah. According to my cousin, they've been delivering something like over a hundred pounds of raw meat and twenty gallons of animal blood two or three times a week," Jack admitted. "It would take a small army to go through that much beef on a weekly basis. And the blood … what the hell do they want with twenty gallons of animal blood?"

Finn felt sick inside. The scientists up there working on some kind of machine were one thing, but this was something else again. That much meat and blood suggested they were feeding animals. But there were no animals at Blue Hills. It wasn't a biology station or a medical research outfit; they were involved strictly in weapons research. Physics and electronics and the like. That's what the Procyon Project was about. At least, that's what people said.

Jack let that lay for awhile. "You think that's strange? Well, get this. They've

Tim Curran

been getting deliveries of books and documents from some university out east. They come by special courier."

"What of it?"

Jack offered him a sardonic grin. "These aren't just any books or documents, friend. They're not technical manuals or blueprints or any of that baloney. These are special." He looked around ever more carefully now, ignoring the posters on the wall that said LOOSE LIPS SINK SHIPS and CARELESS TALK COSTS LIVES. "These are *magic* books."

Finn couldn't believe what he heard then. Not just magic as in pull-the-old-rabbit-out-of-the-hat, but magic as in *black magic.* These were ancient, rare compendiums of arcane lore about vanished religions and forgotten gods, spell books that described how to summon things from beyond space and time.

"You mean, like demons?" he said, his voice dry as chalk dust.

Jack shrugged. "Witch books, Finn. That's what they are. My source told me they got weird names like *Necronomicon* and *De Vermis Mysteriis* ... that's Latin, by the way. These books are old, old, old. Very rare. They were banned by the church centuries ago. Only a few copies remain. Devil books."

"This is goddamn crazy. You sure your *source* isn't having a good laugh at your expense?"

Jack shook his head. His eyes were wide and unblinking, his face mottled with a grayish pallor. No, he looked worried; scared, even. His was not the face of someone who had gotten off a good one.

"Those books are for calling up things ... I can't even pronounce the names. Don't ask me to."

"But what's it all mean, Jack? What the hell is going on here?"

Jack shrugged. "I don't know. They got some kind of machine that sends out waves or something that make people sick. It creates some kind of energy that makes the stars go funny. They're bringing in blood and meat like they got a cage of tigers up there. And they're studying books on devil worship and witchcraft." He swallowed. "I'm afraid to connect the dots on this one."

"Me and you both, brother," Finn said.

ᴛᴊᴀᴊᴉᴀᴦ

They chatted for another hour, then separated to go make their rounds. It was easy and peaceful. Finn relaxed because there didn't seem to be any more activity coming from up on the hill, and that was a godsend. He keyed in at the watch clocks, taking his time, enjoying the night. He saw nothing weird. Everything that had already happened was slowly fading in his mind and he was putting it in perspective—save for the big bug. He still couldn't make sense of any of it, particularly the things Jack told him about, but he knew well enough that some things were better off being left alone.

None of my business what they're doing up there.

Joe Heidigger had offered him a job driving a forklift over at the lumber yard last week and Finn was thinking very seriously about taking him up on it. Maybe it was time for a change. Time to distance himself completely from the war and weapons. God knew he'd served, he'd done his part. Nobody could ask more from him.

The night was nice. Real nice. That was what he liked about the graveyard shift. The quiet, the tranquility. The crickets. The night birds. The lonesome cry of an owl. The solitude put you in touch with yourself. You could think and make sense of things.

He got back to the shack, poured a cup of coffee from his thermos, and settled in. He had high hopes the rest of the night would be quiet. But when he heard the sound of running footsteps he knew that wasn't going to happen.

Sighing, he stepped out of the shack and saw Dr. Westly right away. He was one of the Procyon Project scientists. His game was physics, Finn knew. In the flashlight beam, his eyes were wide, his mouth trembling. "Up there," he breathed. "It's happening up there ... we can't stop it now. We *can't!*"

"Can't stop what?" Finn asked.

"The machine ... it's self-augmenting! It no longer needs us!"

"You're not making any sense," Finn told him.

"We ... we saw the potential for a new weapon. Dear God, but we did! It was a cutting-edge fusion of theoretical physics, particle theory, and witchcraft theorem ... yes, yes, *yes!* How could we know what we were playing at? The elemental forces of chaos we were tampering with?"

By this time, he had grabbed hold of Finn and simply would not let go. His eyes were those of a lunatic, his face wet with rolling beads of sweat, his mouth contorted, his face twisted into a frightened mask of pure animal terror. "We let them through ... yes, we did! But only the insects! I swear, it was only the insects! We had peered through the doorway of multi-dimensional reality into the very heart of a cosmic anti-world! We fed the insects with blood and meat and they got larger and larger! They were not of this dimensional plane ... don't you see? We couldn't contain them. They could utilize four-dimensional space! *They flew right through the walls! Right through them!*"

Finn was getting frightened himself. "Doctor, you have to calm down."

"I can't calm down! I don't *dare* calm down! The machine is still active! It no longer needs us! It draws its energy right from the stars and the atoms themselves!

Tim Curran

Those *things* got into the machine! They took it over! They activated it! It runs because *they* will it!"

"The insects?"

"No, you fool! Those migrating minds from beyond! Those formless, shapeless entities that want to bring the horror through! The monstrosity from the throne of primal chaos! That living primordial mass of nuclear cataclysm—"

Westly was out of his mind, completely out of his mind, and Finn wasn't too far behind him.

The rumbling starting again.

Shit.

The earth shook and he heard a roaring sound from up on the hill as Westly continued to rant on and on. Then a shock wave of sorts knocked him off his teetering feet and nearly punched the wind out of him. It came with a great booming noise. It felt like Blue Hills had been picked up and dropped. He had the same sensation as you get from riding an elevator down many floors. The vibrations followed immediately.

From the vicinity of Building A and Building B, he heard screaming.

Finn got to his feet and hobbled up the road even though his belly was flopping and his head felt like it was filled with a storm of pillow down. He had a hell of a time staying on his feet, but somebody needed help, and he was going to help them.

The vibrations were coming from up on the hill, moving in oscillating waves that made him feel like his bones were hollow and he might drift off into the sky like a helium balloon at any moment.

"Don't!" Westly cried. *"Don't go up there!"*

"I have to!" Finn told him.

The world around him had become a threatening, evil thing. Nothing was right. The stars were drawing down again and the tree branches undulating like tentacles, reaching up toward the sky. Buildings A and B leaned this way and that like narrow tombstones. They were wiggling like loose teeth. He tried to blink it away, but it remained, growing more distorted by the moment. The landscape became an abomination. He saw shadowy dark structures like obelisks and spheres and cylinders rising in the distance. And then—

A whirring sound as swarms of those nameless insects filled the night sky and then a great flapping as of immense leathery wings and he saw other things flying above him, just over his head … save that they were glossy and black, anthropomorphic but lacking anything that might be called faces.

Westly screamed at the sight of them and Finn himself could only stand there, a numb and mute witness to the grim intersection of worlds.

The vibrations grew stronger and stronger.

The sky became a whirling, spinning vortex of thunder and flashing lightning.

The rumbling became the roaring of freight trains, as if the mother of all tornados was bearing down on them. There was a deafening shearing, ripping sound like static electricity crackling and popping. The air went hot as a funeral pyre, then cold as Arctic wastes.

It was like trying to breathe warm, wet oatmeal. Then a searing hot wind hit him, driving him to his knees next to the shrieking form of Westly. The wind was peppered with flakes of ash like a blizzard.

It came with incredible force.

The hill that Buildings A and B occupied had risen like the cap of a monstrous mushroom now, and as he watched, the roofs of both exploded into fragments with a blinding blue flash of light that carried the fragments straight up into the night.

Then the sky above them split open in a luminous aperture like blazing sunlight seeping through a crack in a drawn shade. The hole widened, fanned out, consumed the sky and became a great and glowing gash of sucking, vacuuming wind that dragged both Westly and Finn along the ground, trying to draw them up into the cataclysmic heavens, which had become a huge and discordant vortex of spinning, twisting cyclonic matter.

Something was coming through that gash.

Something that had come to devour the world, to suck its blood and gnaw on its cold yellow bones.

Westly went absolutely hysterical at the sight of it, screaming and screaming, making strange signs with his hands. His speech was frenetic and garbled, but Finn heard this much: *"It's coming for us! It's coming for all of us! The primal nuclear chaos! Dear God, help us ...Yog Sothoth spare us! Nyarlathotep! Iä ... ngai ... ygg ... IÄ! IÄ! THE EYE OF AZATHOTH! I SEE IT! I SEE IT OPENING!"*

Finn just waited there, speechless, mindless, helpless.

This was the end result of the Procyon Project, the ultimate triumph of weird machines and banned books and blood and meat—to call down this godless, hideous nightmare from the subcellar of reality, this writhing haunter of the dark, this seed of atavistic dread, this living atomic furnace. Yes, this is what they'd been trying to do all along. This was the power they were trying to harness and the force they wanted to weaponize.

They had been trying to bring this atomic placental nightmare to term.

Finn thought for one insane moment that the full moon was being birthed from that gash. But it was no moon unless the moon had gone misty, indistinct and nebulous, a fluttering pale orb like a bleached and decomposing eyeball. And like a cyclopean eye, the thing began to iris open lengthwise, swimming closer and closer, filling the sky ... and he saw something in there, something begin to unfold like the petals of some degenerate flower. Squirming, slithering things like fleshy ropes of afterbirth, unwinding and reaching out, growing and lengthening and dividing a thousand times until above the hill there was a forest of pulsing, whipping, transparent roots that seemed to reach for miles.

And beneath them … a phosphorescent chasm. A fungoid, hissing miasma that began to erupt and open like a mouth, slowly, ever slowly. A birth canal. There was something alive in there, a roiling river of cremating pink hunger. Something alive with a glaring and ancient intelligence, a cold and alien hunger reaching out from some haunted, charnel dimension. It had come to devour the world.

Finn heard a reverberating, wet mewling, like the agonized cries of some deformed, grotesque infant being born.…

In mere minutes, the thing had divided and expanded like pestilential cells in a Petri dish, a great and squirming tumescent web that was spreading over the heavens, the ravaged husks of Buildings A and B silhouetted against the flashing, blinding, awesome energy of its face.

It had not only filled the sky, but *become* the sky, and Finn was certain he was only seeing the barest fragment of its immensity.

Then there was a rending, rocketing explosion, and the sky sealed back up, and the thing which was engulfing the heavens let go with a huge and deafening eruption of force and matter and disappeared.

When Finn came to some time later, the world around him was filled with smoke and fire. The destruction was everywhere. The buildings were gone. More so, the hills that held them were missing, too. A smoldering, blackened crater had opened up in their place. The land was flattened and gutted as far as he could see, thousands of trees blasted and felled. It looked like the dark side of the moon out there, gray and scarred and lifeless.

Westly was dead.

He lay there, covered in a dusting of gray ash, his hands held before him like gnarled claws, his mouth hooked in a twisted grimace, his eyes bulging from their sockets.

Dazed, numb, half out of his mind, Finn stumbled through flaming debris and a mist of greasy black smoke until he reached the place where the guard shack had been but was no more. It was here he fell to the ground, shaking and feverish. In the distance he heard police sirens and fire whistles.

Jack Coye was the first one to get to him. Like Finn himself, Jack was streaked with windblown ash, face smudged with soot. He gathered Finn in his arms. "Come on, boy, don't check out on me now. Talk to me, kid."

Finn smiled up at him. "Is it gone?" he said.

"Yeah … yeah, it's gone."

Finn breathed in and out for a moment, then managed to sit up. "Whole place went up."

Jack nodded. "Sure, sure. Nothing left. But … did you see it? Did you really see *it?*"

Finn considered the question, then shook his head. He lit a cigarette, remembering that LOOSE LIPS SINK SHIPS and CARELESS TALK COSTS LIVES. "I didn't see a damn thing," he said.

Jack winked at him. "Good boy," he said.

WUNDERWAFFE

BY JEFFREY THOMAS

Die Glocke Hotel was a giant globe suspended between two larger structures in Punktown's business district: the United Worlds Bank and the Paxton Trade Center (for Paxton was the proper name for this Earth-founded colony-city on the planet Oasis). The globe, brassy and featureless on the exterior, was connected to the two flanking buildings by a pair of tubular passageways like enclosed bridges, carrying people to and from the hotel along conveyance belts or, for a fee, in personal shuttle vehicles. The brass orb hung above the street at the halfway point of the immense glassy towers, one of which was silver, the other black, like a titanic angel and colossal demon fighting over a prize between them.

In addition, surrounding the spherical hotel like a planet's atmosphere was a bubble of water held in place with a tension skin. The water was full of exotic fish, jellyfish, and other aquatic life forms. Though the hotel had no actual windows, vidscreens on the interior allowed guests to look outside and see Punktown as if it rested on the bottom of the sea, colorful creatures seemingly gliding like vast monsters between the city's spires.

The detachment of Colonial Forces soldiers assigned to what had been codenamed Operation Wunderwaffe had been instructed to arrive at the upscale hotel in civilian dress, so as not to draw attention to Die Glocke and arouse suspicion. They arrived at different times, over the course of several days, coming by taxi or dropped off by other soldiers in civilian attire. They rode up elevators in either the United Worlds Bank or Punktown Trade Center, entering Die Glocke Hotel from either direction. In their suitcases, the twenty Colonial Forcers carried their uniforms—which were in city camouflage colors of black/dark gray/light gray—their lightweight chest armor, and their helmets. Instead of bulky AE-95 Sturm assault engines, they had sacrificed a bit of firepower for the more compact AE-93 Sturm, which could still fire solid bullets or corrosive plasma-gel capsules, mini-rockets, and ray bolts. The 93s fit better in their suitcases, and anyway, were better suited for fighting in enclosed spaces. Like the inside of a hotel.

Though just who or what they might end up having to fight, Corporal Sia Coyne didn't know.

After the last Colonial Forcer had checked in, regular hotel guests were informed by management that one of the two connecting tubes that upheld the globe had shown some instability, and that they must regrettably vacate Die Glocke so the problem could be rectified.

When the last regular guest had left, and the full hotel staff as well, the only people remaining in Die Glocke were the twenty Colonial Forcers, and a team of six business-suited agents representing both the military and scientific branches of the Earth Colonies government.

Them, and the group of Kalians that Corporal Coyne and the others had taken to calling the Nine.

ᒍᘈᕐᓄᕐᘈᒍᘈ

"I got some tattoos, myself," Sia told the Kalian man she was assigned to protect.

She thought of herself as his warder, in addition to being his guardian. Though technically he wasn't a prisoner, she had orders not to let him leave Die Glocke Hotel should he attempt to do so. Not that he had expressed a desire to do anything but whatever it was he was here to do. She had not been told what that was. Only to stick by him at all times, for half of each day. For the other half, she was replaced by another CF soldier. Two Colonial Forcers had been matched with each of the Nine.

In the vidscreen over the sink, which, unlike a mirror, showed one's reflection without reversing it, she saw the Kalian stiffen up, and raise his eyes to meet hers as she stood behind him. His eyes were entirely black, like embedded obsidian spheres.

In the bathroom of his hotel room—Room 404—he had just finished splashing cold water onto his face. Earlier this morning, pressing his palms against his closed eyes, he had explained that he was suffering a headache. All of the Nine had been complaining of headaches ever since they'd been moved into Die Glocke, three days ago. It didn't seem possible that they could still be feeling discomfort, since they'd been given pain blockers by the medic allocated to Operation Wunderwaffe. Maybe it was their Kalian physiology preventing the meds from working properly?

This Kalian, whom she only knew by one name, Karik, had pushed back the long sleeves of his metallic gold tunic to prevent them from getting wet when he cupped the icy water. That was how Sia had spotted the tattoos: rows of alien symbols in black ink on the pale gray skin of both his forearms. Now that she had called attention to them, he quickly pushed the sleeves down to his wrists again.

She asked, "Are those words from your language?"

"Yes."

"So what do they say?"

"Mom."

Sia smiled and nodded. "Ahh."

The tall, thin Kalian turned to face her, and to her surprise, he smiled down at her, too. It was a very subtle smile, with his full lips pressed together, but a smile nevertheless.

The Kalians were one of those few races that most closely resembled the Earthers, of whom Sia was one. She had heard that they believed their god, Ugghiutu, had seeded these human races across the universe. Everyone else believed it was simply a matter of convergent evolution, because the human form worked. Whatever the case, she found the gray-skinned Kalian to be quite beautifully formed. She figured he was somewhere in his twenties, like herself. He wore his curly black hair down to his shoulders. Most Kalians, both male and female, wore blue head wrappings best described as turbans. Not wearing a turban, particularly if one were a woman, was considered shocking. What did that say about this Karik, then? And the rest of the Nine—none of whom wore a turban, not even the women among them?

"So," Sia said to him, "don't you want to know what my tattoos are?"

"I fear it would be impolite to ask."

"Hm. So you're suggesting it was impolite of me to ask you."

"I suggest nothing, Corporal Coyne."

"My name is Sia. And I don't mind telling you about my tattoos, 'cause I've got nothing to hide."

"Are you suggesting I have something to hide, Corporal Sia?"

"Just Sia. Oh I suggest nothing either, Karik. Anyway, I think my tattoos are more colorful than yours."

"Your skin color itself is very beautiful," he told her, those obsidian eyes intense in their gaze.

This sudden shift from tattoos to skin threw her off for a beat. Sia's

Jeffrey Thomas

ancestors were African, though she herself had never been to that country, nor even to Earth, and she said somewhat warily, "Yeah?"

"Yes."

"Um, okay … thanks. So, as I was saying, on my bicep here I got the emblem of my division." She slapped her left arm through her camouflage fatigues. Then she slapped her other arm. "On this bicep I got the emblem of the Colonial Forces." Next she patted her chest armor, over her abdomen. "Around my belly button I got a metallic gold star."

"What does that symbolize? That your birth is connected to the cosmos?"

"Uh, no…it's just decorative."

"Perhaps not. You may have had a subconscious reason for getting it."

She shrugged, and said casually, "Maybe some time when I'm not all suited up I'll show you my tattoos."

Karik looked away from her quickly. She wasn't offended, didn't worry that he found her repulsive. After all, he had just complimented her. Instead, she thought she sensed his embarrassment. No matter how moderate or modernized he and the other Nine appeared to be, they were still members of a very reserved people.

She asked him, "Is that all you have for tattoos? On your arms?"

"I think I should lie down for a while," he murmured, leaving the bathroom as if he suddenly felt the space was too enclosed for the both of them. "Perhaps a nap will improve my headache."

ᒉᴵᐟ⌐ᴕᐟᐣ

He slept across the room from her, in one of 404's two large beds. From where she sat, she could only see his glossy black hair spilled across his pillow. From time to time, he shifted position under his blanket restlessly. Several times she heard a soft moan. Pain from his headache, or bad dreams?

Sia slumped more deeply in her chair. Her Sturm leaned against the wall beside her, a handgun holstered at her side. But she didn't wear her helmet behind 404's door; it rested on the coffee table, near the remnants of a meal she had ordered from the room's more-than-adequate food processor. The warmth and stillness of the room lulled her. If she listened intently enough, she could detect Karik's deep breathing. Her own breathing seemed to fall into sync with it.

And soon enough, it was as though she fell into sync with his dreams, as well.

Sia was walking through the hallway of what she took to be a cathedral, with high vaulted arches spaced along the ceiling like ribs seen from inside some immense creature that had swallowed her. Also flanking the hallway were stone columns of a strange braided or entwined design. Everything—floor, ceiling, walls, arches, the rows of columns—was carved from a polished black stone. But unlike most stone surfaces, it felt warm, not cool, under Sia's bare feet.

Bare feet? She stopped walking along this seemingly endless hallway to look down at her chestnut-colored body, with the realization that she was naked. Her boots were gone, her black chest armor, her camouflage uniform—which had a protective mesh lining to stop ray bolts and to prevent solid projectiles from penetrating one's flesh. She was utterly vulnerable. All she saw, looking down past her breasts, was the metallic gold star tattoo that enclosed the black hole of her navel. But as she stared at the star, she realized something was different about it. Normally the star had five arms, yet now it had eight instead.

She continued on, bare feet padding stealthily across warm smooth blackness, until finally she decided to look out one of the windows that were spaced between the columns, and through which slanted the long reddish-gold beams that illuminated the cathedral's interior. She thought the day must be ending. She wondered what the view would be. She felt there must be a great city out there, but she couldn't recall its name.

The window was circular, and appeared to have no glass in it; she felt a cool breeze from beyond pass across her bare skin like a ghostly hand. Her skin pebbled with gooseflesh. Before she could reach the window, and gaze upon the scene it revealed, it suddenly closed up like the aperture of a camera lens. She backed away from it, and approached the next window, and the next, but each spiraled shut before she could get close, cutting off another shaft of red-gold light.

Sia feared what would happen if she should startle all of the windows into closing at once. If that happened, and she was swallowed in darkness, how would she find her way out of this edifice?

Sia resumed walking, walking, tempted to call out for another person but afraid to disturb this profound stillness ... and embarrassed about her disrobed state. Might she find her discarded clothing and armor somewhere if she continued exploring? More so than that, she hoped to find her weapons. She didn't know why this was paramount, but it was an intuition, and intuition had always been her most important weapon.

At last the hallway ended in a great staircase of black stone that curved upward, around and around like the inside of a seashell. She climbed these stairs, her calves beginning to ache from all her walking, until finally she

Jeffrey Thomas

arrived at a walkway along the inside of a massive dome, featureless except for one opening at the very center of the rotunda. The sky beyond this eye-like opening glowed blood red as the sun prepared to sink. When that happened, the total darkness she feared would descend.

As she started along the walkway, keeping one hand on the raised lip that served as its railing—lest she become overwhelmed with vertigo so close to the edge—a soft voice came to her. A hiss of air so faint she almost missed it.

"Sia," the tiny hiss said.

She halted and glanced sharply over her shoulder, thinking someone had followed her up the spiraling steps. No one was there, but as she looked around further, she spotted a figure standing on the walkway at the opposite side of the dome. The figure was facing the inner wall, away from her. She then recalled having heard somewhere about "whispering-gallery waves" ... how this phenomenon occurred in certain structures with circular walls, whereby a person might whisper and the sound would be carried to any other point along the curvature of the wall.

"Sia," came the whisper again.

The figure was a man wearing a matching tunic and trousers of metallic golden fabric. He was tall, slender, with black hair falling to his shoulders in unruly curls.

Sia started around the walkway toward the man at a quickened pace, nudity be damned. She was heartened by the appearance of this familiar figure. At the same time, though, she maintained a prudent sense of wariness. She was, after all, a warrior.

The light glowing through the iris overhead was growing dimmer by the second. It had gone from red to purple. Glinting stars had begun to appear.

Sia wanted to call out to the man, but she had almost reached him now and was waiting until they could be face to face. Perhaps hearing her footfalls near him, he began to turn away from the wall ... turn toward her ...

Just as she started to make out his profile, however, the light in the rotunda drained away utterly, as if the circle of sky overhead had been eclipsed. At the same time, a wild gust blew down through the iris, concentrated like a beam, lashing across her nude body, as cold as a polar wind. With it came a howling shriek ... but was that the wind, or Sia's own voice?

ꓛⅢⅤⲟɛꓒⲅ

"Sia," whispered the man leaning over her.

She sat up so abruptly she nearly bumped foreheads with the person bent over her: Private Patrick Birkett. He jumped back a little.

"Easy ... easy," he told her, keeping his voice hushed so as not to wake the Kalian. "I'm just here for my shift, corporal."

"Dung, man," Sia groaned, rubbing at her eyes with the heels of her hands as she rose from the chair. She had a headache coming on, her sinuses feeling packed solid as if the bone of her skull were growing fuller, filling in its gaps.

"Sorry. Looks like you need to hit the sack, yourself." The two of them had been given the rooms to either side of Karik; Birkett in room 402, Sia in 406.

"I think I'll do that ... so long as I don't have any more nightmares."

"Hey, talking about nightmares, you ought to see something. Come here." The young soldier led Sia behind a partition that half-screened the bedroom area from the living room area, again so as not to disturb Karik. Here, he swept his hand over a large blank panel on the wall. The panel came alive as a vidscreen window, and Sia was oddly reminded of the windows that had magically closed up in the cathedral of her dreams.

The vidscreen revealed the city of Punktown beyond, seen through the sleeve of water that enveloped Die Glocke. The city was a familiar view: a dense forest of uncountable gargantuan towers, that because they were silhouetted against the red-gold twilight looked like the ruins of a city charred black by some monumental cataclysm.

Yet Sia noticed something was amiss right away. Before, the aquarium bubble had been filled with pulsing jellyfish trailing delicate silvery tendrils. Ugly comb-fanged fish with spots of green bioluminescence strobing down their sides. Lazily coiling giant sea worms with fluttery membranes like wings arranged along their smooth bodies. Now, the water contained only carcasses. A worm tumbled by in slow-motion, carried on some current rather than through its own volition. Those fang-faced fish hung suspended everywhere, gently carried along like the worm, their green patches gone dark. And the jellyfish appeared to have already started decomposing, leaving only shredded bits of gelatinous membrane and stray tendrils drifting in the water.

"Oh wow," Sia said. "Dung, is this our fault? We booted out the hotel people, and maybe we didn't do whatever it takes to keep these things alive."

"I don't know, corporal ... there's weird things happening all over Punktown, if you see the news."

"There's *always* weird things happening all over Punktown."

"I mean beyond the usual weird."

Private Birkett described one news story he had seen. An unknown life form had appeared at the city's Theta Transport Station. This facility was

337   Jeffrey Thomas

where Punktown citizens could board a craft to take them to a number of known alternate dimensions … or where sentient beings (on friendly terms with the Earth Colonial Network) from those dimensions could conversely come through to visit Punktown. Rather like the Paxton Teleportation Center, although that transportation service only communicated between worlds within this, the so-called Prime Dimension.

According to Birkett, a shuttle pod that had been returning to Punktown from the extradimensional world of Sinan had gone missing, apparently lost between realities. When it finally arrived after an inexplicable delay of three hours, the pod was found to be empty of the passengers and crew it was to have contained. Instead, aboard the transdimensional shuttle was a large creature convulsing in its death throes, as if it hadn't been able to survive such a journey. Birkett said the creature was described as a formless black mass, honeycombed like a chunk of tripe, apparently without limbs or any internal organs. And yet, it possessed two huge wings, black and feathered like those of a condor. So far authorities could only speculate that the physiology of this being or animal had been compromised by the process of transportation from Sinan—or from wherever else it had originated. They were chiding a certain media source for referring to the thing as some kind of winged demon from the spaces *between* dimensions, that had somehow infiltrated the vessel and destroyed or consumed the passengers.

Though where those passengers *had* ended up, the authorities as yet had no theories.

"Thanks for sharing that, man," Sia said. "Now I'm *really* going to have nightmares." She then left Birkett to seek out her own room, her own bed.

ꓱꚔ𐐓ꖴ

"Who is it I'm protecting you from, Karik?" she asked him when her next twelve-hour shift came around. She was edgy and ill-rested. Though she had no memory of the bad dreams she had experienced in 406, she still felt beaten up by whatever they had been.

"First, you must protect me from yourself," Karik told her.

"How's that?"

"I am certain you were instructed not to question any of us about what our function here is."

Her gaze grew hot, her jaw shifting. "Kind of hard to do my job when I don't really know what that job entails. Who the enemy is. Isn't that the most basic information a soldier needs?"

"You would do better to address that question to your superiors than to me. But if they have been vague with you about the form of the potential threat, it is because we have been vague with them about the form of the potential threat. And that is because we ourselves do not know exactly how, if it comes, that threat might take form. That is all I can tell you."

"That doesn't tell me a goddamned thing."

"I am sincerely sorry."

"Whatever you say." Sulkily she went to the VT and activated it, plopped down in the chair she favored and zipped through channels. She came to a porn channel, and stopped there to watch. Appearing three-dimensional in the vidtank, a Tikkihotto male—human in appearance except for the clear ocular tendrils that swarmed from his eye sockets—was thrusting into an Asian mutant with an additional pair of arms and legs, all eight of her limbs wrapped spider-like around him. The Tikkihotto's eye tendrils crept into the woman's mouth, nostrils, and ears in fervent exploration.

"This filth offends me!" Karik blurted, whipping away. "As you knew it would. Why are you being childish, corporal?"

Sia shut the VT off, jumped to her feet, took Karik's arm and forced him to face her. When he turned, he saw her removing her chest armor.

"What are you doing?"

Next she unfastened the top of her fatigues, and tossed that to the floor beside the armor. Beneath that she wore a black sleeveless undershirt. "I told you my name is Sia. Are you afraid to call a woman by her first name? A little too intimate for you Kalian guys?"

"You do not understand me. I do not see women as inferior, as many of my brothers do. But I have a devotion … I am a priest, of sorts."

"I thought you told me my skin is beautiful, Karik."

"It is," he said, looking down at her body as if he couldn't resist the struggle to do otherwise.

She peeled the undershirt up over her head, and now from the belt up wore only a sports bra. "Then why don't you touch my skin?"

"I cannot," the Kalian murmured.

"I'm telling you, you can." She reached out and took hold of his hand. "I want you to," she said huskily. And she pressed his palm to her bared midriff, just above the five-pointed star outlining her navel. He could have pulled his hand away, but he didn't.

They drew closer, and now both his hands were on her … sliding, roaming, around to her back, meeting and diverging in different directions again.

She kissed his neck, and drew in a deep inhalation of his gray skin, which

Jeffrey Thomas

smelled warmly of the spices he ate. She unfastened the high collar of his tunic, and peeled it apart.

"Please," he said, but she didn't know if that meant *please stop*, or *please do this*. And he whispered, "Sia," sounding just like the ghostly voice that had traveled around the rotunda in her dream of him.

She saw that his chest was densely tattooed with rows of black characters, just like his arms. She bent to his breastbone and kissed these lines of ink. Her lips trailing across his quivering skin, she took a black nipple into her mouth while he in turn slipped his hands up under her bra to cup her breasts.

Sia pulled back from him a little to remove his tunic completely, and help him step out of his trousers. She found that his entire body from the neck down was covered with alien words. As if in resignation, he spread his arms outward like those of a human star.

"You must not tell anyone about this," he said. "Not your people … not mine. No one was to have seen these lines. No one was to touch them. To risk compromising their power, I must be mad. I am too weak.…"

"I don't understand a thing you're saying," Sia said, unbuckling her belt. "Just shut up and get in the bed."

ꓤꟷⵓⲉⴹꓤ

She awoke before him, and glanced nervously at the time, afraid that Private Birkett would come to relieve her while she still lay in bed with the Kalian. She saw that she still had a couple of hours before Birkett came. She slid out from under Karik's tattooed arm as lightly as she could. He moaned, but didn't awaken. She got back into her uniform and armor.

She put on the VT again, but with the volume muted. Instead of a porn channel, she opted for a Punktown news station.

What she found being broadcast there was all the more disturbing for having no audio to give it context.

It was apparently a live feed, the camerawork jerky, though whether it was being supplied by a news crew or just some eyewitness on the street, Sia didn't know. And she didn't know what she was seeing.

It was some kind of structure, looming taller than the other buildings in its immediate vicinity. In fact, it was literally surrounded by a ring of identical apartment towers, and Sia realized she recognized them—though Punktown was an immense city and she had never seen all it had to offer, despite having dwelt there all her life. This apartment complex was called the Octoplex. Several times she had even visited a friend in one of its eight apartment blocks, some years ago. Back then, there had been no central structure like the one she was seeing now.

It was entirely black, and it conveyed the impression of being a baroque and complex cathedral. But a cathedral that *moved* ... that throbbed, and undulated, like something organic and rubbery.

She sat forward in her chair, and gawked in disbelief as a part of the black cathedral like a slender tower or minaret, with an entwined design, unbraided itself and revealed itself to be a nest of wildly whipping black tentacles.

The cathedral seemed to edge forward a bit, toward the camera, and Sia noticed then that the whole soaring form appeared to be supported on a base of thick, root-like growths. Did it *crawl* on those? As the black cathedral shifted, its bulk pressed against one of the towers of the Octoplex. The building toppled into the street, where it seemed to explode into a billowing cloud, which rose up as if to veil the monstrosity from Sia's eyes before it could stain her sanity.

"Turn it off," a voice commanded behind her.

Sia jolted, startled, and twisted around in her chair to see Karik sitting up in bed, the VT glow reflected in his black eyes.

"Turn it off!" he repeated. "Before it sees us watching it."

"*Sees* us?" Sia didn't understand, but she touched the VT's remote and shut it off as he had demanded. She had never heard the soft-spoken Karik speak with such force and intensity.

"It has begun," he muttered, looking away. "As we feared. I had hoped it might only be cultists hunting for us, seeking to eliminate us as a threat. This is so much worse." He swung his legs out from under the blanket and stood.

Sia was shaking all over now. "I've been *inside* that thing ... in a dream. You were in it, too. You know what I'm talking about. So what the dung is it?"

Slowly, Karik faced her again. After a moment of hesitation, he said, "It is one incarnation of the Kalian deity, Ugghiutu. God and demon. Creator and destroyer. In the holy text the *Fizala*, Ugghiutu appears to humans as a temple erected to his own worship ... into which they are enticed as sacrifices, willing or unwilling."

"That ... that's your god? Here in Punktown? And my government knew this could possibly happen?"

"The governing body of Paxton was notified by Kalian opponents of the fundamentalist Cult of Ugghiutu that efforts were underway to attempt a summoning, somewhere in this colony. To conjure Ugghiutu here to do what he does: consume ... destroy. Then give forth new life. But new life that would only bring about yet more destruction, in a never-ending cycle."

"And you ... the Nine ... you're the opponents."

"We are an *instrument* of those who oppose the summoning of Ugghiutu onto our plane. We have devoted our lives to keeping Ugghiutu from infiltrating the Prime Dimension."

"So, are you Nine going to be able to stop that thing?"

Karik was getting back into his clothing as he spoke. "If it is possible. If it is not already too late."

"How are you going to do that?"

"Spells from the *Fizala* are what brought him here. There is another book that we hope will send him back, and seal the breach between planes." Karik groaned and pinched the bridge of his nose. The bullet-like headache again.

"How much of a threat is that thing?"

"More than you can imagine, Sia. Soon Punktown might consist wholly of this manifestation of Ugghiutu. But for now, we ourselves are safer in here, in Die Glocke, than anywhere out there in the city."

"Why is that?"

"The rounded shape of this building. Ugghiutu and his brethren Outsiders move best through angles, not curves. It will be harder to perceive us in here. Harder for them to reach through, and try to stop us before we can act. And the building being suspended in the air, buffered with water … these factors too may help keep us shielded from their awareness, until we can strike. But you must not view this entity on the vidtank … or any other entities that might manifest themselves. It opens a means of them viewing us, in turn."

"How could that be?"

"Just believe me. We should have thought to advise your people on such a possibility earlier."

The door to room 404 buzzed, and a voice came over the speaker. "Karik."

"Enter," he said.

The door slid back to reveal a group crowding the hallway beyond. They were a mix of Colonial Forcers carrying their Sturms, and Kalians in metallic gold garments like Karik's. The foremost of the latter was a middle-aged woman with her black hair hanging free, threaded with silver. "It is time to read the book," she announced.

"I have seen," Karik replied.

A burst of sound behind Sia caused her to spin around, reaching for her sidearm. The VT had come on by itself, the vidtank filled with static, the volume full blast with hissing/crackling. Were those vague dark figures moving behind the veil of snow?

Furthermore, the various vidscreen panels along the walls had awakened like windows that had been abruptly flung open by unseen hands. At first Sia thought it must be night outside, but then she remembered it was still day outside. It was the bubble of water around Die Glocke: it had gone completely black, as if it had changed to ink. Luminous red shapes floated here and there through the ink, and those that drew near to the vidscreens revealed themselves to be creatures like fleas the size of a dog, glowing crimson, their many legs paddling in a blur.

"Ugghiutu knows we are here," the gray-skinned woman who had addressed Karik stated. "He has already seen us, through his familiars. We must move quickly."

ᒋᐦᒉᐊᒐᕊ

The topmost floor of Die Glocke hotel contained an indoor pool, which could be closed to create more floor space for functions such as conventions. Such was the case now. The ceiling above them was a high dome; the interior of the brassy orb's upper curve. Sia was, of course, reminded of that other dome from her dream.

All six business-suited government agents were in attendance, and ten Colonial Forcers held a perimeter around the sizable room. The other ten guarded the rest of the hotel. Sia was one of those providing security for whatever ritual was about to take place. She found it hard to fathom that her own people, let alone the Kalians, believed magic was the answer to the threat that had torn its way into the Prime Dimension. She herself was not religious, not even spiritual, had faith only in the solid killing machine she held ready in her fists.

Eight of the Kalians had disrobed and formed a circle, facing inward, none of them exhibiting any self-consciousness now. Young men, older men, young women, one very elderly woman, and even a male child of perhaps twelve. What they all shared in common was that their bodies were covered in a black mesh of Kalian calligraphy. Only one of the Nine did not undress, and stood at the center of the circle in his gold-colored outfit. Sia overheard others refer to this man as the Reader.

As one, the eight Kalians arranged around the Reader spread their arms wide. They were ready. All the observers held their tongues. Held their breath. They saw the Reader open his mouth to speak.

A massive thump caused the room to tremble, and ring deeply like the inside of a great bell. The military team forming a second circle around the Nine looked about sharply, fingers poised on triggers. Somewhere, there was a long, creaking squeal of stressed metal.

But the Reader straightened up taller with resolve, and began reading.

343

That was when Sia realized what she was seeing. What Karik and the other eight in the circle were.

They were a book.

The Reader was facing the twelve-year-old, reciting in a resounding voice full of authority and strength. Yet Sia understood he wasn't reciting from memory, but reading words inscribed across the boy's bony chest. He had apparently only read a single short line, however, when he shuffled a few steps as if rotating on a fixed axis, to face the elderly woman standing to the right of the boy. Even as the Reader stopped pivoting and faced her, the old woman had turned away from him, so that the next lines he read were tattooed across her back.

He continued shuffling around, revolving to the right and further to the right and then to the left, clockwise and clockwise then counterclockwise … then clockwise again, and so on, like the combination of a safe being dialed. Sia was amazed that he could remember all these movements. More amazing was that each of the eight nude figures encircling him had all learned their own precise movements, also revolving this way and that, so that the Reader could follow a line of text from this person's arm to that person's hip, from this person's thigh to that person's buttocks … maybe only getting several words from a young woman's narrow leg, but a long line from a beefy man's chest. All of the Nine moving constantly, turning like intricately meshed gears in one beautifully articulated machine.

Sia stood behind Karik, and whenever he rotated to face in her direction she searched his face, but if his obsidian eyes registered her she couldn't tell. He seemed either fully entranced, or simply so intent on the memorized movements of the strange dance that his focus precluded all else.

The Reader's chanting voice seemed to grow even louder, stronger, and more rapid, the alien words reverberating off the concave ceiling. Meanwhile, Sia could now hear the sirens of police vehicles beyond the thick metal wall … and deep, dull thuds like distant explosions.

The Reader was almost feverish now, his black eyeballs wide and wild, spittle flying from his lips. He turned faster, faster, and so did all the others gears in the organic machine. They were working toward a crescendo. The whole display was making Sia dizzy, almost nauseous, and her own headache was returning. She realized that she was shivering. No … vibrating. The *air* was vibrating.

The room rumbled, shuddered violently. Another screech of tormented metal.

Beyond that, and beyond the chanting, Sia also detected a kind of scratching or skittering sound against the outside of the dome. Like the Reader's voice, it too intensified by the moment. Then, with a flicker, a single huge vidscreen that encircled the entire room in a band came on. What it showed was that same inky blackness, populated by so many of those monstrous fleas—*thousands*—that their combined red glow shone on the glossy floor. The creatures were massed thickly against the dome, staring inside, clawing at the exterior of the brass orb with their blurring legs.

The room—the entire hotel—lurched. The floor was left tilted at a slight angle.

Through the chanting, the scratching, the quaking, Sia heard the soldier on her left cry out, "The supports!"

The Reader shouted the last word he read from the living book; shouted it at the top of his lungs. Amplified by the rotunda, it sounded like a detonation. And when he went silent, the echo of the final word still ringing in the air metallically, the eight Kalians surrounding him were all facing outward, whereas at the start they had been facing in.

This left Karik facing Sia directly, and at last his eyes met hers with recognition, as if he had just woken from a dream. He smiled at her. It was a very subtle smile, with his full lips pressed together, but a smile nevertheless.

The vidscreen, with its view of the contaminated aquarium bubble, went dead, cutting off the blood-red bioluminescence. And then from somewhere outside Die Glocke, somewhere in the city of Punktown, there was a tremendous howl … or wail … or roar … though there really was no word to describe it in terms of sounds known to the human ear.

"Oh my God," Sia said, in awe of the cry … in awe of the fury and agony it seemed to convey. Her gaze still locked with Karik's, though neither of them now was smiling, she let her Sturm hang by its strap to clamp both hands over her ears.

As the monstrous cry finally tapered away and faded, with wavering reverberations as if the sound were falling away down a bottomless pit, there followed a great crack like a cannon blast—much closer at hand.

Die Glocke, sheared away from the two connecting passageways that had upheld it, plummeted like a cannonball itself toward the pavement so many floors below.

ꝺ‖ꝶꝼꞓꝺꞟ

Sia regained consciousness as if jarred from a nightmare, gasping as she emerged from vague visions of a city that was composed entirely of one enor-

Jeffrey Thomas

mous ebony building. A building writhing and alive … sentient. A crawling city that meant to grow and spread across the whole of the globe.

She was greeted by a cacophony of agonized screams, approaching sirens, and the chatter of automatic gunfire. Lifting her head, she saw that Die Glocke Hotel lay on its side, the floor slanting up beside her like a wall. The closed swimming pool had split open; she lay in its shallow water, cupped in the rotunda's curved wall. A whole section of the actual wall of the hotel's top level had broken away, like the shell of a giant brass egg. She could see the city out there, and several of the other members of Operation Wunderwaffe who had survived the fall.

These soldiers had climbed outside the wreckage, where the shattered orb lay in a thin inky pool: the burst bubble that had once enclosed the hotel. The soldiers were firing at the dog-sized fleas that lay scattered on the pavement, paddling their legs helplessly as if out of their element. From where she lay, propped up painfully on one elbow, Sia also saw a number of other life forms that had previously been concealed by the black fluid, since they didn't glow as the flea-things had done. These larger creatures were globs of honeycombed tissue, sprouting feathered black wings. They flopped horribly, like dying fish exposed to the air. As she watched, she saw Private Birkett step nearer to one of these entities, point his Sturm, and shoot it with a capsule of green-glowing corrosive plasma. Within moments, the blob-like life form—convulsing even more frantically—began to dissolve. Before even a minute had passed, it had vanished altogether, leaving only a steaming smudge.

Sia pulled herself to her feet, battered and wrenched but apparently with nothing broken. She had lost her helmet, and blood trickled into one eyebrow, but she swiped it away as she turned in a circle to survey the immediate damage.

A government agent split into halves by one of the panels that had covered the pool. A Kalian woman moaning, fighting to remain conscious as she clutched the end of her severed leg in both hands. A Colonial Forcer kneeling beside the twelve-year-old Kalian boy, holding his hand as the child wept quietly, either physically or emotionally unable to rise.

As Sia completed her unsteady little circle, she spotted him … only a few paces away.

She staggered to him, and slowly sagged to her knees beside him. There was no need for urgency; it was clear that Karik was dead.

He sat up with his back supported by the slanted floor, his head canted to one side as if his neck had been broken. His eyelids were half closed, or half open. From under them glistened his eyes of volcanic glass. A length of brassy metal, a curved support joist, had impaled him through the upper chest like a dragon's claw. Blood had flowed heavily down his abdomen, obscuring much of his tattooing there. The wound itself was torn through the Kalian inscriptions, these words of power that had been devised to counteract the potent text in the book called the Fizala.

Sia took Karik's limp hand, and whispered, "You did it. Okay? You did it."

But she looked again toward the broken wall, and the city of Punktown beyond. With night descending, the sky had turned a lurid red-gold. Yes, the Nine had banished Ugghiutu, and sealed the rent through which he had come. Yet now the pages of the living book had been ripped. Were there others out there in the city who could step in to replace those pages, should that entity or any of his brethren Outsiders be summoned again?

Emergency vehicles came floating down from the sky, their sirens combining into one banshee wail, and Sia found herself reaching up to cover her ears again, and closing her eyes, as if to block out any nightmares that might return.

Jeffrey Thomas

ABOUT THE EDITORS

Brian M. Sammons has been writing reviews on all things horror for more years than he'd care to admit. Wanting to give other critics the chance to ravage his work for a change, he has penned a few short stories that have appeared in such anthologies as *Arkham Tales*, *Horrors Beyond*, *Monstrous*, *Dead but Dreaming 2*, *Horror for the Holidays*, *Twisted Legends*, *Mountains of Madness*, *Deepest Darkest Eden*, and others. He has edited the anthologies; *Cthulhu Unbound 3*, *Undead & Unbound*, *Eldritch Chrome*, *Edge of Sundown*, and *Steampunk Cthulhu*. For the *Call of Cthulhu* role-playing game he wrote the book "Secrets," has contributed to both *Keeper's Companions*, wrote a companion scenario for the *Keeper's Screen*, and has had scenarios in the books; *Terrors From Beyond*, *The San Francisco Guidebook*, *Houses of R'lyeh*, *Strange Aeons 2*, *Atomic Age Cthulhu*, *Island of Ignorance*, *Punktown*, and *Doors to Darkness*. He is currently far too busy for any sane man.

For more about Brian, you can find his infrequently updated webpage here: http://brian_sammons.webs.com or follow him on Twitter @BrianMSammons

Glynn Owen Barrass lives in the North East of England and has been writing since late 2006. He has written over a hundred short stories, most of which have been published in the UK, USA, France, and Japan. He also co-edits anthologies for Chaosium's *Call of Cthulhu* fiction line, *Eldritch Chrome* (co-edited with Brian M. Sammons) being the first release this year, to be followed by *Steampunk Cthulhu*, *Atomic Age Cthulhu*, and more. He also writes material for their flagship roleplaying game: *Call of Cthulhu*.

Details and news of his latest fiction appearances can be found on his website 'Stranger Aeons: The Domain of Writer Glynn Barrass.'

ABOUT THE ARTISTS

Interior Illustrations

M. Wayne Miller has become a well-known name in the field of horror illustration. Not to be limited, Wayne is equally adept with science fiction, fantasy, and young adult themes, welcoming the opportunities of each genre and, frequently, combining them all. His list of clients has grown long indeed, and Wayne intends to continue his quest to learn and grow as an artist and illustrator.

Front Cover Artwork

Vincent Chong is an award-winning freelance illustrator and designer. Since 2004 he has brought his creative vision and distinctive visual style to a wide range of projects from book and magazine covers to CD packaging and websites. He works for clients all around the world, and illustrates the works of renowned authors such as Stephen King. Vincent is the recipient of a World Fantasy Award, as well as receiving the British Fantasy Award for 'Best Artist' on multiple occasions. He has also been shortlisted for Hugo and BSFA awards. In 2010 he released his first art book, Altered Visions: The Art of Vincent Chong. You can learn more about Vincent at his website, www.vincentchong-art.co.uk and blog, vincentchongart.wordpress.com.

About the Authors

Loyalty

John Shirley won the Bram Stoker Award for his story collection Black Butterflies, and is the author of numerous novels, including the best-seller *Demons*, the cyberpunk classics *City Come a-Walkin'*, *Eclipse*, And *Black Glass*, and his latest, new from Simon & Schuster, the urban fantasy novel *Bleak History*. He is a screenwriter, having written for television and movies; he was co-screenwriter of *The Crow*. He will be in Prime Books' *The Year's Best Dark Fantasy and Horror* anthology, this year, and his story collection *In Extremis: The Most Extreme Short Stories of John Shirley* from Underland Press has been getting rave advance reviews. His novel *Bioshock: Rapture*, telling the story of the creation and undoing of Rapture, from the hit videogame *Bioshock* is about to come out from TOR books.

The Game Changers

Stephen Mark Rainey is not the infamous Stephen King antihero Mort Rainey, but the far more nefarious author of the novels *Dark Shadows: Dreams of the Dark* (with Elizabeth Massie, HarperCollins, 1999), *Balak* (Wildside Books, 2000), *The Lebo Coven* (Thomson Gale/Five Star Books, 2004), *The Nightmare Frontier* (Sarob Press, 2006, and in e-book format by Crossroads Press, 2010), and *Blue Devil Island* (Thomson Gale/Five Star Books, 2007); three short story collections; and over 80 published works of short fiction.

White Feather

T.E. Grau is an author of dark fiction whose work has appeared in numerous anthologies, including *Tales of Jack the Ripper*, *The Best of The Horror Society 2013*, *Dark Fusions: Where Monsters Lurk*, *World War Cthulhu*, *The Dark Rites of Cthulhu*, *Suction Cup Dreams: An Octopus Anthology*, *Dead But Dreaming 2*, *The Aklonomicon*, *Urban Cthulhu: Nightmare Cities*, and *Horror for the Holidays*, among others; and such magazines and literary journals as *LA Weekly*, *The Fog Horn*, *Eschatology Journal*, and *Lovecraft eZine*. His two chapbooks, *The Mission* and *The Lost Aklo Stories*, will be published in early 2014 by Dunhams Manor Press. In the editorial realm, he currently serves as

Fiction Editor of *Strange Aeons* magazine. T.E. Grau lives in Los Angeles with his wife and daughter, and can be found in the ether at *The Cosmicomicon* (cosmicomicon.blogspot.com).

To Hold Ye White Husk

Wilum Pugmire has written many books of Lovecraftian horror, including *Gathered Dust and Others* and *Encounters With Enoch Coffin* for DRP. His next book will be the short novel, *The Revenant Of Rebecca Pascal*, written in collaboration with David Barker and to be published as illustrated limited edition hardcover by Dark Renaissance Books this Spring. He will have stories in new anthologies such as *Black Wings III* and *IX*, *Searchers After Horror*, and *A Mountain Walked*. He dreams in Seattle.

Sea Nymph's Son

Robert M. Price (Selma, NC), professor of scriptural studies at the Johnnie Colemon Theological Seminary, is the editor (with Jeffery Jay Lowder) of *The Empty Tomb: Jesus Beyond the Grave* and the *Journal of Higher Criticism*. He is also the author of *Top Secret: The Truth Behind Today's Pop Mysticisms*; *The Paperback Apocalypse: How the Christian Church Was Left Behind*; *The Reason-Driven Life: What Am I Here on Earth For?* and many other works.

The Boonieman

Edward M. Erdelac is the author of the acclaimed Judeocentric/Lovecraftian weird western series *Merkabah Rider*, and the novels *Buff Tea, Coyote's Trail*, and *Terovolas*. His fiction has appeared in over a dozen anthologies and periodicals including most recently, *Swords and Mythos, Kaiju Rising, After Death, Steampunk Cthulhu, The Dark Rites of Cthulhu*, and *Star Wars Insider*. News of his works and other writings at http://emerdelac.wordpress.com

The Turtle

Neil Baker used to be a filmmaker and animator who occasionally dabbled in writing. Now he is a writer who does a bit of filmmaking on the side. Either way this doesn't bode well for his family's prospects.
He has recently launched a new publishing house, April Moon Books, and their first publication, *The Dark Rites of Cthulhu*, will be out in April.

The Bullet and the Flesh

David Conyers is an Australian science fiction author and editor with over fifty short stories in various anthologies and magazines, many of which are collected in his e-books *The Entropy Conflict*, *The Uncertainty Bridge* and *The Nightmare Dimension*. David is the author of the Lovecraftian espionage science fiction series featuring his ongoing character, Major Harrison Peel, collected in *The Impossible Object*, *The Weaponized Puzzle* and *The Eye of Infinity*, with many more additions planned. He is the editor of the anthologies *Extreme Planets*, *Undead & Unbound*, *Cthulhu's Dark Cults* and Cthulhu Unbound 3. David recently became the Art & General Editor of Ireland's Albedo One magazine.

David Kernot is an Australian author living in the Mid North of South Australia and when he's not writing, he's riding his Harley Davidson through the wheat, wine, and wool farming lands. He writes contemporary fantasy, science fiction, and horror, and is the author of around forty published short stories in a variety of anthologies in Australia and the US, including *The Year's Best Australian Fantasy & Horror*, and Award Winning Australian Writing.

Broadsword

William Meikle is a Scottish writer with over a dozen novels published in the genre press and over 200 short story credits in thirteen countries. He is the author of the ongoing *Midnight Eye* series among others, and his work appears in a number of professional anthologies. His ebook *The Invasion* has been as high as #2 in the Kindle SF charts. He lives in a remote corner of Newfoundland with icebergs, whales and bald eagles for company. In the winters he gets warm vicariously through the lives of others in cyberspace, so please check him out at http://www.williammeikle.com

Long Island Weird—The Lost Interviews

Charles Christian is former barrister and Reuters correspondent turned award winning technology journalist, newsletter editor, blogger, publisher, poet, conference speaker, storyteller and science fiction author. 'UrbanFantasist.com' is his creative website and blog. His most recent collection of science fiction and fantasy short stories *This is the Quickest Way Down* was long-listed for three national and international book awards. He was also the founding editor of the widely read *Ink Sweat & Tears* poetry webzine and he has performed his one-man autobiographical monologue The Boy with the Bomb beneath his Bed at venues and festivals in the UK and United States.

The Yoth Protocols

Josh Reynolds is a professional freelance author whose credits include novels, short fiction and audio productions. As well as his own work, he has written for a number of popular media tie-in franchises, including Games Workshop's *Warhammer Fantasy* and *Warhammer 40,000* lines. He can be found online at http://joshuamreynolds.wordpress.com/.

A Feast Of Death

Lee Clark Zumpe is a reclusive author leading a life of obligatory asceticism in a two-bedroom, one-bath concrete-block cave-dwelling in the most densely-populated county of enigmatic and exotic Florida. He resides with his wife, his daughter and an embarrassingly extensive collection of Silver and Bronze Age comic books.

Afflicted at an early age with a compulsion to compose intricate, engaging falsehoods, Zumpe began scrawling out fiction and poetry to stave off inevitable madness. His work has been seen in magazines such as *Weird Tales*, *Space and Time* and *Dark Wisdom*, and in anthologies including *Horrors Beyond, Corpse Blossoms, High Seas Cthulhu* and *Cthulhu Unbound Vol. 1*. Zumpe is rumored to have a doppelgänger who has assumed his identity and who currently masquerades as an award-winning entertainment columnist with Tampa Bay Newspapers.

The Ithiliad

Christine Morgan works the overnight shift in a psychiatric facility, which plays havoc with her sleep schedule but allows her a lot of writing time. A lifelong reader, she also reviews, beta-reads, occasionally edits and dabbles in self-publishing. Her other interests include gaming, history, superheroes, crafts, cheesy disaster movies and training to be a crazy cat lady. She can be found online at www.christine-morgan.org

The Sinking City

Konstantine Paradias is a jeweler by profession and a writer by choice. His short stories have been published in *Unidentified Funny Objects! 2*, Third FlatIron's

Lost Worlds Anthology and the *Battle Royale-Slam Book* by Haikasoru. He is perfectly aware that he has a writing problem, but he can quit like, whenever he wants, man. His short story 'The Grim' has been nominated for a PushCart Prize and his comedic time travel piece, 'How You Runined Everything' is included in Tangent's 2013 Recommended Reading SF list.

The Shape of a Snake

Cody Goodfellow has written five novels and co-written three more with John Skipp. He received the Wonderland Book Award twice for his short fiction collections, *Silent Weapons For Quiet Wars* and *All-Monster Action*. He was a contributing editor at Substance, the world's first CD-ROM zine, and cofounder of Perilous Press, a micropublisher of modern cosmic horror.

Mysterious Ways

CJ Henderson was the creator of both the Jack Hagee hardboiled PI series and the Teddy London supernatural detective series. He was also the author of *The Encyclopedia of Science Fiction Movies*, several score novels, plus hundreds of short stories and thousands of non-fiction pieces. In the wonderful world of comics he wrote everything from *Batman* and *The Punisher* to *Archie* and *Cherry Poptart*.

He also wrote under the name Robert Morgan.

CJ Henderson passed away in July of 2014. *World War Cthulhu: A Collection of Lovecraftian War Stories* is dedicated to him.

Magna Mater

Edward Morris is a 2011 nominee for the Pushcart Prize in Literature, also nominated for the 2009 Rhysling Award and the 2005 British Science Fiction Association Award. His work has appeared in over a hundred worldwide markets, including *The Magazine of Bizarro Fiction*, Robert M. Price's *The Mountains of Madness*, and Joseph Pulver's *A Season in Carcosa*. Morris lives and works in Portland, Oregon as a writer and bouncer.

Dark Cell
(See the "About the Editors" Section)

Cold War, Yellow Fever

Pete Rawlik's first professional sale was "On the Far Side of the Apocalypse" to the legendary magazine *Talebones* in 1997. Since then his work has appeared in *Crypt of Cthulhu, Morpheus Tales, the Lovecraft Ezine, Innsmouth,* and the anthologies *Dead But Dreaming 2, Horror for the Holidays, Urban Cthulhu,* and *Worlds of Cthulhu.* He is a regular contributor to *The New York Review of Science Fiction* and *Tales of the Shadowmen,* an annual anthology series focusing on heroes from French literature, comics and film. His first novel, *Reanimators* will appear in June 2013 from Night Shade Books.

Stragglers from Carrhae

Darrell Schweitzer is an American writer, editor, and essayist in the field of speculative fiction. Much of his focus has been on dark fantasy and horror, although he does also work in science fiction and fantasy.

Schweitzer is also a prolific writer of literary criticism and editor of collections of essays on various writers within his preferred genres.

The Procyon Project

Tim Curran lives in Michigan and is the author of the novels *Skin Medicine, Hive, Dead Sea,* and *Skull Moon.* Upcoming projects include the novels *Resurrection, The Devil Next Door,* and *Hive 2,* as well as *The Corpse King,* a novella from *Cemetery Dance,* and *Four Rode Out,* a collection of four weird-western novellas by Curran, Tim Lebbon, Brian Keene, and Steve Vernon. His short stories have appeared in such magazines as *City Slab, Flesh&Blood, Book of Dark Wisdom,* and *Inhuman,* as well as anthologies such as *Flesh Feast, Shivers IV, High Seas Cthulhu,* and, *Vile Things.* Find him on the web at: www.corpseking.com

Wunderwaffe

Jeffrey Thomas is the author of such novels as *Deadstock, Blue War, Letters from Hades,* and *The Fall of Hades,* and such short story collections as *Punktown, Nocturnal Emissions, Thirteen Specimens,* and *Unholy Dimensions.* His stories have appeared in the anthologies *The Year's Best Fantasy and Horror, The Year's Best Horror Stories, Leviathan 3, The Thackery T. Lambshead Pocket Guide to Eccentric & Discredited Diseases,* and *The Solaris Book of New Science Fiction.* Forthcoming from Miskatonic River Press is a role-playing game based upon Thomas' universe of *Punktown.* Thomas is also an artist, and lives in Massachusetts.

ABOUT DARK REGIONS PRESS

Dark Regions Press is an independent specialty publisher of horror, dark fiction, fantasy and science fiction, specializing in horror and dark fiction in business since 1985. We have gained recognition around the world for our creative works in genre fiction and poetry We were awarded the Horror Writers Association 2010 Specialty Press Award and the Italian 2012 Black Spot award for Excellence in a Foreign Publisher. We produce premium signed hardcover editions for collectors as well as quality trade paperbacks and ebook editions. Our books have received seven Bram Stoker Awards from the Horror Writers Association.

We have published hundreds of authors, artists and poets such as Clive Barker, Joe R. Lansdale, Ramsey Campbell, Kevin J. Anderson, Bentley Little, Michael D. Resnick, Rick Hautala, Bruce Boston, Robert Frazier, W.H. Pugmire, Simon Strantzas, Jeffrey Thomas, Charlee Jacob, Richard Gavin, Tim Waggoner and hundreds more. Dark Regions Press has been creating specialty books and creative projects for over twenty-seven years.

The press has staff throughout the United States working virtually but also has a localized office in Portland, Oregon from where we ship our orders and maintain the primary components of the business.

Dark Regions Press staff, authors, artists and products have appeared in *FANGORIA* Magazine, *Rue Morgue* Magazine, *Cemetery Dance* Magazine, *Publishers Weekly, Kirkus Reviews, Booklist Online, LA Times, The Sunday Chicago Tribune, The Examiner, Playboy, Comic-Con, Wired, The Huffington Post, Horror World*, Barnes & Noble, Amazon, iBooks, Sony Reader store and many other publications and vendors.

Support Dark Regions Press by ordering our titles directly at: http://www. DarkRegions.com

Made in the USA
Las Vegas, NV
17 January 2023

65809691R00197